F
V86   Vogel, David.
          Married life.

MARRIED LIFE

David Vogel

Translated from the Hebrew
by Dalya Bilu

GROVE PRESS
New York

Translation Copyright © 1988 by
The Institute for the Translation of Hebrew Literature

First published in Israel in 1929–30 by Mitzpeh
under the title *Chai Nissuim*

First English language edition published in 1988
by Peter Halban Publishers Limited

Published by Grove Press
a division of Wheatland Corporation
841 Broadway
New York, N.Y. 10003

Library of Congress Cataloging-in-Publication Data

Vogel, David, 1891–1944.
[Haye niśu 'im. English]
Married life/David Vogel: translated from the Hebrew by Dalya
Bilu.—1st ed.
p.   cm.
Translation of: Haye niśu 'im.
ISBN 0-8021-1129-7 (alk. paper)
I. Title.
PJ5053.V6H313   1989
892.4'35—dc19   89-30649
                              CIP

Manufactured in the United States of America

This book is printed on acid-free paper.

First Edition 1989

10 9 8 7 6 5 4 3 2 1

Part I: The Meeting

1

IN the passage the tap woke up with a roar. In an instant the noise filled all the space around, penetrating the rooms, which were still steeped in the half-light of dawn, and invading the sleeping body of Rudolf Gurdweill.

Perhaps the noise of the tap triggered off an unpleasant dream in Gurdweill a moment before waking, for the first feeling struggling inside him as his senses cleared was one of reluctance: probably the result of the dream, which remained there inside him, on the other side of consciousness.

For a moment Gurdweill lay listening with his eyes closed. But in the meantime the silence had returned and he heard only the click of a door closing in the corridor, picking it up belatedly — in the abstract, as it were — after the sound itself had already faded and died.

Then he turned to the windows and opened his eyes. He saw that the windows were already quite pale with the light of the approaching morning, which immediately increased his desire to go back to sleep. And as if he were fleeing from some danger, he quickly turned on to his right side and pulled the quilt over his head.

Down below, in Kleine Stadtgutgasse, a heavy wagon trundled past slowly, creaking mercilessly and shaking the window-panes like an earthquake. "A coal-wagon from Nordbahnhof," concluded Gurdweill. Now he would never be able to go back to sleep. The creaking narrowed down to two or three maddeningly monotonous sounds, which went on repeating themselves with an idiotic obstinacy in his drowsy mind, although the wagon was quite far away by now, until it seemed to him that they were coming not from outside but from some corner of his own soul. In a sudden panic he jumped up and sat on the bed. He

7

glanced around the room, which was not large, and his eyes fell on the sofa to his right, where his friend Ulrich was sleeping with his face turned to the wall. At the sight of his sleeping friend he felt suddenly and inexplicably wide-awake. And the memory of what he had to do today came crowding into his mind, together with a feeling of oppression. "There's nothing for it! I'll have to go there whether I like it or not!" he said to himself in resignation. He still had time to spare and he lay down in bed again, hoping that he might fall asleep for a little while. But as if to spite him his thoughts went on turning of their own accord around the same unpleasant business, and he could not stop them.

The room was filling with the fine, clear morning of an early spring day. Ulrich sat up and said something in a lazy whisper. Gurdweill pretended to be asleep. He did not feel like talking to anybody now. Through his half-closed lids he watched his friend dressing with negligent, mechanical movements which for some reason seemed to him jerky, absurd and disconnected. "Man is a ridiculous creature," he concluded, "and his absurdity is particularly apparent when he is by himself . . ."

In the end it became difficult for him to go on lying there. He imagined the city streets bathed in the early spring sunshine, and he wanted to be outside. Impatiently he waited for Ulrich to go to work. But the latter, as if to spite him, moved around more than usual this morning, going out into the corridor several times, taking a collar out of the wardrobe, putting it back and taking another one instead, and spending about half an hour cleaning his clothes.

It was about eight o'clock when Ulrich left. Gurdweill leapt out of bed and went over to the window. At the sight of the azure-blue April morning invading the little street he was seized by a fit of high spirits. On a day like this it was good to be alive, to move about, to breathe. For the moment Gurdweill's worries lost their sting; everything seemed easier. He returned to the bed, where his clothes were laid out on a chair, and quickly began to get dressed.

About half an hour later Gurdweill was ready and he

descended the stairs from the third floor with a buoyant step. Outside he was enveloped in the mild morning air, which had a distinctive, undefinable smell, vaguely calling to mind pretty girls who had not yet reached maturity. Everything seemed renewed. The pavement had already been sprayed and the tiny puddles between the cracks were invisibly evaporating and adding freshness to the air. The wagons, the cars, the trams, the terrace houses and the people too — everything shone joyfully in the pristine rays of the sun. Nursemaids in frilly caps and starched white aprons pushed their prams with a kind of secret pride, as if the bonny, smiling babies were the fruit of their own wombs. Gurdweill walked along Nordbahnstrasse and then turned into Praterstrasse. The shop windows were so seductive that he felt a pressing desire to go into each and every one of them and buy all kinds of things, whether he needed them or not, to get into conversation with all the shop-assistants and joke with them light-heartedly. And another desire awoke in him too: to stand in the middle of the street and throw a cascade of gold and silver coins at the street urchins, and to rejoice in their happiness. But all this was beyond his powers; all he had in his pocket was one schilling and a few groschen. And so Gurdweill strolled down the broad, bustling Praterstrasse, looking into the eyes of the passers-by with exaggerated friendliness, as if he had some glad tidings to bring to each and every one of them, until he reached Ferdinand Bridge. He approached a crowd of people who were clustering at the railing, pushing forward and looking down.

"A young girl," a bulky, clean-shaven man turned to his neighbour. "She couldn't have been more than eighteen. I saw her with my own eyes when they pulled her out."

He said it with a certain complacency, as if he was boasting that he had seen the Japanese Emperor with his own eyes.

"Alive?" a reedy voice inquired.

"Not a chance! Dead as a doornail."

"This generation!" interrupted a middle-aged woman in a faded old hat, carrying a bag in her hand. "They're all teetering on the edge. Nothing means anything to

9

them: either they kill themselves or they kill each other. Yesterday a man killed his wife in our own building. Stabbed her to death in broad daylight! She was gone in a second, the poor thing. She never made a sound."

Gurdweill pushed his way to the railing, where two policemen could be seen on the embankment below, standing guard over the drowned girl draped in black, and preventing the circle of curious onlookers from coming any closer. Despite the sudden weakness which had flooded him, Gurdweill went down to the embankment and pushed through the crowd until he was close to the dead girl. Underneath the black cloth, which was not big enough to cover her body, her auburn hair peeped, matted and lifeless, and a bit of pale-blue forehead, which seemed as hard as granite, and on the other side, the toe of a brown shoe, wet and slimy, which had obviously been in the water for many days. The swelling under the cloth seemed big enough for two bodies, and the ground around it was soaked with water. Gurdweill could not tear his eyes away from the black-draped lump. His heart pounded violently.

In the meantime the hearse arrived and swept the onlookers aside. When they lifted the body, the head of the drowned girl was exposed for a moment. There was a scar on the left cheekbone, but the skin of the scar was no different in colour to the rest of the face. The nose seemed excessively long to Gurdweill. "There's no need for the nose to be so long" — the pointless thought flashed through his brain, when the wagon suddenly moved off and someone dug his elbow into his ribs, causing him to feel a short, dull pain. Gurdweill roused himself and remembered that he was in a hurry. He glanced once more at the wet ground in front of him and the smooth waters of the Danube reflecting the blue sky and scraps of white clouds, and began climbing the steps with the dispersing crowd. He suddenly felt very tired, as if after back-breaking physical labour.

"It's no good to be dead on a beautiful spring day like this, young sir, no good at all!" the old woman walking stooped over at his side suddenly exclaimed. And she immediately added, as if it was a sure remedy against

10

death: "And now I must hurry home to make dinner for my sons."

But the beauty of the spring day had been spoilt for Gurdweill. With downcast eyes, his hands stuck in the pockets of his open coat, he walked gloomily along the asphalt pavement by the canal. Within a few minutes he reached the end of Rotenturmstrasse and turned into it. Outside the nearby booksellers he came to a halt and read the names of some of the new books in the window without interest, then he glanced at his watch, saw that it was a quarter past ten, and resolutely entered the shop.

"Can I help you, sir?" asked a red-headed young man with black horn-rimmed spectacles.

Gurdweill asked to see Dr. Kreindel.

The young man disappeared into the passage opposite the door and immediately returned.

"Dr. Kreindel is busy at the moment. If you would be good enough to wait a few minutes, over here —" And he indicated a chair.

This delay was not at all to Gurdweill's taste. He hated waiting more than anything. But he was eager to get the whole thing behind him, and so he sat down on the chair, firmly resolved not to wait for more than fifteen minutes.

There were no customers in the bookshop. From time to time the red-headed assistant climbed a ladder and rummaged busily among the rows of volumes on the shelves, bringing down a pile of books and placing them on the tables below. Next to the entrance, in the cashier's booth, a young woman sat reading. She paid no attention at all to Gurdweill, who was sitting not far from her. In order to pass the time, he tried to read the names of the volumes on the shelves opposite him, on the other side of the long table stacked with books, straining his eyes in the effort. From outside the muffled roar of the city reached his ears. Without any obvious connection, he suddenly remembered the wet ground on the banks of the Danube after they had lifted the body of the dead girl, and his heart contracted. Sitting here and waiting suddenly seemed completely superfluous and pointless. He placed his squashed brown hat on his knees and began

11

rummaging through his pockets for a cigarette, but found nothing. Unthinkingly he turned to look at the young cashier. "She seems completely absorbed in her book," he said to himself, "I wonder if I can distract her by staring hard enough." He fixed his eyes in a concentrated stare on a certain point on her cheek, close to the ear. After a moment the cashier really did become distracted: she passed her hand over her dark-gold hair, cut like a boy's, rubbed her ear, and in the end she turned to Gurdweill and looked at him absent-mindedly. From the expression on her face, it looked as if she was trying to remember something she had forgotten. Then she began reading again. Pleased with his experiment, Gurdweill stood up, as if inspired by a new courage, and informed the assistant that he had no time to wait any longer.

The assistant led him through a narrow passageway, lit by an electric bulb and stacked with boxes reaching to the ceiling on both sides, and after knocking briefly, ushered him into the owner's office. Dr. Kreindel, who was sitting behind a large desk facing the door, jumped up at their entrace as if bitten by a snake.

"How many times have I told you not to disturb me while I'm working!"

"The gentleman has already been waiting for some time," the assistant said apologetically, indicating Gurdweill.

It was only now, apparently, that Dr. Kreindel noticed Gurdweill's presence. After dismissing the assistant with a sweep of his hand, he gave Gurdweill an appraising look and asked him what he wanted, with a trace of his former anger still in his voice.

"My name is Gurdweill," he responded dryly. "I presume that Dr. Mark Astel has already spoken to you about me."

"Ah, yes! Of course!" he said, immediately changing his tone and exposing two gold teeth in the front of his mouth as he spoke. "Dr. Astel, I remember perfectly. Please sit down," — he indicated a chair next to the desk — "So, you want to work for my firm! Very good. What does Goethe say: the love of books is a clear sign of — etc. etc. . . . You write yourself if I'm not mistaken?"

"No!" Gurdweill cut him short. "I don't write at all!"

"No? I was told . . . Never mind, never mind, it doesn't matter in the least. On the contrary, it's even better. Much better . . . Kleist says: Writers are always — etc., etc. I'm sure you know the end of the quotation . . ."

Gurdweill sat looking at Dr. Kreindel's fat face, from which it was hard to tell whether he was speaking seriously or making a joke. The man's sharp little eyes lurking under a low brow were extremely disagreeable to him. An oppressive feeling gave rise to the idea that he would have to spend eight hours a day with this man, day after day, for half a year, a year, and perhaps even longer. He felt a sudden urge to spit on the whole business and get up and leave immediately. But he stayed where he was. He had been out of a job for six months: his sources of loans were running out. He didn't have the courage to reject the possibility of employment out of hand.

Dr. Kreindel went on: "I imagine you are a student of philosophy, sir. A very interesting subject! I love philosophy . . . I studied it for three semesters . . . And I'm ashamed to admit that once upon a time I even wrote a book on the relation between Kant and Spinoza . . . Don't be alarmed, the book was never published. A youthful peccadillo with no harmful consequences . . . In any case I have remained faithful to philosophy to this day. My stocks consist mainly of books on philosophy. You'll find a rich collection here, and all at your disposal, my dear sir, all at your disposal."

Gurdweill suddenly succumbed to an attack of growing melancholy, for which he could see no evident reason. Impatiently he turned to the window on his right, which overlooked a smallish courtyard, a hand-barrow with its shafts resting on the ground, and a blind wall whose upper half was illuminated by yellow sunshine. He felt quite indifferent to the results of the interview. All he wanted was to be far away from here, from this room with its stale, mouldy smell, as if it had not been aired for years, and from this peculiar creature with his meaningless

13

chatter and fictitious quotations, for whom he already felt a definite hostility, as if he had known and disliked him for years. Coming to a sudden decision to put an end to the interview immediately, he turned to face his interlocutor. And then something very strange happened to Gurdweill: instead of Dr. Kreindel's face he saw the alabaster face of the drowned girl, as he had seen it before on the banks of the canal, he saw it quite clearly with the scar on the cheekbone and the matted, auburn hair. A shiver ran down his spine. He stood up and sat down again. He looked closely at Dr. Kreindel's face, and this time he saw it as it was, with its long nose and dark, fleshy chin.

"My nerves are playing tricks on me," he said to himself. "That's all it is — nerves." Then he remembered the fictitious quotations and a weak smile flashed across his face as it occurred to him to respond with a learned quotation of his own.

"Yes, indeed," he said solemnly, "the book trade is a noble calling . . . as Mitzelberg says: the treasures of the human mind find their salvation . . . etc. etc . . ."

"Hee-hee, who did you say, Mitzelberg? Well said, sir! Or should I say — Well said, Mitzelberg!" And suddenly coming to the point: "The matter has not yet been decided. Concerning your employment in my firm, that is to say. First we have to decide if we need additional manpower. If you will be kind enough to drop in in a few days' time — in two weeks' time, shall we say, in the morning, I should be able to give you a definite reply."

Gurdweill said goodbye and left. He was unwilling to admit to himself how pleased he was at the negative results of the interview. As always in similar circumstances he felt as if he had been saved at the last minute from a prison sentence. He needed a job and he had done his duty. What could he do if fate placed obstacles in his way? If only he didn't have to feed his accursed stomach!

It was after ten. Gurdweill felt a disagreeable dryness in his mouth, which came, presumably, from his empty stomach. At the same time he was dying to smoke a cigarette. He crossed Rotenturmstrasse and turned into a side street, where he stood still and counted the coins left in his pocket from the day before. Then he counted them again, although he already knew exactly how much he had. The schilling would do for a simple meal and the rest for cigarettes! He bought a packet of cigarettes and lit one. For a moment he considered going home to work, but immediately decided against it. It would be a shame to lose a single minute of this lovely day. He found himself passing a little park and sat down on a bench. He leant back luxuriously and put his hat down next to him.

Beside him sat a ragged old man with a mangy grey beard making himself a cigarette from the filthy butts lying on a crumpled old newspaper on his lap. Absorbed in his task, with his head bent over the newspaper, he did not notice Gurdweill looking at him.

"Who knows" — the thought came unbidden into Gurdweill's mind — "who knows if I won't end up one day like this old man . . . And so what if I do? What difference does it make?"

He took out a cigarette and offered it to the old man, saying with exaggerated politeness: "Allow me, sir, to offer you a cigarette."

For a moment the old man seemed to hesitate, then he stretched out his hand and took it. He turned it over and examined it gleefully on all sides, stuck it between his lips and removed it to look at it again, and then tore off a bit of newspaper, wrapped it carefully around the cigarette, and put it in the pocket of his ragged coat.

"A thousand thanks, young sir! May God reward you! I'll keep it for tonight, before I go to sleep. That's when it tastes the best — when I'm in bed at night."

"Would you believe it," he immediately continued, "I went to see a doctor once, in the hospital at Neuhaus, a long time ago, ten or twelve years, and he told me to stop smoking. It's poison, he said. He was a clever man. Every mouthful of smoke you swallow, he said, leaves a black spot inside you as big as a thumbnail. He actually showed me the spot on a white handkerchief. I saw it with my own eyes. But I couldn't stop smoking. I stopped for half a day and that was the most I could manage."

And he went back to rolling his cigarette.

15

The clatter of trams and carts coming from the street had a muffled, somewhat distant sound. Some boys were throwing a big brown football around on the little field in the middle of the park. Opposite the park, on the other side of the trees, a woman leant out of a top-storey window and shook a white sheet into the street, looking from side to side to make sure that there were no policemen watching. The old chestnuts were suddenly full of tiny buds.

Gurdweill felt a thousand miles away from the cares of the city. He could have gone on sitting idly on the bench forever, but the pangs of hunger began to gnaw at his stomach, and he got up and went to the bar of the nearby Hotel Metropol to have a bite to eat.

2

THAT afternoon, at about three o'clock, Gurdweill
was on his way to his regular café, where he hoped
to find a "victim," i.e. some acquaintance from whom he
could borrow money. If he was in luck, he would use the
money to go out of town to Kahlenberg or the Prater.

In the narrow, shady Tiefer Graben, a quiet street in
the heart of the city, full of leather warehouses and textile
wholesalers, workers in their shirtsleeves were loading
huge crates on to wide, flat wagons. While this was going
on, the heavy cart-horses with tufts of hair above their
hooves munched steadily and gloomily from the feed bags
tied around their heads. A cleaner in wooden clogs with a
long pipe dangling from his mouth sprayed the pavement
with a rusty hose. In one of the doorways a maid in a white
apron stood calling over and over again in a long-drawn-
out voice: "Flo-ckieee come he-eeere!" But the little brown
dog with his long back and short crooked legs was busy
chasing a cigarette butt blown by the wind and showed no
inclination to go home. A sturdy labourer called teasingly
to the maid from the opposite pavement: "Why don't you
come and sleep with me tonight, pussycat?" Then a heavy
truck came roaring down the road and swept Flockie aside.

A pleasant, pungent smell of cured hides and freshly
dyed cloth wafted out of the open warehouse doors. All
around there was a sense of people busy at work, of quiet,
strenuous effort, and Gurdweill felt an urge to go up to
the labourers and help them load the crates, to lend a
hand and shoulder and overcome the resistance of the
heavy load. At that moment he saw himself as an outcast,
excluded from the masses of humanity helping to keep the
world going. Like all those unfit for crude physical labour,
he imagined that it was the only way to achieve perfect

17

fulfilment. Gurdweill stood at a distance and watched the workers enviously. No, of course he could not compete with men like these! He glanced contemptuously at his thin, short body, which seemed to him to be made of nerves and brains alone, and moved away. He had not taken more than a few steps when it seemed to him that he heard someone calling his name. He turned his head but could not see anyone he knew. He set off again and suddenly felt a slap on his shoulder.

"*Servus*, Gurdweill!" cried Dr. Astel jovially from behind his back. "How are you? Did you go there this morning?"

"I went."

"And what happened?" inquired Dr. Astel, bending his long thin body over Gurdweill.

"Nothing happened."

"What do you mean?"

"He told me to come again in two weeks' time. In the meantime he'll think it over."

"To hell with him! The hypocritical scoundrel!"

Only now Gurdweill noticed Lotte Bondheim, who was waiting a few steps away.

As he went up to the girl he managed to ask Astel in a whisper if he had any money, and to get a positive reply.

"Where were you going, Gurdweill?" asked Lotte.

"I was just wandering around the streets," he lied for no particular reason.

"In that case, why don't you come with us? We're going to the Prater."

"Of course, of course," Dr. Astel made haste to agree, although he didn't seem delighted by the idea. "The three of us will go to enjoy the splendours of nature!"

They walked to Franz-Josefs-Kai to take a tram.

Dr. Astel belonged to the category of people who always manage to give the impression that they haven't got a minute to spare, and who add a peculiar air of irritable officiousness to whatever they say or do, as if it were the most important thing in the world. Now he began talking animatedly, to the accompaniment of quick, jerky gestures, about a certain Zukerberg (it was the first time Gurdweill

18

had ever heard his name), who had found his wife in a café in the company of one of his friends, and slapped her face in public and then gone home and tried to shoot himself. Lotte was fascinated by the story, and questioned him closely about the details, as if it had something to do with her. They got on to the tram and rode to the last station in the Hauptallee, not far from the third café.

The air here was fresh and somewhat moist. The earth was already touched with green. The long, straight boulevard was almost deserted. Once in a while a car drove silently past, or an elegant carriage whose proud horses trotted over the asphalt in perfect unity. Occasionally a horse-rider rode past on the riding-track at the side of the road, and his horse's hooves thudded dully on the loose soil.

Lotte hung on the arms of both young men. For some time they walked down the boulevard in silence. Then Lotte said, giving Gurdweill a sidelong glance from her grey eyes: "Actually, Gurdweill, it's a long time since we met." And she immediately added, half seriously, half bantering, "I was already beginning to miss you."

"Well," said Gurdweill with a smile, "you didn't miss me too badly, I imagine."

"You can never tell . . ." she replied. And in a burst of enthusiasm: "Oh, how wonderful it is here, children. So wonderful that suddenly you don't know where you are . . . You feel as if you have just this moment emerged into the world and that you are seeing everything for the first time. At moments like these people are ready to perform uncommon deeds. Deeds of self-sacrifice and heroism, or the opposite: bestial deeds, murder, for example . . ."

"Hold your horses, my girl!" cried Dr. Astel. "I sincerely hope you're not planning to murder me . . ."

"No, no! You have nothing to fear!" retorted Lotte with a hint of contempt.

Suddenly she freed herself from their arms and jumped up and planted a kiss on Gurdweill's mouth.

"It's Gurdweill who's in danger, not you!"

"In that case murder me too, Lotte, darling Lotte, I

19

beg you . . ." Dr. Astel implored, twisting his face into a ludicrous grimace.

"Too late, my dear! You're a coward!"

Gurdweill took Lotte's hand and placed it in Dr. Astel's.

"Come along, children, make friends now and live happily ever after."

"Why don't you mind your own business Gurdweill?" Lotte snapped irritably in a sudden change of mood and pulled her hand away. "It's got nothing to do with you! What rudeness! Interfering in other people's affairs . . ." And turning to Astel as if she were addressing him alone: "Come on, I'm thirsty. Let's go into the café . . ."

"But we can't leave Gurdweill on his own," said Dr. Astel with a coaxing smile.

"It makes no difference to me. He can come with us or go wherever he likes . . ."

Gurdweill smiled to himself and made no reply. "There's no point in taking any notice," he said to himself. "Women will be women."

After he had taken a few steps back along the boulevard Lotte announced: "Actually, I'm not so thirsty after all . . . Perhaps we should walk a little longer and then have something to drink. What do you think?"

And they strolled back the way they had come. She asked Dr. Astel for a cigarette, lit it and blew out long wisps of smoke. As she did so, her full lips rounded into a little circle, adding a particular charm to her fresh, pretty face. She held the cigarette expertly between her third finger and her little finger, and puffed on it without a pause. Suddenly she grew sick of it and threw it far away. She smiled at Gurdweill, who was walking on her right.

"You aren't angry with me are you, Gurdweill? About what happened before, I mean. Please don't be cross. Let's be friends again. Please, please," she clapped her hands like a little girl, "don't be cross! Tell him not to be cross, Astel!"

"But who said I was cross?" laughed Gurdweill. "I'm not in the least!"

"Really and truly not? I'm delighted to hear it! What

do you say, children — why don't we go to the Wurstel-Prater?" But the minute she saw their reluctant faces she changed her mind, and they went on strolling as before. After a while they sat down on a bench.

A train crossed the bridge over the boulevard, invisible from where they sat, chugging and puffing and panting like a chorus of asthma sufferers. It left a palpable silence behind it. Behind the still bare trees the blood-red orb of the exhausted sun appeared and disappeared. An invisible swallow, too, chirped a few times and fell silent. There was already a slight chill in the air as evening approached.

The three of them sat in silence. Dr. Astel seemed in a bad mood today: he hardly spoke, which was very unlike him. Lotte leant her head against his shoulder and played with her bag which was made of rough snake-skin. In the end she jumped up:

"What's the matter with the pair of you today? You're boring me to tears!"

It was growing dark and cold. They got up and started back. Gurdweill regretted having accompanied them. He could already taste in advance the feeling of futility which invariably remained with him after a few hours spent in the society of others. It was a pity he hadn't come by himself! As soon as they arrived at the tram stop, he would say goodbye.

But when they got there, he gave way to the temptation to drop in to the third café "for just a minute," angry at his own weakness a moment later. His face took on a hard expression and the lines at the sides of his mouth deepened.

They sat on the open terrace which was slightly above ground level and which was almost empty. Gurdweill sipped his coffee, which seemed to him tasteless, mechanically. His need to be alone, no matter what, suddenly became irresistible. He glanced at his watch and recoiled: Damn, he had completely forgotten, he had an appointment he couldn't miss at seven . . .

"Wait a minute," said Lotte, "We're all going in a minute."

And with sincere regret: "What a shame you're not

free. I was going to ask you both to come and have tea at my place."

"You can come later, when you're free," suggested Dr. Astel.

No, he couldn't promise anything. There was no knowing how long it would take . . .

Gurdweill took the tram with them to Franz-Josefs-Kai, where he got off after borrowing a small sum of money from Dr. Astel.

The city was shrouded in a dull orange glow from the electric and gas lights. The streets were full of people, streaming out of the shops and businesses and hurrying home. Corrugated iron shutters came down with a deafening crash. At the tram stop the newspaper-sellers announced the headlines at the tops of their voices, running after the receding trams and pushing their rolled-up papers through the windows. Here and there a barmaid could be seen crossing the street with a tray full of glasses of beer from a nearby tavern.

The rush and hurry infected Gurdweill too, along with all these people who had just finished working the whole day long. Although he did not have anywhere in particular to go, he pushed through the crowds and squeezed on to one of the packed trams. With one foot on the platform and one in the air, his body plastered against the broad, sweaty back standing in front of him like a wall, he reached the Schottentor, where he got off. For some time he walked back and forth in front of the Vienna Banking Company building without knowing what to do next. In the end he got on to a tram and rode back the way he had come and went home.

3

"A bottle of beer, Johann, and the evening papers!"

The blond waiter, who was standing not far off with his back to him, a dirty napkin under his arm, hurried off to bring his order.

It was nine at night. One by one the *habitués* of the little café near the university assembled: students and minor officials who sat in the same chairs night after night, and ordered their coffee as if they were finishing off their evening meal at home. These customers were as much a part of the café and its particular atmosphere as the ragged, threadbare velvet sofas around the walls and the dark, dirty, marble tables. It was rare for a "stranger" to appear here.

Perczik attacked his veal cutlet in its dark brown gravy with gusto, cutting piece after piece off the whitish meat surrounded by a rim of transparent yellow fat with his blunt knife and swallowing them avidly. His short, plump fingers worked diligently and his lips were red and shining with fat. From time to time he took a sip of the foaming beer. He was in an expansive mood, as always when a hearty meal was set before him, and ready to discuss all kinds of lofty questions: even his heart seemed to soften, and he spoke without stopping as he chewed, his eyes darting to and fro under the thick eyebrows which met over his nose.

"It's completely superfluous, I tell you . . . and any sensible person would say the same, unless he were a liar. What good does it do, for example, to a man with toothache? Or someone who hasn't eaten for two days? Will you give him Madame Bovary to read? Or show him pictures by Rembrandt, etc.? The truth is that art only interests the rich, the snobs who want something to decorate their

23

houses along with the rest of their unnecessary possessions
. . . nobody else needs it at all."

And Perczik jabbed his fork in the air to underline his
words.

Gurdweill sat with his head down, mechanically drawing floral patterns on the tabletop and rubbing them out
with his finger. Perczik's roast veal did not interest him in
the least; he had eaten two full meals today, hearty meals,
you could even say, in comparison to other days. But the
latter's good mood and concern for the fate of art and the
sufferings of humanity provoked him.

"What are you going on about, Perczik? Why should it
concern you? If anyone's got a toothache let him go to the
dentist. And art will get along fine without you too. You'd
do better to give me a cigarette."

"A cigarette?" Perczik's voice dropped. "In a minute."

He took the leather case out of his pocket, opened it and
offered it to Gurdweill. There was only one cigarette in it,
and that was half empty of tobacco.

"Here you are! It's my last one," he said pleadingly.

"No thank you!" Gurdweill rejected the offer. "You can
smoke that one yourself! Tell the waiter to bring some good
ones."

He had no alternative. The veal and the beer suddenly
lost their flavour. "It's always the same," reflected Perczik
bitterly, "when you sit at the same table with these scroung-
ers. You should avoid them like the plague!"

The waiter opened a new pack.

"Will ten Khedives be satisfactory?"

"No, no!" Perczik waved them away, as horrified as if
he were being asked to mount the gallows. "Haven't you
got any Memphis? I prefer Memphis . . . a mild, pleasant
taste . . . Give me three!"

"And what about me?" said Ulrich with a laugh. "I smoke
too, you know!"

"Since when do you smoke? You never used to."

"I do now."

"In that case, of course . . . With pleasure . . ."

"A light, Perczik!" Gurdweill commanded.

"I haven't got any matches," lied Perczik.

Ulrich lit a match and gave Gurdweill a light.

"Memphis!" teased Gurdweill. "Who smokes Memphis today . . ? It's time you started smoking Khedives, Perczik! A hundred dollars a month!"

"What hundred dollars a month?" Perczik defended himself. "Who earns a hundred dollars a month? I'm happy if I earn thirty . . ! It's all a big lie . . . Do you think it's so easy to earn a hundred dollars a month?"

"Nevertheless, you'll lend me two schillings," said Gurdweill with a smile, looking him straight in the eye.

He knew that it was a lost cause, but he wanted to see him squirm.

"Two schillings?" Perczik stopped eating as if he had been struck by lightning. "I haven't got it! I swear to you, I haven't got it! I've hardly got enough to pay the waiter. I haven't even got the money to give my wife for housekeeping tomorrow . . . I didn't make it to the bank in time today . . . I'll have to run and change my last five dollars first thing tomorrow morning."

"In that case, you can give me one schilling," persisted Gurdweill.

Perczik pushed his plate away, leaving his meat unfinished, and gulped down a glass full of beer.

"They don't even let you eat in peace," he reflected furiously.

He put his hand into his trouser pocket, removed the big bills from his wallet, and pulled out the wallet with what was left in it.

"Bring me the bill, Johann!" he called crossly.

After paying his bill there was little more than a schilling left.

"This is all my money!" he showed Gurdweill.

"Fine! Lend me the schilling and keep the change for yourself. In any case, you won't be able to do anything else with it."

"If you really need a schilling so much," Perczik made one last attempt to rescue his money, "perhaps you can wait until tomorrow. I can't go home without a penny in my pocket, now can I? I'll bring you a schilling here tomorrow evening with pleasure. I need something to give the boy in the morning when he goes to school too. You don't expect me to send the child out of the house without a penny! Without a penny until lunchtime!"

"Don't be so obstinate Perczik. I'm not worried about you. You'll find a way out I'm sure. Now give me that schilling!"

Gurdweill took the coin and examined it carefully on both sides:

"First let's see if it's genuine. There's a lot of counterfeit money going around . . ."

Perczik lit himself a cigarette and smoked it in silence, trying without much success to hide his anger. In the end he said with artificial friendliness:

"Look here, Gurdweill, I'm not an expert at giving advice. That's not my line at all, as you know. But nevertheless I consider it my duty to tell you that it's time you changed your way of life. The time for fantasies is past. We're not eighteen-year-old boys any longer, for God's sake! I was a dreamer and a loafer too once, as you know very well, but everything has to end sometime! One year, two years, five — how long can a person go hungry? And what the hell for? Perhaps you can explain to me: what for? It's not worth it, I tell you! First you have to fill your stomach — the rest comes later! In my opinion, you should look for a job. That's my honest opinion. You can't live from hand to mouth forever. What do all the young writers do? One works at this and another at that. I was lucky, I found work on a newspaper — and I snapped it up! They don't pay a person a decent salary — but it's better than nothing and you can go on working for yourself at the same time. Look at me. Only last week I finished a long story! You can go on writing, believe me!"

Gurdweill heard Perczik's words as if they were coming from another room. His attention was elsewhere. A strange girl had entered the café and seated herself opposite them, three tables away. She placed three books in black cloth covers, evidently library books, on the table, ordered coffee, and glanced at the people around her. Gurdweill could not take his eyes off her. He suddenly felt a vague unease, as if at the premonition of disaster. There

26

was nothing extraordinary about her appearance. She was neither particularly beautiful nor particularly ugly: one of the flaxen-haired, fair-skinned Viennese girls you met in their thousands in the street or the little cafés after working hours. But for some reason she made a powerful impression on Gurdweill. And when he encountered her penetrating, steely-blue glance, he was forced to turn his eyes away.

In the meantime Perczik stood up and said goodbye.

When he left, Gurdweill whispered to Ulrich:

"Did you see the new girl? At the third table on the left?"

"I saw her. What about it?"

"What do you think of her?"

"Nothing in particular. A girl like any other."

"No! There's something about her you've missed. Something of the old Viennese tradition. The Biedermeier period. Look at the line of authority in the bottom half of her face. I'd like to meet her."

And a moment later, rather hesitantly:

"Maybe you could try to introduce yourself to her?"

"Nothing easier. Watch me."

Apparently sensing that they were talking about her, the girl glanced at the two men from time to time as she sipped her coffee.

Ulrich stood up and threaded his way through the tables as if he was on his way somewhere else, and suddenly came to a halt next to the girl. He bowed and said with all the politeness at his command:

"Pardon me for disturbing you, Fräulein. My friend would like to meet you. Will you allow me to introduce him?"

The girl glanced first at Ulrich and then at Gurdweill. She seemed taken with this direct, businesslike approach. The stern, definite cast of her features softened into the shadow of a smile. She said only: "Good!"

Ulrich beckoned and Gurdweill approached. He tried to adopt a self-confident air, but his efforts succeeded only in upsetting his inner equilibrium and making his movements look stiff and ridiculous.

Ulrich introduced him:

27

"Herr Gurdweill, allow me to introduce you to Fräulein . . ."

"Baroness Thea von Takow."

They asked her permission and sat down. Gurdweill felt hollow inside. He knew he should say something but he didn't know what to say. He felt like someone about to make a speech who had forgotten how to begin. For some reason Ulrich too said nothing. The silence became oppressive and embarrassing. In the end Gurdweill pulled himself together and said:

"You don't come here often, I think?"

As he spoke it seemed to him that his voice was lower than usual, almost a whisper, and he filled with rage against himself.

"No. I just happened to be passing."

There was another pause.

The Baroness was not unaware of her new acquaintance's state, and it gave her a strange, cruel pleasure. Gurdweill racked his brains energetically to find something to talk about: he would ask her if she was a student.

"Would you like another cup of coffee, Fräulein?" He was horrified to hear himself saying instead.

To his relief, she refused.

Be careful, you idiot! He castigated himself. You haven't got the money to pay for it!

A wave of inexplicable sadness suddenly flooded him, washing away his awkwardness and embarrassment. He felt as if he had known the Baroness for a long time.

"You know, Fräulein," he said, looking directly into her face, "it sometimes happens that you meet someone and you immediately feel that there is already a definite, permanent relationship between you, good or bad, but the kind of relationship which is usually only created by years of living together. In these cases the first part is already over, it has already taken place in secret. Have you ever had that kind of experience? Meeting someone, for instance, and knowing right away that you have to avenge yourself on him for something, or the opposite: feeling that you owe a debt of gratitude to some stranger you have just met for the first time in your life? Strange, isn't it?"

28

The Baroness listened in silence. In Gurdweill's words, not in their content but their tone, there was a note of suppressed sadness which was unconsciously absorbed by the listener. In his utter seriousness he seemed to be taking a step towards the essential heart of things, and revealing a measure of their mystery.

Gurdweill went on, as if compelled by some hidden force:

"And sometimes you meet someone for the first time and you feel instinctively that he is the source of the sorrow without which you cannot exist, that it has been flowing from him to you through invisible channels all your life . . . and you are attached to this man as inseparably as a shadow . . ."

"You may be right," said the Baroness, her fingers mechanically playing with her books, "the truth of such things can never be proved. But with regard to what you said about needing sorrow in order to go on living — I must beg to differ. This is an individual matter. To me it seems, on the contrary, that a man needs a little happiness. That it is happiness, and only happiness, which keeps him alive. I, at least," the Baroness smiled, showing strong teeth, "live only by and for happiness."

"Certainly, certainly," Gurdweill eagerly agreed, "it's not the same for everyone of course."

The Baroness glanced at her wristwatch. She suggested going for a little walk. They paid and left. Outside Ulrich left them immediately. He was tired, to his regret, and he had to get up early.

When they were alone the Baroness asked Gurdweill where he lived. She herself lived in the opposite direction, in Während, on the other side of the Gürtel.

In the mild spring air a pure, gentle stillness seemed to drop from the darkening sky. The deserted streets looked as if they had just been swept. The city was sinking into sleep in the orange glow of the streetlamps. From time to time, at increasing intervals, a tram split the silence like a nightmarish awakening. A distant train emitted a long, muffled hoot. And for a moment the imagination was captured by long journeys through the soundlessly

29

breathing night, strange cities populated by millions of human beings.

Gurdweill, who was short and thin, walked beside the woman who was a head taller than he was. From time to time, as they walked down Währinger Strasse, he glanced at his companion and thought to himself: A tall, handsome woman, but obviously hard. She'll probably give a lot of pain to anyone close to her. Gurdweill felt a wonderfully pleasant sensation together with a terrifying uneasiness. The girl gave off a vague but definite sense of menace. It was a strange new mood for Gurdweill, but at the same time it was clear to him that he had experienced it before, perhaps in his infancy. Certain events, too, connected with this mood trembled at the threshold of his memory. Gurdweill almost touched them, but then they sank back into the depths of his mind, like a fish leaping out of the water and disappearing into it again before you could do more than glimpse it.

He took off his hat and bared an untidy fringe of hair and a white, domed forehead.

"When I was a small child," he said as if to himself, "I imagined the world as a big, bottomless sack full of holes . . . People struggled inside it, trampling each other and getting entangled with each other like crabs, and falling out of the holes into God knows where . . . This scene would often come before my eyes, with nightmarish clarity. It terrified me. And strangely enough, precisely at night, and especially on dark nights, I would feel reassured. I could hide in the darkness and feel safe and hidden . . . Even now I prefer dark, moonless nights."

"Who knows, perhaps you're a lunatic," said the Baroness, and for some reason she laughed loudly.

Her laughter sounded hollow, as if it came from inside an empty barrel, and Gurdweill felt a little hurt.

"No," he answered simply, "I'm not a lunatic."

On the alley corners the prostitutes sauntered to and fro, dangling their handbags and staring at every solitary male. The Baroness gave them a quick, appraising look and made an unclear gesture with her hand. When they moved away she burst out with sudden emotion:

30

"I hate them! I could kill them! I can't understand how any man could bear to touch them. Only scum would have anything to do with them."

A suspect hatred, Gurdweill reflected, and said nothing.

In the meantime they had already reached the Volk-soper, which was locked up and silent. From here it was not far from the Baroness's house. They walked slowly, in the middle of the street.

Suddenly, to his astonishment, Gurdweill found himself saying:

"You know, Baroness, I feel that we would make a good couple . . ."

The Baroness replied with a laugh:

"Perhaps. I've got nothing against it. I like you."

She stood and looked him over from top to toe, as if he were a child who had said something cute. Then she rumpled his untidy hair.

"You've got nice hair, Herr Gurdweill."

A torrent of warmth struck his heart. His hat slipped from his hand and fell on to the street. He bent down to retrieve it and as he did so he seized her hand and kissed it ardently. She did not protest. At that moment a car's hooter made them recoil and jump on to the pavement. They continued on their way. Gurdweill was beside himself. He felt like dancing in the middle of the street. "Now I'll be able to walk with her like this every night," he said jubilantly to himself. "From time to time we'll sit down on a bench and she'll rest her head on my shoulder. How beautiful she is! And I'll embrace her . . ."

"Here we are," the Baroness stopped outside a five-storey house. "It's late. Tomorrow I've got to go to the office."

They arranged to meet the next evening, in a different café, and said goodbye. When they heard the doorman's shuffling feet and the rattle of the keys, the Baroness bent down and kissed Gurdweill hastily on the mouth, and disappeared into the blackness of the doorway.

Gurdweill remained rooted to the spot. None of it seemed real to him. His lips stung as if they had been burnt and his mind was completely stupefied. There was

31

no room in it for even the shadow of a thought. His heart beat like a hammer, it hammered in his hands, in his legs, his head, as if it had leapt out of his chest. Something had just happened, something wonderful, something incredible, but perhaps it had happened not to him but to somebody else, outside him. Gurdweill stood facing the locked door, concentrating on the inside of the house into which the Baroness had disappeared. He imagined he heard her footsteps on the stairs. He listened for a while and he kept on hearing them. He looked up and imagined he could see a light going on in one of the windows on the second floor. Yes, that must be the window of her room . . . In the end he moved away. But after a few steps he stopped again and stared straight ahead of him, into the next street, as if he were searching for something. On the sign stuck to the wall on the corner, which was illuminated by the streetlamp, he read uncomprehendingly the name of the street. He read it again and again but nothing sank in. Opposite him there was a man standing leaning against the wall.

"I suppose he must be hungry . . ." the thought flashed through his mind. Gurdweill walked slowly on, swaying slightly, and without realizing where he was he reached Nussdorfer Strasse. Aha! he suddenly remembered — the Währing district! He had just been in the Währing district! It was written on the sign, in so many words! And she, she lived in Schulgasse number 12. The Ba-ro-ness The-a von Ta-kow, 12 Schulgasse. Not thirteen or eleven, but exactly twelve . . . Six and six, seven and five, eight and four — they all made twelve! Thea von Takow, Rudolf von Takow — no, von Gurdweill . . . the Baron Rudolf von Gurdweill! Ha, ha, ha! Gurdweill burst into loud laughter, which somewhat cleared his head. A new part of his life was beginning. He could feel it in his bones. This evening was a milestone. One thousand five hundred miles up to here. A station. And from here on! He felt a powerful urge to do something, to go somewhere unfamiliar, to argue with people and beat them, to prove to them that everything was for the best, that nothing was wrong or distorted, that they should rejoice with all their hearts, rejoice and give

32

thanks for every breath they took, for the immeasurably great gift which had been given to man, who was utterly unworthy of it. He wanted to share with others the joy in life which filled him to overflowing.

Gurdweill searched for cigarettes in his pockets but found none. Cunning fellows these cigarettes — he smiled to himself — sometimes they like to play hide-and-seek with you. On the other hand he found in one of his jacket pockets a schilling about whose existence he had completely forgotten. He went into a little tavern in Währinger Strasse and bought five cigarettes from the waiter. But his palate was so dry with thirst that it made the cigarette smoke taste bitter. He sat down and ordered a tankard of beer.

At this late hour there were only a few customers in the bar. A man and a woman were sitting in a corner with grey haversacks on their backs which they had not bothered to remove. They were taking turns in drinking from the same glass, very seriously, without exchanging a word. A worn-out married couple — decided Gurdweill — with nothing left to say to each other. Next to his table in the middle of the smallish room two men were sitting by themselves, each with a gigantic glass of beer in front of him. One of them, opposite Gurdweill, was sitting like a stone, with his head lowered, completely absorbed in the drink in front of him. When Gurdweill sat down, the latter stole a quick glance at him, and immediately went back to staring at his glass, as if he could see some marvellous sight in it. With long pauses in-between, he took big, angry gulps, and lowered his head again, without wiping the foam off his unkempt moustache.

Poor devil, thought Gurdweill compassionately, he's probably drinking in despair. He felt an urge to strike up a conversation with the stranger, to speak to him coaxingly and lighten his heavy heart. As for his own great joy — he was hoarding it up in his heart for later, when he was alone, like a child saving sweets and enjoying the pleasure of simply knowing that they were there. Suddenly he wished that the man would rouse himself, become excited, get up and begin abusing him as if he were some inferior creature. He

33

was ready to pay for the favour which had been bestowed upon him, a favour of which he was certainly unworthy. He picked up his glass and set it down with a deliberate bang. The man opposite him did not move. A few minutes ticked slowly by on the clock hanging on the wall. It was forty minutes past midnight. The man and the woman with the haversacks got up and left. Gurdweill finished his beer and was about to leave too. And all of a sudden the man opposite him said in an apathetic, slightly hoarse voice, without raising his head:

"You, young man, are you married? No? Well, I could have told you that myself. I can tell with one look."

He fell silent for a moment and then continued:

"Don't get married, young man . . . I urge you. As long as a woman isn't sure of you she's sweet as pie, you can twist her round your little finger. But the minute you put a ring on her finger — it's all over! She begins kicking like a mule — and you can't do a thing about it. It's a law of nature, young man! Reason won't get you anywhere with them. Am I right or not?"

"Not all women are alike," ventured Gurdweill.

"You think so? No, I say. They're all the same!"

He took a gulp from his glass and repeated emphatically:

"No! There's not a scrap of difference!"

"Look at me," he added after a moment and pointed at his grey, puffy face. "No, no, look properly. Well, what do you say? You can't say I'm ugly, now can you? No one would believe you if you did! And look what happened to me! The first one, the late Fritzl, was only half of it. Here I was the swine. I was a real swine, I admit it frankly. But she too, that Fritzl — she wasn't fit for a dog to eat — believe me. She had two, Herr Mentzl from the railways and the welder Poldy — two lovers aren't a lot, I grant you. And when I came back from the Italian front in 1918 — she was dead. She was a sweet soul that Fritzl — but a real slut. Here — I won't say a word. May God have mercy on her dust! Good! So I took Gustl . . . Won't you have another, Herr Doktor? This time it's on me! No, I insist! Schurl, bring the Herr Doktor another beer! So — now

34

comes Gustl. 'Gustl,' I say to her, 'that's it! Finished and done with! From now on you've got me to deal with — I'm telling you straight. And I know what I'm talking about! From now on men don't exist as far as you're concerned. Not one! You start with one — and before you know it it's two, three, five — and there's no end to it! And so — that's it!' That's what I told her, right? And what do you think, Herr Doktor? I'll be damned if it helped!"

Gurdweill was feeling tired. He still had a long way to go home. But for some reason the man interested him.

The latter continued, his eyes which were already dull and bleary, fixed on Gurdweill:

"You see, Herr Doktor, you're a clever man — I could see it at once! You can't pull the wool over Heidelberger Franzl's eyes! So what I say is, and you'll understand me I know: once a woman starts playing around, she's a goner as far as I'm concerned! A beating or two won't do any good — and when Heidelberger Franzl leaves his mark you feel it for a month of Sundays, believe me! But scandals in public — that's something else again. Heidelberger Franzl won't get his name in the papers, no sir! Man is not a swine, and order must reign!"

The customers were all leaving one by one. The waiter appeared with a broom and started overturning the chairs on the tables. Someone yawned loudly. A desolate silence began to invade the room. Gurdweill stood up.

"You're in a hurry, I see," said Heidelberger Franzl. "Wait a minute, I'm leaving too."

Outside he said: "You live in 17 Liechtensteinstrasse too, don't you? I've seen you there a few times."

No, he only visited the shoemaker Vrubiczek from time to time.

"So that's it! But you're a student, Herr Doktor! I saw it at once. I've got an eye for these things! Well, I see you're in a hurry — it was an honour, Herr Doktor! Glad to have met you! I'm always glad to talk to a clever man. Next time you're at Vrubiczek's, drop in on me. Heidelberger Franzl is your brother!"

Gurdweill turned towards the Schottentor. He dragged

35

his feet; he was very tired. The day which had passed felt as long as a week. But beneath his enormous weariness a great joy flickered. He did not dare to examine the event in detail now, when his senses were stupefied with weariness and drink. When he reached home at two o'clock in the morning, he dropped into bed like a dead man and fell asleep at once.

4

THE next morning Gurdweill woke at ten. A wave of happiness immediately struck him in the face. He had slept well and felt fresh and full of energy.

Ulrich had already left. The dark, cloudy day outside did nothing to dampen Gurdweill's spirits. In his imagination he joyfully went over every single detail of yesterday's great event: Baroness Thea von Takow appeared before him as large as life, tall, erect, blonde, and even beautiful in her navy-blue wool coat with the black-jacketed library books in her hand and in the light of her person everything took on a new significance. Everything now strove towards a definite aim. Life no longer groped shamefaced in the dark, as it had seemed to do up to now. It had become open and clear, it had a firm, visible outline. It was suddenly clear to him that his long, difficult journey had deliberately led him, with all its vicissitudes, straight to this point.

Gurdweill rose and began shaving himself carefully and lovingly. He suddenly seemed particularly precious to himself, in need of devoted care and attention. You might say that at this moment he felt respect for himself. Even his face did not seem ugly to him — not in the least ugly. His nose was where it should be, a well-developed, manly nose; the eyes were fine, the brow, the hair — not bad, not bad at all. As for being short — this was not such a terrible disadvantage. The facts spoke for themselves! Frau Fischer, the deaf old landlady, came in with her broom — without knocking first, as usual. Gurdweill did not realize she was there until she was standing beside him.

"Herr Gurdweill is making himself handsome again, I see," the old woman said in a hoarse whisper, exposing a few black stumps of teeth. "I do like to see a man

shaving. My dear departed husband," — she never omitted the epithet "dear" when referring to any member of
her family, alive or dead — "my dear departed husband
always let me stand next to him and watch when he
shaved. Aie, aie, aie!"

She leant the broom against the wall and began wiping
the cupboard and the backs of the chairs and the bed with
a damp cloth, only in the places exposed to the eye. After a
moment she came back to Gurdweill and sighed deeply:

"Sick and tired, that's what I am! Aren't you sick and
tired, Herr Gurdweill?"

No, Gurdweill was not "sick and tired." He smiled to
himself without replying.

"You don't know what it's like, Herr Gurdweill," the
old woman went on, "when a person grows old. Aie, aie,
aie! You can't fall asleep, you hear the clock striking three
o'clock, four o'clock . . . On the twenty-fifth of July I'll be
seventy-one — seventy-one years old and not one day less!
How old would you say I was to look at me? Quite a bit less,
I'll be bound!" — Gurdweill assented with a hypocritical
nod of his head — "And you know what, Herr Gurdweill,
at night I think of you — you don't know how much I
think of you! Pssss!" She flapped her hand energetically
to indicate an amazing amount. "Now you're a decent man,
Herr Gurdweill, a very decent man, if I may say so. Do you
think of me too? No, of course you don't . . . Ah, well . . .
I'm an old woman, a widow. It's ten years now since my
second dear husband died." And after a short silence she
added: "You should get married too, Herr Gurdweill. A
person gets sick and tired of being alone. Sick and tired!
Psssss!"

"What was your second husband's profession?" asked
Gurdweill, who had finished shaving and was busy sharp-
ening his razor for the next time.

"What was that?" The old woman inclined her head towards him and pointed to her left ear. "I'm a little hard of
hearing. From the day that my dear second husband died
I've been a little hard of hearing."

"His trade," Gurdweill put his mouth to the old woman's
ear and shouted, "What was your second husband's trade?"

"Why are you shouting like that, Herr Gurdweill? I can hear you, I can hear you very well! Aalbert (she pronounced the name with a heavy stress on the first syllable) — the son of my first dear departed husband, you know — is apprenticed to a tailor. He's a good boy, Aalbert is. In two years' time he'll have finished his apprenticeship. It's a fine profession is tailoring."

Gurdweill began to wash his face and the old woman proceeded at her leisurely, sloppy pace to make the beds. Her wispy grey hair, which had come loose from its braid, wagged about on her neck like the short, thin, pointed tail of some tiny animal. After a few minutes she approached him again:

"Today, Herr Gurdweill," she said in her usual whisper, "I feel well, thank God. My second breakfast went into the lower stomach, thank God!" — she patted her belly. "When food goes into the upper stomach" — she pointed to her ribs — "aie, aie, aie! It lies like a stone. It hurts the whole day long and I can't take another bite. But today I feel as healthy as a young girl!"

Gurdweill knew this speech off by heart. He had heard about the old lady's two stomachs and the rest *ad nauseam*. But today he felt kindly disposed and he listened with enjoyment, as if he were hearing it all for the first time. She went on chattering. Now she was telling him, as she did every morning when she came to tidy his room and he was still there, about the news she had read in the *Journal*, especially the murders and catastrophes, which were the only things that interested her and for whose sake she bought the paper. Wagging her head sympathetically, she told him about the officer who had murdered his mistress in Paris, "shot her in the head with his pistol five times he did, and she died on the spot, poor little thing," and about an earthquake in China, where three thousand people had been killed and three thousand had been left "naked and without a roof over their heads, aie, aie, aie!" and about a bank robbery in broad daylight in the heart of Chicago.

Gurdweill finished getting dressed and went into the kitchen to make himself tea. He decided to stay at home and work. He had a great desire to work and a feeling

39

that his work would go well today. When he returned with the sooty kettle, the room was tidy and the old woman on the point of leaving. But she came back and stood before him with her broom and cloth, and said with a certain hesitation:

"My Siedl says that I should put the rent up by five schillings. Prices have gone up, Herr Gurdweill, you know that yourself. But I told her: Herr Gurdweill is a quiet, decent man. We'll give him another month. The room is really an excellent room. You see for yourself, Herr Gurdweill! Big and clean — you won't find half a flea here, not if you search all day long."

"I can't manage it at the moment. I'll talk to your daughter about it."

Now the old woman heard every word.

"That's quite all right, Herr Gurdweill. Not now, but next month. And it makes no difference if you talk to Siedl or me. No difference at all. The room's for nothing, even with the extra five schillings! Where will you find such a nice big room for forty schillings? And for two people! It's only because you're such a decent man."

"Good," said Gurdweill, "we'll come to some arrangement."

He borrowed a small sum from the old lady and went downstairs to buy himself something to eat and cigarettes. Then he sat down to work.

After working for about two hours, he stood up feeling pleased with himself. There were still six hours to go until the meeting, he couldn't write any more, and he had no idea of how to fill in the time. It occurred to him to empty the ink from one ink-pot into another: a completely superfluous labour. His hands were stained with ink and he went to scrub them clean. Then he cut the sheets of paper into short pages and arranged them in exaggeratedly neat piles. He took care not to let any page project and made sure that the edges were as even as the pages in a bound book. All this took up no more than twenty minutes. He remembered that his old manuscripts needed tidying up too. He had been meaning to do this for some time, but he had never got around to it. He took a bundle wrapped in crumpled, dusty brown paper out of the cupboard, and undid the string. But after rummaging through the parcel for a few minutes he grew bored and tied it up again and put it back in the cupboard. He glanced at his watch: a quarter past two. Would he find Dr. Astel at home now? Sometimes he was at home at this hour. And if not — it would be a walk anyway. Gurdweill set off and walked to Karlsgasse, a fifty-minute walk in the mild air under the cloudy sky, where he did not find Dr. Astel at home. But he did not regret it in the least. Now he would go home and try to work a little more, and in the meantime the day would pass. He crossed the Opern Ring and turned for some reason left, in the direction of Herrengasse, instead of going down Kärntner Strasse, which was the shortest way home. In front of the entrance to the Hofburg he bumped into Lotte Bondheim, who was frankly delighted to see him and invited him to accompany her home, if he was free. She had to pick something up there, and afterwards they could go for a walk, or sit in a café, whatever he liked. She would take an umbrella too, because she was sure it was going to rain. Spring days were always liable to turn rainy. And especially today, with the clouds hanging right over your head. And she had a new hat on too — he hadn't even noticed, which was not nice of him at all! He, Gurdweill, never gave her a second glance. She was sure that he didn't even know what colour her eyes were! What, he did know? It must be a coincidence. Pure chance! And what about her hat? Did it suit her? Yes? She was glad to hear it. His opinion meant a lot to her. He was the only man she knew who understood anything about feminine attire. Blue always suited her, pale blue. She had woken up this morning in a somewhat melancholy mood, probably because of the weather. Cloudy days always had a bad effect on her. And the idea came into her head to buy a new hat! That was always a distraction. Going to the shops, trying the hats on, choosing. And now she felt better. So, did he really like the hat? He did! And she would do as he said and pull the brim down a little to the left. But Gurdweill seemed a little absent-minded today — was anything the matter? No, no — she noticed at once. She knew she was right. Well, if it

41

was a secret, she wouldn't press him, naturally. What a pity that he hadn't come for tea the day before yesterday! But he surely wouldn't refuse her now! She was really glad she had met him. She had peeped into the café earlier on, thinking she might find Dr. Astel there. Had Gurdweill seen him today? No?

And thus they arrived at Myrten Gasse, where Lotte lived.

"You must come up with me, Gurdweill," she pleaded, "we'll rest a minute, have some tea, and then go on."

Gurdweill deliberated for a moment. He remembered too, that he had to find someone to borrow money from for this evening. In the end he gave in and went up with Lotte.

There was nobody at home. Lotte peeped into the kitchen and said: "The maid must have gone out to buy something. She'll be back in a minute."

She ushered Gurdweill into the drawing-room and went out to make the tea.

A moment later she came back dressed in a loose, flowery kimono, and sat down next to Gurdweill on the sofa.

The latter remarked, as if to himself: "It really is strange . . ."

"What's strange?" inquired the girl.

"Meeting by chance like that, I meant. I was in Kärntner Strasse and I intended going home to work. And for no reason at all, I turned this way. The wrong way, in fact . . ."

"Perhaps it isn't the wrong way at all . . ." said Lotte with a meaningful smile.

Gurdweill took a cigarette from the open box on the smoking table next to the sofa and Lotte lit a match for him. Then she went out and came back with a silver tray holding tea, a china jug of milk, rolls and butter.

"Do you like tea with milk? No?"

With dainty, graceful movements she spread the rolls with butter and poured the tea. They drank silently. A muffled, distant roar rose from the streets outside and underlined the stillness in the house. Weak sunrays filtered through the clouds for a moment, and touched the keys of the grand piano in the corner without making a sound. Lotte lit a cigarette and blew the smoke out straight in front

42

of her. From time to time she cast a sidelong glance at her guest, as if she were trying to guess his thoughts. Suddenly she stood up and took a step towards the middle of the room, changed her mind and sat down on the sofa again. She gathered the folds of her robe together, as if she were feeling cold, and leant against the back of the sofa, in a semi-reclining position.

Gurdweill asked in a voice which was slighly louder than usual:

"And your mother, isn't she at home in the afternoons?"

"Sometimes she goes out to a café or to visit one of her friends. She's a modern woman, my mother. Even more than I am. But I think you know her, don't you?"

"Yes. You once introduced me to her."

Lotte sat up. She looked at Gurdweill as if she wanted to say something, but she didn't say anything. After a minute she asked about his work. He said he was working a little.

And as if suddenly remembering that he was pressed for time, he took out his watch and said: "Half past four. I have to go home."

Lotte looked offended.

"If you want to go, go . . . Nobody's keeping you."

"Your work's very important, of course," she added mockingly. "Nobody wants to stand in the way of your work . . ."

She began to play with the cigarette box on the table, moving it about and in the end trying to set it on the upturned box of matches. Her restlessness was obvious to Gurdweill, although he could see no reason for it. Suddenly she burst into loud, staccato laughter, leapt up from the sofa and ran to the window. She remained there, slightly stooped, looking out. From the back, Gurdweill noticed her slumped shoulders heaving slightly, as if she were silently sobbing, and he felt guilty, although he did not know why. He said in a coaxing voice:

"You wanted to go out yourself, didn't you, Lotte?"

Lotte did not answer right away. Then she said, without turning her head, that she didn't feel like it any more.

Gurdweill sensed vaguely that he should stay with her for a while. If he did, something in the situation might

43

become clearer. Nevertheless, as if in spite of himself, he stood up and announced:

"I have to go now."

Lotte accompanied him to the hallway, and offered him her hand without a word and without looking at him. He had the impression that she was waiting impatiently for him to go. But he did not see a window on the second floor opening when he emerged into the street. And he did not see Lotte sticking her head out of the window and staring at him until he turned into Lerchenfelder Strasse.

5

O N his way home Gurdweill tried without success to
find the reason for Lotte's strange behaviour. He
went over everything he had said in her house in his
mind: there was nothing that could have given her the
least offence. In the end he came to the conclusion that
there was nothing behind it but her own nervousness, and
he felt a little sorry for her, for this Lotte, who was actually
a very sweet girl, a dear soul, and for whom he had long
felt sentiments of the warmest friendship.

In the meantime the sky had partially cleared. Between
the murky clouds patches of deep blue appeared, fresh
and clean. Gurdweill remembered happily that there were
only three hours left until the meeting, and unconsciously
he quickened his pace, as if to reach the appointed hour
sooner.

At home he found a letter from his sister in America
waiting for him, with a ten-dollar bill folded inside it. It's
come at just the right time, thought Gurdweill. He would
be able to pay a few debts, and re-open old sources of
loans. And most important of all: he would not go to the
meeting empty-handed. Apart from the concrete benefits
involved, Gurdweill saw the fact that the unexpected letter
had arrived today of all days as a favourable omen. Without a doubt, this was the beginning of a new, happy time.

The money-changers in the vicinity were already shut,
but Gurdweill remembered in time that it was possible to
change money at the railway station too. Then he bought
himself a new collar and a bite to eat and went home again.

Soon afterwards Ulrich returned. He too had brought
food, bread, butter and sausage, and they sat down to eat.
Ulrich told him that he had seen Lotte at the café half an
hour before, and that she had asked him to give Gurdweill

45

her regards and to ask him to drop into the café that evening if he was free. She was sitting with Dr. Astel and seemed in high spirits.

"She's a pretty girl," added Ulrich. "Especially her eyes, they're quite extraordinary."

"Yes, very pretty," agreed Gurdweill absent-mindedly.

"I hear that she's already officially engaged to Dr. Astel," remarked Ulrich, and after a moment he added: "It doesn't seem like a good match to me."

"In these matters you can never tell in advance. There are always surprises. Anyway, why shouldn't it be a good match? Dr. Astel seems very much in love with her. And presumably she loves him too."

"I wouldn't be so sure."

"Why on earth not?" Gurdweill became unreasonably excited. "Tell me why not? She's maybe a little eccentric, perhaps. But in that respect she's no different from a lot of other people in our generation."

"That's not what I'm talking about. In my opinion, she's too good for him. And besides, I don't think she loves him."

"How on earth do you know? On the contrary!"

But in his heart of hearts he knew that Ulrich was right and he was wrong.

After eating Gurdweill stood up and began putting on his coat. Ulrich asked if he would come to the Café Herrenhof later.

"No, I'm meeting someone." (He was too shy to say her name.)

"The girl from yesterday?" asked Ulrich simply. And in order to give pleasure to his friend, for whom he felt true affection, he added: "She's very nice. There's a hidden charm about her, which you don't notice right away."

Gurdweill arrived at the café fifteen minutes early. He selected an empty table in the corner opposite the door, and ordered coffee. The few customers scattered around the square, smallish room, all seemed like old acquaintances and well-wishers to him, although he was seeing them for the first time in his life. He would have been delighted to shake them all by the hand and ask after the health of their families. He could not understand his former bitterness towards people like them. Weren't they all — all of them without exception — simple and good and deserving of love?

When the waiter brought his coffee Gurdweill asked him if the Baroness had not already been there this evening. He described her in detail — her face, figure and clothes. It gave him a peculiar pleasure to talk about her to this stranger.

"She's my fiancée, you see . . ." he concluded.

"No young woman of that description has been here. She's not one of our regulars."

"And could you tell me what the exact time is now?"

"Eight o'clock."

"In that case she'll be here directly. She's supposed to come after eight . . . she's very punctual . . ."

Gurdweill sipped the coffee and watched the door vigilantly. He smoked a cigarette, and then another one, and the Baroness did not come. It was already a quarter past eight. Perhaps it was the wrong café? — the doubt flashed through his mind. No, impossible! They had definitely arranged to meet in the Café Alserbach! He could not possibly be mistaken!

At that moment the Baroness entered the café. She walked straight up to him, as if she had known in advance that he would be sitting in precisely that corner. Gurdweill leapt up and went forward to meet her, his face radiant.

"I'm not late am I?" smiled the Baroness and held out her hand.

"Yes, you are late. Because I've been waiting since yesterday . . ."

"But not all the time here, I hope. That would have been rather boring."

She sat on the upholstered seat against the wall, took a packet of cigarettes out of her bag, lit one for herself and offered one to Gurdweill. She inhaled the smoke avidly, like an addict who had denied herself too long, and ordered black coffee.

Gurdweill was full of various things he wanted to say to her, but his tongue seemed stuck to the roof of his mouth.

47

He sat opposite her and gazed at her tenderly, smiling weakly with pleasure and embarrassment. The Baroness finished her coffee and asked him what his first name was.

"Ah, Rudolf," she said. "Rudolfus, Rudolfinus! My cousin's name is Rudolf too. He's taller than you by two heads — but he's an ass."

"I — I'm very glad that he's an a-ass . . ." stammered Gurdweill with an idiotic smile.

"What? You're glad that my cousin's an ass?" The Baroness burst out laughing.

"I only meant," Gurdweill recovered and tried to correct himself, "What I meant was . . . That's not what I'm glad about, of course . . . I didn't express myself properly . . . I imagine him tall and skinny, with straight, oiled hair parted in the middle, his shoes always polished until they shine. Patent-leather shoes. And when he looks at anyone he inclines his head slightly to one side, like a chicken, and puts on a very dignified expression — because, of course, he's really nothing but an ass . . ."

"You've described him very well — but never patent-leather shoes. Brown ones. And you forgot the gold-knobbed cane . . . 'Dorothea' — he always calls me 'Dorothea' because it sounds more dignified and traditional — 'Dorothea' — he says, ridiculous and pompous as an old man, 'you are the scion of an ancient race. Your ancestors were Crusaders, don't forget! You must be on your guard against the Jews. The city of Vienna has become Judaized from one end to the other. Blood doesn't matter any more. They're poisoning the air. But for them, we would never have lost the war.' And all the time he himself is running after a little Jewess who's turned his head completely."

"And do you obey him, Baroness?"

"In what respect?"

"Preserving the purity of the race?"

To this the Baroness responded with a loud burst of hard, unruly laughter.

"You know what," she said suddenly and irrelevantly, "Why don't you just call me Thea? Titles bore me."

Gurdweill gave her a grateful look. For some reason he suggested having a brandy. A spirit of recklessness entered

48

him: his pale, slender, feminine hands sought some object to hold, to absorb the energy coursing through them, and underneath the table they found one of the Baroness's unresisting hands. The waiter brought two little glasses of brandy, and Gurdweill emptied his in a single gulp. The Baroness announced that the next day, Saturday, she did not have to go to work because her "General" (which was what she called the lawyer for whom she worked) had gone away for the week-end, and she could stay out a little later tonight.

"Good, wonderful!" enthused Gurdweill.

They talked and fell silent and began talking again — talk which was apparently trivial, but was nevertheless full of a kind of hidden significance — and the time flew by as imperceptibly as an open plain by the side of an express train.

It was already eleven o'clock. Both of them at once suddenly felt the need to leave the café. Gurdweill called the waiter and paid him.

Outside the Baroness linked her arm in his, and they walked silently down Alserbachstrasse and turned into Sechsschimmelgasse. Suddenly she said, half seriously and half jokingly:

"You'll marry me, won't you, Rudolfus? I fancy you and I don't mind saying so."

Gurdweill was astonished. Such a possibility had not even crossed his mind. She was certainly an interesting girl! The way she said it — so simply! He had never heard anything like it before . . . He made haste to reply: "Of course! Of course! I'm ready! I've got no objections!"

And after a moment: "But what about your family? They won't give their consent will they?"

"My family?" she exclaimed scornfully. "Who? My cousin Rudolf? And what about me — where do I come in? I'm used to doing as I see fit! And by the way, my father is a very nice man. You'll meet him and see for yourself. I know he'll like you."

They walked down the slumbering streets, discussing the matter at length. The Baroness wanted a "real" wedding, in other words, a religious ceremony "according to the Jewish tradition." In order to do this, she would have to convert to Judaism, which did not seem to present any problems as far as she was concerned. She did not want any unnecessary delays, and they agreed to "take the necessary steps" and get married as soon as she was converted. To tell the truth, Gurdweill felt a certain flicker of uneasiness at the changes which were about to take place in his way of life, but he immediately suppressed it as groundless. Now, he thought with boundless happiness, now the dream he had been cherishing in his heart for so long would come true! Within a year! Or even two! And from who? From her! A son from her! Two ancient races! (For Rudolf Gurdweill came from an ancient Jewish family. He could trace his descent to a great and famous rabbi from Prague.)

So great was his joy that he stood still and embraced the Baroness in the middle of the street.

"A son," he whispered ardently, "you'll give me a son, won't you?"

The Baroness gave him a strange look and smiled without saying anything. It seemed ridiculous to her that this little man wanted a son . . .

They were in an ill-lit side street. It must have been about half past midnight. In the desolate silence their footsteps echoed with a hollow sound. Not far off the signboard of a hotel sticking out into the lane twinkled with orange bulbs. From the open door of the hotel a tongue of light protruded on to the paving stones and climbed halfway up the opposite wall. Gurdweill felt his companion's footsteps slowing down without understanding why. When they reached the hotel entrance she stopped. She bent down to Gurdweill as if he were a child and whispered:

"Why don't we celebrate our wedding night now, my little fiancé . . ."

It was only now that he noticed the brightly-lit hotel, which had previously escaped his attention. He felt as if the ground was slipping from under his feet. A dull flicker of rebellion stirred inside him and died down immediately. Before he knew what was happening they were already in front of the receptionist's desk. Gurdweill signed the register mechanically: Rudolf Gurdweill, born on such and such a date, in such and such a town, and his wife . . .

With an expression of total indifference on his tired, sleepy face the bellboy led them up the shabbily carpeted stairs and showed them into a square, sparsely furnished room on the second floor.

"If you need anything, just ring here!" He pointed to an ivory button next to the door, and pocketed the tip which Gurdweill offered him.

The Baroness made herself at home, glancing at the water jug to see if it was full and lifting the blankets to look at the sheets. Gurdweill was suddenly assailed by an alien, hostile spirit, reeking of sordid affairs and unexpected accidents — the spirit of all such squalid hotel rooms, and for a moment he came to his senses. The whole business, you had to admit, was rather strange. Before he could turn around, he found himself in a new, ambiguous situation, no longer in control of his actions or capable of directing them at his will. What was he doing here in this strange and disagreeable room? For a moment he regretted the whole thing and wanted to run away. He felt a kind of shame. This was not the way to begin the new stage in his life! He stood in the middle of the room with his coat on, his hat in his hand, as if he were on the point of leaving. Then he turned to face his companion, who had removed her hat in the meantime and loosened her long flaxen hair. He felt very embarrassed. He looked for somewhere to put his hat and in the end he put it back on his head. He went up to the window and drew the curtain and looked outside without seeing anything. Then he returned to Thea, who was already sitting on the bed and undoing her shoes. Her long, jutting chin twitched spasmodically and her bosom heaved. Gurdweill sat down beside her on the bed. She immediately left her shoes alone and turned to face him. There was a cruel, bloodthirsty expression on her face. She fixed him with eyes flashing like spears, as if to subdue him completely, and with one swift movement she threw herself back and stuck her teeth in his elbow, like a beast of prey. Gurdweill let out a strangled groan. He felt as if he were about to faint with pain and desire at once.

51

He sensed his strength draining out of his body. Flaming red daggers danced before his eyes and sweat burst from his brow. At the same time he wished that it would go on forever, that the pain would increase a thousandfold, that it would annihilate him entirely. No woman had ever made him feel like this before.

Thea suddenly jumped up.

"Get undressed, Rudy!" she commanded in a slightly husky voice, and she herself began tearing off her clothes and throwing them on a chair. Then she seized hold of Gurdweill, lifting him like a doll, and laid him on the bed.

At half past five in the morning, after seeing Thea home, Gurdweill dragged himself through the dead streets. Taking small, slow steps he tottered down the middle of the street, his head heavy and at the same time absolutely empty. Fresh morning breezes whipped across his face, suddenly changing direction and buffeting him from the side and the back, trying to rob him of his hat. He took it off with a mechanical movement and abandoned his rumpled hair to the wind. A row of big carts, piled high with vegetables, trundled slowly towards the market; the heavy wheels creaked and scraped on the street, vanquishing the stubborn silence. High up on their perches the drivers slumbered, huddled in sacks against a possible rainfall and the morning chill, withdrawn into themselves like lifeless bundles. It seemed as if they had been driving thus for years on end, driving on and on without a pause. The lamplighters bobbed up in their filthy cloaks, zigzagging from one side of the street to the other, and putting out the gas lights with the long bamboo poles they carried on their shoulders like tremendous spears. From time to time a solitary milk cart emerged from a side street, the big tin containers lined up one on top of the other, or a closed bread van from the "Hammer" or "Anker" bakery. Here and there people were already waiting for the first trams: prostitutes with wilted, tired faces, their unmade-up eyes naked and wrinkled. How depressing they looked in their garish, crumpled dresses, their gay hats awry. Women from the poorest of the poor, one with a bundle of morning papers wrapped up in a bottle-green shawl, one with a huge basket of vegetables. A few workers. The newborn morning invaded the street with a pale, milky light and everything seemed strange and dreamlike to Gurdweill. The night had left him with a feeling of measureless oppression, strangely combined with a kind of reckless hilarity. He was already on the quay, and suddenly he stopped dead and laughed to himself with a lopsided grin on his face. Anyone who saw him would surely have thought him drunk. He set off again, crossed the Ferdinand Bridge, and stopped to wait for a tram. With lustreless eyes he looked at the two prostitutes waiting there, and the picture of the hotel room in which he had spent the night rose up before him. The memory gave him such a disagreeable feeling that he was forced to avert his eyes. But at the same time he was filled with a great longing for Thea. For a moment he imagined that he would never see her again, that he had parted from her forever, and he felt utterly abandoned, fatally ill, and completely useless. At that moment he could have burst out crying. Gurdweill now knew, without the shadow of a doubt, that he was enslaved to her, to this strapping, blonde girl, forever, and that without her he was a broken vessel, fit for nothing. He moved away from the tram stop and walked down Praterstrasse on shaky legs.

When he entered his room it was already morning. And from the next-door room he could already hear the yells of "Aalbert," the old landlady's grandson, and his Auntie Siedl, fighting as they always did when the boy spent the night in their house.

6

I T was now two weeks since Gurdweill had met Thea.
There were only ten days left to their wedding, which
was to take place on the Jewish festival of Lag B'Omer.
The necessary documents were already in the possession of
the congregation's "Marriage Bureau," and every evening
after work the Baroness went to the rabbi for instruction
in the Jewish religion. She regarded this as a kind of sport,
and after every lesson she would boast of her knowledge,
not without a hint of irony.

It was agreed that Ulrich would look for another
room and that Thea would move in with Gurdweill after
the wedding. Ulrich agreed willingly, despite the housing
shortage which meant that it would not be easy for him to
find a new room.

With the exception of Lotte Bondheim, who for some
reason had kept away from the café recently, most
of Gurdweill's friends had already made Thea's acquaintance. Dr. Astel, who had pretensions to being a
connoisseur, found the Baroness "*superbe,*" as he liked
saying in French. Although she came from an ancient
race, he said, she showed no symptoms of decadence.
She was natural and healthy — "a real Brünhilde." But
when Lotte Bondheim heard the news of Gurdweill's
approaching marriage she burst into a fit of hysterical
laughter. She was in the café with Dr. Astel at the time.
For ten minutes she laughed loudly and wildly, stopping
for breath and beginning all over again, until everyone
stopped talking to stare at her.

"Oh, no," she cried, "it's too ridiculous for words! I've
never heard anything so grotesque in my life! Little Gurdweill is going to marry a Baroness! A big, blonde Baroness!
Ha ha ha! A little baron! One day he'll start a pogrom

54

against us!"

When Dr. Astel tried to calm her down: "What's there to laugh about Lotte? I can't see anything to laugh at . . ." she retorted: "No, of course not, you're too blind to see how ridiculous it is!" And three days later, when she met Gurdweill in the street, she was very pale and down at the mouth, and there were blue rings under her big grey eyes, as if she had just been ill. She asked him gravely if the rumours that he was about to get married were true, and when 'Gurdweill answered in the affirmative she said nothing at all. A moment or two later she parted from him after the exchange of a few banalities.

In the days preceding his marriage Gurdweill was in a daze. He perceived everything around him as if through a fog. The truth was that he was far from the happy and contented state to be expected from a prospective bridegroom. He seemed more like someone preoccupied by a very important matter which required the concentration of all his spiritual resources. And there really were a number of minor matters which demanded his attention, matters which had acquired a new importance in the light of the change about to take place in his way of life. Including the urgent need to find some sort of job.

He had been to visit Thea's father several times. Despite his sixty years the Baron was a strong, erect figure of a man, with the sprinkling of grey at his temples only adding an extra touch of aristocracy to his features. Apart from Thea, he had two grown-up sons, Poldy and Freddy, a second wife, and a fat, lazy, black and white cat, to whom he devoted most of his time. He lived modestly on the income from some fund, drastically reduced by the ten thousand per cent devaluation of the Austrian currency, and on Poldy's salary as a bank clerk. He liked Gurdweill from the moment he met him and invited him over several times to drink black coffee and play chess, which according to Thea was a sure sign of his approval.

Gurdweill met Thea every evening, usually in their café. Once he waited for her outside her office, in Johannesgasse, but she was not pleased. After the boring day's work in the office, she said, she needed a change of air to recover her strength, and there was nothing better for her than a solitary walk in the bustle and noise of the streets . . . Although it seemed a little strange to him, Gurdweill gave in and did not go to meet her again. They had already paid several visits to Gurdweill's regular café, the Herrenhof, where they had arranged to meet this evening, too, but until then he still had a long time — over four hours — to fill in. Gurdweill tried to work for a while, but after writing a few lines he realized that he was not alert enough to work today, and he decided to go outside.

The city was bathed in spring sunshine, the trees in the gardens next to the streets were already in full leaf. Gurdweill wandered pleasantly from street to street, bareheaded, his stick in his hand, the silver-knobbed stick he had once received as a gift from Dr. Astel, which had been hibernating behind the wardrobe and revived with the stirring of spring, to accompany Gurdweill wherever he went until the autumn, as a kind of substitute for his hat, which stayed at home as long as summer lasted.

When he reached the Schottenring it occurred to him to call on the shoemaker Vrubiczek, who lived nearby and whom he had not visited for some weeks now. A peculiar friendship existed between these two men, who had nothing in common as far as age, education or opinions were concerned. Two years before Gurdweill, who had been living in the neighbourhood, had taken him a pair of shoes to mend and entered into conversation with him. And ever since then he had visited him regularly, even after moving out of the neighbourhood.

When he entered Vrubiczek jumped up happily to welcome him:

"So you've turned up again Herr Gurdweill! I was about to inform the Lost Property Office about you! Where have you been all this time?"

Gurdweill sat down on the square stool, on the hollow seat of greasy, black leather which the shoemaker cleared of the shabby shoes stiff with dry mud and the dirty lasts full of nail holes. Vrubiczek took up the shoe lying on his lap and began to attach the heel.

56

"I wanted to come before, but I never had a chance," said Gurdweill. "How have you been keeping, Herr Vrubiczek? And your old lady?"

"Well, well!" replied the shoemaker contentedly. "Couldn't be better! When your shoes fit your head doesn't ache, as it says in the proverb. Yes, my Johann was married this very Sunday — and what more could you want, Herr Gurdweill? The old are buried and the young are married, and that's the way of the world. My old lady's been asking about you: what's become of Herr Gurdweill? Why don't we ever see him any more? And I say to her: if he doesn't come, he's got his reasons. Depend upon it. Who knows, maybe he's taken a wife who keeps him at home, or maybe his business is prospering and he's hard at work."

"My business isn't prospering," said Gurdweill with a slight smile, "but I am indeed about to take a wife."

"Is that so? Then allow me to congratulate you!" Vrubiczek stuck out a rough hand. "You're like a son to me, Herr Gurdweill, a real son! I said the same thing to my old lady only last week. I'm very glad to hear it! A bachelor is like an odd shoe, I always say, however expensive it is, it's fit for nothing! And yourself nearly thirty!"

After a moment he went on: "What do you say, Herr Gurdweill, with all your book-learning? Is there any other purpose to life? Tell me: did you learn anything better from reading all those books? I've been sitting here on my stool and thinking for these forty years, and what I say is: get married, have children, and enjoy life as much as it's given to a man to enjoy it!"

Gurdweill nodded in agreement. He was already familiar with the shoemaker and his clear mind, full of healthy thoughts about every aspect of life, thoughts which seemed to grow out of the depths of the earth itself, as strong and enduring as it was. In Vrubiczek's presence he always felt fortified, more firmly rooted in the soil: a feeling similar to the sensation which overcame him in the countryside, far away from the city and its strains. At these moments he would feel at peace, and everything would become clear and straightforward, like a boldly outlined design.

Vrubiczek stopped working, wiped his hands on his dirty apron and began rolling himself a cigarette. He offered one to Gurdweill as well. Then he looked at him with his clear, true eyes, as innocent as the eyes of a baby but full of wisdom, too, and said sympathetically:

"But you don't look well, Herr Gurdweill. You seem worried about something, too."

"It's nothing. Perhaps I'm a little tired."

He himself did not know why he did not look well. He felt perfectly fit and could only attribute it to his lack of sleep in recent weeks. For some reason, however, he was displeased by the fact that the shoemaker had noticed it.

He sat smoking his cigarette in silence, watching Vrubiczek as he stooped over the inverted shoe, knocking the nails into the heel with rhythmic, monotonous blows. Little by little he sank into a kind of quiescence, a half-slumber of the senses. His elbow propped up on his knee and his chin cupped in his hand, he abandoned himself with a certain enjoyment to this semi-comatose state. His back was turned to the glass door leading to the street, and the noise coming from outside seemed to him to be receding further and further into the distance, until all that remained was a dull, vague murmur without beginning or end. Now a slightly husky male baritone broke into some popular song in the neighbouring courtyard and rose above the murmur. The song was apparently a very sad one, but it did not touch Gurdweill's heart. On the contrary, it seemed to Gurdweill that the man was not singing at all but announcing something, straining his voice so as to make himself heard above the shoemaker's hammering, which for some reason he found supremely ridiculous. "Ah, if only Thea could hear him! How she would laugh! And Vrubiczek himself," he reflected, "sitting here for forty years . . . Yes, forty years on end knocking in one nail after the other — that too is strange and incomprehensible, if you only stop to think about it . . ."

"You know, Herr Vrubiczek," Gurdweill suddenly said in a whisper, without raising his head, which had drooped right down, "once, more than a year ago, I had a strange dream. I dreamt that my left leg was amputated. At first

58

I didn't know why, but it immediately became clear to me that I owed this leg to my sister in America, and the whole thing seemed perfectly natural to me. And I didn't feel the lack of this leg at all when I was walking, because I immediately found a way round it: I remembered the way children hop on one leg with the other one tucked up when they play, and I did exactly the same, to everybody's astonishment. But on the other hand, one of my arms suddenly grew very long, several yards long, so that when I stood on one side of the street I could take something out of a shop on the other. And when I lay down to sleep, I had to fold this arm ten or fifteen times, like you fold a timber merchant's measuring rod, and in the end it really turned into a kind of measuring rod and I was very sorry about it."

Vrubiczek gave him a quick glance as he worked, scratched his shorn grey head with the handle of his hammer, and said nothing. For some reason it occurred to him that Gurdweill was not happy at all, and he pitied him.

In the meantime the singing in the courtyard had died down. Without thinking Gurdweill took a mended woman's shoe down from the shelf, turned it this way and that, examined it closely and returned it to its place. Vrubiczek finished attaching the heel to the shoe and began smoothing and trimming it with his knife, making a curious faint squeaking sound, like a mouse. From time to time he glanced at his guest, who went on sitting slumped on his stool, as if sunk in heavy thoughts. But to Gurdweill it suddenly seemed that Vrubiczek's silence had lasted too long, and that there was some hidden intention behind it, perhaps some resentment against himself. At the same time he decided not to go to visit Thea's father that day, as he had intended doing in the morning. It would certainly be too late now. He took out his watch and glanced at it, immediately forgot what it said, and looked again: quarter past six already! And Vrubiczek was still not finished.

"How late do you work, Herr Vrubiczek?"

"As late as I have to, of course! But usually till about six o'clock."

After a moment he added: "Poor people are not in command of their time. They have to bow to necessity. But I'm going to be finished in a minute. When the spring comes in, you know, the work gets less. The sun, you might say, is bad for the shoemaker. Not that I'm complaining, God forbid. On the contrary, let the poor warm their bones and good luck to them!" And as he saw Gurdweill standing up and taking his cane: "What, going already? No, no, Herr Gurdweill! You must come up with me and join us in a bite of supper! I won't let you go! You can't do a thing like that to me!"

"Thank you very much, Herr Vrubiczek, but I really have to go."

The shoemaker stood up and took off his apron. He said with sincere sorrow:

"No, Herr Gurdweill, I don't want to press you, but I must tell you that you're insulting me. My old lady will be very sorry."

"No, no, it really is impossible," Gurdweill insisted for no good reason. "Please give my regards to Frau Vrubiczek and to Johann. I'd like to invite you to my wedding, this coming Thursday, at three o'clock in the afternoon in Seitenstettengasse. Perhaps you'll be free then."

"I doubt it very much. On weekdays I'm never free, as you know. But I wish you well from the bottom of my heart. It's high time you were married. Give my regards to your intended. Please bring her to visit us one Sunday. If it's a nice day, we'll go for an excursion outside the city."

When Gurdweill left the shop he bumped into Heidelberger, who was about to go into the next doorway. The latter recognized him immediately and called out cheerfully:

"Good evening, Herr Doktor! How are you? I'm glad to see you! I've just this minute come home from work."

He invited Gurdweill to come up with him. Gustl was a good cook. Before he married her she used to cook for the gentry. They would eat and then go down for a chat over a glass of beer. Gurdweill explained that he was in a hurry, but Heidelberger pleaded with him so energetically to come in for at least half an hour, that in the end he agreed.

They went up to the third floor and Heidelberger opened the door with the key he took out of his pocket.

"Good evening, Gustl!" he shouted as soon as he crossed the threshold into the dark passage. "I've brought a visitor. The Herr Doktor has done me the honour! Is supper ready?"

From a door to the right of the entrance a woman of medium height appeared with the sleeves of her white blouse rolled up to above the elbows. Because of the dim light Gurdweill could not see her face properly. She said in a voice which seemed to him extremely sharp:

"Very pleased to meet you, Herr Doktor! Welcome! Everything will be ready in a minute!"

And she shut the door behind her.

Heidelberger ushered him into a small dining-room furnished with plain but strong furniture and pulled out a chair from the table in the middle of the room. "I have to wash a bit after work. Excuse me a minute," he said and went back into the passage, closing the door behind him.

Some kind of exchange between the husband's rough voice and that of his wife immediately ensued, but Gurdweill could not make out a word of it. He felt unsure of himself and ill at ease, and wondered what devil had persuaded him to enter this alien household. As if to give himself courage, he lit a cigarette and glanced quickly around the room and its contents. His eye was caught by a group of photographic portraits on the opposite wall. One of them, a large picture in a black frame, was the portrait of an old woman with a crumpled face, a sunken mouth and a mean, penetrating look in her eyes. This look was aimed directly at Gurdweill and made him feel distinctly uncomfortable, as if the person staring at him were alive. She must be his mother — he concluded — no doubt about it. Next to this portrait was one of Heidelberger in army uniform with a bristling

61

moustache, and a third picture was a group portrait of men in uniform.

Heidelberger's wife returned with a tablecloth and cutlery to lay the table. She was about twenty-six years old, not at all ugly, with quick movements in spite of her rather bulky body, and lively, darting eyes.

"Please don't get up," she said politely to Gurdweill as he pushed back his chair to make room for her, "don't trouble yourself, Herr Doktor!"

And she added with a significant smile and a twinkle in her eye:

"A diligent housewife never disturbs her guests."

Working briskly and deftly the young woman laid the table, stealing covert glances at the visitor as she did so. Gurdweill felt as if he had taken a seat to which his ticket did not entitle him in the theatre or some such place, from which he was in danger of being ejected at any moment. He said in an embarrassed, apologetic tone:

"*Gnädige* Frau, I'm really not in the least hungry and I beg you not to trouble yourself on my account. And besides, I can't stay long. I have to leave in another fifteen minutes at the most. Please forgive me for having disturbed you."

Heidelberger's wife, who was unaccustomed to being addressed as "*Gnädige* Frau," was evidently impressed. She paused for a moment in her work, stationed herself in front of him with her bosom swelling, and said, for some reason lowering her voice:

"Surely you're not serious, Herr Doktor! It will be an insult to me if you don't stay and eat with us. Franzl will blame me for it. He'll say that I don't know how to behave myself in society. Why bring shame on our humble home, Herr Doktor?"

She seemed to be making an effort to speak the kind of language she had heard in the houses of her domestic employment, without any admixture of common Viennese slang, and gave the impression of reciting some lesson she had learnt by heart in a foreign tongue for which she did not normally have any use.

In the meantime Heidelberger came in, clean and

spruce with his moustache neatly combed. His wife appealed to him:

"Franzl, the Herr Doktor refuses to stay and have supper with us. You talk to him —"

"That's enough!" he interrupted her, "You do your work and don't poke your nose in when nobody asked for your opinion!"

He sent her to fetch three tankards of beer from the tavern and while she was gone he engaged Gurdweill in conversation, overwhelmingly friendly and garrulous as ever, asking his name and religion, and telling him boastfully that he was a foreman in a big machine factory, and earned a handsome wage. Gustl returned with the beer and they pulled their chairs up to the table. Heidelberger ate heartily, with evident relish and appreciation of every dish. From time to time he urged his guest in his gruff voice, speaking with his mouth full:

"Eat up, Herr Doktor, eat up! Eating comes first — I always say — and everything else comes afterwards!" Although Gurdweill was not hungry he ate everything on his plate in order not to give offence, and heaped praise on the food, which was, in fact, very well prepared, to the delight of Gustl, who beamed with gratification.

"Didn't I tell you?" her husband chimed in. "Didn't I tell you she was a first-rate cook? You have to give her that! Say what you like about her — but that's one thing she knows how to do! A woman who can't cook and keep house isn't worth tuppence — that's what I say and nobody can deny it!" He took a gulp of beer and added:

"But what else do I say? That's not enough! A woman has to know that she's got a husband! That's what she has to know first of all!" He seized his wife, who was sitting next to him, by the shoulder, and showed her to his guest, as if she was some inanimate object: "What do you say, Herr Doktor? Nice, eh? You'd like a bit of jam like that yourself, I dare say? . . . Hee-hee-hee! . . ." He let go of his wife and slapped his guest affectionately on the back. "Well, we'll see! You mean a lot to me, Herr Doktor, because you're a clever man! I saw it at once! Who knows, hee-hee, who knows . . . One day,

Herr Doktor, one day, only because it's you, mind . . .
Heidelberger Franzl is your brother!"

And he burst into loud guffaws of laughter.

"What nonsense you talk, Franzl," said Gustl, smiling
coyly. "How can you say such things in front of visitors?
What will the Herr Doktor think of us?"

As she spoke she did not take her eyes off Gurdweill,
who was sitting opposite her, and it seemed to him that
she even winked once or twice with a kind of sly promise.

"Shut your mouth, Gustl!" commanded her husband.
"Don't interfere in matters that are none of your business!"

Gurdweill was embarrassed. And in order to pretend
that the whole thing was a jest he said with a smile:

"Not a bad joke, I must admit, not bad at all."

"A joke, you say?" retorted Heidelberger. "Maybe it's
not a joke . . . who knows, hee-hee . . . When I say something, I mean it! You're my friend, and when a man's my
friend, hee-hee . . . But she's a nice bit of jam," he jerked
his head in the direction of his wife, "you can't deny it,
eh?"

Gurdweill muttered with his eyes fixed on the table:

"She . . . she's very pretty, of course."

"So you see! And apart from that, hee-hee-hee . . ."

Gurdweill stood up and said that to his regret he
would have to leave now as he was pressed for time.
Heidelberger and his wife rose too. It was nearly eight
o'clock, and evening was already seeping through the
dark blue window and filling the room with shadows.
Heidelberger put his arm around his wife's waist and
cried with a rather hoarse laugh: "And now, Gustl,
give the little lad a kiss! He won't say no . . . Franzl's
got eyes in his head!" And he pushed her towards the
astonished Gurdweill and brought their heads together.
Before Gurdweill could break away, Gustl planted a kiss
on his lips, at the same time pressing herself against him
so closely that he could feel every curve of her warm
body.

"That's it, that's it! Harder now, ha-ha-ha, my little
Herr Doktor!" bellowed her husband. In the end she

64

drew away, blushing hotly, and said apologetically:

"Please forgive us, Herr Doktor. Franzl has taken leave of his senses today. But he's a good man, I can tell you straight!"

Gurdweill stood there for a moment completely at a loss. His heart pounded. He mumbled something in a whisper, smiling a twisted smile. Then he turned his head from side to side, as if looking for something. He avoided looking at Heidelberger or his wife. In the end he remembered his cane, which he had left at the door, and went to take it.

When they parted, Heidelberger said:

"Don't think badly of me, Herr Doktor, and come and see us whenever you like. My home is always open to you! It's a pity you're in a hurry today, but I won't try to detain you. Don't forget, Franzl Heidelberger is your friend and brother! You'll come again soon, won't you?"

And Gustl chimed in:

"Yes, yes, it will give us great pleasure."

He promised to come soon and left. His hosts accompanied him to the passage and opened the door for him. He hurried down the stairs almost at a run. Outside the streetlamps were already on. Gurdweill strode rapidly towards the Innere Stadt; he had arranged to meet Thea at eight o'clock and he was already quarter of an hour late. His embarrassment gradually subsided and he occupied his thoughts in attempting to clarify the strange scene which had just taken place. Heidelberger had for some reason attracted his interest from the first time they met, that night in the bar, and his curiosity had now increased a hundredfold. He could not find a satisfactory explanation for his host's behaviour. He did not know if it stemmed from perversion, or if it really was a strange expression of friendship and hospitality, as practised to this day in various nationalities — or if it was both these together. The woman herself — although she was undoubtedly attractive, "a healthy, natural female," which at some other time may well have aroused his appetite — had not made any impression on him. On the contrary, the contact with her lips and body had left him with a disagreeable taste, almost approaching revulsion. Nevertheless, he decided to follow the development of the episode through to the end.

7

GURDWEILL arrived at the Herrenhof half an hour late for his appointment. In an alcove by the window Thea was already waiting in the company of Dr. Astel and Perczik. They were engaged in an animated conversation, and the minute Gurdweill entered the café he was flooded by a disagreeable feeling, as if they were conspiring against him. Perczik's presence, above all, made him suspicious.

Dr. Astel greeted him with false heartiness:

"Hey, Gurdweill, what kind of behaviour is this? Since when do ladies have to wait for their cavaliers?"

To this sally Gurdweill made no reply. He turned to Thea with a conciliatory air:

"It's not my fault if I'm late. I was detained." As he spoke Gurdweill noticed a sly smile crossing Perczik's face, which he imagined, for some reason, to be directed at him.

"Never mind, Rudolfus, you're not very late," said Thea. "If you had been, I would have been really angry. But why are you standing? Sit down!"

Gurdweill brought a chair from a nearby table and placed it next to Thea.

"Oh, hullo Perczik," said Gurdweill in a surprised tone of voice, as if he had just noticed his presence. "How are things in the *avant-garde* nowadays? Are you still raking in the dollars?"

"What's that got to do with anything?" retorted the latter angrily, stroking the corners of his mouth with his thumb and forefinger in embarrassment. "But you're apparently in a bad mood today . . ."

"I'm in a bad mood? Not at all! On the contrary!"

"Perczik's no longer getting paid in dollars, but in African pounds," Dr. Astel chimed in.

Perczik pulled a sour face but said nothing.

67

While Gurdweill sipped the piping hot coffee the waiter brought him, Dr. Astel picked up the threads of their interrupted conversation, which was about the role of coincidence in life. Dr. Astel was a lawyer and making speeches was his profession. He loved hearing himself talk, and never missed an opportunity to hold forth, especially when women made up part of the company.

"It all comes down to our own limited understanding, my dear lady," pronounced Dr. Astel with the self-importance and confidence of an expert. "We are able to perceive only the visible, external aspect of things, and that too only in fragments, in incomplete bits and pieces, whereas the inner connection, the unifying thread, is invisible to us. And what follows from this? That those phenomena which we call coincidences are also part of the chain of cause and effect, and that they are absolutely inevitable. It may seem, for example, that coincidence A which happens to X, and coincidence B which happens to Y, could change places, so that A would happen to Y, and B to X. Not so! These things follow an iron rule. Just as chemical element A combines with B and not with C, when two things meet and combine in the world there's nothing coincidental about it except in terms of our own limited vision."

Thea asked with a smile:

"So do you think, for instance, that even the fact that we two met is a result of some inner necessity?"

"Of course. I'm certain of it."

A wild, remote possibility, too vague to define, flashed across both their minds at once, and was gone again before they could catch more than a glimpse of it.

"The truth of these matters can never be scientifically established. They're always open to different interpretations," remarked the Baroness. And turning to Gurdweill: "And you, Rudy, haven't you got anything to say?"

"No, I've got a bit of a headache," said Gurdweill, who did not feel like talking due to the black mood which had suddenly and inexplicably descended upon him. He longed to be alone with Thea, somewhere else, with nobody to disturb them, but she was apparently enjoying herself and showed no signs of wishing to leave the café. Leaning back with his face to the window, the bottom half of which was covered with a heavy, hairy, wine-red curtain, he sat and smoked and tried to make out, through the slit in the curtains, the profile of a passer-by in the light breaking out of the café and climbing up the opposite wall, where the shadows of the people sitting inside were printed. For some reason, he remembered with a pang the mean look in the eyes of the old woman in the portrait in Heidelberger's house. Yes, the whole affair was very strange, including the fact that he had agreed to go up to Heidelberger's place, whereas he had stubbornly refused to go home with Vrubiczek, who was his friend . . .

In the meantime Ulrich and Lotte Bondheim came in, intoxicated by the chilly spring air. The two women surveyed each other for a moment as Dr. Astel introduced them. Gurdweill sensed clearly that Lotte did not take to Thea, and for some reason it seemed quite natural to him that this should be so. As if he had known it all along.

As she sat down in the place vacated for her by Dr. Astel, opposite Thea, Lotte said:

"I've already heard a lot about you, Baroness, and I'm glad to meet you."

At the same time she noted complacently to herself: badly dressed, and no beauty either! Her nose is too short, her chin too long and flat. And those little eyes, without any eyebrows, have a hard look. I wouldn't change places with her, not even to be a Baroness . . . Gurdweill will get what he deserves from her, the miserable creature.

She gave him a pitying look and said:

"And you, Gurdweill, you've completely deserted your old friends, eh? You've quite disappeared from view!"

"I've been here a number of times without seeing you," he replied in a tone of self-justification. "I heard you weren't too well. Are you better now?"

"But of course! What choice did I have? If I'd waited for you to visit me I could have waited for ever!"

"Some of the blame is mine," said the Baroness with a smile. "I take up a lot of Rudolfus's time. You're not angry with me on that account, are you, Fräulein?"

69

Lotte noted: a vulgar, common accent. She calls him Rudolfus . . . that's all that was missing . . . And aloud she said:

"No, no, Baroness, why should I be? On the contrary!" And to Gurdweill:

"But you look shocking! I've never seen you look so bad. Perhaps you're the sick one!"

"Me? What an idea! I'm fit as a fiddle!"

"I can't see anything wrong with the way he looks," said the Baroness.

"Yes, but the Baroness has only known him for a couple of weeks, unless I am mistaken . . ."

"Indeed, but when I first met him he looked even worse . . ."

This discussion about his looks made Gurdweill feel ill at ease. Behind the words, innocuous enough in themselves, a secret battle was raging, and the battlefield, unfortunately for him, was Gurdweill himself. In a sudden decision to put an end to it, he said:

"What difference does it make what I look like! The main thing is that I feel strong and healthy. The rest doesn't matter a fig! After all, I'm not a baby who has to be weighed every week!" he concluded with a forced smile.

"Who knows!" said Lotte provocatively. "Maybe you are a baby . . ."

Dr. Astel, who was busy talking to Ulrich and Perzcik, caught the word "baby" and asked:

"What baby? What baby are you talking about, ladies?"

"Just a baby," Gurdweill quickly replied. "And the question is: should he be weighed twice a week or is once enough? What do you think?"

"Hmm, if you have to know right away, I'll go and make a telephone call immediately . . . if not we can put it off till later."

The exchange was not very witty, but it was enough to turn the conversation in a new direction. "Right away, right away of course," laughed Lotte.

The Baroness smiled a faint, triumphant smile. She suddenly knew with absolute certainty that Lotte was mad about Gurdweill, but at the same time it was quite clear to her that she had the upper hand. "Not bad at all," she thought. " 'A temperamental little Jewess,' as my cousin Rudy would say. Well, let's see who's the stronger!"

She took a packet of cigarettes out of her bag and offered it to Lotte, giving her a look of triumphant self-confidence which was met with one full of suppressed hostility. "She's probably more beautiful when she's angry," thought Thea. "Bright colours must suit her . . . We'll tickle her a little when we get the chance, this little girl . . ."

Lotte fumbled in the packet for a moment, her fingers trembling slightly, before she managed to take out a cigarette. She asked:

"Do you smoke a lot, Bar-o-ness?" (She never omitted the title, which she pronounced in an emphatic, faintly ironic drawl.)

"No! From forty to fifty a day . . ."

"In that case you must be an exceedingly nervous woman."

"Are you sure, my dear? — You'll allow me this intimacy, I trust? After all, we're going to be great friends soon, I feel it in my bones. Actually, I'm not nervous at all. Not in the very least! Smoking gives me pleasure, and I see no reason to deprive myself of any source of pleasure whatsoever . . . But people with weak nerves should abstain, there I agree with you."

Lotte shot her an annihilating glance and did not reply.

Dr. Astel suggested going to a wine-cellar. Perczik immediately stood up and began taking his leave, saying that it was getting late, to his regret, and his wife was waiting for him at home . . .

"Have you got enough money on you?" asked Gurdweill frankly. "Because I myself am clean out of cash today."

"Leave that to me!" said Dr. Astel. "Everything will be all right. Luckily for us, we don't have to count our pennies . . . Which reminds me of a story about my friend Bloch . . ."

And he sat back and began in a calm, deliberate voice to tell his story:

"A year ago I spent a few days in Berlin, where this

71

Bloch stays. When I arrived I wrote him a note and arranged to meet him in the morning in a café. I must tell you in advance that the man is far from poor. His father owns a bank in Berlin and gives him a generous allowance. To cut a long story short: I met Bloch as arranged and we spent an hour in the café. Then he invited me to have lunch with him — not at home, since he was on bad terms with his wife, but in a restaurant. Outside the restaurant he suddenly stopped, took out his wallet, and began counting and recounting his money. He had about two hundred and fifty marks, I remember. 'Why are you counting your money?' I asked in surprise. 'Just to be on the safe side,' he replied. 'I always count my money before entering any place where you have to pay.' And he told me the following story: when he was fifteen years old, still at high school, a funny thing happened to him. (They were then living in Dresden, where he was born and stayed until he was eighteen, when his parents moved to Berlin.) There was a girl there, of his own age, a pupil at a girls' school, whom he used to see almost every day on his way to school and who occupied his thoughts continuously for months on end although he had never met her face to face. He was much too shy to approach her, even though he longed to do so. And then, one Sunday afternoon at the beginning of summer, he met a friend in the street and stopped to talk to him. After a few minutes the girl came up to them and his friend introduced him to her. It transpired that she was his cousin, and that the two of them had arranged to go on an excursion into the countryside together. But his friend immediately informed her that he had to stay at home and would not be able to keep his promise. Upon which the girl proposed that he, Bloch, accompany her instead — an invitation which, as you may imagine, he was only too happy to accept. When they were already sitting in the tram, and the conductor came to take the money for their tickets, Bloch recalled that he had only one mark with him — barely enough to pay for the tramfare for the two of them there and back. What was he going to do now? The girl would certainly want to have something to drink in the hot summer weather, and perhaps to eat too! He was

72

too embarrassed to tell her that he didn't have any money with him. In the meantime the girl saw a friend of hers at the station and called out to her from the window, inviting her to join them. She immediately agreed. Bloch paid for her tramfare too, out of good manners . . . And he was left with twenty-five pfennig, just enough to pay for his own fare back."

Dr. Astel called the waiter and ordered aquavit. Then he continued:

"When they arrived at their destination, no sooner had they descended from the tram than the two girls wanted an ice-cream. They went into an ice-cream parlour and ordered two portions. Bloch pretended that he didn't like ice-cream and ordered nothing for himself. When they had finished they ordered another two helpings. The ice-cream was delicious, they said, and they simply couldn't understand how Bloch could not like ice-cream . . . How could anyone not like ice-cream! . . . It was the best thing in the world, etc. Bloch was desperate, he felt as if he was sitting on a nest of vipers and scorpions and racked his brains in vain to find some way out. Suddenly he had an idea. He saw two youths passing outside, apologized to the girls and said that he had to leave them for a moment to speak to a couple of acquaintances he had just seen in the street, stood up and went outside and ran . . . And from then on," concluded Dr. Astel, "he never goes into a café or a restaurant or the like without counting his money at the door, even though he always carries more than enough on him."

"What about the girls?" asked Thea.

"He never saw them again. He began taking a different route to school and lived in constant fear of bumping into one of them. Fifteen years have passed since then, the girls are married women with children, but he still feels the same old fear stirring inside him whenever he has to go to Dresden, which he tries to avoid as far as possible. As for ice-cream — he feels nauseous at the very mention of the word. It's enough for a woman to express the desire for an ice-cream for her to lose all her attraction as far as he's concerned. He can't wait to find an excuse to get away

73

from her, and he never sees her again. He only married his wife after ascertaining that she hated ice-cream as much as he did. This Bloch," concluded Dr. Astel, "is a strange character altogether. I could go on telling you about his peculiarities and eccentricities for a week."

"A sick man," said Gurdweill, "a complete neurotic."

"And now let's go, people!" urged Dr. Astel. After deciding to go to the Opernkeller they got up and left the café.

It was about half past ten. The noise in the streets was already growing weaker, as if there were holes gaping in it. The asphalt stretched out before them, swelling and gleaming with a nocturnal glitter. The passers-by were reflected in it as in a distorting mirror, squat and dwarf-like or exaggeratedly long and thin. Rays of an orange coloured light issued from the luxurious cafés, a glaring, arrogant light, so bright that when you entered it your eyes shrank and blinked momentarily in pain. The revolving doors disgorged people from one side and swallowed them from the other, like some strange machine. In their garish uniforms the doormen bowed ceremoniously, making sweeping gestures with their arms as if they were opening great doors in the air. Fragments of jazz, foxtrots and tangos came reeling from all directions, flying around you like invisible bats and leaving you slightly stunned, your arms and legs throbbing in time to the tunes. In the middle of all this the solitary policemen idly patrolling the street looked superfluous, pitiful and forlorn.

With small steps they walked down the middle of the street: Dr. Astel and Lotte at the head and behind them, at a distance of ten paces or so, Gurdweill, Thea and Ulrich. Thea chatted to Ulrich while Gurdweill was sunk in thought. His thoughts ran along these lines:

"People rush to places of amusement and dancing and bawdiness not always out of any real appetite for pleasure, but more often in the need to escape. Most of these people are unhappy, sick of their lives, unable to stand themselves ... Burdened by daily cares, boredom, or simply fear, an obscure fear of which they are not even aware — a fear which unconsciously robs them of their peace

74

of mind, drives them relentlessly on, and prevents them from looking directly and courageously at the commotion in their souls and all around them. The rootlessness grew even worse after the war, until it sometimes seems that all these people are actually sorry they survived . . . Perhaps there is a need for a new religion," he reflected, "a religion capable of stopping these fleeing masses, of returning them to themselves, bringing them back to nature and healthy simplicity . . ."

A gentle melancholy seeped through Gurdweill, touching and not touching him — a melancholy which gave him a certain pleasure and which perhaps might better be described as a subtle kind of happiness. It was good, after all, to be able to walk through the streets on a mild spring evening, with close, devoted, kind-hearted people — yes, kind-hearted in spite of themselves, to walk like this without end or aim. Gurdweill sensed the touch of Thea's arm linked in his, and he felt secure, as if he had finally set foot on dry ground after months at sea in a lost ship. And then he heard Thea saying to Ulrich: "Yes, he's a handsome man . . . He could be attractive to women . . . But Lotte doesn't seem too keen on him . . ." He knew immediately who the subject of their conversation was, and he felt a faint echo of his previous distress upon entering the café. No! He, Gurdweill, without any ulterior motives, did not consider Dr. Astel handsome. That nose, too long and heavy for his narrow face, which looked as if it was pulling the whole balding head downwards — that could hardly be called handsome . . ! And the little eyes, too, with their nondescript colour, like two oblique, Mongoloid slits, which always seemed to have a different expression to the rest of his face — could anyone really claim that they were attractive? But women apparently thought otherwise. They were usually attracted to him. His elegant clothes, made by one of the best tailors in town, certainly helped. Women liked that sort of thing. In any case, making an impression on the female sex in general proved nothing either to a man's credit or discredit. You could even say that it was more to his discredit than his credit . . .

In the meantime they reached their destination. After

descending a number of steps they entered a low-ceilinged, spacious hall, fitted out in a deliberately plain, rustic style, and crowded with people. They looked around for a while before selecting a spot in the corner, and sat down at a square, brown table of sturdy oak.

"I take it you've got nothing against Malaga wine, ladies?" said Dr. Astel heartily. "It's heavy and a little sweet like a summer evening in Vienna . . ."

As far as she was concerned, said the Baroness, there was no need to order sweet wine for her. She drank spirits too, with pleasure . . . And the stronger the bet-ter . . . But she liked Malaga too. It was a very good wine.

And to Lotte: "How about you, my dear?"

"I?" said Lotte, with every intention of insulting her, "I, my dear Baroness, dislike all forms of alcohol. I may drink a little occasionally, but only in order to be sociable, and without deriving the least pleasure from it. Drinking isn't womanly, in my opinion."

Thea, who had guessed that Lotte would say something along these lines, was highly amused.

"Why not?" intervened Ulrich. "It's not nice for a wom-an to get drunk, but a drink or two? That doesn't detract from their femininity or attraction. On the contrary — all it does is make the blood flow a little faster, making a pretty woman even prettier and more lively."

The waiter uncorked the dusty bottle and Dr. Astel, as the host, poured. He ordered another bottle immediately. They clinked glasses and drank. The heavy wine soon lit a fire in their blood, their faces grew flushed, their voices grew louder, bolder and more animated.

Two men passed close to their table and greeted the Baroness with what seemed to Gurdweill excessive friend-liness. They sat down at a table not far off, which had just been vacated. Gurdweill looked at them suspiciously. These men were involved in Thea's past, an alien, un-known past in which Gurdweill had no part and which, without admitting it to himself, he hated. She had not told him anything about her past, and he had not asked, perhaps out of a secret fear that he might hear something

76

very painful which was better left alone. But any man she had known previously and without him was antipathetic to him in advance, arousing a profound hostility which he preferred not to examine too closely.

He poured a glass of wine down his throat and lit a cigarette. He kept stealing sidelong glances at the two strange men.

The effect of the wine on Lotte was immediate. She was sitting on Gurdweill's left and she put her arm around his neck, an arm bare to the armpit, smooth, pale and shapely, covered with a fine down from the elbow to the wrist, and whispered into his ear, breathing hotly and swallowing half her words:

"She doesn't . . . you'll see . . . in the end you'll find out . . . she doesn't love you . . . a woman sees these things at once . . . she's heartless . . . you'll see later . . ."

But Gurdweill paid no attention at all to what she was saying. He suddenly saw that the two men were smiling at Thea. It even seemed to him that they were making signs to her with their glasses and winking at her. A kind of burning, heavy lump suddenly rose in his gorge and shot into his head. Cold shivers ran down his spine. He pushed back his chair and went over to their table before anyone realized what was happening.

"What do you think you're doing?" he demanded in a hoarse, trembling voice. "Be so kind as to stop that vulgar winking at once!"

"Wha-at?" The two men jumped up. "Get lost! What the hell has it got to do with you?"

Thea came running up and grabbed Gurdweill's raised arm before he could strike them.

"Leave them alone, Rudolfus!" she ordered in a commanding voice. "What are you looking for fights for? You're drunk. These men are acquaintances of mine."

Dr. Astel and Ulrich, too, came up to hold him back. But their attempts only increased his rage. He struggled to free himself from his friends, flushed and shouting:

"I'm not drunk, I tell you! I'm not drunk at all! How dare they make obscene signs at a decent girl in the company of her friends? What unheard-of cheek!" In

77

obedience to a gesture from Thea the two men sat down again with contemptuous smiles.

Gurdweill, too, was led back to his seat. He sat shooting annihilating looks at his enemies, who were drinking their wine and laughing and joking as if nothing had happened. His anger had not yet subsided. It seethed inside him like a dense poison without finding an outlet. He bitterly regretted not having had the chance to hit them, the scoundrels, and teach them some manners. He poured himself a glassful of wine and drank it down in one gulp.

"What devil got into you all of a sudden, Gurdweill?" said Dr. Astel, who hated scenes, placatingly. "You surprised me, I must say. You really surprised me! I would never have thought you capable of it!"

Lotte kept repeating in a whisper, as if talking to herself: "It's not worth it . . . you'll see . . . you'll regret it . . ."

"How dare they stare like that! What rudeness! I'm not drunk, but you're a couple of cowards! Yes, cowards!"

"What, aren't they allowed to look in this direction? You can't stop them from looking!" said Thea.

"Looking! You call that looking! Civilized people don't look at a decent girl like that!"

But this was only a pale echo of his former rage, which had faded in the meantime to a painful kind of bitterness. The whole thing suddenly seemed unimportant, as if it had nothing to do with him. He bowed his head in resignation. He no longer heard what was said to him, except as a muffled sound coming from another room. A sudden pallor covered his face and he felt like crying. At the same time a scene from another time and place flashed into his mind. His mother was standing next to him and placing a cold compress on his brow. He was ill in bed. His mother bent over him and for some reason he placed his hand on her back. The first touch of the compress was icy cold and made his teeth chatter, but gradually he felt its soothing effect: his headache was a little better. His mother straightened up and remained standing beside him. She smiled at him very lovingly. Then she asked: "Is it a little better, baby? Soon you'll be fine again!" But Gurdweill said nothing. He lay looking at his mother's delicate face, its pure, transparent skin, and he did not want to open his mouth to speak. He was glad that she was there next to him, looking after him and loving him. Gurdweill saw all this as if he were split in two: one observing and one lying sick in bed. And the strangest thing of all was that Gurdweill's appearance as an infant was no different from his appearance today. It seemed to him, too, that the sick Gurdweill was unshaven, and he felt a quick pang of regret. The whole scene was over in half a minute. He did not see the events taking place one after the other, but all at once, one next to the other, as it were. And suddenly everything disappeared. His hand was playing absent-mindedly with the empty glass on the table and his head was hanging on his chest. Suddenly he felt a tremendous heaviness in his head and a dull pain. He raised his head and fixed his eyes on Thea with a puzzled, glassy look:

"We're not such heroes ... When it comes to a little headache we're not such heroes, are we?"

And a moment later: "Ah, Th-Thea, pour me a little wine! M-mother's gone ..."

"What are you mumbling about, rabbit?" laughed Thea. "What mother?" ("Rabbit" was her pet name for Gurdweill, on account of his shortness and quick movements.)

"Oh, never mind!" Gurdweill collected himself. "Let's go soon, eh?"

"Just a little longer!" replied Thea. And in a whisper: "The two of us will go and enjoy ourselves afterwards, won't we?"

And she looked deliberately at Lotte, as if she wanted her to understand.

"Yes, yes," answered Gurdweill mechanically without taking in a single word.

The heat in the cellar and the drink coursing through their limbs made them feel drowsy and relaxed. Lotte leant against Dr. Astel and laid her head on his shoulder, smiling a sad, resigned smile.

"Why are you all so silent?" cried Dr. Astel. "A little life, gentlemen! Gurdweill, Ulrich!"

"There's no point in getting worked up," said Ulrich.

Dr. Astel raised his glass and peered through the dark red liquid at Lotte, and since he could not see anything, he drank the wine and raised the glass to his eyes again.

"Ah, yes," said Ulrich, brandishing his glass, "that's what I always say! Gurdweill is my witness, right, Gurdweill? The world, I say, is like a single garment for an entire family . . . A large family, ranging in size from the baby in the cradle to the man in his prime . . . And the garment is too big and long for one, ha-ha-ha! And for another too short and narrow — too short and too narrow, gentlemen!"

Before Gurdweill's eyes flashed the picture of a hulking youth wearing a child's green striped coat, barely reaching his waist and splitting at the seams to expose strips of white vest. He nodded his head and smiled a satisfied smile.

"An excellent metaphor," said Dr. Astel half seriously and half jokingly, "I'll make a note of it for future reference."

Addressing himself for some reason exclusively to the Baroness and gesturing with his hands and head, Ulrich continued hoarsely:

"And here, Fräulein, you come up against something final! Reason, will — everything evaporates! A man must needs be content with his lot in life — and hold his tongue! And if not, if he refuses to be satisfied — why, he is free to shake his fists and kick his legs as much as he likes, until he gets tired and stops . . . You may say: but look at so-and-so — he struggled and he prevailed, he succeeded in changing his life! To this, my dear Baroness, I would reply: the person in question was only a pawn obeying the secret commands of another. He only appeared to be in control of his actions — and appearances don't count!"

"But this" — interrupted the Baroness — "is a philosophy for tired old men! If you don't mind my saying so, young men with blood in their veins don't concern themselves with calculations — they act! What are all these calculations good for? At the most — writing books for old maids and weak, impotent men — a miserable surrogate! Real, vibrant life wants nothing to do with calculations! What matters is passion, boldness, force!"

"This view of life," intervened Dr. Astel, "is a product of our generation. The soil in which it grew up is obvious. It is an utter negation of all civilized values. But man, in my opinion, is not an animal. Precisely those calculations which you, madam, relegate to weaklings and old men, are what distinguish human beings from the rest of the animal world. And don't forget that all the aeroplanes and automobiles, etc., which are the pride of our generation, are based on calculations too!"

"Enough arguments!" said Lotte. "It's time to go home. I'm tired."

Dr. Astel called the waiter and paid the bill. It was half past midnight when they left. The street lay bare in the night, spotted with light from the lamps. A sharp, cold wind blew between the walls, rattled the shop shutters, seeking escape like a trapped animal. From time to time it whipped a spray of rain like a wet broom across their faces. The women's dresses billowed like sails. The gaslight flickered in its cages, dancing and dying down and flaring up again. The policemen were suddenly seen to be draped in orange rain capes, making them look a little less important. Solitary cars drove past, their mud-guards glittering in the rain. Above their heads the lights of the advertisements went on and off, red and blue and purple, completely in vain.

The cutting wind sobered their fuddled minds a little and brought them back to reality. There was no hope of a tram at this hour. The group made haste to say their goodbyes. Thea seized Gurdweill by the hand, as if he were her property, and cried to Lotte:

"You'll come and visit me, won't you my dear, at home — from next Thursday on, Kleine Stadtgutgasse — but you know, of course! But I'm sure we'll see each other before then in the café. If you're free, I'd be delighted if you came to our wedding . . . next Thursday, at three o'clock in the afternoon, in Seitenstettengasse . . . Do come!"

Lotte did not reply.

Thea and Gurdweill turned away in the direction of the Schottentor.

8

THE next morning Gurdweill went to see Dr. Kreindel. This time he was not kept waiting. Dr. Kreindel greeted him with exaggerated joy, almost embracing him in his enthusiasm.

"Ah, at long last! I was getting impatient. Please sit down, Herr . . . er, Goldwein."

"Gurdweill!" Gurdweill corrected him.

"Ah, forgive me, Herr . . . er, Gurdweill. You have a strange name, sir. A rare name . . . Melodious and rhythmical: Gurd-weill . . . even a little mystical . . . No need for any title or degree, anything of that kind would be completely superfluous . . . The name speaks for itself. A name of that kind is a guarantee of greatness, if I may say so, without a drop of flattery. Better than the most brilliant pseudonym . . . Have you written anything good lately, Herr Goldwein — oh, forgive me! — I mean Herr G-Gurd-Gurdweill?"

Gurdweill was by now seething with suppressed rage. What a buffoon the man was — and what a scoundrel! He said curtly:

"I've already told you that I don't write at all! In any case, it's irrelevant. I came to see you, sir, on another matter entirely."

"Of course, of course," Dr. Kreindel cut him short, and even gave him a friendly pat on the back. "I know very well what you came for. Don't upset yourself, Herr Gold — er — Gurdweill! We'll come to that, of course. There's plenty of time for that! More than enough — it doesn't take me long to wrap up worldly matters — a couple of minutes one way or the other — that's my nature! But the spiritual side of things is something else entirely! Here time means nothing to me — we can chat at our leisure, like old friends! You understand me, Herr

Gurdweill, you understand me very well, I know you do, hee-hee-hee. Both of us are intelligent, well-educated people — no, no, don't demur, sir, that's the exact truth of the matter: intelligent, well-educated people! I insist upon it! This is the correct definition of what we are and what we have in common. In addition to which, we're the same age too. You, sir, are twenty-eight or nine, according to my estimation, and I am thirty-two years old — in other words, as close as makes no difference! And the main thing is: we understand each other. It isn't every day that you have the good fortune to meet a man — hmm — a man on your own level . . . not so, Herr Gurdweill? As Schiller put it so well: a soul may sometimes seek its mate for a generation without . . . hee-hee-hee . . ."

Gurdweill sat looking at him throughout this speech, and it suddenly seemed very strange to him that he should be sitting there and listening to the nonsense of this man with his gold teeth and malicious smile. Gurdweill's face was paler than usual and there was a dull gleam in his eyes. He felt a painful emptiness in his skull, as if there were a hollow space inside it and a cold wind was blowing through it . . . His silver-knobbed cane was standing between his legs and he fingered it unconsciously. For some reason he remembered his quarrel with Thea's two acquaintances the night before, and he was overcome by distress. He must have been really drunk. He had made a fool of himself in front of Thea. No, the idea flashed through his mind, as if it were in some way connected to yesterday's fiasco — no, there was no hope of getting a job from this man! He stood up and said decisively:

"I'm sorry, but I'm in a hurry. I would like to know if I may hope to obtain employment here, or if I should look elsewhere."

"God forbid!" The book-seller too rose from his seat. "Hope? Of course you may hope! The job is already in your pocket, my friend! I've been waiting for you, as I told you before. The salary is one hundred and eighty schillings a month. At the beginning. You'll get a raise later. If that suits you, you're my man."

After brief negotiations they agreed that he would start

the next day at a salary of two hundred schillings a month, "only because he, Dr. Kreindel, was not prepared to lose a man like him, a kindred spirit, etc . . ."

Gurdweill said goodbye and left the shop. He turned absent-mindedly towards the Kai, walking rapidly as if he had no time to waste. Anxiety gnawed at him, even though he still had a whole day of freedom in front of him. In a secret corner of his soul he was disappointed by the positive results of the interview. He was flooded by a wave of nostalgia for the days of recent months, days which were all his, every single minute of them, to do as he liked without any stranger interfering. Despite their poverty and the petty cares which filled them, these days now seemed to him flawlessly beautiful, worth their weight in gold — and now they were over. From tomorrow he would have to spend eight hours a day with that scoundrel, that buffoon, day in and day out, every day the same as the one before. Life, it seemed, had laws of its own, which could not always be adapted to suit the heart's desires.

It was midday. The sun shone down on the city, which was fresh and sparkling from the night-long shower. The shops and businesses began disgorging crowds of people, who invaded the pavements and packed the trams. Gurdweill, who had not noticed that he had begun to retrace his footsteps a few moments before and was already walking down Rotenturmstrasse, now found himself next to St. Stephen's Cathedral. The Cathedral clock struck once, with a deep, hollow sound. He took out his watch and set it to the clock: a quarter past twelve. Thea would be leaving her office now for lunch, it occurred to him, and he might bump into her. He knew that she hated surprise meetings, but nevertheless, with a rather hesitant heart, he quickened his step. When he reached the turning into Johannesgasse, he glanced furtively down the street, out of the corner of his eye and without stopping. He walked on for about twenty paces, turned on his heel and passed Johannesgasse again, this time without turning his head, and then he walked back again and passed it for the third time. He stopped a little way off and scanned the crowds milling to and fro. No, Thea was nowhere to be seen. Perhaps she had left a few minutes before. He continued slowly towards the Ring, turning to look back from time to time, and decided that he might as well stroll over to Dr. Astel, who lived not far off. He passed a shop selling various steel instruments, and stopped to look at the shaving gear in the window. Gurdweill had a weakness for shaving instruments, especially good razors. He already had three razors at home, but he still wasn't satisfied. As soon as he had a bit of money, he had made up his mind to buy himself a real English razor and a decent razor-strop. And in the meantime, he always stopped outside the display windows of shops of this kind to choose and deliberate: he couldn't make up his mind whether to buy a razor with an ivory handle for twenty schillings, or one with a plain black handle, which cost as much as the first, but whose blade was probably better. He would gladly have bought all the razors and shaving accessories in the window, and in other shop windows too, if only he had the money. As he stood there deliberating, he remembered that he had to take one of his razors which was blunt to be sharpened, and at the same moment he heard a familiar voice. He turned his head and saw Thea standing behind him, with a tall man. Gurdweill felt a stab as if someone had stuck a needle into him. But he recovered immediately and scolded himself: What! Have you gone mad? She's allowed to talk to someone! Or maybe even that's a sin, you idiot! Nevertheless, he was eager to know who her escort was — not out of any desire to spy on her, God forbid, no one could accuse him of that, but simply out of curiosity. Perhaps the man was an acquaintance of his, Gurdweill's, too. He would not try to hide, he could make it look as if they had met purely by chance. All this flashed through his mind with the speed of lightning, and he began pushing his way through the crowds of people on the pavement, almost knocking over an old woman, who cursed him roundly, in his haste to reach the kerb. He crossed the street without looking round and began running along next to the kerb, keeping an eye on the opposite pavement to make sure they did not disappear

85

from view. After running two hundred yards or so Thea and her escort were left far behind, and he recrossed the road and began walking towards them. He walked slowly, as if he were enjoying a stroll. But his heart was pounding and beads of sweat broke out on his forehead, because of his run or his excitement or a combination of both. From a distance he saw the man walking next to Thea, a well-dressed, pleasant-looking stranger in his prime. He greeted them with a deep bow and was about to continue on his way when Thea stopped him:

"Where are you going, Rudolfus?"

With an archness which may have hidden some slight embarrassment she introduced them: "Rudolfus Gurdweill, my intended, a young writer with a promising future, and Dr. Ostwald, my General."

"General — you exaggerate, madam," protested Dr. Ostwald with a modest smile.

"Why don't you come home with me, rabbit?" Thea suggested. And when she saw him hesitate, she added: "See us to the tram, anyway. You're not in a hurry are you? You can decide then."

They set off. Dr. Ostwald walked with a confident tread, full of a sense of his own importance, as if to say: "Here walks the famous, successful lawyer, to whom the mysteries of the universe are as familiar as the palm of his hand. He says nothing, but everyone knows . . ." He offered Gurdweill a "Corona" from a gold cigar case with a slightly patronizing air, as if he were a younger friend. They exchanged a few polite, insignificant remarks. Gurdweill rather regretted the whole business. He didn't like being with Thea in the company of anyone else. Strangers acted as a kind of barrier between them. And Thea herself, whenever anyone else was with them, seemed different, not the way he knew her. She spoke differently, laughed differently — and he didn't want to see her like that. Even in the company of her family she was not the same Thea.

When they reached the Opera the lawyer, who was travelling in the opposite direction, said goodbye. Thea and Gurdweill stood and waited for the tram. Gurdweill had not yet decided whether to go with her or not. He wanted two contradictory things: to be with her and to remain by himself. As always when he had difficulty in making up his mind, he knew that it was best to let events take their course. At the last moment the issue would resolve itself, either by an inner instinct, which with blind, groping feelers always sought what was right and best for him, or by the intervention of some unexpected external factor which had not yet been taken into account.

Thea asked him what he thought of her "General."

"He seems like a decent chap. But a bit of a snob, I should imagine."

"Although," he added after a second's pause, "you can't really judge by first impressions."

"Your verdict is right in general, rabbit. But sometimes he loses control of himself. And then he's like a different person. He's got secret appetites, all nicely wrapped up and hidden away under that elegant suit. In any case, he's not uninteresting when you know him well. Well, are you coming or not?" she asked as she saw the tram approaching.

"No," the word escaped from his lips.

"Oh yes, I forgot to tell you, I've got a job, from tomorrow," he added when she was already on the tram.

Afterwards he crossed the Ring and approached Karlsplatz. He would go to Dr. Astel's anyway, although it was already doubtful if he would find him at home. Some of the paving stones on the square had been torn up where they were repairing the tram tracks, and the ripped-up stones were lying one on top of the other next to the long cut, which had exposed the dark yellow soil below. "In any event," reflected Gurdweill as he walked over the loose, soft soil, "in any event it would be better to work for a man like the 'General' than my buffoon." At that moment his eye was caught by a group of people clustering next to the fence around the little garden in the centre of the square. He went up and pushed his way through the little crowd. A policeman was bending over a young woman sitting propped up against the fence. She appeared to have fainted, and her face was deathly pale. Her black hat had slipped sideways and her head was drooping and wobbling to and fro, as if it were about to drop off. The policeman supported her head with one hand while attempting to force a glass of water into her mouth with the other, but her lips were clamped shut and the water spilled down her chin and dripped on to her dress. In the end her eyes opened a slit, revealing two lines of white, and then the lids came down again. After a moment she opened her mouth and drank what was left of the water in the glass. Her eyes opened too and she looked around her in bewilderment. She tried to lift her limp hand as if to protect herself, and mumbled something unintelligible. Gradually she recovered her senses, and an embarrassed expression appeared on her face. "Please, it's nothing," she murmured in a barely audible whisper, "a little weakness, only a little weakness." She tried to get up, leaning on her hands, but her hands were too weak to support her and she fell back with a guilty smile. "I'll just rest a minute," she whispered apologetically, glancing around as if she were pleading for her life. Her eye fell on Gurdweill and rested on him for a moment. Gurdweill felt something like a sudden push from behind, took a step towards the policeman, who had already straightened up and set about dispersing the crowd, and said firmly:

"I know this woman, officer! She lives in my neighbourhood, in Heinestrasse. I'll take her home."

Later he himself was astonished at his strange behaviour and the urgent inner necessity which prompted it, a necessity which brooked no refusal. In any event, the policeman believed him and accepted his offer with some relief. Gurdweill bent over the woman and whispered as he helped her to her feet:

"Forgive me, madam. Don't be alarmed. I'll take you wherever you want to go."

The woman gave him a grateful look and stood up obediently. She was still very weak, her legs failed her, and she hung with all her weight on Gurdweill's arm. He led her slowly away, and when they were a little distance from the policeman and the curious crowd, which had begun to disperse with an air of disappointment at the way the drama had ended, he said in a gentle, reassuring voice:

"Why don't we go into the park first so that you can rest, and afterwards I'll take you home."

The woman made no reply.

At the entrance to the park he bought an orange from a hawker, after which he led her to an unoccupied bench. They sat down. Gurdweill was suddenly overcome by embarrassment. He didn't know what to say. He began to peel the orange and to offer her one segment after the other. "Her hands are small and pampered, so she obviously comes from a good family," he concluded. He felt a little ashamed, ashamed for this strange woman, as one sometimes feels ashamed when somebody else does something wrong or says something ridiculous in a company of which you form a part. He waited for the stranger to wreak her anger on him, in one way or another. He wished she would hurry up and get it over, so that she would feel better. But she took the orange segments from his hand and ate them silently, as if in spite of herself, staring blankly in front of her as if she were thinking of something very far away or not thinking at all. From time to time Gurdweill stole a glance at her without uttering a word. And suddenly she turned to look at him and said in a weak but clear voice, with a faint, sickly smile:

"I trust you, sir. I feel that you are a decent man. But I dare not . . . really, I dare not trouble you and take up your time. You're not angry with me, are you?"

"Of course not," Gurdweill reassured her, "it's nothing, nothing at all! My time is my own today and I'm only too happy to put myself at your disposal, madam!"

The woman went on chewing. She chewed slowly, without relish, like a child being fed against her will. Her body had apparently recovered, but her face was still rather pale, like slightly smoky ivory. It was a pretty face, a delicate, oval face with tired brown eyes. She smiled quietly to herself, like a child comforted after weeping. Gurdweill felt happy and purified. He felt as if he could touch the secret threads joining him to all the pure, suffering souls in the world.

Suddenly she shuddered convulsively, as if she were feverish. She turned to him wildly, with an expression of great, animal fear on her face, and the orange segment dropped from her fingers to the ground.

"I'm afraid," she said in a strangled voice, "I'm so afraid!" She gripped his hand. "Oh God, he'll kill you! He's capable of it. He killed my child . . . it was him, I know it was. They tried to tell me that he died of diphtheria, but I know better. He kills everyone close to me . . . everyone who wishes me well. He wants me to be alone in the world . . . without anyone to protect me . . ."

"What? Who? Calm yourself, madam, I beg you," said Gurdweill, himself infected by her agitation, "calm yourself, please, nothing will happen . . ."

"No, no, you don't know, sir! He sees everything and knows everything. Oh my God — he could pass by here now and kill you . . ! He could easily pass here by chance . . . No, no, we must get away at once . . . If he should see us together . . ! Please take me home, sir. I know he's not there now."

In a sudden excess of energy she leapt to her feet and pulled Gurdweill up after her.

Gurdweill went with her. He was full of fear — not because of the imaginary man but because of this strange woman, who seemed to him unbalanced in her mind. Her sudden fear and the strange things she said were like an alien wind blowing from beyond some frontier of sanity, from the domain of nightmare and horror. But perhaps she was not mad at all? Perhaps there was something real behind it all? For a moment he regretted having embarked on this adventure. However, it never occurred to him to make some excuse and run away. They hurried out of the park, with the young woman darting terrified looks in all directions, as if they were being pursued. She clung tightly to Gurdweill's arm. But the further they receded from the park the calmer she grew, to Gurdweill's astonishment. As they approached the Ring her footsteps slowed down. Her terror of a moment before seemed to have been completely forgotten. Gurdweill now found the courage to ask her for her name and address.

"Frau Franzi Mitteldorfer," she replied with a strange smile. "Neubaugasse 27."

"No, no, sir," she immediately corrected herself. "I won't lie to you. My address is Stumpergasse 14. Tram number 61."

Gurdweill stared at her in perplexity and said nothing. He led her to the tram stop, which was not far off, and then got into the almost empty tram with her. When they sat down the woman said apologetically:

"The spring weather is a little exhausting. This is the third time I've fainted this year. Fortunately for me the two previous times it happened when I was at home. My mother was there. I was standing in front of the wardrobe, it was in the afternoon. I wanted to get dressed and take the baby out for a walk. And all of a sudden I felt as if the room and the furniture were about to collapse. The wardrobe was teetering, it was going to fall right on top of me. And a kind of tongue, a long, pointed, dark purple tongue began dancing in front of me, reaching out to touch my face and filling me with an inexpressible fear. After that everything was blotted out. I woke up on the sofa with a terrible pain in my right elbow. My mother was standing next to me. At first I couldn't understand why I was lying on the sofa and I wanted to get up. But I didn't have the strength. I had to go on lying down for another half an hour."

"But my dear lady, haven't you been to see a doctor?" asked Gurdweill compassionately.

"The doctor says that I'm suffering from general exhaustion and anaemia. A leftover from the birth of my son. He says I should go to the country to convalesce for a few months. But times are hard. My husband isn't earning much at the moment. I can't afford such luxuries."

"Before, on Karlsplatz," the woman continued, after a short silence, "I felt a sudden panic at the crowds and the traffic. I suddenly had the feeling that the cars and wagons were leaving the street and coming on to the pavement, on to me. I was about to turn around and run . . . and what happened after that you already know, sir."

In the meantime they reached their stop and got off the tram. From there it was a five-minute walk to her house.

Gurdweill accompanied her and climbed the stairs to the third storey with her to her front door. As he was about to say goodbye, the door opened and an elderly woman with a rather heavy body and sparse grey hair sticking to her scalp appeared.

"Mother!" cried the young woman, indicating Gurdweill. "This gentleman brought me home. I felt a little unwell on Karlsplatz, a giddy spell, and the gentleman kindly took care of me and accompanied me home — wasn't that good of him?"

Both women now pleaded with him to come inside and rest a while and have a cup of coffee, until in the end he agreed.

They ushered him into a living-room furnished in bourgeois taste, and seated him next to a round table. The old woman left the room to brew the coffee.

From the windows which opened on to a broad courtyard rose muffled, rhythmic hammer blows, apparently from a carpentry shop, and the howls of a dog. There was an antique, stuffy and slightly sour smell in the room, which reminded him of the distinctive smell of the historical museum for weapons and military uniforms. After a moment it was joined by the pungent aroma of boiling coffee filtering through the doorway. Franzi Mitteldorfer removed her hat and tidied her boyishly cropped grey hair opposite the mirror on the cupboard door. Suddenly a baby began to cry from the next room, and the young woman hurried out after begging her guest's pardon and handing him a big, thick photograph album. Gurdweill opened the album mechanically and read on the thick, grey-green frontispiece, in red ink and a round, fair hand: "To dear Franzi," etc. He did not read the verse which followed, written in the same fair hand. Suddenly he felt that he was a thousand miles away from himself, from his way of life, his usual environment, and even from the city of Vienna itself — as if he had been miraculously removed to a remote and foreign country, and set among the people of an unfamiliar race. The cries of the baby in the next room died down, but the carpenter in the courtyard below went on hammering. The first picture in the album showed a youth standing, strong and slender, with his hair parted in the middle and a downy growth on his upper lip. His face told Gurdweill nothing. He turned the page and saw another picture of a seated girl with a high bosom beneath a white blouse and thick blonde hair covering her forehead in a heavy fringe. The girl was apparently trying to smile, but succeeded only in twisting her lips into a peculiar grimace.

In the meantime the door opened and the old woman entered bearing a tray with coffee cups, which she placed on the table. Immediately afterwards her daughter came in with a baby in her arms. The baby was about eight months old, with fat cheeks and a pointed forehead crowned with a quiff of thin, colourless hair standing up like a coxcomb. The baby smiled toothlessly and brandished a plump little fist in Gurdweill's face, to the delight of the two women.

"He likes you, the little treasure," said the young mother, pushing a curl out of her eyes with her free hand. "Fritzi, my little one, the gentleman found mummy in the street and brought her home to you so that you wouldn't cry, and now she's going to stay with you forever and ever."

They drank the aromatic coffee and Gurdweill became acquainted with the details of the little family's life: that Franzi's husband worked in a large textile concern, that the old woman was a widow and Franzi was her only child, but that she was not strong, as Mr. Gurdweill had seen for himself, especially since giving birth to Fritzi, etc. etc. . . . .

Gurdweill stood up to leave. He pinched Fritzi on his smooth, fat cheek, the baby cupped Gurdweill's nose in his clumsy hand — and an alliance was cemented between the two of them. The women thanked Gurdweill again and very warmly invited him to visit them, and he said goodbye and left.

It was already almost four o'clock. When Gurdweill stepped outside the sky was grey and overcast. Through an open window on the ground floor he saw an old woman ironing sheets with her spectacles pushed up on to her forehead and her naked eyes red and suppurating. A little boy stood on the kerb peeing into the street. From somewhere near at hand a voice crowed hoarsely and

93

ironically: "Rags and bones, pots and pans!" Gurdweill looked about him in surprise without finding the source of the voice, until he discovered a parrot in a cage on the sill of a ground-floor window, repeating the lesson he had learnt from the rag-and-bone men in the morning. Gurdweill smiled to himself and continued on his way. He wondered whether to take a tram home or go on walking through the streets. A car sped past, leaving a trail of suffocating stench in its wake. Tired, dragging notes from a piano somewhere above him dropped into the quiet alley with a somnolent effect. No, Gurdweill concluded the thought that had been simmering beneath the threshold of his consciousness — no, he would not go home now. What would he do there? He had no desire to work today. From tomorrow a long line of dreary days would begin. Ah! — he flapped his hand as if to chase away a troublesome fly. He came out into the other end of Gumpendorfer Strasse, far from the centre of the city, a very long, narrow street, full of traffic. The laughing face of the baby he had just seen flashed before his eyes, and he was overwhelmed with happiness. It had been years since he had been with a baby. None of his friends had babies. He had had to content himself with looking from afar at the babies in the streets and parks of the city. And now he had a new friend: little Fritzi! Yes, he would drop in on them again. And who knows, perhaps in a year's time, one year's time, or even less, he too . . . Gurdweill did not dare take this happy thought to its conclusion. Without thinking he found himself standing and waiting for a tram and then riding towards the city centre. And half an hour later, as if in spite of himself, he was home.

When he opened the passage door he was greeted by the old landlady, who was shuffling to and fro in her slippers in the semi-darkness like some panic-stricken chicken woken from its sleep in the middle of the night. In her usual whisper she said:

"Herr Gurdweill, aie, aie, there's a letter for you. The postman has just left. This very minute. You didn't meet him? Aie, aie, aie! What a pity! A registered letter. From Berlin, he said. I signed for it. It's on the table in your

94

room. I just fell asleep, a little afternoon nap, and now —
my upper stomach, psssss!"

Gurdweill left her standing in the passage and went
into his room. So — there was a reason why he had hurried home, against his will, in the middle of the afternoon!
Enclosed in the letter from the editor of the literary
magazine was a cheque for fifty marks. The editor sang
his praises and predicted a great future for him. The
story was already at the printers and would appear in the
coming edition, which they would send him, of course, as
soon as it came out. And would Gurdweill for God's sake
hurry up and send him something new without delay, etc.
etc. . . .

Gurdweill felt like a hero. Although this was not the
first time he had heard his praises sung by an editor, he
always felt the same elation, the same tremendous surge
of hope, which faded as suddenly as it had appeared.
Especially when he sat down to work and experienced
the usual difficulties (always, as if to spite him, exacerbated
after praise!), stopped, despaired, took courage and began
again, recognized all his flaws and shortcomings, and
reached the certain, depressing conclusion that he would
never, ever, succeed in expressing everything that was in
his heart, and expressing it the way he wanted to, exactly
as it floated before his eyes — and what good would the
praises of others do him then?

But today he was happy in spite of it all! Thea was
his, exclusively, undeniably his! (He firmly suppressed
certain doubts which were beginning to flicker in the
darker corners of his soul.) And in a few more days, yes,
in nine more days — everything would be finalized! Then
a new life would begin, a life laid out in straight, neat lines,
a life of calm and contentment. In his leisure time he would
be able to work to his heart's desire. From now on he would
work in a different way entirely! He would charge in and
attack, aim straight for the heart of things, for the central
point — and without a doubt he would prevail!

"And what about Dr. Ostwald, for example . . ?" A
doubt succeeded in suddenly breaking through into consciousness.

Gurdweill started up from the sofa, where he had absent-mindedly seated himself, and began pacing up and down the room.

"What? What about Dr. Ostwald?" he said to himself angrily.

"Yes, yes, precisely Dr. Ostwald!"

"Well, what about him? A decent man, apparently, and nothing more! Thea's been working for him for the past two years and they're friends — and that's all there is to it!"

"But those acquaintances of hers in the wine-cellar" — Gurdweill interrrupted himself — "they were insolent scoundrels! Absolute scoundrels! They should have been taught a lesson!"

A quick, blurred scene flashed before his eyes: he, Gurdweill, towered wrathfully above them while they cringed and knelt and begged his pardon. And this curious scene made him crush the editor's letter which he was holding in his hand. The rustle of the paper returned him to reality. What nonsense! he said to himself with a gratified smile. He went up to the table and proceeded to straighten out the crumpled letter, meticulously flattening it with the edge of his hand as if it were a matter of the utmost importance. After that he glanced at his watch: it was twenty to six. He went over to the window and drew the grubby net curtains aside. A fine drizzle was falling imperceptibly from the sky, wetting the street so that it glistened blackly. There was a half-open window on the second floor of the building across the street, the Hotel Zum Nordbahnhof. In the depths of the room Gurdweill saw the profile of a naked woman, presumably standing in front of a mirror. The woman was powdering her naked body with a big puff, while a man in his shirtsleeves circled round her, a lighted cigarette in his mouth. Every now and then he stood still, removed the cigarette from his mouth, and kissed her on the nape of her neck and her back, and then resumed his circling and smoking. After a while the woman disappeared into a part of the room out of Gurdweill's field of vision. "What a swindle!" the thought flashed through his mind. Nevertheless he went on standing there and looking out, waiting with a pounding heart. A few minutes later the woman appeared again, already half dressed. Gurdweill turned away from the window and sat down on the sofa. There was a hot, tingling feeling in his limbs. Scenes of intimacy between him and Thea rose up in his imagination, among which for some reason loomed the memory of a cheap, old-fashioned picture depicting a man sitting bowed over a table, as if sunk in thought — a picture which must have penetrated his unconscious mind from the walls of one of the nocturnal rooms he had visited with Thea, although he could not now remember where. He saw this picture with great clarity, as if it were hanging on the wall before him, and he did not like it in the least. On the contrary, it seemed to him excessively ugly, even repulsive, but it persisted in intruding on his thoughts with a pointless obstinacy which resisted all his attempts to banish it. In the end he lit a cigarette and went over to the window again. In the hotel window opposite there was no longer anything to be seen. "They must have gone out by now," he concluded to himself. He went on standing there for a while and then decided to shave. He was still properly shaved from the morning, but nevertheless, he reflected, he should shave again in honour of his last day of freedom, and also because he had to get up early to go to work the next day and he wouldn't have time to shave.

It took him about twenty minutes to shave. Afterwards he stood in front of the mirror to change his tie to a black one with white stripes which he had recently received as a gift from Dr. Astel and which he was now going to wear for the first time. It was seven o'clock. The grey, rainy day was already drawing to a close and the room was steeped in twilight. Gurdweill stood in front of the mirror and feasted his eyes on the new tie, which he considered handsomer than his own greenish one. Suddenly it seemed to him that someone was standing behind him. He shuddered. He whipped round and found Frau Fischer. "For God's sake!" he hissed through his teeth.

The old woman asked him if he wanted a cup of coffee. She had just brewed a pot and there was enough for him

too. And her coffee was good, as Herr Gurdweill knew for
himself! Pure coffee, without anything mixed in! Her dear
departed husband had adored it. You could search every
café in the city for coffee like hers, he would say — and in
the end you wouldn't find it! And she might as well take
the opportunity to tell him — she went on, scratching
with one finger behind her ear — that her Siedl said that
Herr Gurdweill had not yet paid this month's rent and it
was already past the twentieth! Not that she was pressing
him, God forbid — nothing could be further from her
thoughts! On the contrary, if he didn't have it now, she
would gladly wait. She would even wait for a few weeks.
She trusted Herr Gurdweill — pssss! No one more. She
only wanted to remind him, in case he forgot. Because
Herr Gurdweill had other things on his mind, of course
. . . As for the coffee, she would bring it at once, it was
still hot. Standing on the stove. No? What a shame! Such
good coffee!

Gurdweill told her he would pay the rent the next
day and went out. He set out for the Innere Stadt at a
leisurely pace, although he was a little hungry since he had
not eaten lunch. He would have a bite in town, he thought,
there was still plenty of time. With conscious enjoyment
he abandoned his bare head to the fine, invisible drizzle
falling from the sky like flour through a sieve. The streetlamps were already on, since evening had already invaded
the streets, and above his head, at the level of the flames,
the fine, swarming drizzle was as clearly visible as a slanting
shaft of dust coming through the window on a bright
summer sunbeam. Outside it seemed like autumn now,
although it was not cold. He reached the Danube canal,
where the fractured reflections of the gaslights shimmered
on the water. The water looked very black and cold and
uninviting. The shops were already shut, with an occasional illuminated display window striking a garish, jarring
note. The bright lights of the city centre were a little
dimmed by the rain. The wet asphalt, glittering like a black
mirror, reflected the passers-by with their legs above their
upside-down umbrellas, and two rows of upside-down
buildings on either side of the street.

Feeling quite content, Gurdweill turned out of Rotenturmstrasse into a side street and went into a little
restaurant he knew to have supper before going to meet
Thea.

9

HE had to be there at three, and it was already two (in the morning Gurdweill had gone to work in Dr. Kreindel's office as usual): in other words he only had an hour left — minus half an hour to get there, and so all that remained was half an hour. Which meant he had better start getting ready at once.

Ulrich had moved to Rembrandtstrasse the day before, but right now he was there in the old room with Gurdweill. Dr. Astel, too, was supposed to come to the room, so that they could all go together, but if he failed to make it in time, he would go straight there, as arranged. There was not much time left.

Ulrich was as excited as if it were his own celebration. He could not sit still, kept on getting up and sitting down again, and wandered around the room getting in Gurdweill's way, smoking one cigarette after the other and giving advice. Wearing black in honour of the occasion, freshly shaven and powdered with a bluish talc, he was all nervous anticipation. It was a Thursday, an ordinary day of the week like any other, albeit blazingly hot for the time of the year — but at the same time it was a special day.

Gurdweill first polished his shoes. They were no longer new, the patent leather was wrinkled and had fine cracks in it, but after an energetic polishing their appearance was somewhat improved. Then he washed his face and the upper half of his body and put on the white shirt his brother-in-law Poldy had lent him for the occasion, a shirt with a front and cuffs as stiff as steel. A stiffly starched collar, of course, and a black bow-tie: the day demanded a black bow-tie, and fortunately he had one, old but black, in his possession, and did not have to borrow one. A black

suit, needless to say, was obligatory for the occasion, and
Gurdweill wore one: the jacket was his own property
(ancient and shiny, but never mind!), and the trousers
also borrowed from his brother-in-law, and accordingly
far too long for Gurdweill since the former was as tall
as a telegraph pole. But the problem had been solved:
the night before he had turned up the hems about eight
centimetres, stitched them up roughly, wet them and left
them all night long under a heavy weight of thick volumes
to press them flat. But when the trousers were on him,
and he went for some reason to look out of the window,
Ulrich, who was sitting on the edge of the sofa opposite
him, discovered a hole in an immodest place, exposing a
shining white circle the size of a button — to Gurdweill's
dismay, but also to his great relief. For imagine if the hole
had only been discovered later, when he was already there!
And in front of strangers! Now, at least, the damage could
still be repaired! Gurdweill quickly pulled off the trousers,
took a needle and thread out of the desk drawer, and sat
down to mend the hole. Which was easier said than done:
his fingers were clumsy, the starched collar cut mercilessly
into his neck and chin, the shirt-front was as unyielding as
armour; the sweat poured down his tomato-red face and
trickled under his shirt and over his chest in slightly chilly
rivulets, like crawling columns of loathsome insects. At last
the job was done and Gurdweill completed his toilet with
no further mishaps. He placed a stiff bowler hat (it too
the property of his brother-in-law), the likes of which
he had never worn before, on his head. The hat was
too small for him and perched on the top of his head
as if it did not belong there, giving him an extremely
ridiculous air. When he looked into the mirror Gurdweill
could not restrain himself and burst into loud laughter.
Ulrich laughed too, rolling his eyes grotesquely. Then
they hurried off. They strode rapidly down the street.
Gurdweill in his finery felt as if he had been confined
in a narrow barrel, boiling hot, sweating and panting,
frequently wiping his face with the handkerchief he kept
clasped in his white-gloved hand, skipping every now and
then in his haste. The sun blazed as if it were the middle

of July, although it was only May, the asphalt on the pavements was melting in places, revealing black spots and giving off invisible steam, and it felt soft beneath their feet. They seemed to be pushing through the dense air, as if they had to cleave their way by force. It did not occur to either of them that they could have taken a tram, as if the invention of this form of transport had completely slipped their minds. In the end, after a very strenuous walk, they reached their destination on time.

The "other side" were already waiting in the vestibule, which was open to the street. They included: first of all, Thea, of course, draped in a kind of white veil; her father, the old Baron, tall and erect, with a military bearing; her two brothers, Poldy and Freddy, tall as their father and dressed in black as he was. With them were also a young couple, who were introduced to Gurdweill as relations of the family, and an old aunt of aristocratic appearance.

They had to wait for the conclusion of a marriage ceremony in the great hall of the synagogue, from which the muffled singing of a choir now burst, to the accompaniment of the deep bass notes of an organ, which seemed to be borne towards them from a vast distance away. The solemn singing poured into the steep, winding Seitenstettengasse, filling it with a carefree, dreamy atmosphere not at all compatible with the coarse profanity of the wretched Jews struggling to make a living there by selling rags and second-hand clothes.

Gurdweill was exhausted from running. His ridiculous clothes made him uncomfortable and restricted his movements. He could not rid himself of the feeling that he had put on some disguise in order to attend a fancy-dress party. But since it was the middle of a boiling hot day, and the street was full of Jews milling about with bundles of clothes on their arms or backs, and opposite him, on the other side of the street, a short, fat Jew with a pointed beard and a black silk skullcap, round and high as a kettle, was standing idly in the doorway of a shoe-shop and looking around him with a smug, stupid expression on his face — Gurdweill felt the absurdity of his situation all the more sharply. The whole thing was superfluous,

102

absolutely superfluous, and completely irrelevant to the business at hand. And on top of everything else one of his gloves, which he had taken off and was holding in his hand, now slipped out of his fingers and fell to the ground, obliging him to bend down in his tight-fitting clothes and pick it up. At least it was cool in the vestibule, he thought.

His father-in-law said something to him and he replied mechanically. Thea's relations stood a little apart and conversed among themselves. Gurdweill did not notice that the singing from within had stopped. Dr. Astel arrived, greeted everyone heartily and kissed the women on their hands. And straight afterwards the uniformed beadle informed them that their turn had come.

Shortly after that they were standing beneath the bridal canopy in the small hall of the synagogue. A short rabbi with a neatly trimmed little beard read whatever it was that he read, and Gurdweill, whose mind was now quite clear, reflected gladly that it would soon be over and he would be able to take off his clothes. The rabbi read "Behold thou," and waited for Gurdweill to repeat the words after him one by one, but the latter suddenly remembered his childhood lessons and read the whole sentence triumphantly by himself, slipping the ring on to Thea's finger as he did so. The rabbi glared murderously at Gurdweill as if he had deprived him of his rightful due, looking like someone who has exerted all his strength to lift a heavy sack, only to discover suddenly that it was full of feathers, causing him to lose his balance and fall over backwards. Gurdweill, who was for some reason gratified by the rabbi's discomfiture, smiled broadly for a moment. Then he remembered that he was supposed to be wearing a solemn expression and quickly suppressed his smile. The rabbi went on reading something. The cantor, too, raised his voice in song, and Thea listened to everything with great interest. In the end the ceremony came to an end and Gurdweill felt a sense of liberation. Everyone congratulated them and kissed each other, and even the old aunt gave Gurdweill a chilly aristocratic peck on the cheek. Afterwards they all went to the tram stop and took a tram to Baron von Takow's house.

There was a table laid in the small dining-room with

103

brandy, liqueurs and various sweetmeats. There was even a dusty bottle of 1897 Tokay, the Baron's pride. Apart from that, there were oranges and the first cherries of the season — all tastefully arranged. "Ladies and gentlemen, please!" said the Baron and led the old aunt to her place at the head of the table. They toasted the bride and groom, ate the fruit and the sweetmeats, conversed, drank a second and a third toast, the younger members of the company in particular, and the heat in the room became intolerable. The Baron regaled them with tales of military life and ancient "court secrets," his apple cheeks covered with tiny red veins and beads of sweat breaking out on his square forehead underneath his short, bristling grey hair. The old aunt spoke about her late husband, the Baron von Hochberg, who was a General in the Hussars. After that Dr. Astel skilfully turned the conversation to more modern topics. Gurdweill felt suffocatingly hot; nothing interested him. He was waiting for the moment when he would be able to go out into the fresh air without breaking the rules of etiquette. At long last it was almost six o'clock and the old aunt rose from her seat. Everyone began to say goodbye. Ulrich and Dr. Astel, too, took their leave. Gurdweill immediately asked his brother-in-law for another, soft shirt, went into the next room and changed his armour. He felt as if he had just been released from prison. The young people, Gurdweill and Thea and her two brothers, decided to go to the cinema before supper. It was cool in the cinema, but the film was sentimental and uninteresting, and he was glad when it was over and they went outside again. Gurdweill's wedding day, the day which marked the beginning of a new chapter in his life, was also the most boring and oppressive day he had ever spent. Everything about it was uncomfortable and stifling and irritating. His true liberation only came at ten o'clock, when the family meal was over and they could go home. Thea took only a small bag with her — the rest of her possessions were to be transferred the next day — and left with her husband, Rudolf Gurdweill, for his home, the room in the old widow Fischer's house in Kleine Stadtgutgasse.

Part II: The Beginning

10

THE summer came to an end, an arid, almost rainless summer. The dry, yellowing leaves whispered in the parks and boulevards, some of them on the branches above but most on the ground below, rustling in every passing breeze. The nights were already chilly, and when dawn broke a fine, delicate layer of frost was quite often to be seen, sprinkled like icing sugar over the paving stones and the ragged patch of lawn on the banks of the Danube canal.

All over the city ruddy, tanned faces were conspicuous in the crowds: the faces of those who had recently, or only yesterday, returned from the country, the beaches, and the mountains — or those who had spent all summer in town but taken advantage of the many swimming pools of the city and its environs to bathe and roast themselves in the sun. The season of theatres, opera and cinema shows began, the cafés filled up, and the offices and factories started working at full capacity.

In the parched, rainless summer those forced to remain in the city had breathed not air, but a kind of molten orange metal, full of the suffocating stench of petrol fumes mingled with melting asphalt. And they had complained bitterly of their lot. But now that the summer was dying there was an ache in their hearts — precisely the hearts of those who had suffered from it the most.

It was eleven o'clock on Sunday morning. Gurdweill had risen early to put in a few hours' work while his wife slept, and now he was sprawled, fully dressed, on the couch which served as his bed at night, and upon which the pillows and blankets were still piled. Thea had woken up a few moments before in a good mood, jumped out of bed and snatched him from the table, sweeping him up from his chair as if he were a one-year-old and swinging him to and fro in her arms, she in her long nightgown and he in his clothes and shoes, bouncing him in her arms like a baby and dancing round the room, shouting and laughing wildly: "My little bunny rabbit! You're a cute little thing after all! You're the child of my old age, that's what you are!" As always when she picked him up in her arms, Gurdweill was unwilling. He felt a peculiar pleasure, mixed with a vague kind of shame, shame before himself, before Thea, and before the whole world, as if the most private part of his being had been exposed in public — and he was unwilling. But he could not protest. He only repeated from time to time, pleading and demanding at once, with a weak, twisted smile: "Stop it, Thea! Please let me go!" But Thea did not put him down until he became too heavy for her. Then she exclaimed, panting for breath: "Well, rabbit, I couldn't carry you round like that all day long!"

Now she stood naked in front of the washstand, while Gurdweill lay sprawled on the couch next to the opposite wall, with only her back visible to him. Her head turbanned in a towel to keep her hair from getting wet, she scrubbed her back with a rust-coloured rubber sponge, and her buttocks quivered lewdly. Gurdweill puffed on his short pipe — lately he had taken to smoking a pipe — his face pale and tired. In the past six months he had aged, the lines at the sides of his mouth had deepened and a few faint wrinkles had appeared on his fine, white forehead. He stood up and went over to his wife and stroked her affectionately on her wet back. She said in a tone of command, without turning her head:

"Go and make coffee, Rudolfus! I'm famished! Is there any butter left?"

"N-no."

"Then go down and buy some!"

"But the shop's shut. You know yourself . . . it's Sunday . . ."

"What? The shop's shut?" She turned round abruptly, an ominous expression on her face. "Why didn't you go before?"

Gurdweill stood facing her, small and skinny, his eyes

on a level with her full, white breasts, which had a faint tracery of bluish veins under their delicate skin. He was silent. "Naked people are a little ridiculous when they're angry . . ." — the idea popped into his head. "Ridiculous, definitely ridiculous, and not very imposing at all . . ." But Thea screamed:

"I must have butter! Even if you have to search the whole of Vienna! There must be a shop open in Praterstrasse!"

And she pushed him towards the door.

And Gurdweill, naturally, went to look for butter. He searched for a long time until he found some in Novaragasse, in a little Jewish shop, which he entered furtively through a courtyard. After about half an hour he was back at home. Thea was still naked.

"Did you get it?" she asked as soon as he opened the door. "What took you so long?"

Her anger subsided slightly at the sight of the butter.

"Well, what are you waiting for? Go and put the water on for coffee!"

Gurdweill poured the coffee for himself and Thea, spread the butter, and they sat down to eat. He ate in silence, since he knew that Thea was already irritated, and anything he said would only provoke her further. Thea chewed her food with a hearty appetite. Quiet settled on the house, broken from time to time by the distant rattle of a tram in Heinestrasse or Nordbahnstrasse. After appeasing her initial hunger, Thea inclined her head towards the breasts exposed between the gaping lapels of her dressing gown and said:

"I've decided to have an operation, rabbit. I don't want such big breasts. They get on my nerves."

Gurdweill stopped eating and looked at her in surprise. He didn't know whether she was speaking seriously or making fun of him. He waited for a moment, and since his wife said no more he tried cautiously to object:

"But why, my dear? They're beautiful just as they are. Really beautiful . . ."

"Nonsense, rabbit, you don't understand the first thing about it!" Thea interrupted him. "If I tell you they're too big, you can take it from me that I know what I'm talking

109

about. It's not a difficult operation, there's no danger involved. I've already spoken to Dozent Schramek — you know him yourself! He said it's a very easy operation, child's play . . ."

And she started describing the operation to him in great detail, with such relish that she even forgot her coffee and bread and butter. It was obvious that imagining the operation gave her particular pleasure. But Gurdweill was appalled. He could not bear such scenes, either in reality or imagination. "How can a woman want to have operations all the time?!" he thought. "A couple of weeks ago it was an operation on her nose, also quite unnecessary, and now it's an operation on her breasts!"

"But we haven't got the money for it," he remarked.

"There's no need," replied his wife, with her mouth full, "at any rate, not right away. Dozent Schramek has a sanatorium, as you know, he's my friend and he'll do it for nothing. And even if we have to pay — we can do it later on, one day when we've got the money."

Gurdweill was silent, since nothing he said would have made any difference. Thea wanted to have the operation at the end of the week, and it was plain to him that she would get her way. He was sorry about her breasts, which he liked the way they were, and afraid of the risks inherent in any operation. He was unable to finish drinking his coffee. He sat playing with his knife for a while, then filled his pipe and lit it. In the meantime Thea finished her breakfast.

"Go and roll me a cigarette, rabbit!" she said as she stood up. "And clear the table while you're about it!"

She stretched, lit the cigarette that Gurdweill offered her, and stretched out on her back on the couch, like a satisfied animal. Gurdweill cleared the table, washed the dishes, and put them away under the washstand, which served them instead of a sideboard. Then he returned to his desk. He sat puffing on his pipe and glancing covertly at his wife, whose white, nearly naked body gave off an invisible mist of eroticism, powerful and tormenting. His head grew heavy, he felt drunk. "So that woman there," he reflected vaguely, "is my wife . . . my wife . . . my wife . . ."

110

when suddenly, in the midst of these reflections, he felt a fierce pain in his heart, as if it had been pierced by a sharp object. And before he could defend himself, he was overwhelmed by a torrent of mixed-up memories, all kinds of different things which he always tried to suppress in his consciousness, things which were no mere product of his fantasies and fears but whose reality, unhappily for him, had been forced upon his notice by circumstances too obvious to ignore — and which would not allow him to return to his thoughts of a moment before. Gurdweill suddenly saw a number of his acquaintances, and some strangers too, a whole crowd of men, approaching Thea one by one, his wife Thea, lying half naked on this very couch next to the wall, and she was smiling at them, showing them her breasts, holding out her arms to them . . . Gurdweill could not bear the sight, but he was compelled to look, to see everything. And together with the terrible, unendurable pain, the sight gave him a strange, inexplicable pleasure . . .

His pipe, dropping from his lips and falling on to the table with a clatter, woke him up. Thea was lying and smoking. Gurdweill stood up. His breath came in heavy pants, and he felt giddy. He went up to his wife and began kissing her and scratching her like a wild beast. His savage excitement and despair brought tears to his eyes. Thea said only: "What's got into you today, rabbit?"

Afterwards he tidied his clothes and went on sitting next to his wife on the edge of the couch. There were still tears in his eyes, and his whole being was suddenly enveloped in a great sadness. All of a sudden he felt so abandoned, so alone in the world, so forlorn. Unconsciously, as if asking for help, his hand stroked his wife's warm thighs. He looked straight in front of him without seeing anything, and murmured, as if to himself: "Ah, if only it was all a little different, just a tiny little bit different, how wonderful everything would be . . ."

"What on earth are you mumbling about, rabbit?"

Gurdweill did not reply: perhaps he did not even hear the question. He shrugged his shoulders as if in resignation to his fate. He knew that it never would be different.

Thea jumped off the couch and went up to the mirror hanging over the washstand. With both hands she lifted her breasts up and weighed them for a moment, as if she wanted to know exactly how much they weighed. Then she got dressed.

On Sundays, as on other holidays from work, when they weren't invited to Thea's parents for lunch, they usually prepared themselves a simple meal at home. Their salaries were insufficient for their needs, and they were always short of money. Especially Gurdweill. For Thea spent almost all their earnings, his and hers, on herself. She never denied herself anything she fancied. And then she would always come and ask Gurdweill for money. For their daily needs there was nothing left. Even though he was now earning two hundred and twenty-five schillings a month at Dr. Kreindel's, which was quite enough for one person to live on, especially a person whose needs were as modest as Gurdweill's, he never had a penny in his pocket and was always begging for loans of nonsensical sums of money, as before, in order to buy himself bad tobacco or a slice of bread. He was actually even hungrier and more debt-ridden than before.

The relationship between himself and Thea was set from the first day. Immediately after the wedding Thea informed him, without beating about the bush, that he had better not harbour any illusions about marriage changing her way of life in the slightest degree . . . She was free now, as before, to do as she saw fit . . . And she did as she saw fit. She spent most of her free time, in the evenings after work and on holidays, not with Gurdweill but in places and circumstances unknown to him. Her comings and goings were her own affair. And if at first it seemed rather strange to him, not at all as he had imagined married life to be, in the end he acquiesced, since there was nothing else he could do. As for the jealousy, which at first had tortured him incessantly — he fought a constant battle against it, and even seemed to succeed. That is to say: he did not succeed in actually uprooting it, but in pushing it into a corner of his soul, where it lay in waiting to ambush him whenever the opportunity arose. He would look for

112

excuses for his wife's behaviour, give her the benefit of the doubt, interpret the plain facts in a special light, more convenient to him and, above all, he tried his best to ignore this nightmarish corner of his soul. But an unrelieved malaise now lay heavily on his being, as if he were bearing within him the seeds of a dangerous, fatal disease. He shrank completely into himself, and walked about enveloped in gloom and in the grip of constant inner tension. There was a kind of invisible barrier separating him from the world. And it was very seldom nowadays that he could forget himself and show a cheerful face in the company of his friends.

Although he tried as best he could to conceal the actual state of affairs between himself and Thea, his friends knew the truth. As outside observers, their perceptions were sharper and more comprehensive. They saw many things of which Gurdweill was ignorant. As time went by even those friends who had been taken in by Thea at the beginning realized what she was really like, and they pitied him. Thea finished dressing. She put on her coat and hat, ready to go out. It was nearly one o'clock. She said to her husband, who was still sitting passively on the couch:

"I'm going home for lunch, rabbit. Would you like to come with me?"

But he understood from her tone that she didn't want him to. Besides, they hadn't actually been invited and he said no.

"Have you got any money?"

"No. I've only got a few groschen. Maybe twenty."

"Where on earth has all the money gone?"

"You know I'm broke," he said apologetically. "Yesterday I gave you three schillings. And I paid for the butter too — and that's all there was."

"But I need money! You have to do something! Go and ask Frau Fischer — maybe she'll give you something."

"I can't," said Gurdweill, fumbling with his pipe. "We still owe her last month's rent. Apart from which, I've already borrowed about ten schillings from her."

"But what am I going to do?" Thea sank despairingly into a chair. "I have to have some money. And there's no

113

money at home either. I saw Poldy yesterday. They haven't got a penny."

After a moment's thought she said:

"Look here, Rudolfus, perhaps you should go and ask the old lady anyway. Can't you see how much I need the money?"

"I can't, my dear, I really can't," Gurdweill begged. "She won't give us anything, I know she won't. This afternoon I'll go to town and try to borrow some money."

"I'm telling you that I need it now. Now, this minute!" screamed Thea furiously, stressing every word. "Can't you understand, you idiot!"

Gurdweill was silent. In his embarrassment he took his tobacco pouch out of his pocket and began to stuff his already full pipe with its half-cracked bowl. "Money, money," the word hammered in his head. "Where to get money?" He stood up and went over to his wife, who was sitting at the table with her head in her hands. He stood behind her and tried to placate her. He stroked her back and said gently:

"I'd do it with all my heart, my dear, if only I could. You know I would . . ."

Before he knew what was happening, a stinging slap landed on his left cheek. Sparks shot from his eyes and his head felt as if it were being uprooted from his body. For a moment he thought that the house was collapsing and the ceiling was crashing on to his head. The precise location of the pain was not yet clear to him. All this took no more than a few seconds. Then he felt a distinct burning on his left cheek and saw Thea, as if through a fog, walking to the door and going out. For a while he went on looking at the door through which his wife had disappeared. The square patch of sunlight lying on the floor at an oblique angle to the door drew his eyes to it. It seemed to him intensely hot and shining. Gurdweill took a sudden step forward, bent down, and felt the patch of sunlight on the floor. "It's not so hot," he mumbled to himself, "it's only my imagination." He straightened up and remained standing where he was. His thoughts shied away from that other place. Nothing had happened there. Everything was as usual there. But

114

in spite of himself his hand went up automatically to the side of his face and came to rest on the burning cheek — and as if a floodlight had suddenly been turned upon it, the whole scene rose vividly before his eyes. He felt a dull pain in his cheek. "She must have stood up first, because she was sitting down, and she couldn't have done it sitting down . . ." the irrelevant thought occurred to him. And he was immediately overwhelmed by a great shame. He glanced distractedly around the room, to make sure that nobody had seen. At that moment he felt even more ashamed for Thea than for himself. She would probably be ashamed to look him in the eye, he thought. And Gurdweill was almost ready to run after his wife, who could not have gone far, to appease her and ask her to forgive him. He took a step towards the door. Then he turned round abruptly, and caught sight of his reflection in the mirror above the washstand. His face, usually so pale and downcast, was bright red, as if lit by a hidden flame. Overcome by a great weariness he lay down on the couch and lit his pipe, which he had been holding in his hand all this time.

At that moment the old landlady entered the room without knocking, as usual. Gurdweill remained lying on the couch.

"So the young lady's gone out, has she?" she asked, although she must have seen her leave. "A fine wife you've married, Herr Gurdweill," she added, stationing herself next to the couch, "a very fine wife, psssss! I always told you that a decent man needs a wife. Two are better than one, aie, aie, aie! If only my dear departed husband was alive, what would I lack for now? And without him what am I worth? A worn-out old woman alone — it's awful, just awful!"

"Could you possibly lend me just one more schilling, Frau Fischer?" The words suddenly burst out of Gurdweill's mouth, and he sat up.

"I understand, Herr Gurdweill, I understand. There's no need to yell. I'll fetch it at once. A decent man like you!"

She left and returned with the schilling. Then she tidied

the room, chattering incessantly in her irritating whisper, and in the end she went away.

Gurdweill remained in the room for a little longer, then he washed his face as if to cleanse it of some stain, took up his cane and went out.

11

OUTSIDE Gurdweill felt a slight sense of relief. Al-though the profoundly humiliating, depressing thing that had happened to him at home was still there inside him, lurking behind his every thought and struggling to emerge from repression into consciousness at the first opportunity — its sting was somewhat blunted at the sight of the magnificent, sun-dappled autumn day. It was as if he had held an object in his hand, its shape and colour fully exposed to view, and then put it away in his pocket.

It was early in the afternoon. The closed shops and warehouses and few people in the streets made the city seem unlike its usual self — as though it had been swept clean and carefully spruced up in preparation for some special occasion. Gurdweill strolled slowly and aimlessly from street to street and alley to alley, his bare head bowed, the hand holding his cane swaying like a pendulum in time with his step. Here and there the doorways revealed a watchman in his shirtsleeves, reading a newspaper and relaxing at his post. These simple people seemed to Gurd-weill amazingly contented, calm and carefree, enjoying their day of rest to the full and imparting their own inner serenity to the buildings and streets. In a few of the quiet streets, their dark-grey asphalt glittering in the sun, boys were playing football or taking turns to ride a bicycle — boys with flushed faces whose bare, sunburnt knees were dirty and scarred. Occasionally a motorcar drove past, scattering them to the pavements with short blasts of its hooter. The quiet streets and his own steady pace gradually permeated Gurdweill with a melancholy calm. He had always felt a delicate love for this city with its air of faint sadness, both mocking and innocent at once. He

117

loved its winding, capricious streets, its magnificent buildings, as proud as they were modest, its parks and gardens steeped in a sweet sadness, and its chain of encircling hills, already tinged with the dark, cloudy bleakness of the distant alpine crags. He loved its frivolous, high-spirited inhabitants, and the air of frothy, light-hearted gaiety which permeated it. He had lived here for twelve years, ever since he came of age. And the autumn in Vienna! The autumn days were wonderful, a little grey and cloudy in the morning and with a mild, gentle warmth in the golden, transparent afternoons. The sky was a deep, still azure, and a few feet above the ground delicate white threads floated aimlessly in the air — a sure sign, people said, of more warm days to come.

Gurdweill had no wish to see any of his friends now, and he instinctively avoided the streets in which he might have encountered them. He found himself walking behind the Börse, crossing the Schotten Ring, and continuing along Porzellangasse. There he stopped by force of habit outside the cinema and looked at the posters on either side of the entrance. But the programme did not interest him and he turned away, intending to go into the nearby Liechtenstein Park, when someone tapped him on the shoulder:

"Ah, Herr Doktor! What an honour, Herr Doktor!"

Gurdweill recoiled in fright, and turned around.

It was Franzl Heidelberger with his wife Gustl, who smiled at Gurdweill as if he were an old friend.

"And how are you, Herr Gurdweill?" Heidelberger beamed with pleasure. "Why don't you come and visit us?"

"Well, er, I was going to . . ." Gurdweill stammered, "And how are you?"

"Very well, Herr Doktor!"

And Gustl chimed in: "Very well! We were already wondering why we never see you, Herr Gurdweill."

"Yes indeed," Franzl took over, "I've already remarked on it to Gustl several times. Gustl, I say, whatever's happened to Herr Gurdweill to make him forget his friends? Could it be that we insulted him, I say, that we didn't treat him with the respect he deserves? And now you must come

118

up and visit us. Now that I've caught you, you won't get away so easily!"

Gurdweill tried to make excuses, but Franzl insisted:

"No, no, Herr Gurdweill, nothing will help you. You're completely at our disposal now. No excuses!"

"Of course, of course, Herr Gurdweill!" his wife joined in. "Surely you won't deprive us of the honour!"

"Hold your tongue, Gustl!" Franzl quickly put her in her place. "Nobody asked for your opinion!"

And turning to Gurdweill, he said in a tone that brooked no refusal:

"And now, my friend, you're coming home with us!" And he added with a sly wink, which Gurdweill did not notice: "You go up first with Gustl. I'll join you right away. I'll just drop into the café for a minute, and I'll be with you in a jiffy."

Gurdweill accordingly set off with Gustl, who seemed highly satisfied with this turn of events. She relaxed immediately and became freer in her movements and speech. She chattered away, laughing all the time, and told him that they were on their way home from a visit to her uncle who lived nearby. She had mentioned Herr Gurdweill only yesterday. You might even say that she had missed him. A few days before she had even dreamt about him, ha, ha, ha! And Herr Gurdweill had deprived them of the pleasure of his company — it really wasn't nice of him. And she gave her escort a warm, inviting look.

They soon reached the house, which was not far off, and climbed the stairs with Gustl leading the way. Gurdweill decided to accept the situation and make the best of it, despite his earlier disinclination for company.

After his first visit to their house he had never been there again. Once he had met the two of them by chance in town and stood talking to them for half an hour, and another time he had met Franzl alone and gone to a tavern with him for a glass of beer. And once, after visiting Vrubiczek, he had knocked on their door without getting a reply. Gustl's looks had improved over the past six months: her face was tanned and also somewhat thinner, which suited her better.

She opened the door and ushered him into the same scrupulously clean room as on his previous visit.

"Please sit down, Herr Gurdweill. Over here," she indicated the sofa as she removed her hat, "it's more comfortable on the sofa."

"I'll just shut the window a little," she added immediately, "the noise from the street is quite deafening . . ."

Gurdweill was not yet seated. He took a few steps and rubbed his hands together as if he felt cold. Then he stood next to the table. Absent-mindedly he took his pipe out of his pocket and put it back again. An inner restlessness had him in its grip, as if in the face of some impending disaster. Like an animal facing its predator he watched the woman's movements, which had suddenly grown lax and careless. He heard her murmur something about coffee, but it took him a while to understand what she had said. He stammered, "No . . . there's no need . . . not now . . ." All of a sudden Gustl seemed exhausted, and she sank on to the sofa, her face flushed. And the next minute, without knowing how it had happened, he found himself sitting beside her on the sofa, his hands fumbling with her dress. She only whispered in a weak, drowsy drawl, "No-o-o, no-o-o . . ." and lay back on the sofa . . .

Gustl tidied her hair in front of the mirror, a satisfied smirk on her flushed face. Gurdweill felt uncomfortable and slightly ashamed, and if it had been possible, he would have left at once. He was still sitting on the sofa. In his embarrassment he took out his pipe again and began stuffing it with an air of great concentration. Then he got up and stood vacantly next to the table, afraid to glance in Gustl's direction. She approached him from behind and stood beside him, where she appeared to hesitate for a moment and then planted a hasty, burning kiss on his left cheek. She was the first to break the tense silence:

"If you'll excuse me, Herr Gurdweill, I'll go and make the coffee." And she slipped out of the room.

Gurdweill sat down on a chair. A clatter of dishes rose from the kitchen, and immediately died down again. He suddenly remembered the morning's slap and felt a dull ache in his left cheek. "Ah, nonsense!" he exclaimed aloud and tried resolutely to distract his thoughts from the unpleasant memory and concentrate all his attention on the woman with the baby in her arms, whom he could see standing at one of the windows of the brown house opposite.

This was the first time he had come into physical contact with another woman since he had met Thea. And this time, too, he had not really been responsible: it had happened of its own accord, as if he had been impelled to act by some power outside himself. Gurdweill did not admit his guilt. He was in a strange, unfamiliar state of mind. He felt as if he had been momentarily relieved of a number of things which had been troubling him, like a man shut up in a small, stuffy room who had opened the window for a moment to breathe fresh air. Various insults which had sunk to the bottom of his heart like stones had now found some sort of compensation. And it seemed that Thea's domination of him, too, was no longer complete. So Gurdweill was not yet absolutely lost, and there was no need for him to despair. What had happened had restored his balance to a certain extent and rid him for a while of the constant pressure. All this Gurdweill felt obscurely. Suddenly he was seized by an exhilarating sensation of confidence, such as he had not experienced for a very long time. He felt as if his true, private, essential worth had all at once been restored to him, his worth as a man, and for a moment he was confident that from now on everything would go smoothly. In his mind's eye he saw Thea sitting and waiting for him impatiently at home. She opened a book and put it down again, too impatient to read. Then she lay down on the couch and lit a cigarette. She took a few puffs, threw it down, and jumped up again. She went out to ask the landlady exactly when he had left the house and whether he had said anything about when he would be back. Gurdweill saw and heard everything in his imagination. He heard the old lady reply in her usual whisper: "Ah, a decent man, Herr Gurdweill, a very decent man, aie, aie, aie! And quiet and friendly — psss!" Thea went back to the room and looked out of the window, turned away and paced about the room,

121

took up the book again, opened it, and in a brief moment of distraction, when her attention was caught by something in the book, the door opened and he walked in. And Thea jumped on him and fell lovingly round his neck: "My darling, precious little rabbit, where have you been all this time? I felt as if a whole year had passed since I saw you. And I was afraid that something had happened to you. I suddenly felt so terribly lonely that I thought I would die. The world seemed empty to me, as if there was nobody in it. No, no, my darling, you must never leave me alone again. I can't bear the loneliness. Without you I'm bereft, I'm nothing. From now on you must never leave me. I'll go with you wherever you go." And Gurdweill replied in a coaxing voice (his lips actually moved): "Of course, my dearest, of course. Do you think I like being on my own? Don't you know how much I love you? Don't you know that I'm always ready, every minute of the day and night, to give my life for you?" "And Gustl?" "Ah, that was nothing! It was only because I was so miserable. It doesn't mean a thing. It was only because I thought you didn't love me and that I didn't count for anything with you, and my suffering was too great to bear . . . That's all! How could you believe for a single minute that Gustl means anything to me? But now that I know that you love me, it's all over and forgotten. Let's not talk about it any more."

All this time a happy smile illuminated Gurdweill's hollow face. He looked like a baby who had been given his favourite toy after crying for it for hours, and who was now playing with it and smiling contentedly to himself. Gurdweill's face was lowered to the table, and his fingers were playing nervously with his pipe which had gone out in the meantime, when Franzl burst noisily into the room.

"Well, Herr Doktor, I hope you haven't been too bored?"

He twirled his moustache and winked slyly.

Gurdweill looked up at him with a bemused expression on his face and smiled stupidly. At first he couldn't understand who this man was and what he was talking about. He fixed his eyes on one of the buttons on Franzl's coat, which was hanging by a thread and seemed about to fall off at any minute and roll on the floor. Gurdweill

122

waited for the button to fall with a peculiar impatience. Let it fall and get it over! Why was it pretending to be so innocent? As if it didn't know! It was taking its time out of spite. Just because Gurdweill wanted it to fall now, it wouldn't!

"Gustl didn't make too much of a nuisance of herself, hmm? We all know what women are like . . ." continued Franzl.

"N-no, not at all . . ." said Gurdweill absent-mindedly. And he stuck out his finger and pointed straight at the loose button, saying firmly, like a doctor to a recalcitrant patient:

"You must have it fixed at once! It's going to fall off!"

Franzl grasped the button between his finger and thumb, pulled it off and laid it on the table. Gurdweill looked at the shining black button as if it were a deadly enemy, and smiled triumphantly. Then he suddenly laughed aloud as at some private, highly amusing thought, stuck his extinguished pipe into his mouth, and said between his teeth:

"And so, Herr Heidelberger, what kept you so long?"

"Did it really take so long?" Franzl, too, laughed. "I only went to buy cigarettes. But then I got such a thirst that I had to have a tankard of beer. Gustl!" — he raised his voice in the direction of the door — "Get a move on! Is that coffee going to take all day?"

"I'm coming, I'm coming!" Gustl cried from the kitchen.

"A nice bit of jam, Gustl, eh?" Heidelberger turned to his guest again with an ambiguous smile. He slapped Gurdweill on the shoulder: "How do you like her, brother?"

"Not . . . not bad, I must say," replied Gurdweill in some confusion. Gustl's face floated before his eyes for a moment, very close to his, a flushed face with glazed eyes and wild hair, the face of a cave woman.

"Ha, ha, ha!" Heidelberger laughed complacently.

Gustl brought the coffee. She put the tray down on the table and went to open the window. Then she poured the coffee. From time to time she smiled affectionately at Gurdweill, who was sitting opposite her.

123

"And how is your old lady?" inquired Heidelberger.

"Well. That is . . . very well, of course."

"And we're still with the bookseller, are we?"

"Yes, I'm still there."

"You forgot to put in sugar, Herr Gurdweill. Here!" said Gustl and offered him the glass bowl.

"Funny thing, books," Heidelberger philosophized between sips of coffee. "It always amazes me where people get the patience to write so many books or read them either — aren't I right? When you think how many millions and millions of books there are in the world, in all those languages and countries — it can drive you round the bend! I'm not talking about science books, mind. That's something else again. People need science to know what's what. But what about the others? All those story books! I'm blowed if I understand what anyone needs them for! When I myself, for example, see a book like that a mile away I begin to yawn. You can believe me, Herr Doktor, I'm not exaggerating in the least!"

He took a few sips of coffee, put his cup down, and continued:

"There was a bloke in the military hospital — believe me, he could read three books a day! He lay next to me for two months, his leg was smashed up too, full of shrapnel, and I'm telling you, Herr Gurdweill, without any exaggeration, he must have read a thousand books! It was that Sister Steffie who always brought them to him. Once I said to her: 'Tell me, Sister Steffie, why don't you bring me one of those books too? I want to see what it's all about.' So she brought me one. It was called *An Out Of The Way House* or something like that, I couldn't swear to it — but the long and the short of it is, I read two pages, and believe me — that was quite enough! I couldn't take another word of it. But my neighbour gobbled it up in one afternoon and licked his lips into the bargain! 'What's it about?' I asked him. 'What are they all on about? I want to know too, for once!' And all he could say was: 'Oh, it's so beautiful, it's so beautiful! You have to understand!' But what is there to understand, Herr Gurdweill, I ask you? What? You're a clever man, please explain to me, who on earth cares if

124

somebody or other wants to marry some woman and then he marries her or doesn't marry her? Or if somebody else is a thief and cheats people on the sly and in the end he's caught, or he's never caught at all? Tell me, why should anyone be interested? Am I right or aren't I?"

Gurdweill smiled in embarrassment. He didn't know what to say. For a moment the kind of book in question seemed slightly ridiculous to him too. At that moment he felt like a man who suddenly finds himself among savages who have never seen a civilized person before, and they look him up and down and poke him all over as if he were the savage, not they.

Gustl chimed in:

"My gentry were also always reading. The mistress would lie on the sofa and read, and the master would often read too. Once I peeped into one of their books and it was about this girl, and how this elegant young man seduced her, and dishonoured her (Gustl was now speaking in the refined language she had picked up from her "gentry" or, perhaps, from the book she had read), and afterwards abandoned her for another woman. And so she was sick at heart and wouldn't be consoled, and she was pregnant by him too. And then this other woman came and wanted to give her money, a great deal of money, but she refused to take it. Because she said: 'Your husband or nothing!' In those very words. She gave it to her good and proper! She was a proud one and no mistake! And then it came close to her lying-in time and she was very desperate and she went and bought a pistol and waited in the night for her seducer and shot him three times until he fell dead. And then she ran and threw herself into the Danube. It was a good book. Very sad. It made me cry my eyes out."

"Stuff and nonsense!" pronounced Heidelberger. "What does a woman understand? What's interesting about all that rigmarole?" And to Gurdweill:

"You see, Herr Doktor? You see what a load of rubbish it all is! What's it got to do with anything, I ask you? Only fools can write stuff like that, for fools like them to read. Now aren't I right?"

"One can't generalize," said Gurdweill evasively. "There

125

are better books, too. And the main thing is: as long as there are people who enjoy reading them, books should be written. And if there are some people who don't find them interesting, that's no proof that books in general are worthless. Just like a healthy man with two good legs, for example, can't see the need for crutches, although a legless man would be lost without them. That's the way it always is. People are different both physically and emotionally, and the same goes for their needs: each according to his own nature."

"Quite right! Herr Gurdweill has spoken very wisely, and you can't possibly disagree!" exclaimed Gustl enthusiastically.

Gurdweill got up to go.

"Well, I'll have to be running along now."

"What's your hurry?" protested his host. "Stay a little longer! Once you're already here . . ."

"Yes, Herr Gurdweill, do stay," Gustl joined in.

But Gurdweill was firm. Suddenly he felt restless and wanted to get back home as soon as possible. In his heart of hearts he was certain that Thea was waiting for him there. He was sure of it because he wanted it to be true with all his heart and soul, and nothing in the world could have detained him a moment longer.

"In that case, *servus*, brother!" Heidelberger gave in. "Regards to your old lady from Heidelberger Franzl! Why don't you bring her to visit us one day? I'm curious to meet her. And as for you — don't keep us waiting too long! Come next week, or even before, if possible — whenever you like! Gustl is always at home . . ."

"Yes, Herr Doktor, I'm always home these days. I'll be delighted to see you!"

And she pressed Gurdweill's hand meaningfully.

12

BY the time he got home it was almost six o'clock. Thea
was not there, and Frau Fischer informed him that she
had not been in all day. Instead of his wife, the morning's
slap leapt upon him the minute he entered the room, as if
it had been hanging in the air all this time, waiting for his
return. Totally dispirited Gurdweill sank into a chair next
to the table — the very chair upon which Thea had been
sitting before the slap. How ridiculous his hasty return now
seemed to him! He was overcome by a despair from which
there was no escape. Everything seemed to him pointless
and worthless: he himself, down to his last thought and
deed, and all the people and objects around him. And
it seemed to him that it would always be the same, for
all eternity: empty, futile, meaningless. Automatically he
rummaged in his coat pocket for his tobacco, as if it could
rescue him. With no idea what to do next he sat puffing
on his pipe until a cloud of dirty, dark-grey smoke formed
above his head, filling the room and escaping through the
open window. Gradually the twilight penetrated the room
and a profound silence reigned, a painful, gnawing silence.
It was the day of rest, and the groaning and creaking
of the packed, heavy trams below was stilled. There was
nothing but the muffled, distant roar of the city itself,
which was perceived by the abstract imagination rather
than the senses, as if it rose intangibly from his very
soul. Gurdweill sat without moving and smoked. But the
life-blood was still coursing through his veins, the will to
live still stirred somewhere inside him — and the acuteness
of his despair accordingly grew weaker and was gradually
transformed into a light, and even, to a certain extent,
agreeable, melancholy. Yes, even a pinpoint of hope, the
palest reflection of a hope, began to spread through his

soul like a blood-transfusion. There were still a number of things that could be changed! There were still pockets, here and there, of expectations. Even, for example, a child ... This child, it was true, had not yet come into the world, and there was no knowing when he would come. But if he did, even if it took a year or more ... And why not? Thea was healthy and so was he! Then things would surely be better! Apart from the fact itself — and Gurdweill's heart almost burst at the thought of it — it was only natural for a child to bring its parents closer together. Thea would stay at home more and she would love the child, their child. Perhaps they would even be able to afford an apartment, a two-roomed apartment with a kitchen, at the very least ... they would have to! You couldn't stay in one room with a child ... And he himself had his own work to do, he would have to get down to it as soon as possible, and for that he would need a corner of his own, too. Yes, he would work hard, he would dedicate himself to his work, his wife and his son (there was no doubt that it would be a son!). And if he worked properly he would earn enough to make a decent living and he would no longer have to be a slave to Dr. Kreindel or anyone else! And Thea too, in the last resort a worn-out woman, would be able to stop working for that lawyer of hers and devote herself completely to their child ...

The frenzied strains of a piano burst out of a neighbouring apartment. Gurdweill recognized it immediately as a highly sentimental Chopin waltz. In wild pursuit and flight, the notes broke into the silent room, as if deliberately invading it through some hidden crack in the ceiling; they whirled about the room, clashing with each other and mingling with the dense dusk air and the smoke of Gurdweill's pipe. And suddenly the figures of Thea and the child began spinning giddily before his eyes. Thea's hair streamed wildly through the air, touching him as she came closer and whipping his face, which gave him great pleasure. And the child, his and Thea's son, golden-haired like her, gold as the skin of an onion, danced with his mother, his round face flushed with excitement, laughing aloud with delight. Gurdweill

128

suddenly remembered that he had bought a little motor-car for the baby and left it in the kitchen — how could he have forgotten it until now? And so he got up and went into the kitchen — the kitchen of his father's house, and discovered to his astonishment that the little car had disappeared. He was certain that he had left it there, in the left-hand corner, between the dresser and the wall, and now it was gone. Gurdweill searched all the other corners too, he even opened the doors of the dresser — but all in vain. An inexpressible sorrow overwhelmed him. Suddenly he knew that he would die of this sorrow, and the knowledge in itself did not depress him: all he wanted was for it to happen as quickly as possible, for he could not bear the terrible sorrow for another second. And then it suddenly occurred to him that he had seen a fine, long, black radish in the dresser, and he could give this radish to the baby . . . surely it would make him happy, such a fine black radish! Gurdweill opened the dresser again — yes, it was still there! He took it and felt it and weighed it in his palm: it was hard, firm and heavy — an excellent radish! But as he continued to examine it, he saw that the tail of the radish was wagging to and fro, slowly but steadily, just like an animal's tail, and suddenly the tail turned into two, three, innumerable tails, all wagging away, and getting entangled with each other, and tickling his palm until he burst out laughing. And suddenly Thea was standing before him, seething with fury. She snatched the radish out of his hand and cried: "What, were you going to give him a radish? The baby's dying of thirst and you were going to give him a sharp-tasting radish? And what do you think Dozent Schramek would say?" She began pushing the long radish into his mouth, shouting as she did so: "You eat it yourself, yourself, yourself!" . . . Gurdweill felt as if he were going to choke, his mouth was full of radish and he couldn't breathe. "This is the end of me," he thought . . .

There was a knock on the door and then another, and the door opened. The room was in darkness, illuminated only by the light in one of the hotel windows opposite. Gurdweill was sitting with his profile to the door,

129

withdrawn into himself, his head resting on the table, like some dark, shapeless bundle.

Dr. Astel and Lotte Bondheim came into the room.

"Hello, Gurdweill, is this how you welcome visitors?" Dr. Astel cried to the dark lump next to the table.

Gurdweill awoke with a jolt.

"Sorry, the light, I forgot to light the lamp . . ." he stammered. "I don't know what happened to me . . . But sit down, children, please sit down!"

He stumbled round in the dark as if searching for something, and then took the oil-lamp from the bedside table, next to the stove, and set it down on the big table in the middle of the room, saying as he did so:

"Very good, excellent! What a good idea, to drop in like this, a wonderful idea!"

He lit the lamp and held out his hand to his guests. They sat down, Dr. Astel next to the table and Lotte on the couch. Gurdweill, still covered in confusion, bustled about as if there was something important and urgent that he had to do.

"Where's Thea?" inquired Lotte.

"Thea? She'll be here any minute," said Gurdweill decisively. "No doubt about it. She went to visit her parents. And you, my dears? How are you?"

And turning to Lotte:

"When did you get back from the mountains? Did you have a good time there?"

"Yes, not bad at all! And you? Is everything as usual?"

"Yes, everything's as usual — of course it is! But you, Lotte, you look really well, and I'm happy to see it, very happy indeed! So, tell us, how did you pass your time there? Oh, of course! I completely forgot: tea or coffee — which do you prefer?"

"Nothing at all!" replied Lotte. "Please don't bother. We've just had something in the café downstairs."

"Sit down, sit down, there's no need for anything," confirmed Dr. Astel.

"And Thea? What's she up to?" inquired Lotte.

"Nothing special. Working as usual," said Gurdweill.

"But you," said Lotte in a sincerely sympathetic tone, "you don't look very well, Gurdweill. Is anything wrong?"

"Nothing at all. I don't think I look any worse than usual."

Gurdweill, who for some reason could not endure any reference to his ill looks, quickly changed the subject. "Did you come straight from home?" he asked, and immediately regretted the question, which seemed to him indiscreet.

"No, we were in the Prater," Lotte replied simply. "We would have come before, but we were afraid we wouldn't find you at home on a day like this!"

"Actually, I wasn't at home. I only got back about half an hour ago."

Gurdweill seated himself on the edge of the couch, close to Lotte, gave her an inquiring, sidelong look, and said with a smile:

"You've grown prettier! Much prettier! And a new hat too, which suits you very well!"

"What's this, Gurdweill?" laughed Lotte. "Are you beginning to pay me compliments in our old age? I never knew you so gallant before!"

"It's got nothing to do with compliments! I'm only saying what I think, without a trace of flattery."

"We all know that Lotte's beautiful — it's a well-known fact," said Dr. Astel.

"You too?" cried Lotte archly. "The pair of you are conspiring against me!"

After which she began to ask Gurdweill about the literary work he was currently engaged upon. A few weeks ago, when she was on her vacation, she had read the last story he had published, and it had made an unforgettable impression on her. It was an excellent story, absolutely first-rate! She meant every word! Dr. Astel agreed with her, although he pointed out a few imperfections, which while not detracting from the value of the story, he should nevertheless try to avoid. Gurdweill

131

complained that he had no time to work. When he came home in the evening he was exhausted and he couldn't concentrate properly. And for this reason he was hardly getting anything done. He did not tell them, of course, that Thea had once torn up the manuscript of almost an entire story in a rage, and that ever since he had been obliged to work in secret, when she was sleeping or when she went out, and to hide his manuscripts from her. He did not tell them, but Dr. Astel and Lotte sensed for themselves that Thea was to some extent to blame for his inability to work as he would have wished.

Suddenly Thea put in an unexpected appearance. She greeted Lotte like a long-lost friend, almost embraced her, and seemed delighted to see her.

"I'm so glad to see you both!" she said. "I was thinking about you only a moment ago in the street."

Gurdweill was pleased that she had chosen precisely this moment to come home. He was a little uneasy himself about meeting her after what had happened, and he imagined that the presence of strangers would be especially welcome to Thea, since she would surely be even more ashamed than he was. But Thea showed no signs of shame. She seemed to have forgotten the entire affair. Turning to her husband she said:

"Why haven't you offered our guests a cup of tea, rabbit?" Her voice was gentle, and a wave of warmth flooded his heart.

"I offered them tea and they refused. But I can make some now. I'd be glad to."

The guests refused again.

Thea took off her black felt hat and threw it on to the bed. After pushing her straight flaxen hair back with a practised hand, she looked like a plucked chicken. Thea was far from beautiful, and some people might even have considered her ugly. Her ugliness was particularly striking now that she had removed her hat and pushed her hair severely off her brow. Her colourless face seemed naked. It was a long face, with a rather high forehead. The distance between her little snub nose and her flat, rectangular chin seemed immense, taking up almost half her face, a blank, empty space hardly interrupted by her inconspicuous lips. Something was lacking in this space — perhaps a big moustache . . .

Thea lit a cigarette from the flame of the oil-lamp, pulled up a chair opposite Lotte, and sat down and crossed her legs.

"You have a new hat, I see. A bit too light for you, I think. A darker one would suit you better . . ."

"No," said Lotte. "I tried a darker one and it didn't suit me. Besides, everyone thinks that this one looks good on me. It's the men's opinion that counts . . ." And she smiled.

"The men's opinion? What do men understand?" Thea protested. "The men have been smitten with blindness," she pronounced in biblical style and winked at Dr. Astel.

"Come, come, Thea, don't exaggerate," said the latter. "What is female beauty for if not for men? I'd like to see you get along without men!"

"We would manage without them very well, I assure you!"

"Maybe you would, as an exception to the rule. But other women wouldn't agree with you."

"What's the point of all these silly arguments?" Gurdweill intervened. "Men and women were created for each other, they need each other, and that's all there is to it."

"And you, Lotte," said Thea half seriously and half mocking, "aren't you thinking of getting married soon? It seems to me that I heard some rumour to that effect . . ."

"I'll have to consult you about it first," smiled Lotte. "With all your experience . . . already married for six months!"

"My experience is confined to the rabbit, which is hardly a basis for generalization . . . Or perhaps you intend marrying him? That I certainly couldn't recommend!"

Gurdweill was not enjoying the conversation. He smiled in embarrassment and gazed at his shoes as

133

if they held the solution to some perplexing riddle. The couch suddenly felt hard and uncomfortable.

"You're no basis for generalizations either, Thea," said Dr. Astel jokingly. "What's wrong for you may be just right for some other woman . . ."

"Have you got a cigarette?" Gurdweill interrupted him, noisily getting to his feet.

He took the cigarette and stationed himself next to the table, leaning against the head of the bed.

"Guess who I met this afternoon, rabbit — Perczik. He sent you his regards. We went for a little walk together. A ridiculous person . . ."

Gurdweill thought to himself: now him too, that little rotter! He knew only too well what Thea meant by "ridiculous." Whenever she called anyone "ridiculous" it was a sure sign that she was interested in him. Why did she have to tell him these things! "He's not in the least ridiculous," he said. "Only a little limited."

But he regretted the words before they were out of his mouth, and berating himself silently for his idiocy added aloud:

"Everyone's a little ridiculous, if you like. Each in his own way."

"He told me some strange stories," Thea continued with a meaningful smile, "about his family life. Fascinating . . ."

"What would you like to do now, children?" said Dr. Astel and stood up. "Why don't you come down with us for a while? It's such a lovely evening!"

They all agreed. It was already eight o'clock. Dr. Astel was hungry and suggested that they go first to a restaurant and then see what they felt like doing afterwards. And he led them to a good restaurant on the corner of Heinestrasse, where they all ate heartily except for Gurdweill, who had no appetite. Then they went to the Prater.

Crowds of people were streaming in and out of the Prater, which was illuminated with a garish, orange light, milling about like a swarm of ants. A Sunday crowd of workers, clerks, and servants, avid for excitement and adventure to see them through the six dreary, monotonous days ahead. The Prater roared and shrieked with thousands of clashing voices, inviting the crowds with its hustlers and organ-grinders, clowns with painted faces, monkeys, dwarfs, gigantic Fat Women; its fake Indians and Negroes, its part-time athletes with their bare, muscular arms like butchers in an abbatoir; its still wax figures in glass cases, acrobats in flesh-coloured tights; its conjurers and magicians and sword-swallowers — invited with its deafening cries and blinding lights: "Don't miss the opportunity of a lifetime! Come in, ladies and gentlemen, come in!" There was a flea-circus, there were all kinds of swings and roundabouts, shooting ranges with boring prizes for the winners, tawdry circuses and cinemas showing "Westerns," a roller-coaster, a Ferris wheel, merry-go-rounds, cheap cabarets, hawkers selling piping-hot sausages, pastries and fruit, bars, sprawling drunks, prostitutes of the worst kind — everything to satisfy the naïve and simple tastes of the lower classes. But behind all this, behind the entertainment hawkers and their customers, lay grinding poverty, suffering and disease, and they were the true, permanent nucleus, the quintessence of it all — Gurdweill sensed this with a terrible clarity as they passed the entrance to the Volksprater, and his throat constricted as if all the oxygen had suddenly drained out of the air. A deathly loneliness seized hold of him, and an angry vein began hammering almost audibly in his temples. He gripped Lotte's arm with such suddenness that she cried in alarm: "Gurdweill, what's the matter?"

"Nothing, nothing!" he whispered as if to himself and immediately added, "It must be the crowds . . ."

Thea and Dr. Astel walked on ahead, with Lotte and Gurdweill following. They passed under the railway bridge and entered the Hauptallee, where the widely spaced streetlamps cast a pale, insignificant light in the dense darkness rising from the clumps of trees bordering the avenue. It was a cool, starry evening, and here the chilly air was slightly damp. The further they penetrated into the avenue the more muffled the clamouring voices of the Volksprater sounded, like the distant roar of some

135

gigantic factory. Lotte and Gurdweill walked in silence.
Here and there the smothered laughter of hidden lovers
broke out of the trees. From time to time a solitary policeman loomed unexpectedly out of the darkness, just like
one of the gangsters against whom he was supposed to
protect them — popping up under their noses as if he
had sprung straight out of the ground, staring grimly into
their faces, and then crossing to the other side of the road.

Suddenly Lotte said in a gentle voice:

"I thought about you often, Gurdweill. Over there
in the mountains. I had a lot of time to think, and the
stern silence of the mountains is conducive to thought. I
thought that your fate will be a hard one, an extraordinary
one . . ."

She paused for a moment and then went on:

"I don't know why, but ever since we met I've
sensed something dark and mysterious about your
being, of which you yourself may not even be aware. Perhaps I could call it 'your metaphysical being' . . . I've never
felt anything like it in anyone else. And it makes me feel
afraid. Not afraid of you, but afraid for you . . . Recently
this fear has become more frequent, almost constant. Not
like before, when it would flash through my mind and then
go away again immediately. Now it's settled down inside
me and it won't go away . . . Sometimes when I'm busy
doing something, reading a book, sewing, talking to someone — all of a sudden I become very upset, for no obvious
reason, and soon afterwards the fear comes into my mind:
'Perhaps something's happened to him!' . . . And I can't
rest until I've seen you or found out that nothing's happened . . . It's as if you're in some permanent danger . . ."

"Not a moment's peace," thought Gurdweill.
"Wherever I go it's always the same . . ." But
Lotte's warm words did something to dispel his loneliness
and depression nevertheless. Unconsciously he gave the
girl's arm a grateful squeeze. With a pretence of gaiety he
exclaimed:

"Nonsense, Lotte! There's nothing for you to worry about. What can happen to a wicked old man like
me?"

Lotte was silent. They passed the third café and continued walking, crunching the gravel beneath their feet. It must have been about half past nine. Thea and Dr. Astel turned around and came to meet them, and Dr. Astel invited them all to come home with him and have a drink. The invitation was accepted, and they took the next tram back to the city centre.

13

Dr. Mark Astel was in partnership with his elder brother, who had a reputation as an excellent lawyer. For over a year now his name too had appeared on the bronze plaque on the door of 7 Wollzeile: "Dr. Richard and Dr. Mark Astel, Certified Lawyers, Criminal and Mercantile Law," etc. He had been born and brought up in Vienna in a bourgeois family. His education had proceeded smoothly from high school to university, and at the age of twenty-two he had received his diploma without any particular difficulties or outstanding academic achievements. His future was mapped out in accordance with his family traditions and his own steady character: so his father, who was also a lawyer, had lived, so his brother lived, and so Dr. Mark Astel, too, would live, a comfortable, affluent, bourgeois life, without any upsets or scandals. In the war, too, he had been lucky. He had been taken prisoner a few weeks after enlisting, and spent the duration in a P.o.W. camp in France. He had been working for his brother for six years, from the day of his discharge from the army, and everything was going well apart from his affair with Lotte Bondheim, who led him on and rejected him in turn, according to the whims of her volatile moods, and made it impossible to get anything settled.

He had an apartment of his own in Karlsgasse with three spacious and tastefully furnished rooms, a kitchen and a hall, which he had received two years previously from his brother, when the latter married and moved into a bigger place.

The visitors were shown into the drawing-room, where they were immediately greeted by the slightly stale, chilly air characteristic of unused rooms.

Glancing about her as if to emphasize that she had never been there before, Thea cried:

"What a lovely apartment, Doktor! If it were in my nature to be envious, I would envy you for this place!"

"Which would not prevent me, of course, from feeling as comfortable in it as before," laughed their host.

He placed a pot-bellied bottle of Benedictine liqueur and two bottles of Muscatel wine, which he took out of a glass-fronted cabinet, on the table. Then he fetched polished, dark-blue goblets, with stems as long and slender as those of flowers, a box full of cigarettes, and an assortment of snacks from the supply which he always kept handy.

"We can have tea or coffee too, if you wish," he said and sat down at the table.

Lotte removed her hat and autumn coat and poured the drinks, playing the hostess. "She's changed a little over the past few months," thought Gurdweill, observing her graceful movements, "she's calmed down." And he was sorry, for some reason, that she had calmed down. She sat next to Gurdweill. They clinked glasses and drank, and then they drank again. Soon the drawing-room became cosier; tongues were loosened and wagged without constraint. Dr. Astel began telling jokes, indifferent by now to the fact that most of them were rather *risqué* for mixed company. He was an excellent raconteur, and everyone laughed loudly and freely, as if they had just been released from invisible chains. Gurdweill's laughter rose above the rest, very shrill and piercing, and he went on laughing after the others had stopped. His excessive merriment seemed to stem not from the jokes themselves, but from some inner need to laugh, which had now found an outlet. He sat with his shoulders hunched and his head dropping on to his chest, shuddering with laughter. Anyone seeing him might have wondered how such a skinny little body could contain so much loud laughter . . . Thea leaned back in her chair, crossed her legs, clasped her hands behind her head, and gazed at some invisible point just below the ceiling. Her face was red. Lotte played mechanically with her empty glass, while Dr. Astel played with the cigarette box and went on telling jokes.

139

After a while Dr. Astel got up and fetched bigger glasses, which he filled with wine.

Gurdweill emptied his glass in one gulp, without looking at anyone. Then he let his head fall to his chest again and began humming a tune to himself.

"Wake up everybody!" cried Thea. "Why so gloomy? Mark! (Lotte noticed that she called him by his first name.) Rabbit! What's the matter with you men?"

Gurdweill raised his head slightly and looked stupidly at his wife. He even smiled a hurt, foolish smile which looked more like a tearful grimace. Dr. Astel started singing a popular ballad. His voice was pleasant, though not strong. He sang tastefully, flaring the nostrils of his huge nose. Thea hummed in her rather coarse, discordant voice. Then Lotte joined in too. But they sang without any real enthusiasm, as if they were under some obligation to do so, and in the end they fell silent.

Suddenly Gurdweill spoke, and they all turned to look at him in astonishment, as if some dumb creature had suddenly opened its mouth. Without lifting his head he said, as if it were all perfectly obvious:

"The little things aren't important, of course . . . that's what I've always said . . . not important at all . . . But still, they're necessary . . . necessary for — for — the main thing! That's it! But what if the main thing itself is missing — what then, eh?" He raised his head inquiringly. "What happens if the main thing itself is missing? . . . Pour me a bit of wine, Doktor! Hee-hee . . ."

He took a gulp of wine and continued:

"Take, for example, a baby . . . A baby is something concrete, it exists, that's obvious . . . And if a person's got a baby, he buys it a toy . . . A teddy bear, a little car, a r-radish, yes, why not, a black radish too, hee-hee . . . Babies like radishes too! To play with, of course, only to play with . . . But if there's no baby, can I eat the radish myself? And what if I don't like radishes? If I don't like them at all? What then, eh? Dr. Kreindel always says: 'Instead of little people standing up, big people should sit down, in the words of Schiller . . . Hee-hee,' he likes quoting, Dr. Kreindel! And Thea knows it too."

140

"What on earth are you talking about, rabbit?" laughed Thea. "Come, let me give you a kiss! You're really cute today!"

And she inclined her long body sideways to kiss him. But Gurdweill leant backwards, as if to evade a blow.

"Not that!" he said. "Not that! This isn't the time for that sort of thing ... Right, Doktor? You're my friend, I know, even if you are a little sly and crooked like all the advocates ... and even a little stupid — don't deny it! It's the truth!" Gurdweill cut the air with his hand for emphasis. "But I like you anyway! I definitely like you!"

And he smiled complacently.

Dr. Astel laughed. "My dear Gurdweill," he said, "you're very generous with your compliments!"

"Don't mention it," said Gurdweill, "it's nothing at all!"

And he stood up, stepped round the back of Lotte's chair, and stationed himself on the other side.

"Lotte," he said, "you're a pure soul. Let's drink a toast together, you and I."

He took somebody's glass from the table and clinked it against hers. Lotte looked at him pityingly.

"Come on, Lotte, drink up!" urged Gurdweill. "Don't you want to drink with me? You wouldn't insult me, would ,you?"

Lotte took a little sip of wine. Thea put her arm around Dr. Astel's neck and whispered something in his ear. "Later," he said audibly, "later!"

Gurdweill seated himself on the sofa opposite and began again:

"You all think I'm drunk, admit it! Everybody always thinks that everybody else is drunk or mad ... But I'm only cheerful ... very cheerful indeed! I can laugh too, if you like: ha ha ha! Isn't that so, Thea? My mother always used to say: a child should play with other children and be cheerful! And now I'm cheerful, as you see ... of course I am! And if any of you would like to dance, I'm ready! ... Ready and willing! Right away!" He stood up and went over to Thea. "Do you want to? All you have to do is say: I want to."

"What?" she laughed.

141

"Nothing! Just be cheerful . . . Because I love you very much, you know I do."

"I'm not sad at all, rabbit! You can see for yourself that I'm perfectly cheerful!"

"Good! Very good! And you don't hold anything against me? . . . Everything's forgotten? . . . You see, I was afraid that you had some grudge against me . . . But now everything's all right!"

"Don't drink so much, Gurdweill!" cried Lotte, and took the glass from his hand. "What's the matter with you? Have you gone mad?"

"I'm thirsty, that's all!"

He grabbed the bottle and pressed it to his lips, but Dr. Astel snatched it away from him before he managed to take more than a gulp or two.

"Shame on you, Gurdweill! We still drink from glasses here!"

Gurdweill smiled patronizingly. "Who needs glasses?" he said. "You know what, Doktor, why don't we all have another drink, and then you can play something on the piano for us, eh? Thea and I want to dance . . ." And he giggled loudly.

Lotte had begun sobbing soundlessly. At first nobody noticed, but now they saw that her shoulders were heaving. The gap between her hands, which were covering her eyes, revealed the quivering of her full red mouth and the trickle of tears dripping from its corners. The church clock on Karlsplatz struck twelve, deliberately and inexorably, as if pronouncing an irreversible sentence. Dr. Astel leapt up, rushed over to Lotte, and began tenderly stroking her hair and back.

"What is it, Lotterl," he coaxed as if she were a baby. "Did somebody hurt you? Never mind, you'll feel better soon. Believe me, the bad feeling will go away in a minute."

Thea stood up too, and began pacing about, sniggering to herself. A door in the passage closed with a bang. Lotte wiped her flushed face with a handkerchief and tried to smile:

"Please don't make a fuss. It's nothing. Just nerves . . . But I'm all right now. Really, I'm fine!"

142

Gurdweill stood at the opposite end of the table, where Thea had been sitting, and observed the scene with intense interest, a grave expression on his face. Something was evidently not quite clear to him here. Why had Dr. Astel suddenly gone over to stand next to Lotte? He should have been doing something else entirely!

In the meantime Lotte calmed down completely.

"It doesn't make sense," mumbled Gurdweill to himself. "No, it doesn't make sense at all . . ."

He went up to Lotte, raised his finger in the air, and announced:

"The night is made for joy! If you don't laugh at night you won't laugh by day either!"

Lotte took a sip of wine and said: "Come and sit next to me, Gurdweill. You really are the most cheerful of us all . . ."

"You shouldn't drink, my dear," Thea exclaimed with a hidden sneer, "it's bad for your nerves. Some people just can't take it."

Lotte pretended not to hear.

Dr. Astel sat down at the piano and strummed a tune from some new operetta, playing softly because of the lateness of the hour, while Gurdweill beat time with his foot on the floor. He even began swaying clumsily where he stood, which made him look quite ridiculous since he did not know how to dance. When Dr. Astel finished playing, Thea, who was standing next to the piano, said loudly so that everyone would hear: "You wanted to show me your flat, Doktor! Do you want to do it now?"

And Dr. Astel retired with Thea to the next room, while Lotte looked after them suspiciously. The sound of Thea's laughter immediately breaking out cut dully into her flesh, like a blunt knife. Unable to sit still, she jumped up and went over to Gurdweill, who was still dancing on one spot, humming a tune to himself through his nose. In the next room the laughter died down abruptly. Lotte seized Gurdweill's hand and pulled him to the sofa.

"Sit down with me, my dear. It's so hard, so hard . . ."

Gurdweill sat down rather unwillingly and whispered: "Ah, yes, Lotte! Yes, of course . . ."

143

Mechanically he placed his hand on her head and began slowly stroking her hair, as if to console her for something. His stroking hand gave her a feeling of inexpressible pleasure, and she suddenly seemed about to burst into tears again. But she controlled herself. A heavy silence came from the next room.

"Where did Thea go?" asked Gurdweill.

"Thea?" Lotte flared up instantly: "You need Thea now? Don't worry, she won't get lost!"

She flung herself away from him: "You're a fool, a hopeless fool! You deserve everything you get, and more! You're all the same . . . You stick like leeches to whoever makes your lives most miserable!"

"What?" asked Gurdweill, who had not heard a word she said.

Lotte sat weeping silently. The tears poured down her cheeks, one after the other, and she made no effort to wipe them away or to stop their flow. No one in the world could have consoled her. At that moment Lotte felt utterly abandoned, alone in the middle of the night in the big, black world with a man who was not only drunk but infatuated with another woman, a woman who tormented him and made his life a misery. Gurdweill lay down on the sofa with his head in her lap and in a moment he was fast asleep. Lotte was flooded with pity both for herself and for this dear tormented soul, sleeping in her lap like a baby. She bent over him and pressed her lips to his hair. Then she got up carefully and placed a dark red velvet cushion under his head, went over to the window and looked out at the empty street. From the next room the voices of Thea and Dr. Astel became audible again. Lotte dried her eyes and went and sat at the table. The two of them entered the room.

"Look, Rudolfus has fallen asleep! We must go home, it's late," said Thea and shook Gurdweill without succeeding in waking him.

"Let him stay here," intervened Lotte. "Why drag him home when he's so tired?"

"It's all the same to me — if the Doktor's got no objections, that is."

144

"But of course, Thea, of course! You can stay too, if you wish. You can both sleep in my bedroom, and I'll make up my bed on the sofa."

Thea refused. She could not get a decent night's rest except in her own bed.

The two women therefore put on their coats and hats and Dr. Astel went out with them to accompany them on their way.

14

THE window overlooking the small courtyard reflected a murky autumn day, assailing the soul like a heavy fog. On the ruddy brick wall opposite the solitary, invisible palace which had somehow miraculously landed up in this commercial courtyard in the heart of the city, cast a vague, blurred shadow; and the frequent shifting of this shadow seemed to indicate that a strong wind was blowing outside, one of those blustering winds typical of the city.

Dr. Kreindel sat at his ease in an upholstered arm-chair in front of the large desk in the middle of the office. He was smoking a thick chocolate-brown cigar, from which he had not removed the gold and red band. Rudolf Gurdweill, his secretary and "right-hand man," who was sitting at another desk next to the wall, was smoking too; but he was smoking a thin cigarette of an inferior brand — which seemed to sum up the difference between their respective situations. Dr. Kreindel could afford other luxuries, too — such as giving vent to a bad mood due to the gloomy autumn day on the one hand, and on the other, the loss of the two thousand schillings he had been obliged to give his wife that morning to buy a new, modern fur coat, although she already had a perfectly good one which had cost him ten thousand only two years before.

Dr. Kreindel removed the cigar from his mouth and gazed for a moment at the column of ash on its tip. Then he turned it around to the tip of his sharp nose and avidly sniffed the warm, aromatic ash. As he did so he reflected, with a note of resignation in his voice: "They're all incorrigibly extravagant . . . you won't find a sensible person among them . . . They've got nothing in their heads but rags and tatters!" As if he had come to a sudden decision, he flicked the ash into the large conch shell which served him as an ashtray, stuck the cigar back into his mouth, and cast a glance at Gurdweill, who was sitting bowed over his desk, writing.

"Have you written to Rowohlt Publishers yet, Herr Gurdwein?" (When he was in a bad mood he always got Gurdweill's name wrong, by one letter at least. Gurdweill had grown accustomed to it in the course of time and no longer took any notice.)

"The letter must be sent this morning. Without delay!"

"It's already written," replied Gurdweill without turning his head.

"Good!"

And after a short pause:

"How is your wife, by the way? I met her in the street the other day, about two weeks ago, to be exact . . . She didn't look bad at all, hee-hee, in fact she was positively radiant . . ."

Since Gurdweill said nothing, he continued:

"Yes indeed, my friend, this world was created for them and them alone. Women, I mean . . . They really get the best of it. What does Heine say? 'Noble creature, over all flesh placed by God to reign . . . etc.' Do they have spiritual conflicts like we do? What have they got to worry about except enjoying themselves? And while we wear out our brains and dry them up with philosophical questions and so on, they run after worldly pleasures . . ."

"Who wears out his brain with philosophical questions?" inquired Gurdweill, turning his head around. "No one that I know . . ."

"Come, come, my friend, don't be so modest!" Dr. Kreindel smiled into his cigar, happy to have succeeded in provoking Gurdweill into speech. "But how well I understand your modesty! No one better! Both of us are made of the same clay, after all . . . No, no, don't deny it! It's the simple truth! As for the quality of modesty, I know it in all its shades. You could say that I know it inside out . . . In the words of Lichtenberg: 'The genius hides in the seclusion of his room, but his perfume . . . etc.' Wonderful, eh? . . . But to return to the matter we were discussing before: women,

147

at any rate, aren't interested in philosophy — here I agree with you completely. Of course I don't know your own wife well enough to judge. Perhaps she is and perhaps she isn't — you know best. But as for the rest of them, taken as a whole — including my wife, of course — their interests lie in another direction entirely . . . 'either in the marrow or in the bone' as the old Chinese proverb has it."

"But Dr. Kreindel, you have an inexhaustible fund of quotations," sneered Gurdweill. "And what a memory!"

"What, my memory, you say — oho! I was already well known for my memory in primary school — a perfect memory! I was famous for it! Memory, he says, as if he's just discovered America! I could quote you from memory, for example . . . hmmm . . . the whole story you published recently, word for word, hee-hee . . ."

At the sound of these words Gurdweill was seized by a terrible nausea, as if some loathsome worm was crawling over his body. He immediately lit the stub of his cigarette, which had gone out in the corner of his mouth, and drew on it deeply. But he had to go on listening nevertheless.

Dr. Kreindel continued in a tone of tremendous satisfaction: "Not a bad story, by the way. Well written — nobody could say anything else. First of all: the style! A classic, noble style . . . the style of a Baron born and bred, one might say! Goethe, no less, hee-hee . . . I assure you, if I had to write the same story myself — I would choose the very same style! A pure, refined style — pearls! I always knew that I could rely on you from that point of view, my dear Herr Gurdweill. What does Mörike say? 'Once you love a person, then love . . . etc.' You can finish it yourself, I'm sure!"

Gurdweill could endure no more. The blood rushed to his head. "If he goes on one minute longer, something will happen . . ." He pushed his chair back so loudly that Dr. Kreindel jumped: "What is it, Herr Gurdweill? Are you trying to bring the house down, or what?" But Gurdweill's rage had already subsided. "Let the idiot talk as much rubbish as he likes! What difference does it make to me?" he said to himself, forcing a smile to his lips. And as if to punish himself for losing his temper, he added: "It can't do any harm to hear what else he has to say . . ."

"As far as the story itself is concerned," continued Dr. Kreindel in the same calm tone and with the same satisfied smile, "the conception, sequence and ordering of events — do I have to sing their praises to you? You know yourself that they're first-rate, above criticism, hee-hee! And as Klopstok says: 'What the artist himself says about his work is . . . etc.' The hand of a true artist is evident throughout. In me, my dear Gurdweill, you have a devoted reader! A reader who pores over every letter and never misses a thing! That's the kind of reader you need, hee-hee-hee . . . In other words, a reader whose mind and spirit match yours, a twin brother like me, who can understand what you're trying to say! And you don't have to look far for that reader, not at all! Here he is sitting and talking to you! However far you looked, you wouldn't find another like me! And why bother to look? We both know that nobody needs more than the one, right reader. And him you already have in me, and in me only, hee-hee-hee . . . And if I'm mistaken, you've already said yourself, my dear Herr Gurdweill, in this very story: 'Only man, man the creator, gives things their value' . . . etc. A fine phrase, eh? A pearl, hee-hee-hee!"

Gurdweill suddenly burst into loud, wild laughter and Dr. Kreindel joined in immediately, as if this were the signal for which he had been waiting.

"Excellent, excellent!" exclaimed the bookseller in the midst of his laughter.

"Herr Doktor," said Gurdweill at last, "since we're twin brothers, you should offer me a good cigar. I'm surprised you haven't yet realized that I, too, would enjoy one of your cigars."

"Well said, Herr Gurdweill, hee-hee, well said, twin brothers indeed! . . . A cigar, you say . . . With pleasure! But this afternoon. I haven't got any more on me now. That girl, Gertrude, in your story, whose love for Reinhold is only aroused when he's blinded in his right eye, she's a really interesting character . . . A rare psychological phenomenon, just waiting for a true artist like you.

To tell the truth, hee-hee, as far as I'm concerned you hit the nail on the head there . . . I had exactly the same thing on my mind for some time before the story appeared, and I came to the same conclusion as you did — the very same conclusion, believe it or not! You said exactly the same things that I had in mind. Let me tell you that if I didn't know you were an honest man, if I didn't know that such a thing was out of the question — I might even have suspected you of stealing my ideas! Don't take offence, my dear Gurdweill, it's only a manner of speaking, of course, to illustrate how similarly our minds work — that's all!"

Gurdweill sat facing Dr. Kreindel and looked at him with a smile. He wanted to see how far his employer would go if he didn't stop him. But Dr. Kreindel was already on the point of concluding. His excitement had waned, and besides, he felt that Gurdweill had missed the point and his words had been wasted on him. He only asked: "And what are you writing now, my friend?"

"I'm not writing anything," said Gurdweill innocently, "I've finished all the letters."

"Not bad, hee-hee-hee . . . What does Novalis say? 'The profound mystery of a word, which . . . etc.' But that's not what I meant, of course. I was referring to your creative writing, hee-hee. What literary work are you engaged upon at the moment?"

"I'm not engaged at present, nor will I be engaged in the future, upon any literary work at all."

"But why not?" Dr. Kreindel began to get excited again. "I can't believe you said that seriously! Impossible! You won't deprive me of that great pleasure! The only pleasure, you might say, that I have in the world! Why, it's exactly as if I were the writer myself! Just like here in the office, when you apparently do all the writing, but the real writer is me . . ."

At this moment Dr. Kreindel's wife, a vivacious little blonde, burst into the room, bringing with her a cloud of perfume and a gust of chilly autumn air. She immediately began talking rapidly, as if she were continuing a conversation begun outside.

"Isn't it wonderful? And see how it suits me! Look,

Paulerl!" she cried, pointing to her new fur coat. "Feel how soft it is! I put it on at once, it's quite chilly enough to wear a fur coat, isn't it? And it's so light, as light as a feather! You don't even feel it — no more than a bath robe. And now I need a new hat to go with it, a little felt hat, perfectly plain . . ."

"Sit down for a minute, my dear," interrupted her husband, who had risen to greet her when she came in. "How can Herr Gurdweill do his work when you create such a commotion?"

"Ah, Herr Gurdweill!" She finally noticed his presence in the room and offered him a hand in a white woolly glove. "Please forgive me. I didn't see you sitting there in your corner, ha ha ha! And what do you think of my new fur coat? I've just bought it, this very minute!"

Gurdweill cast an expert eye on the brown and white fur and pronounced: "Very nice! It suits you very well, madam."

"Doesn't it! Feel it please, Herr Gurdweill! The latest fashion!"

"But the hat doesn't go with it . . ." said Gurdweill deliberately. "It needs something simpler, a little cloche, black I'd say . . ."

"Of course, of course, I'm going to buy one right away! You see, Paulerl, Herr Gurdweill is an expert on women's fashions. He thinks I need a new hat too!"

"Very well, my dear, you shall have one. But what's the rush? You can buy it this afternoon. There's plenty of time for it this afternoon. The hat won't spoil in the meantime!"

"No, no, I have to have it right away! This afternoon I won't have time. At three the manicurist's coming, and then at five I'm meeting Malvina Holtzer — you know her, she just came back from Munich yesterday."

"But it's already twelve o'clock," Dr. Kreindel tried again. "Time for lunch!"

"It won't take long," his wife insisted. "Fifteen minutes at the most. The shop's right next door. You go home and I'll follow you straight away."

Dr. Kreindel had no alternative. Having failed to postpone this latest extravagance to the afternoon, at least, he

151

was obliged to hand the money over there and then, and his wife was gone in a flash.

Gurdweill gave him the letters to sign, took his hat and coat, and left the office. In the shop the cashier stopped him with a smile.

"Are you off to lunch already, Herr Gurdweill? Perhaps you'd like to go to a concert this evening? I have two tickets. Beethoven's Ninth with Salk."

"What's this, Fräulein Koppler, are you trying to seduce a married man?" joked the ginger salesman, who had just finished emptying a carton of books and was stretching luxuriously.

"It's none of your business, Herr Rudel. I wouldn't try to seduce you, at any rate."

"What a pity! But perhaps you would allow me to seduce you?"

"What nonsense you always talk, Herr Rudel!"

"I don't know yet if I'll be free this evening," said Gurdweill. "I'll tell you this afternoon."

The girl seemed a little offended, and Gurdweill made haste to add: "Actually, there's no reason why I can't say yes right now. At any rate, I'll do my best to be free."

"No," said the girl, "I completely forgot that an old childhood friend has asked me several times to get him a ticket to the Ninth with Salk ... I'll phone him first, he's sure to jump at the chance. But if he's busy, I'll let you know this afternoon, Herr Gurdweill."

"Fine," Gurdweill smiled at her and made for the door. "We'll leave it at that then."

In fact, he did not have the least desire to go to a concert, and had only made his half-promise to please the girl, who for some reason seemed to him unhappy.

For the past two weeks Thea had been in Dozent Schramek's sanatorium. The operation on her breasts had been successfully performed. Gurdweill visited her almost every day after work. During all this time she had been in a good mood, treating her husband with a degree of affection which gave him new hope and serenity. In his free time he was able to work on his writing without anyone to disturb him, and his satisfaction at the way it was going, too, contributed to the improvement in his general frame of mind. The constant feeling of oppression had grown somewhat lighter, and during this period he took in the world around him with alert senses, and the fresh vision of a man just released from a long term of imprisonment. Although Gurdweill was conscious of this inner liberation, he mistakenly attributed it to all kinds of other reasons, because his soul recoiled from the plain truth and because there was something stronger than the truth, which prevented it from penetrating his consciousness. He thus deluded himself into believing that the change stemmed from his own maturity, which had now reached a higher level in the natural course of its development, without any relation to external factors — and he was content with this explanation.

When he had the money, he would eat in a little restaurant not far from the office. He now entered this restaurant, which was not very full, sat down in his usual place and was immediately served. As he was eating his soup, which gave off a bad smell of stale fat, a spark of his previous wrath against Dr. Kreindel suddenly flashed through his mind, and his appetite vanished. He laid down his spoon and pushed the bowl away from him abruptly, making such a noise that the woman in widow's weeds opposite him, who had not taken off her black gloves to eat, recoiled and raised her head in astonishment. At that moment it seemed to him quite impossible to go back to the office and see that swine's stupid face once more that day. He would call the office as soon as he finished eating and say that he had a headache — and to hell with them! This unexpected decision calmed him down immediately and even gave him a pleasant feeling of revenge. Now he would be free as a bird the whole afternoon! He hurried to finish his meal and pay the bill. But in some hidden corner of his conscientious soul remorse had already begun to gnaw. Yettie Koppler the cashier and her invitation to the concert popped into his head, where they suddenly assumed an exaggerated importance. You can't possibly insult that poor girl, he said to himself — she's expecting you ... No! — he

153

pulled himself together — I won't go back! Not today! And he rose resolutely to his feet and marched out of the restaurant.

15

FOR a while Gurdweill strolled aimlessly along Franz-
Josefs-Kai, stopping now and then to look idly into the
shop windows. Then he crossed the street to the bank of
the canal. Resting his chest on the railing, his coat collar
raised, he looked down at the dark, wind-swept surface of
the water, which seemed to him to exude all the piercing
cold of the city. Two policemen, apparently in training,
were standing in a swaying boat, one of them rowing
vigorously with a single oar, bending the upper half of his
body, while the other stirred the water with a long pole, as
if searching for something on the river bed. "They're looking for someone who's going to drown himself tomorrow
or next month," it occurred to Gurdweill as he watched
them from the bank, "although it hasn't even entered that
person's head yet to put an end to his life . . ." As he passed the tram stop next to Stephanie Bridge, he recognized
Franzi Mitteldorfer's mother. He had never gone back to
visit the young woman who had fainted in Karlsplatz about
six months before, although he had resolved to do so
several times.

He went up to the old woman, who recognized him
immediately, and asked her how her daughter and the
baby were.

"Ah, what a tragedy!" the woman began to sob. "What
a tragedy! You had better not ask me, my dear young
man. Who could ever have imagined such a thing! It's
been two months now. At first we thought it was only
a passing nervous crisis. She's such a delicate little thing,
poor baby! You saw her yourself, Herr Gurdweill — she
was always the same, nothing to her at all! But from the day
little Fritzi was born her nerves broke down completely."

Gurdweill felt that his heart was being squeezed in a

155

vice. He grasped the situation immediately. Even then, six months before, he had realized that the young woman was troubled in her mind, and foreseen some kind of catastrophe.

The old woman continued, speaking with profound pain:

"We thought it would pass. We decided to send her to the country with the baby, even though things are very hard at present, as you know. My son-in-law doesn't earn much. But we were prepared to make the effort. My son-in-law loves Franzi very much. He's a good man, he doesn't drink or gamble, he spends all his free time at home. We were going to borrow some money from friends and pawn a bit of jewellery, not that we've got too much, but still — and then the catastrophe happened!"

"And where is she now?" asked Gurdweill sympathetically.

"Where is she? She's over there!" The old lady gestured vaguely behind her. "They took her away! Took her by force! I would never have given her to them of my own free will — as you can imagine. But they took her against my will! I couldn't stop them. And now she's been there for two months, the poor baby."

Gurdweill guessed where "there" was, but he wanted more details.

"But how could they take her? Did she do anything violent?"

"What are you talking about, Herr Gurdweill?" the old woman protested. "How can you imagine such a thing? That weak, delicate baby — violent! Nothing of the sort! She didn't lay a finger on a soul. I was busy in the kitchen and she was still in bed. It was about ten o'clock in the morning. My son-in-law was out of town on business for a couple of days. I was just about to take her some breakfast when she walked through the kitchen and into the passage in her nightgown. You have to go through the kitchen from the bedroom, you know. I imagined that she was going to the lavatory, which is on the landing, and that she would put on a shawl or a coat, and I didn't try to stop her. After a few minutes I suddenly became uneasy.

156

I ran to the landing and she wasn't there, and I knew right away that a catastrophe had happened. I ran down the stairs and rushed outside and saw a little crowd of people on the corner of Gumpendorfer Strasse. My heart told me immediately that I would find her there. And there she was, dressed in nothing but her nightgown, standing pale and silent in the middle of the crowd. A policeman had already arrived on the scene, and there was nothing I could do. He took her straight to the closest police station and she never came home again."

The old woman burst into tears again.

"I went home," she continued after a short pause, "to get her clothes. I left Fritzi with the caretaker, a kindly soul whose husband died about a year ago. So I took her clothes over to the police station. She was sitting there on a bench, the poor baby, staring silently in front of her as if none of it had anything to do with her. I dressed her and she let me do it, she was completely apathetic. And when I was finished, all she said was: 'We're going home now, mummy. Victor (that's her husband's name) will be cross with me for taking so long. He's hungry.' But she didn't move. And she didn't mention Fritzi. 'Of course we're going home,' I said, 'where else should we go?' But they wouldn't let her go home. 'The district doctor has to examine her first,' they said. And so they took her to his office. And after he examined her the doctor said: 'My dear lady, I have to inform you, to my regret, that your daughter's nervous condition is very bad. She requires medical supervision. We'll send her to the General Hospital. For a few days, a fortnight at the most. She'll be under the care of Professor Wagner-Jauregg — don't be alarmed, dear lady, it's only the ward for nervous disorders.' You can imagine how terrified I was. My heart stood still. You must have heard rumours about Wagner-Jauregg yourself, how he doesn't care a fig for human life! At first I couldn't say a thing. I suppose I must have gone pale too, because the doctor made me sit down and told someone to fetch me a glass of water. But Franzi didn't turn a hair, as if it had nothing to do with her. I began pleading, arguing — all in vain! 'It's a clear case of depression,' the doctor said, 'melancholia

157

with anxiety neurosis and suicidal tendencies. She requires professional supervision. What will you do if she jumps out of the window one night? In addition to everything else, you live on the third floor! Can you undertake to hire two nurses to keep an eye on her twenty-four hours a day? Well then!' And he phoned the hospital and half an hour later the ambulance came and took her to the Wagner-Jauregg ward. I went with her, of course. She was silent all the way. But afterwards, when we were there and I wanted to say goodbye, she suddenly burst out crying: 'Mummy, where am I?' 'You're in the hospital, my child, you're ill,' I replied, feeling as if I was going to faint. 'I don't want to, mummy, I don't want to! I'm not sick! I want to go home!' she screamed and threw herself about. I fainted, and when I recovered she was gone."

The old woman dried her eyes. Gurdweill was very touched by her story. He looked at her compassionately.

"And do you think that she stayed there?" the old woman continued bitterly. "Three days! That's all! They said: 'There's no room here! This is only a temporary station, for a few days, and from here they're sent there. It can take a few weeks, even months, you can never tell in advance with this disease, sometimes two months and sometimes six, too, and there's no room here.' I objected, I cried, I begged, I even spoke to the Professor, to Wagner-Jauregg himself. And he said: 'We'll see. If it's possible, she can stay with pleasure. But if the directors say there's no room, presumably they know what they're talking about, and my intervention won't help. Over there, by the way, the conditions are better than they are here. Our building is old and there everything is new and up-to-date and adapted to the needs of the patients. It's just the name that's frightening. Pure prejudice!' And when I came to visit her the next morning, I was told that she had already been transferred to Steinhof. And she's been there ever since."

Gurdweill was silent. After a moment he asked:

"And how is she now? Is she any better?"

"How should I know? Who knows! The doctor told me last week that she's much better and that if she continues

158

to make progress she'll be able to come home in two months' time. I myself can't tell. At first she refused to eat. She wanted to die of hunger, she said. They had to feed her artificially. She was indifferent to everything, and just imagine, she didn't even want to see me when I came to visit her. She didn't even ask about the baby, she just sat there in silence. Now she talks a little and eats whatever I bring her. Once, early on, I took the baby with me. I thought she would be glad to see him — but she didn't take any notice of him at all. And I never took him again. My son-in-law goes once a week, he's too busy to go more often. A few days ago she asked me to bring her oranges. Now she waits for me, she looks out of the window on the days when she thinks I'm coming — the nurse told me so. A few days ago she even asked the nurse about the baby. But she always wants to come home. Saying goodbye is heart-breaking. She won't let me go. She begs me to take her home with me, she runs after me crying. When I come home from there I'm ill for two days. I can't bear to see my baby suffering."

"What block is she in? I'd like to visit her."

"At first she was in number nine, but last week they moved her to number seven. The nurse said it was for less serious cases. I myself can't tell the difference. They're all poor sick creatures."

Gurdweill decided to go straight to Steinhof, and said goodbye to the old lady, who advised him in parting to say that he was a relation of her daughter's — for otherwise they would not let him in.

He went to call the office. And just as he was thinking that it would be better if someone else phoned, Ulrich, for example, he bumped into his friend Ulrich outside the public telephone booth.

Ulrich had lost his job a few weeks earlier and spent his time wandering about the city, sitting in cafés, and occasionally writing a poem. For the time being he was eating at his uncle's and he had not yet felt the pinch. He was always elegantly dressed and usually in high spirits.

"So you're not going to work — why not?"

"As far as Dr. Kreindel's concerned, because I don't

159

feel well. As far as you're concerned — because I don't feel like it. In any case I have to go to Steinhof. Why don't you come with me?"

"Of my own free will? Not a chance! Who have you got there?"

"A girl I know. I've just heard that she's there. And where are you off to?"

"Herrenhof. I haven't read the paper yet today. Why don't you join me there afterwards?"

"I won't be back before five. It's a long way."

"Don't worry! I'll still be there."

Gurdweill bought a bar of chocolate and some oranges and got on to the tram. The journey took about three-quarters of an hour; he had to change trams twice, standing crushed between working-class women carrying hot food in baskets and knapsacks for their sick relations. The institution was situated outside the city. It stood in large grounds on the top of a hill and was conspicuous from a distance — a secluded, self-contained city surrounded by a high iron fence, with the golden dome of the hospital church gleaming dully against the cloudy sky. The closer he came to his destination, the more uneasy he felt — an uneasiness which was tinged with fear. When the tram finally jolted to a stop and the noise of its engine died down, a terrible silence fell. Life came to a standstill. The passengers seemed dazed, uncertain whether to dismount or stay in the tram. And suddenly a blood-curdling shriek rent the silence, the high, continuous, animal-like shriek of a woman which seemed to come from far away, beyond the broad valley sweeping down at the foot of the institution. An icy tremor passed through Gurdweill and for a moment his heart stopped beating. Then there was silence again, a silence more profound than before. An old woman next to him exclaimed, to no one in particular: "Poor sick people — they're suffering." Gurdweill got off with the rest of the visitors, paused for a moment next to the tram, and then approached the gate. From the other side of the fence there was a loud burst of mocking, demonic laughter, mingled with the high, clear voice of a woman singing a merry tune from an operetta. Gurdweill

160

could not make out the words, but he was familiar with the tune, which everyone was singing in the city below. And hearing this merry song here made a profoundly depressing impression on him, as if it alone expressed all the sorrow and anguish of the inmates, and of humanity as a whole.

The brawny gatekeeper, with his terrifying moustache bristling like a pair of horns, pointed to the white administration building opposite the gate, where the visitors had to obtain entrance tickets. With the ticket in his hand, Gurdweill postponed entering the block a little longer, and wandered about the neat, criss-crossing gravel paths, alongside which ran narrow rails for transporting the food from the kitchen to the blocks dotted around the grounds. Among the many trees, lawns, and flower beds loomed handsome white stucco buildings, two or three storeys high, set rather far apart and surrounded by high wire fences. Autumn was very evident here. The trees were already quite bare and the fallen leaves lay in crumpled yellow piles next to the paths. The air was sharper, colder. Here and there he encountered nurses in their grey uniforms and caps, hefty guards, and inmates walking arm in arm with their visitors. They all wore the dull, stupefied expression which seemed peculiar to the place. "Here's the other side of the coin!" said Gurdweill to himself. "Only three-quarters of an hour by tram, and here you have the true face of life — life in all its nakedness!" He felt as if he were in another world, with different laws of life and death, a place in which the preoccupations and concerns of the ordinary world below had no meaning. But a clock struck three with a heavy sound and he remembered that he had to go in before it was too late.

A passing nurse showed him the way and he pressed the bell. A hefty nurse with a coarse, red face opened the door and locked it behind him. He followed her up to the first floor. The nurse opened a door to a long, bright corridor and then locked it, too, behind them.

"Wait here!" She pointed to a door on his right. "I'll call her."

And she called loudly into the echoing corridor:

161

"Frau Mitteldorfer! A visitor! Get dressed!"

Gurdweill waited next to the door of the visitors' room. His heart pounded. All the doors on the left were locked. From time to time a nurse walked down the corridor. A woman patient, evidently one of the less severe cases, wandered about eating a large apple. She gave Gurdweill a sidelong glance and smiled foolishly. Afterwards, when there was no one else in the corridor, she approached him and offered him the half-eaten apple.

"Have a bite, my dear, it's good!" she said with her mouth full. "Wouldn't you like to be my sweetheart? Whose husband are you?"

She addressed him with familiarity, in a common accent, and seemed very pleased with herself. The smile never left her grey, flabby, unattractive face. Gurdweill now became aware of the peculiar smell — a strong, sour, disagreeable smell — which permeated the corridor and rose overpoweringly from the hospital uniform of the woman next to him. It was an absolutely distinctive smell — a combination of odours which he had never smelled before. A key grated in a lock and the woman darted off, saying: "*Servus*, sweetheart! I can't stay now, but I'll always be happy to give you an apple! See you later!"

Diagonally opposite a door opened. A nurse appeared with Franzi Mitteldorfer behind her. A hotch-potch of female voices spilled into the corridor, prominent among them a weeping voice and a laughing one. He caught a glimpse of a spacious room, with a row of white iron beds, part of a barred window, and a group of half-naked women clustered round one of the beds.

Franzi Mitteldorfer hurried up to Gurdweill. She had evidently dressed quickly and carelessly. One of her clumsy, white, woollen stockings had slipped over her felt slipper, exposing a pale, skinny calf. Without greeting him, in a kind of speechless bustle, she seized his hand and pulled him into the visitors' room, where one of the patients was already sitting with an elderly woman. There were three small, round tables in the room and a number of upholstered chairs and benches. Franzi led him to a table in the corner, at a distance from the two women,

162

and they sat down. Her face immediately crumpled in soundless weeping, and she whispered without looking at him:

"Well, what's going to happen now? Perhaps you can save me? Nobody in the whole world wants to save me! Not even my own mother. See what I look like, see how I suffer here," she looked fearfully around her, "and nobody wants to save me!"

Her large brown eyes strayed hither and thither with a vague, terrified stare, and her fingers played ceaselessly with the edge of her coarse, striped gown.

Gurdweill could not utter a word. His heart constricted with pain. He did not even know if she recognized him or not. One after the other he took the bar of chocolate and the oranges out of his pockets and placed them on the table. He began peeling one of the oranges and offering her segment after segment. She nibbled them unwillingly and immediately put the pieces down on the table. Then she began her dry-eyed weeping again.

Gurdweill pulled himself together and said:

"Please eat, it will do you good."

"How can I eat," she sobbed quietly, "when I want to go home and nobody in the world is willing to help me? I hoped that you would help me, like you did that time in Karlsplatz, but now I can see that you too have hardened your heart like a stone. No one in the whole world! They've left me here to suffer all by myself! They beat me and scratch me. Not the nurses!" she quickly corrected herself with an animal fear, "don't think that I meant them! The nurses aren't allowed to hit us, even if they want to! I never said that the nurses hit me! But the women hit me and pull my hair. The women here are bad. They're really sick, insane! They yell and scream all the time and don't give you a moment's peace. They have to lock them up in the cage-bed or the padded cell."

Suddenly she smiled slyly and nodded in the direction of the two women: "One of them's sitting right there."

Gurdweill gave her another orange segment, and then a second and a third, which she swallowed automatically.

163

She even took up the pieces she had left on the table and ate them.

"And what for?" after a moment she began again. "Such idiocy! I could slap my face for it! How could I be such an idiot? Don't think that I don't know it! Who doesn't know that it's forbidden to go outside without your clothes on? Any baby knows that! But I forgot all about it ... I didn't realize what I was doing ... Such carelessness! I only wanted to see if it was raining and then go back inside again ... So I got up and went out ... And I simply forgot that I was naked and that it's forbidden to go outside without your clothes on ..."

Suddenly she got up, and standing facing him with her back to the wall, she began reciting with a strange, tearful pathos, stressing every word and wagging her finger solemnly:

"You mustn't go outside without your clothes on! You mustn't go outside without your clothes on! You mustn't go outside without your clothes on!"

She repeated this phrase over and over, as if to engrave it indelibly on her memory so that she would never forget it again.

Horror crawled like a worm down Gurdweill's spine, and a cold sweat broke out on his forehead. He turned to the two women sitting on the other side of the room, as if to enlist their help, but they had not even noticed that anything was wrong. The patient sat silently eating the dishes arranged on the table in front of her, while the older woman stroked her hair and whispered to her all the time. "That woman eats without stopping," he thought absent-mindedly. Then he stood up and went over to Franzi Mitteldorfer:

"Come," he stammered and took her hand, "come along ... soon the visiting hour will be over, and we still have a lot to talk about."

He was afraid to look into her face. He kept on seeing the stocking falling sloppily over her brown felt slipper.

She let him lead her back to her chair like an obedient child. She appeared to have calmed down a little. She even smiled to herself with a satisfied expression.

Gurdweill said: "One of your stockings has fallen down. You had better pull it up."

"Oh, my stockings! I was in such a hurry . . . I didn't have time to fasten them. And I've lost my garters too. You can't put anything down here for a minute without somebody stealing it."

She bent down and pulled the stocking over her knee with an impatient movement.

Gurdweill offered her a piece of chocolate, which she rejected.

"I'll eat it later. And now tell me, what's going to become of me? You can see for yourself what it's like here. Just listen to the screaming and wailing over there! Tell me yourself, how can anyone survive here? The sanest person in the world would go out of his mind if they put him here, I promise you! And what's the wonder? All you hear all day long, all night long, is screaming and wailing! And what's going to become of me? I ask you — what? I feel that I'm going insane. If I stay here any longer I'll go insane in the end. Nobody could stand it. It's already been ten weeks, ten weeks," her face twisted again in the dry-eyed weeping which tore at Gurdweill's heart, "ten weeks, ten weeks!"

Gurdweill felt as if he was about to burst out crying himself. He felt actual, physical pain. It seemed to him that he had never yet experienced so deep and sharp a sorrow and that there was no sorrow in all the world to compare with it. He clenched his teeth and forced back the tears that were choking him.

Franzi repeated with stubborn monotony:

"Ten weeks, ten weeks!" Without thinking he took an orange segment and put it in his mouth. The cold, sour juice revived him somewhat. At first, however, he did not know what he had in his mouth, and he removed the chewed-up segment and held it in his hand. After studying it intently for a while he realized what it was and immediately threw it under the table. Then he put his hand on the sick woman's arm and said in a pleading, coaxing voice:

"Calm down, my dear, calm down, I beg you. Here you are, have an orange. You'll see, everything will be all right.

165

You'll soon go home. In a few days' time, you'll see. Just keep calm and then the doctor will send you home himself, when he sees that you're calm and well again. You must eat everything and be calm."

"No, I can't, I won't," the poor girl sobbed, "not one more day! Not one more hour! I have to leave now! I can't bear it for another minute! I'm going out of my mind here! I don't want to go mad, I don't want to! You're to blame, all of you, for bringing me here! I have to go home immediately! This very minute! Otherwise it will be too late! Because I'll go really mad here and then they'll never let me out! Everybody's abandoned me and nobody cares. And you don't want to rescue me either. And I hoped that you would! And now nobody wants to! Who can I turn to, tell me, who can I turn to now? Steinhof, Steinhof! Now I'll be ashamed to show my face outside. Everyone will point their finger at me, as if I was a murderer! From now on nothing can save me! Everything's lost! Steinhof! With the crazy people! And all for such nonsense! For such nonsense!"

Her hand was on her forehead all this time, as if she had a headache. Gurdweill asked compassionately: "Does your head hurt?"

"My head hurts! My head hurts all the time! Everything hurts me here! I have to suffer so much! So much! At home I would have recovered long ago, and here I get sicker from day to day! I beg you, my dear, take pity on me, I beg you," and she began stroking Gurdweill's head and cheeks.

"I cast myself on your mercy, before God, save me! I'll never forget it! Save me before it's too late. I'm still young, I want to live. I don't want to go mad here and stay here for the rest of my life. I can't tell you how terrible it is here! I go down on my knees to you" — and she really did go down on her knees — "save me while there's still time."

Gurdweill raised her to her feet and seated her on the chair. He was deathly pale and his whole body was trembling. He was prepared to do anything for her, but he didn't know what he could do. His mind was a blank

166

and he didn't have the ghost of an idea. In a hoarse voice he said:

"I'll try to do something. I'll do whatever I can. But now calm down. Please calm down."

"You must go and talk to Dr. von Eichendorf right away — our head doctor, the director of the hospital. You'll find him in the administration building now. He isn't here every day, but today he has his reception hour. Three times a week he has a reception hour, and you can talk to him. Press him. He'll do anything if you press him . . . One of the patients was released a few days ago. Her family put pressure on him and it helped . . . and she was really very sick. She was always screaming and crying. But her relations pleaded with the head doctor and he let her go home. Everything depends on Dr. von Eichendorf, our Director. But in the name of God, don't say that I sent you! You mustn't say that on any account! Because if you do you'll spoil everything." And she looked over her shoulder to see if anyone had heard.

At that moment Gurdweill believed her. Perhaps she really would be better off at home. Perhaps she would recover sooner.

"I'll talk to the Director. I'll do whatever I can."

"Then you must go now!" she urged. "I want to know what he says right away. Come back and tell me what he says."

Gurdweill glanced at his watch.

"There are only five minutes left. I won't be able to come back. I'll go and see Dr. von Eichendorf as soon as the visiting hour is over."

He offered her another orange segment, as if it were some kind of panacea. Franzi put it mechanically into her mouth and chewed pensively for a moment, before beginning to wail again:

"Now you see, it is already too late . . . If you'd gone right away, I could have gone home today . . . You would have taken me home like last time . . . And now it's too late . . . Now I'll have to wait again . . . God only knows how long I'll have to wait! And I'm getting worse every day . . . Now I'll get really sick and then I'll never go home. The

167

really sick people never get out of here! Up to now I kept my head above water, I struggled: I thought they would take pity on me and send me home . . . But now I can't stand it any more . . . Now I'll have to get really sick . . ."

"No, no! You won't get sick!" Gurdweill protested. "You'll get better soon and go home. I'll talk to the Director."

"With the Direc . . ." Franzi broke off in the middle of the word and started from her chair. The door opened and the nurse came in to say that the visiting hour was over.

Gurdweill rose to his feet, collected the chocolate and the remains of the oranges and gave them to Franzi, who said fussily to the nurse: "Just a minute, Sister Charlotte, there's something I still have to say to him."

And to Gurdweill, in an urgent whisper: "Go to him now! You know who . . . Plead with him! Tell him I have a baby at home and I have to take care of him . . . For the baby's sake . . . Go right now! You'll find him there now."

She accompanied him to the end of the corridor and signalled to him with her head and her free hand to go directly to Dr. von Eichendorf. Before the door closed he caught one last glimpse of Franzi Mitteldorfer's sharp, hollow face, her straying, haunted eyes, her wild, wispy hair. He noticed, too, that the stocking on her right foot had slipped down again and fallen over her slipper. His heart broke to leave her thus, in such inhuman suffering. But the door shut and everything was over. The nurse accompanied him down the stairs and locked the front door behind him.

Outside he stood still for a moment, next to the door, to take a breath of fresh air. He felt as if a long time, several days perhaps, had passed since he had entered that door. His limbs ached with weariness and his face was as pale as if he had just recovered from a serious illness. Franzi's doleful refrain rang in his ears: "Ten weeks, ten weeks!" And: "You mustn't go outside without your clothes on!" Other disjointed phrases, too, filled his head and he did not even feel the thin, slanting rain which had begun to spatter against his face. For a moment he

168

wondered whether he should really go to see the Director. But he immediately rejected the absurd idea, and began rummaging in his pockets for a cigarette. All he found was a little stub, which he looked at absent-mindedly before lighting it and moving off.

He had not gone far when he heard a terrible shriek — the same shriek as before, but closer this time. He stood still, petrified. The shriek died down abruptly, as if interrupted in the middle. The only sound to be heard was the faint rustle of the fallen leaves at the sides of the deserted avenue, which Gurdweill took in at the same time as he became aware of the rain. With a feeling compounded of horror and avid expectation, he waited for the shriek to come again. But it was not repeated, and he started walking slowly towards the exit.

The number 6 tram was very crowded again, but Gurdweill did not notice. He was haunted by a feeling of guilt towards all those tormented creatures he had left behind in their misery. He saw himself as a deserter, and was slightly ashamed of the sense of relief which he had felt the moment he emerged from Franzi's block, and even more intensely, the moment he walked out of the Steinhof gate.

A crude, nasty female voice exclaimed next to him:

"Don't push young man! If you want to travel in comfort, go by car!"

Gurdweill turned his head slightly to the right, in the direction of the voice, while the rest of his body remained stuck like a brick in a wall. But all he could see was the slightly curved surface of a broad, endless back clothed in a black, hairy coat.

The voice continued:

"Yes, you! You in the black hat!" Someone giggled, and Gurdweill became conscious of the fact that his right elbow was digging into something soft and warm. The vision of a huge, spongy breast attached to some ugly woman popped into his head and he felt a violent revulsion. With all his strength he tried to draw his elbow in, but his efforts came to nothing apart from a slight jarring of the immense back in front of him.

169

Soon after this the tram reached the last stop. The passengers began struggling towards the door. Before getting out, Gurdweill turned himself to the right, as a man turns to see the stone against which he has just stumbled, and saw an elderly woman, short and fat, with a faint black moustache and a hairy mole on her chin. It seemed to him that she was the same woman who had been sitting in the visiting room with the other patient. Immediately a vision of the room floated into his mind, with the sick woman chewing dumbly and above her, on the orange wall, a portrait of Kaiser Franz-Josef. He got off and walked to the number 59 stop, to take a tram to the Ring. On no account could he remember if he really had seen the orange wall and the portrait of the Emperor or not, and this uncertainty nagged at him obstinately. For he was curious to know if his imagination had been playing tricks on him and hanging a picture of the Kaiser on a blank wall, or instead of a picture of someone else entirely, for example, that of some famous psychiatrist who trimmed his beard in the same fashion as the Kaiser: two pointed prongs, one on either side of the chin clean-shaven in the middle — thereby creating a certain resemblance between them? What a pity that he hadn't taken a closer look when he was there! But what did it matter to him, in any case? What possible difference did it make? He got into the tram and sat down in the only vacant seat, close to the door. He put his hand in his jacket pocket and pulled out a whole cigarette, which he had overlooked before, and was absent-mindedly about to light it when someone said:

"This isn't a smokers' coach, young man! You should have gone to the last coach for that!"

The coarse voice seemed familiar. He raised his eyes and saw the same squat woman with the moustache and the hairy mole sitting opposite him and looking straight at him with her mean eyes. Gurdweill was flooded with rage. At the same time he felt his stomach contract, as if he had swallowed something particularly disgusting. He was about to jump off when the tram started moving and he was forced to stay where he was. He removed

170

the cigarette from his mouth and put it back in his pocket. Then he sat back, deliberately assuming a pose of ease, crossing his legs, and started staring intently at the mole on the woman's chin. After staring for a few moments, his rage subsided. There were three hairs sprouting from the mole, one of which was white and the other two black. He counted them a few times and could not find more than three, only one of which was white. But they were all thick and hard as wire — this was obvious at first sight and required no further examination. It would be interesting to see her face, reflected Gurdweill with a certain satisfaction, if someone were to unexpectedly take hold of one of those hairs with a tweezer, or simply between his fingers — and he felt a kind of tremor in the fingers of his right hand — the white one, or one of the black ones, and pull it out! Gurdweill glanced at the woman's eyes as if to see the effect on her of the imaginary attack. Almost certainly, he continued his train of thought, if all three were suddenly pulled out at once, she would feel not only physical pain, but even a twinge of grief, as at the loss of some limb. At first she might even see herself as uglier without them, until she reconciled herself to their absence . . .

"Tickets please!" cried the conductor, and interrupted Gurdweill's reverie.

Outside darkness was beginning to fall, and the street-lamps went on. The tram stopped and the woman opposite stood up. Before she got off, she sent Gurdweill a parting glance full of hostility. He looked through the window to see if it was still raining, but the pane was so steamed up that he couldn't see a thing. Not long afterwards the tram stopped at the Ring, the last stop, and evening came down on the city.

16

GURDWEILL decided to walk to the Café Herrenhof, which was not far off. Cold and stinging, the fine rain drizzled on his face. He took a short cut, passed the back of the Burgtheater, and soon found himself in Herrengasse. The sight of the people he encountered in the rainy streets, preoccupied with their daily cares as usual, came as something of a shock. He thought it strange that none of them seemed aware of the real, terrible suffering lying in wait for human beings with every step they took, in comparison to which all kinds of everyday aggravations were as nothing. On the other hand, he said to himself, it's probably for the best — otherwise it would be impossible to go on living . . .

Ulrich was still sitting in the cafe, in a window alcove, with Perczik, who was reading *Der Abend* and smoking.

"You certainly take your time, Gurdweill," Ulrich greeted him with a mild reprimand, "it's a quarter to six. I was just about to go. Well, what was it like over there?"

"Nothing special," Gurdweill answered unwillingly as he sat down. "Sick people."

But Ulrich was not satisfied. "What about your friend?" he asked.

Perczik put his newspaper down and pricked up his ears: perhaps there was material here for a feuilleton.

"My friend," said Gurdweill vaguely, "is sick too. Presumably. Otherwise she wouldn't be there."

"Do they let anyone in?" Ulrich tried again.

"Where, where?" Perczik pounced.

"The Rothschild Hospital," said Gurdweill, irritated by Perczik's curiosity. "*Café au lait*, Herr Krieger."

A shadow of annoyance crossed Perczik's face. He knew very well where Gurdweill had been, and was eager to hear what he had to say, but Gurdweill refused to say anything. He inquired with a show of sympathy: "Is your wife feeling better? I heard she wasn't well."

"Yes, thank you!"

"Is she at the Rothschild Hospital?"

"If you like . . ."

Perczik despaired of drawing Gurdweill into conversation and took up his paper again. Ulrich realized that Gurdweill was very upset and left him alone for a while. Then he said:

"Lotte dropped in about half an hour ago. She'll be back at six. She wants to see you."

Gurdweill was silent. He sipped the coffee the waiter placed before him apathetically. Through the gap between the curtains he saw people passing with their umbrellas up: so the shower was not yet over. Sadness beyond measure filled him. "Yes," he reflected, "man is a puny creature — he can be driven mad by a cloudburst or a mosquito." He looked at Ulrich, as if to find support for this private conclusion. He saw that the latter's chin was cleft as usual, cleft with a kind of self-important smugness, and that his black and white striped tie was impeccably tied and lay right in the middle of his chest as if fixed there with invisible nails. All these childish efforts suddenly seemed ridiculous to him. And as if in grotesque contrast, the contorted, fear-ridden face of Franzi Mitteldorfer appeared again before his eyes. His heart began to pound.

"Did she stay long?" he asked, as if to distract himself. "No. She didn't even sit down. She only asked about you and said she would come back later. She asked you to wait for her. And here she is!" he looked towards the revolving door, where Lotte Bondheim at that moment appeared.

She approached their table with a hurried tapping of her high heels, casting her eyes about for a place to put her dripping umbrella. Perczik took it from her, stood it underneath the table, and chivalrously gave her his seat.

Gurdweill looked at her inquiringly as she sat down beside him, and found that her face was drawn and had grown paler since the last time they met, which touched his heart.

"How are you, Gurdweill? I haven't seen you for ages!" She smiled faintly. "If we meet so seldom, in the end we won't recognize each other . . ."

"There's no danger of that," said Gurdweill seriously. "Not as far as I'm concerned, anyway."

"And how is Thea? Will she be staying at the sanatorium much longer?"

This question apparently escaped of its own accord and made Lotte wring her brown glove nervously between her fingers (although Gurdweill was too ashamed to admit the truth, all his friends knew, from Thea herself, the real nature of the "illness" which had sent her to the sanatorium).

"About ten days longer, I imagine. If everything's all right . . ."

Gurdweill disliked talking about his wife to other people in general, and particularly to Lotte, who he knew was hostile to Thea.

Lotte went on compulsively:

"I meant to visit her but something always prevented me . . . before you turn around the day's gone . . . And you, Ulrich," she interrupted herself with an evident effort, "you're still sitting here exactly as I left you an hour ago. How long can you people go on sitting in cafés? Don't you ever get tired of it?"

"My dear lady," said Ulrich with a smile, "sitting in cafés is a barrier against the enforced activity which makes our lives miserable . . . The last stage before the pure Nirvana of our Master Buddha . . . People like us always have the mistaken feeling that they are wasting time, missing something irretrievable . . . As if a man had a set amount of things to get done in a set amount of time . . . The harmful influence of our materialistic generation, a generation of physical labour and advanced technology . . . But the minute you enter a café, you're on holiday — the yoke is lifted from your shoulders, snapped in half! Like a workers' strike, where inactivity is the rule . . . Look, what I hate most of all is the compulsion to work. Work itself, any work whatsoever, could be enjoyable if only people didn't make it a moral duty . . . The first question they ask you,

174

these self-appointed detectives, is always: 'What do you do? What's your profession?' I'd like to reach the stage where I could answer, without any shame or self-deception: 'Me? I do nothing, sir! Nothing at all! I live because God gave me the breath of life, right? As for all the rest I'm not under any orders and I haven't got a clue. I don't have to do anything! I live — and that's all I'm obliged to do . . .' This doesn't apply, of course, to the poor wretches who have to work for a living. They deserve our pity. I'm only talking about people who are provided with the necessities of life, but nevertheless feel obliged to work — in order to pay not for their food, but for the air they breathe, as if they owed some eternal debt for their very right to exist!"

Lotte had stopped listening long ago to Ulrich's lecture, which did not interest her in the least. All this time she kept her eyes fixed on Gurdweill, who sat looking down at the table as if sunk in thought. In the end she said:

"Ulrich, you talk just like a leading article in the *Neue Freie Presse*. You should write it down and send it to them and get paid for it."

"Writing is work too, madam!" retorted Ulrich without reacting to her sarcasm. But in his heart of hearts he was hurt. He took out his cigarette case and offered her a cigarette, as if to show that he had not taken offence.

Gurdweill said: "Things are so complicated, and people too, even those who seem the simplest. You can't measure them all by the same yardstick."

It was impossible to tell if his words were a response to Ulrich, or the conclusion of some other, private train of thought. No one answered him. Soon afterwards Lotte announced that she had to go home and asked Gurdweill to accompany her. They paid and stood up. Ulrich and Perczik left the café with them and set off in another direction.

It had stopped raining, but the street was shining with a wet, black gleam as if it had been coated with black lacquer. For a while they walked in silence. The shops were closing and iron shutters were coming down everywhere with a deafening clatter. Gurdweill sensed intuitively that Lotte was sad, and for some reason she seemed to him at that

175

moment very pathetic and in need of help. Pity welled up in him. "How unhappy she is, this Lotte," he reflected, "she, too . . ." And he immediately caught himself up on the "too" and tried to explain it away. It was vital to remove himself from this "too" and connect it to everyone else but him. He linked his arm with hers.

"This afternoon I went to Steinhof," he said gently. "I was visiting a friend. Over there you feel as if you're suddenly faced with the absolute nothingness of everything. One little screw comes loose — and instantly the naked core is revealed . . ."

Lotte said nothing.

They reached the Ring, where cars and packed trams were rushing to and fro. The Parliament building stood facing them with pompous arrogance, a closed fortress casting the heavy boredom of politics on the passers-by. Policemen patrolled its magnificent façade, guarding the emptiness within. In the distance, beyond Schottentor, like eyes opening and closing, coloured electric lights went on and off, advertising Schicht soap and Salamandra stoves. A crowd of curiosity-seekers clustered round a huge furniture van which had lost one of its wheels. What did it all amount to? Nothing. When one turned one's mind in a certain direction, it was all completely meaningless . . .

Gurdweill and Lotte had to wait a while before crossing the Ring. When they reached the back of the Parliament building, next to the dark garden on the left, where occasional showers of heavy raindrops fell from the boughs of the trees overhanging the fence, Lotte said:

"One should put those things out of one's mind . . . Healthy people with healthy instincts never think of such things, as far as they're concerned they don't exist — and but for them the world would come to a standstill. As for the others, they're already sick themselves . . ."

Healthy people! — thought Gurdweill — he did not have the least desire to be one of those healthy people. Besides, they, too, were sick themselves . . . sick without knowing it . . .

By now they were already walking up the rather steep incline of Lerchenfelder Strasse. Lotte leant with all her weight on Gurdweill's arm. In a pleading tone she said:

"But everyone wants a little happiness and peace of mind . . . Life can be so hard . . ."

And after a moment she went on warmly:

"I don't mind admitting that I'm an egoist. Should I be ashamed of it, Gurdweill? How many years have I got to live? I want to live them! To squeeze the last drop out of them! Perhaps it's in the nature of a woman. But I can't endure suffering. I'd even be capable of hurting my fellow men, if it would only help me to avoid suffering myself . . . I admit it freely. Does that make me wicked? Certainly no worse than others. And why should I be better than them? For that one has to pay a price, to give up personal happiness, which I refuse to do . . . And I won't be satisfied with a little either. I want it all! Everything that life can offer, I demand for myself! Because nothing else exists but for this life! I don't believe in anything else and I don't want to either! Life as it is, the life that reveals itself to us through our five senses, is good enough for me! Life is beautiful, extraordinarily beautiful, and I want to enjoy it to the full!"

After this outburst they walked on in silence. When they were not far from Lotte's home, she suddenly felt an urge to sit in a café for half an hour. She could spare another half an hour for him. And it would be a special pleasure for her — she added in a half-serious, half-joking tone — a rare treat, in view of the fact that they met so seldom nowadays. Gurdweill agreed willingly. He was even rather pleased by the invitation, since he was feeling tired and irritable and hoped to recover his spirits in the company of Lotte, who was now in a quiet, somewhat melancholy mood.

It was a small, third-rate café, half empty at this hour of the evening. The little waiter bestirred himself at their entrance and showed them with a flourish to a corner table, as if he had been reserving it especially for them. In the next room someone was playing fragments of tunes on the piano. Gurdweill ordered coffee for two and cigarettes, glancing as he did so at the sign hanging on the opposite wall: "Aryan Nature Lovers Meeting,

177

Neubau Branch." A picture flashed through his mind of tall, Aryan teachers in green jackets and short, dirty leather trousers, with bare, bony, sunburnt knees and long, curved pipes sticking out of their colourless, stupid faces: "Nature Lovers." The waiter brought the coffee and cigarettes, and Gurdweill heard the President of the Society say: "And now, gentlemen, I give the floor to our honoured member Herr Eigermeyer, after which, with the permission of all those present, we shall go on to discuss the items on the agenda of the meeting." Herr Eigermeyer rose to his feet and began in a somewhat rusty voice: "The great and particular importance, gentlemen, which cannot be sufficiently emphasized, of the establishment of special branches of our society for the organization and education of Aryan youth to the love of nature and fresh air and a proud, healthy, natural life in the spirit of the teachings of our Saviour Jesus Christ and their preservation from the undesirable foreign elements which — hmm — which have penetrated into our midst from the East, and which are taking over everything — I must stress, gentlemen, everything, all the economic and intellectual professions, and in the end even the last, precious possession remaining to us, the glorious nature of our beloved country . . . My heart bleeds, my friends . . ." And when he came home Herr Eigermeyer would wake his wife and tell her in a casual, nonchalant tone that he had made a speech lasting half an hour at the meeting tonight. He wasn't one to blow his own trumpet, as she very well knew, but all the members of the society had praised the clarity of his ideas and the precise, economical way in which he had expressed them . . . His wife would yawn lengthily, listen inattentively, and fall asleep again while he took off his clothes and got into bed with a feeling of profound self-satisfaction.

Gurdweill found it highly agreeable, even soothing, to picture this scene in a mood of ironic detachment. He smiled and took a sip of coffee. Not far off the waiter stood leaning against a table, apparently deep in thought. But the moment Lotte finished her coffee and put a cigarette into her mouth he rushed up to offer her a light.

Perhaps Lotte was affected by Gurdweill's strange mood, or perhaps she was following her own train of thought — in any case she said:

"There's something peculiar about the atmosphere here. As if everything in the world had suddenly narrowed down and been reduced to one simple, basic thing — something limited, animal, down-to-earth ... It reminds me of a remote tavern in a mountain village." Lotte rounded her lips and blew out a puff of smoke. Then she continued:

"You sit in a place like that in the daytime or the evening. There are only a few customers. Some of them are playing cards with a ragged, worn-out pack, and others are brooding over their beer and scratching themselves in secret. The mountain people are slow-witted and slow-moving, you know, as if they have to carry one of their own mountains around on their backs ... They haven't got much to say for themselves, and you sit there and look at them and suddenly you realize that the whole world with all its complications is slipping through your fingers ... Simply vanishing into thin air ... And all that's left is this little tavern with the handful of people in it and the giant mountains around. It's an extraordinary feeling, I'm telling you. And at that moment you're not in the least sorry for losing the world, despite the great fear that seizes hold of you with the realization of your utter aloneness ... On the contrary, the fear itself gives you extra courage, because from now on you've got nobody but yourself."

She fell silent and sucked on her cigarette, which had gone out while she was speaking. Gurdweill hurried to light a match for her. The piano in the next room had stopped playing.

"And nevertheless," said Lotte, "when you're back in town again, with all the crowds around you, you don't want to renounce the least little bit of it. And it all seems quite natural and self-evident again ..."

Lotte suddenly sensed that she was talking round and round the point, without touching on the matter that lay like a heavy stone on her heart. Nothing she had said so far expressed what was most important to her, for she had no words with which to express it. And so she felt dissatisfied and fell silent. She now had a powerful urge to reveal her soul to Gurdweill. She wanted him to see her as she really was, without any barriers, so that he would sense her soul in all its subtlest folds and nuances without her having to explain her feelings in words, which falsified and confused things rather than clarifying them. But at the same time she was suddenly sure that Gurdweill would never know her properly, because she counted for nothing with him, because he took no more interest in her than in any woman who passed him in the street. And a torrent of resentment surged up in her against the man sitting opposite her, curling a lock of his hair around his finger as if it were the most important thing in the world.

"Well, Gurdweill, you're not a great hero, are you? That's one thing nobody could suspect you of being!" And she laughed mockingly.

Gurdweill stared at her in bewilderment: "A hero? Why a hero?"

"Because. You probably think you're a hero."

"Me? I've never thought so. The idea has never even entered my head."

"It makes no difference!"

All at once the urge to tease him left her. She felt miserable, discontented. Everything suddenly seemed pointless, even sitting there with Gurdweill, who seemed a thousand miles away. His hollow face, too, seemed utterly strange to her, as if she had just set eyes on it for the first time in her life, and the distance between her and this face opposite her seemed too vast to traverse. Perhaps she should give up the whole affair and make a quick, clean break. But Lotte was afraid of making a break. Beyond it was a gaping void, containing nothing worth a moment's interest. Lotte was afraid of looking into this void. And so she wanted to try again, with all the means at her disposal. Gurdweill's marriage could not last long. Not from Thea's side either. She would not last long with anyone, never mind someone like Gurdweill. Besides the fact that she didn't love him, she didn't know him at all, she didn't know the first thing about him. (Lotte, by the way, derived a certain consolation from this conviction. She was confident that she herself was the only person in the world who really knew Gurdweill, and consequently, from this point of view at least, he belonged to her exclusively.) Sooner or later, things were bound to explode. Of that she had no doubt. But when and how? Whenever she thought of this inevitable end, a shiver would run down Lotte's spine. For it was clear to her that these two people would not part without some dreadful catastrophe. And since Gurdweill was the weaker, he would probably be the one to suffer. Perhaps, too, because he was the one who loved. But did he really love her? — Lotte interrupted herself — how could anyone love Thea? Especially Gurdweill? It was impossible. She fixed her eyes on him, as if to find the answer in his face, but in vain. He sat and smoked, his head resting on his hands, utterly opaque. When he felt her eyes on him, he said rather absent-mindedly:

"You think too much, Lotte. It won't do you any good. All this soul-searching — what does a pretty young girl like you need it for?"

Lotte was silent. After a moment she said that it was late and she had to hurry home. When she parted from him in front of her house, she said:

"I really wanted to talk to you about something else, Gurdweill, but today I didn't have the chance. Some other time, perhaps. When will we meet again?"

"I can't make any appointments, Lotte. You know how busy I am. But on Sunday afternoon I'll be at home. If you're free, why don't you drop in with Dr. Astel?"

"With Dr. Astel!" thought Lotte bitterly. "Was he really such a fool, this Gurdweill, or was he only pretending to be one?"

And she slipped inside without another word.

181

17

A blustering wind, spotted with flurries of rain, lashed icily at Gurdweill's face, drummed on the tin signs and closed shutters, and swayed the electric lights festooning the city like strings of orange pearls. Weather in which a man would have been well advised to hold on to his hat: a precaution which Gurdweill in his absent-mindedness failed to take. And all of a sudden he was chasing ridiculously after the article in question as it flew down Lerchenfelder Strasse, a foot above the ground, diving to the pavement only to take off again at his approach, as if on purpose to mock and torment him. Gurdweill pursued it steadily, bending down from time to time with his hand outstretched to snatch it from the air. Then it began bowling along on its rim like a wheel, and in the end it flew up, turned over once like a strange black bird, and dropped down dead on the pavement. Gurdweill pounced and put his foot on it. Exhausted and out of breath from the chase, he picked it up and shook it and scolded it aloud.

"Have you gone out of your mind?" he demanded crossly. "Don't ever do that again!"

Then he cleaned it as best he could and glanced at his watch. It was a quarter past eight. Suddenly the whole scene at Steinhof appeared before his eyes again, as if there were some hidden connection between it and the time on his watch. He was seized by fear, and felt a sharp pain in his left side. He thought of his room and it seemed horribly empty. What would he do at home now? It was still early. But he went on propelling himself through the driving wind nevertheless, swinging his hat in his hand, and suddenly he found himself close to the University. Ah, yes! he remembered — it was high time to pay a visit to Vrubiczek! He hadn't been there for ages. If he was in luck, he would find him at home. But, of course, he might be out. He might have gone with his wife to the cinema, or to some other place. Since the doubt had entered his mind, it was certain that Vrubiczek would be at home ... Gurdweill pushed this last thought down as far as it would go, somewhere in the region of his toes, and would not let it rise into his consciousness, since he did not want to tempt fate, which disliked adapting events to human wishes and expectations. At the same time, he kept repeating to himself in the part of his brain where thoughts were clear and definite: "It's certain he won't be home, it's certain he won't be home," in order to get the better of fate indirectly, as it were, by assuring it: "You see, I know in advance that I won't find him in, there's no room for surprise and disappointment here" ... because the fear of going home alone was growing stonger all the time, and he hoped that in Vrubiczek's presence he would recover his peace of mind.

Vrubiczek was at home.

"Julia, Julia, look who's here," he cried with undisguised delight, helping the visitor off with his coat. "It's an ill wind indeed that blows nobody any good!"

The old couple were in the middle of their supper. A spirit of sheltered tranquillity pervaded the small, simple dining-room, together with the aroma of roast meat and herb-flavoured soup. Gurdweill swallowed his saliva. The old woman drew up a chair to the table.

"Please don't trouble, I can sit anywhere. I don't want to disturb you in the middle of your meal."

"On the contrary," said the woman, who was in her fifties, on the short side and with a beaming, kindly face. "Now that you're here, you must eat with us."

"No, thank you, I've already eaten," Gurdweill for some reason lied. "I had something to eat a few minutes ago."

"Please join us nevertheless, Herr Gurdweill," Vrubiczek seconded his wife's invitation. "You can't refuse. The stomach is elastic, it stretches like leather soaked in water. In any case you won't get much. I've already eaten most of it myself."

Gurdweill was persuaded to eat with them. They were

183

already on the meat course, but Frau Vrubiczek brought him a bowl of soup from the kitchen.

Afterwards Vrubiczek took the napkin from his knees, wiped his heavy, grey-streaked moustache, and asked:

"How are you, my dear fellow? And how's your old lady?"

"Fine, fine! Thea's in a sanatorium." The last sentence escaped him against his will, and he regretted it immediately.

"What did you say? A sanatorium?" exclaimed Vrubiczek, full of concern. "How can you be so calm about it? What's the matter with her?"

"Nothing serious. A little operation with no risk involved. Already successfully performed, by the way."

Frau Vrubiczek, coming back into the room from the kitchen, was horrified to hear the word "operation." Nothing in the world alarmed her so much as the thought of an operation, however minor. There was no doubt in her mind that she would rather die than allow anyone to operate on her.

"What did you say? An operation?" she cried from the doorway, in evident alarm: "Who's had an operation? Where?"

"My wife," replied Gurdweill. "There's no danger."

"Where? Where?" the old woman pressed.

"On . . . on . . ." Gurdweill stammered, blushing, "on her nose, of course. Where else would they operate on a healthy woman like her? They took out her adenoids."

"But she had an operation on her adenoids last summer, didn't she?" asked Vrubiczek. "Does that mean that they grow again?"

"In the summer they operated on one side, and now they operated on the other. Presumably it was necessary — Dozent Schramek is an expert on adenoids . . . He said that if they didn't operate at once it would grow so big that it would block up her whole nose. Ha, ha, ha — those adenoids are devilish creatures, it seems!"

And for a moment they all saw a loathsome, purplish-black creature, about the size of a bean, swelling immensely inside the dark cavity of an imaginary, free-floating nose.

184

The old woman sighed deeply:

"Operations, operations — the worst thing in the world. I think that if I was told I had to have an operation I would die of fright before I reached the operating table. And then again: can you trust the doctor? He's only human, after all! They're always making mistakes and cutting out the wrong thing, perfectly healthy organs! I've heard of a number of such cases. And sometimes they even do it on purpose, out of spite. What do they care? It's all a game to them. Do they feel the pain?"

"Come now, Frau Vrubiczek, that's a little exaggerated. Anyone can make a mistake of course, but doctors don't harm their patients on purpose."

"My old lady," said Vrubiczek, "is terrified of operations. It's an old sickness with her — ever since her sister died after an unsuccessful operation. Twenty years have passed since then and she's still inconsolable. But you can't generalize from one case. Sometimes you get a shoe so worn-out that it's beyond repair — and then everyone blames the shoemaker, who tried to mend it and failed! The opposite can also happen, of course — when a shoe that could still be mended falls into the hands of a bad shoemaker. But you can't generalize from that."

"No, no," protested Frau Vrubiczek, who was standing by the table, her eyes wet with tears, "you always see the best in people because you see them from a distance, and from a distance a bit of glass can glitter like a diamond too. I begged them not to operate. Sturdy as an oak she was, Herr Gurdweill. You can ask Karl," she jerked her head in her husband's direction, "he knew her well. We'd already been married a good few years. Lovely as a summer's day she was — nineteen years old! And those murderers took her and cut up her stomach. I shouted at them: Leave her alone! There's no need for an operation! She'll get better of her own accord! Have you ever heard the like, a person has a stomach-ache and they immediately take out their knives! Everyone said: The doctors know! If the doctors say it's cancer, then it's cancer. And the only cure for cancer is surgery. That girl would still have been alive today, I can promise you, just like you and me, if not for those doctors! What do they care? One person less in the world! So what?"

She collapsed on to the chair next to her and began again:

"And do you think, Herr Gurdweill, that they let her off with one operation? Two! Two operations, one after the other, the poor girl! The first, they said, had succeeded, but they needed another one. A very complicated pheno- menon, they said, a rare phenomenon, and one operation wasn't enough. Have you ever heard the like? It's perfectly obvious to me that the first time they cut in the wrong place! I'd stake my life on it! So they cut her up again, and she died. What else? Who could go on living after having their stomach cut up twice over? Not even the strongest man in the world!"

"Enough, Julia," her husband coaxed her, "you can't bring her back. Instead of upsetting yourself like this, why don't you make us something to drink? Coffee, for example? The living take precedence over the dead, my dear, and we must take care of their needs first of all."

He began rolling himself a cigarette with his calloused fingers, while his wife shuffled into the kitchen, dragging her feet like a much older woman. In the doorway she paused, and turning to face them, pronounced:

"All I'm saying is that you should never trust doctors. If you get sick — wait for it to get better of its own accord. There are plenty of good old home-remedies, I'm not saying anything against them — that's something else! But doctors — I would never let anyone dear to me anywhere near them!"

And she left the room.

"Women," said Vrubiczek tolerantly. "The older they get, the weaker their brains become."

He offered Gurdweill a tin of tobacco and cigarette papers. "So the operation's safely over?"

"Yes, it's over."

"And when is she coming home?"

"In another week or ten days, I think."

"That's good," said the shoemaker. "I'm glad to hear it!"

Gurdweill didn't know what was so good about it, and at

that moment he didn't particularly care. The meal he had just eaten made him feel pleasantly tired and heavy. And the wind beating incessantly against a rattling window-pane made the warm, bright house and its kindly, simple occupants seem doubly sweet. When the wind subsided for a moment the quiet hiss of the gas light immediately made itself heard. And from the kitchen, too, came a mysterious murmuring sound.

The events of the day lost some of their sharpness. Everything seemed simpler, easier. Perhaps there was no cause for despair after all. How good it would be if Thea were sitting here beside him, kind and contented, both of them together sheltered from the chaos of life . . .

Frau Vrubiczek brought the coffee.

"And how's Johann?" Gurdweill inquired. "I haven't seen him for ages."

"No complaints!" replied Vrubiczek. "He's a good lad, he works hard and enjoys life with his young wife. What else can you ask for? He doesn't come and see us so often now, of course. A young woman wants her husband to spend his time with her — and quite right too. When we were a young couple ourselves, we were jealous of every minute too, weren't we, Julia?" Vrubiczek stroked his wife's cheek affectionately in memory of those good old days.

Here's a man who can be said to be happy! Gurdweill reflected with a certain satisfaction.

As he drank his coffee, his head bent over the table, the vision of a summer's morning many years ago, on the banks of a river, suddenly interrupted his thoughts. He must have been a very small child. He was not alone on the river bank, and his mother was not with him — of that he was quite certain. But someone was definitely there with him, because when he tried to reach the water's edge someone stopped him, someone said: "Little boys aren't allowed to go too close, little boys can only look from a distance!" No, it wasn't his mother — the voice was coarser, a nanny or a maid. In any case, the voice jarred on his ears — he remembered it clearly. And suddenly there were rafts sailing down the middle of the river, directly underneath the sun, and one of the sailors, his naked torso brown as leather, his legs bare to the knees, beckoned him from his raft, which was sailing so slowly that it seemed to be standing still. He even called out something which Gurdweill did not catch because of the distance. He was seized by a passionate desire to sail on the raft, and he began shouting and crying and jumping up and down, until the person with him dragged him forcibly away from the bank . . .

The whole scene perplexed Gurdweill profoundly. There was no river like the one he had just seen in the town of his birth, and no one ever sailed down it on a raft — so where did the memory come from? Perhaps he had read something like it in a book, or heard the story from someone else, and the memory had taken root in him as if it had actually happened to him?

"If that's the truth, it's no good at all!" he announced out loud and then, startled by the sound of his own voice, looked around him with baffled eyes.

"It's the truth, my friend," confirmed Vrubiczek, thinking that Gurdweill was referring to what he had just said, "but what's so bad about it?"

"What? How can you ask?" exclaimed Gurdweill uncomprehendingly. "When your memory becomes confused and brings up strange scenes as if they had happened to you yourself, completely out of the blue . . ."

At that moment Johann came in without knocking.

"Ah, Johann!"

"Alone?"

"And where's Mitzi?" His parents greeted him.

Johann took off his hat and flung it boyishly on to the sofa. Then he kissed his mother and shook hands with his father and Gurdweill.

"Mitzi?" he repeated with some embarrassment. "She's fine . . . She wanted to go to . . . to the pictures, and I didn't feel like it. And how are you, Herr Gurdweill? Everything all right?"

He gave Gurdweill a strange, nervous look, and Gurdweill saw at once that he was annoyed about something.

"Yes, not too bad. Things could be worse," he replied, looking closely at Johann.

The lad fell on to a chair as if he were exhausted. His mother, who was sitting next to him, stroked his head.

"I'm so glad to see you, darling. Are you hungry?"

Johann shook his head.

"But you'll have a cup of coffee? I'll go and get it right away. Just imagine: we were talking about you this very minute. The minute before you came in. What a shame that you didn't bring Mitzi. Herr Gurdweill could have met her, too. You haven't met her yet, have you, Herr Gurdweill?"

"Who?" asked Gurdweill absent-mindedly. He was busy scrutinizing Johann, whose angry expression, for some reason unknown even to himself, interested him keenly.

"My daughter-in-law! Mitzi."

"No, not yet."

"Mitzi went to the pictures," repeated Johann mechanically, looking down at the table. "She wanted to go to the pictures, but I didn't feel like it."

His mother's caresses appeared to be having a soothing influence on him. He bowed his head and seemed on the point of falling asleep.

"I'll bring your coffee in a minute," she said and left the room.

Vrubiczek stood leaning against the cupboard and smoking silently. He seemed deep in thought. From time to time he let out a long curl of smoke, which was almost the same colour as his moustache and seemed like some kind of extension of it. Now he said firmly, like a judge pronouncing sentence:

"See here, Johann, a woman can't go out by herself! If her husband neglects her, she'll look for another man in the end . . . And that's all I have to say on the matter."

Johann stared coldly at his father for a moment as if wondering what business it was of his. Then he apparently came to his senses and said:

"Of course. But she wanted to go to the pictures . . . and I couldn't go with her . . . Let me have a cigarette too, father!"

189

His mother came in with the coffee. "Take off your coat, Johann. Otherwise you'll catch cold when you go out."

"Yes, yes!" said Johann with a sudden spurt of activity. "But I have to go right away. I only came for a minute. I have to get up early for work. It must already be late. What's the time, Herr Gurdweill? Ten o'clock?"

"Ten o'clock exactly!"

"Then I must be off! I have to meet Mitzi outside the cinema, too. I'll just drink my coffee and then I'll go. You put in too much sugar again, Mother! You know I can't stand such sweet coffee! One lump is always enough for me. And you, Herr Gurdweill, will you stay or leave with me? Oh yes, I forgot to tell you: my boss raised my salary. From now on I'll be getting seventy schillings a week: what do you say to that? Beginning this week."

He drank his coffee in big gulps and jumped up.

"Well, Herr Gurdweill — you want to stay a little longer, don't you?"

"Why drag Herr Gurdweill away, Johann?" said his mother. "You may have to leave now, but Herr Gurdweill can stay with us a little longer. We haven't seen him for ages."

But Gurdweill stood up to leave. He had seen in Johann's eyes that he wanted him to leave with him.

There was no light on the stairs. Vrubiczek led them to the head of the staircase with a candle and waited for them to descend the two floors. Then they groped their way down the third flight in the dark and went outside. The wind hit them in the face like a cold, wet cloth. Johann seized Gurdweill by the arm.

"I want to talk to you, Herr Gurdweill! I have to talk to you! I can't talk to my father. It's about Mitzi, my wife."

His voice trembled slightly.

"Yes, of course," said Gurdweill.

"We can go and sit somewhere," suggested Johann, "only if you're free, naturally, and if you really want to. I was very glad to find you there. I can't talk to my father. We can go and sit in some café, or tavern, whichever you prefer, and talk with nobody to bother us."

190

"Of course I want to," said Gurdweill.

Gurdweill felt in advance something of the distaste and embarrassment usually felt by the sensitive and fastidious when obliged to listen to the secret troubles of others, especially those concerning the relations between man and wife, which were not meant for a third person's ears. And despite his curiosity, he was for some reason afraid of hearing this confession.

"What will you drink?" asked Johann, as they sat down at a round table in a dimly lit and almost deserted little tavern on the corner of Wassergasse.

Gurdweill asked for a beer and Johann ordered half a litre of wine for himself.

For a while Johann was silent. He sat opposite Gurdweill, staring at some point in the distance behind him. It was apparently hard for him to begin. Gurdweill, too, evaded his companion's eyes, not wishing to embarrass him. In these cases — it occurred briefly to Gurdweill — it's better not to look into a person's eyes. Later on, if he regrets his frankness, he can always delude himself that the other person didn't hear everything, that he didn't hear the most important part.

The waiter brought their order and Johann took a big gulp of wine, as if to give himself courage.

"I don't know," he began in a whisper, "if they're all the same, or if it's only her . . . but I can't take it . . . I won't stand for it . . . Something terrible's going to happen . . . I'm not responsible for my actions any more."

He breathed heavily.

"At first I couldn't believe it. I didn't want to believe it. But I saw it with my own eyes. With my own eyes. Is it possible that they would walk down the street arm in arm, and go into the cinema like that, if there was nothing between them? She told me she was going to the pictures with her sister. Her sister lives not far from us. It was a few days ago. Maybe a week. I made a scene, but she only laughed and called me a jealous fool. She used to know him before we got married, she said, when they lived in the same neighbourhood. An old acquaintance and nothing more. He met her in the street and invited

191

her to go to the pictures with him. Wasn't she allowed to go to the pictures with an old acquaintance? And besides, she said, he was a married man with a child, and what was there to be afraid of? Maybe she wasn't lying. But what if she was? And last night, after supper, she went out again. To her sister's, she said. I let her go, but I followed her. She went into number 55, where her sister lives. I waited outside for a quarter of an hour, or half an hour, I don't know how long. Mitzi didn't come out. Then I went up to the second floor and knocked on the door. Nobody answered. I knocked again and again and nobody answered. Evidently there was nobody at home. So where had Mitzi disappeared to? I hadn't seen her leave the house. I went downstairs and waited outside for another half an hour, an hour, and she never came out. Then I hurried home. Mitzi had just come in. She hadn't even had time to take off her coat. Her face was all flushed, as if she'd been running. I asked her how her sister was. On purpose I asked her. She said that her sister was fine. They had gone out for a walk. Soon after she arrived. On such a lovely evening, she said, who wants to stay inside? And then her sister had walked her home. She kept laughing and she seemed all excited. But I hadn't seen them coming out. And I was standing there all the time. In a place with a good view, right opposite the front door. They couldn't possibly have come out without my seeing them. But I didn't see anything. I saw her when she went in, of that I'm positive. It was her, Mitzi. I saw her clearly. Besides, I was walking behind her and I couldn't have been mistaken. But how and when had she left the building? I don't recall seeing two women coming out of number 55 in all the time that I was standing there. It's a small street and you can see everything. And another thing: if her sister really had seen her home, as she claimed, I would have had to meet her close to the house, because I arrived right after them, by the route she would have had to take home. The shortest way from her house to ours. And besides, I kept on looking around me because I was watching out for Mitzi."

With growing agitation Gurdweill took in his companion's whispered words — words which opened old wounds he thought had begun to heal. Lately he had deluded himself into believing that these things no longer touched him, that he was armoured against them, and now he saw that it was not so. Suddenly he realized that they were still there inside him, unchanged, liable to emerge from their hiding-places at any moment and pounce upon him. Gurdweill felt Johann's torments as if they were his own. Although he had never set eyes on Mitzi in his life, he saw her vividly in his mind's eye, putting on her coat, a grey coat, and saying: "I'm just running round to my sister's for a minute." His soul burned in an agony of jealousy as he asked himself: where had Mitzi been and what had she been doing during all that time? He picked up his beer and drank it. And as if to banish the tormenting doubt from his heart, he said to Johann, who was sitting with his head bowed, drumming his fingers on the table:

"You haven't got any real grounds for suspicion. Perhaps it was all exactly as she said. The fact that you didn't see her coming out doesn't prove anything. She probably came out just when you were looking in the other direction. And precisely because she came out with her sister, you didn't notice her; you didn't see her because you didn't expect to see her with a woman."

Johann stared at him imploringly: "But the uncertainty, the uncertainty! I can't stand it! I can feel it here," he tapped on his chest, "here, like a heavy stone. And if I ever find out that she was lying to me — I'm not saying anything! But there'll be trouble. Something terrible will happen!"

He took a gulp of wine and continued:

"Last night I never slept a wink. Was she with her sister or not? And if not, where was she? It nagged at me until I thought I would go mad. But I'll find out. And then — they'd better look out!"

Three deep, ominous lines appeared between his eyebrows, and the tip of his pointed nose grew sharp and flinty, like some stone-age pick. Who could have imagined that the quiet, kindly Johann, the "good lad" — in his father's words — would be capable of such savage rage? Gurdweill felt a little frightened of him.

193

"Here, have a cigarette," he offered in a conciliatory tone.

Gurdweill now wanted to tell him that his fears were probably exaggerated, that in the end his suspicions would turn out to be groundless, etc. But instead he found himself asking:

"And the man, the one she went to the cinema with — you don't know who he is?"

"The one who went to the pictures with Mitzi? No, I don't. Although I seem to recall her saying that he wrote for some American paper or other. His name is Pe . . . Per . . . — some peculiar name."

"Perczik, perhaps?"

"Yes, that's it. I think that's the name — Perczik."

Gurdweill suddenly knew with absolute certainty that it was Perczik, and he was filled with a terrible rage. He went on interrogating Johann compulsively:

"Was he short? Dark and rather plump? Did he have a grey hat on?"

"Yes. Not tall, and darkish. I didn't notice his hat. I only caught a glimpse of him. What — is he an acquaintance of yours?"

"If it's Perczik, I know him well. But I don't really think it's him . . ."

"Yes, yes, it must be him!" Johann latched on to this possibility as if it held some sort of solution to his problems: "I'm sure it's him! I remember now, I'm almost positive she said Perczik. Has he got a wife and child?"

"He has."

"In that case it's definitely him."

Johann smiled with all the happy relief of a dangerously-ill person after the crisis has passed and he feels that from now on he will recover and live. He even became rather gay and high-spirited. It seemed that now that he was sure it was Perczik, he felt safe from danger. But Gurdweill knew that Perczik of all people was unlikely to take Johann Vrubiczek's wife to the cinema for nothing. And he pitied Johann with all his heart. Because he knew, too, that this was not the end of the matter, but only a brief interlude after which all his doubts would come back to haunt him.

"I'll have to talk to that swine as soon as possible!" he silently resolved. "If he's not in the café tomorrow, I'll write him a note and make an appointment to see him."

"Won't you have something else to drink?" asked Johann. "Another beer, or a glass of wine?"

Gurdweill refused.

"Do have a glass of wine, Herr Gurdweill," urged Johann. "The wine's good. Really good. I must come here one day with . . ." he hesitated for a moment, ". . . with Mitzi. She likes a glass of good wine. Yes, I'll definitely bring her here one day."

"And how are you, Herr Gurdweill?" he suddenly asked, as if he had only now noticed his presence. "Everything all right? And your wife? All going well, I hope?"

Gurdweill nodded.

"I'm glad to hear it! Very glad indeed!" He gave Gurdweill an affectionate pat on his hand, which was lying palm down on the table. "You're a good sort, Herr Gurdweill, I mean it. A really good sort. Please have another drink with me. We meet so seldom." In the end Gurdweill gave in to his pleas and ordered another beer. Johann ordered another glass of wine for himself.

Suddenly Johann asked, without looking at Gurdweill:

"What's he like? What kind of a person is he?"

"Who?"

"That friend of yours, Herr Perczik?"

"He's a writer and a journalist," replied Gurdweill evasively. "I've known him for several years. We run into each other occasionally in a café we both go to. To your health, Johann!" he raised the tankard of foaming beer which the waiter placed before him. "To your health and domestic happiness!"

"Your health, sir!" grunted Johann and fell silent, lowering his head and staring gloomily at the table. Gurdweill glanced at his watch.

"And now, my dear Johann, it's time to go home. It's getting late."

"What's the time?"

"Half past eleven."

"Yes, it's time to go," said Johann and called the waiter.

195

"In any event," he said as he stood up, "I'm grateful to you, Herr Gurdweill, for sparing the time. And if you see Herr Perczik, tell him from me that he'd better cut it out from now on, or he might get more than he bargained for. Let him take his own wife to the pictures and leave Mitzi alone."

"Yes," said Gurdweill, "I'll tell him. And you too, Johann, would be well advised to put the whole thing behind you. Your suspicions are groundless, I'm sure of it." And they parted and went their respective ways.

Part III: Inside and Out

18

THE newspaper burned quickly, with a merry flame, and the twigs did not have time to cach fire. A thick, dirty column of smoke escaped from the stove, which was made of glazed white tiles, into the semi-darkness of the room. The kneeling Gurdweill tried laboriously to fan the flames, but without success.

"Oh, how useless you are!" scolded Thea, pacing the room in her hat and coat, as if she were in the street. "You need lots of paper!"

"I put the coal in a bit too soon and it choked the fire," apologized Gurdweill who stood up to look for more paper.

Through the window a dense fall of thick snowflakes could be seen, flying about like feathers. The sight of the snow made the unheated room feel even colder.

Gurdweill looked for paper in the bedside table, at the bottom of the wardrobe, and came up with only one little piece. As if by magic, all the paper had disappeared from the room.

"Haven't you seen any paper, Thea? There should be a lot of old newspapers somewhere."

"I haven't seen anything!" replied Thea impatiently, still pacing to and fro. "Hurry up, can't you? It's freezing! And why don't you light the lamp?"

"In a minute. I want to light the fire in the stove first, to give it a chance to take. But where am I going to get paper?"

Gurdweill pottered about helplessly. "Take your manuscripts," sneered his wife, "here's something they're good for at last."

Gurdweill did not reply. He climbed on to a chair and stretched out his hand to search on top of the wardrobe.

199

"Will you get a move on, Rudolfus!" Thea goaded him. "Light the lamp first, donkey, so that you can see what you're doing!"

He climbed down and lit the lamp. Then he went to ask the landlady for old newspapers, and came back and knelt in front of the stove again. He had to clean out all the coal and twigs and begin again from the beginning. Thea walked around the room like a stranger. From time to time, however, she glanced in her husband's direction and issued various directions to his back.

When he finally succeeded in lighting the fire, Thea said in a tone of command:

"And now Rudolfus, hurry up and go downstairs! What else do we need? We've still got coffee and sugar. Buy chestnuts, half a kilo of chestnuts, don't forget! And rice, do you hear? And a little cinnamon too. And take the milk bottle with you. And buy some sprats — but good ones! Not like last time! Well, I think that's all. Oh yes, cigarettes, I almost forgot. Get Khedives, fifty, don't forget! And hurry up about it!"

Gurdweill huddled into his old coat and left. When he returned after about half an hour, laden with packages and covered with wet snow, he found his wife still in her hat and coat, just as he had left her.

"What on earth have you done to the stove?" she greeted him, even before he had had time to unload his parcels and shake the snow off his coat. "It's not giving off any heat at all! Don't just stand there — go and see what's wrong!"

Gurdweill went over to the stove just as he was, bent down and opened the door. A blast of heat hit him in the face, which instantly turned red. The snow on his hat began melting and dripping off the brim.

"What do you want?" he ventured to ask. "It's burning perfectly. It couldn't be burning any better."

"What do I care if it's burning! I want it to be hot — make it hot!"

"It takes a while. You know what the stove's like yourself. Once it gets going it will be nice and warm."

He threw another shovelful of coal from the sack into the stove, shut the door and straightened up. A few little

200

puddles of melted snow from his clothes and shoes remained on the floor.

"Where are the cigarettes?"

He took the two dark-blue boxes out of his pocket and handed them to Thea, who opened one of them and stuck a cigarette into her mouth.

"Did you bring pork chops?"

"No, you didn't tell me to."

"Idiot! Did I have to tell you? Christmas comes once a year and he doesn't know for himself that he should buy something decent! Go down right away and get some pork chops! And a little bottle of brandy too. And hurry up about it!"

Unwillingly Gurdweill went out again. We could really have done without the pork chops, he thought. His shoes were worn away at the heels, and although they did not yet let in the water, he had a constant feeling of dampness in his feet, perhaps because of the cold, and it seemed to him that he was trudging barefoot in the wet, dirty snow. If there was one thing he hated, it was leaky shoes. Damp feet, he was in the habit of saying, are the source of all illness. First of all — see to your shoes! Torn trousers don't let in the water, but shoes are another story! But he had not yet had time to go to Vrubiczek to get his heels mended. It was only yesterday that he had discovered they needed repairing.

When he got back to the room he sat down immediately to take off his shoes. No, his feet were not in the least damp. He pulled a chair up to the stove and sat down with the soles of his feet against the smooth warm tiles.

"You're already warming your feet like an old man," sneered Thea, who was only now about to take off her hat. "Perhaps you'd like me to get you a hot water bottle too?"

"It wouldn't do any harm," he joked. "They're cold as ice."

Little by little a pleasant warmth filled the room. Because of the green shade, the dim light diffused by the oil lamp was directed downwards, leaving the upper half of the room in semi-darkness except for a glowing orange circle on the ceiling directly above the lamp.

Thea took off her coat, threw it anyhow on to the couch, came to stand next to the stove, and lit herself another cigarette.

"Do you want one, rabbit?" she offered the box to her husband.

Gurdweill put the cigarette into his mouth. Another eight months, he thought joyfully, or perhaps only seven. You could never tell exactly. And then he would be here, his own flesh and blood, a new little human being . . . He looked at Thea's belly as if it were already possible to see something there.

From the moment he knew that a little embryo was hidden inside it, his wife's belly became sacred to him, more precious than anything in the world. It seemed to him to have a life of its own, apart from the rest of her body, which needed special care and attention. If only it were possible he would have carried it around with him everywhere, this sacred belly, to see that no harm befell it. Whenever he thought of his wife now, whether she was there or not, he would concentrate exclusively on the part of her body which housed the child, the marvellous creation of his and hers and Mother Nature's, who did not yet exist and which existed nevertheless. And at the same time he would reflect with awe on the holiness of women, who had been chosen to bear and give birth to mankind. And not human women only, but the entire female sex of every living creature on the face of the earth — they too were holy.

Without thinking he put out his hand and stroked his wife on her belly.

"What do you think, my dear, a boy or a girl?"

Thea gave him a mocking look and said teasingly:

"Nothing! I can get rid of it too, if I want to. Who's to stop me?"

"You wouldn't do such a thing, I know you wouldn't."

"How do you know I wouldn't? What makes you so sure? If I want to I will — and if you think it's such a pleasure, then carry it around yourself for another eight months!"

"No, no!" exclaimed Gurdweill, deathly pale. "That's

impossible! You're just teasing me. You can't be serious. And if you do it, then . . ."

Gurdweill did not finish the sentence. Nor did he know himself what would happen "then." He stood up and added: "Please stop talking nonsense, dearest. Why say such things when you don't really mean them?"

Thea smiled nastily. She appeared to reconsider, chucked her husband under the chin as if he were a baby, and said:

"Don't get so excited, little one. Perhaps I'll leave it after all . . . we'll see . . ."

And after a moment: "My parents invited me round this evening. You too, rabbit. I didn't feel like going, so I said no. But perhaps Poldy will come here at about half past nine. Are you glad I refused the invitation?"

"Yes, we can go there another time. Tomorrow. This evening I'd rather stay at home alone with you."

Thea suddenly felt bored. The evening stretched before her long and empty. There was nowhere to go. The cinemas and cafés were all closed, and there was no chance of meeting anyone. Everyone was either at home with his family or dining out with relatives or friends.

Thea seated herself on the chair which her husband had just vacated, and pulled him down on her knees.

"Come here, rabbit! Tell me — who do you want him to resemble, you or me?" she inquired with suppressed mockery.

"It doesn't matter," said Gurdweill and kissed her on her hair. "There's no real difference. If he's like you, he might be stronger, and that, of course, is all to the good. And if not, that's all right too. After all I'm not a sickly person, and I'm not a weakling either even if I'm not tall."

"No," laughed Thea, "you're not tall. And you can hardly be blamed for that. Go and fetch me the book on the table. And put the oil lamp here, on the bedside table."

Gurdweill went in his stockinged feet to do her bidding. Then he took his shoes, which he had left standing next to the stove, and began to put them on.

Thea said without turning her head:

203

"Run along, rabbit, and put the coffee on! I feel like a cup of coffee."

"Perhaps it would be better to put it off until later? In an hour or so? You shouldn't drink a lot of black coffee now. It's not good for him . . ."

"Wha-at?!" Thea turned her head. "It's got nothing to do with you! It's my own business! What do you understand about it? Go and do as you're told!"

Gurdweill accordingly went to the kitchen and put the sooty coffee pot on the gas burner.

"Terrible weather, pssss!" said Frau Fischer, who was also busy cooking something. "True Christmas weather. You're a young man, Herr Gurdweill, and you don't care; but what about me? Aie, aie, aie! In old age a person feels the snow as if it was falling right inside his body! Warm rooms and warm clothes don't help. Yes, yes, Herr Gurdweill! I didn't make it up, don't think it was me. It was my dear departed husband who said it. A wise man, my second husband, psss! And now I feel it in my body, right here," — she pointed to her back, encased in a thick woollen jacket and wrapped in a big red shawl — "and here" — she pointed to her thigh — "and that's apart from my stomach, of course."

The old woman's shrivelled head with the wispy grey hair sticking lifelessly to the skull looked tiny in comparison to the swollen cumbersome body. She reminded him of a plump, round chicken with its head buried under its wing.

"The only thing that keeps me going," she continued in a whisper, "is a good cup of freshly ground coffee. There's nothing to beat it! But for my coffee I'd have been dead long ago. An old woman alone. Pssss!"

Gurdweill's own coffee had begun to boil in the meantime and he grabbed hold of the coffee pot and quickly transferred it to the room, where he placed it on the table. Thea was still sitting next to the stove, reading and smoking.

"Pour the coffee out! No, first open the brandy!"

Gurdweill silently obeyed. He knew that she should not be drinking coffee, let alone brandy, in her present condition, but there was nothing he could do about it. After serving her he lay down on the couch and lit his pipe.

"Aren't you having anything to drink, rabbit?"

"I don't feel like it at the moment. I'll have something later."

Everything will still turn out for the best, Gurdweill reflected. Now with the baby coming. She's not really bad . . . only a little capricious, just like all her sex. She'll love him too when he comes.

Gurdweill liked lying there on his back and puffing on his pipe. Especially in the middle of the night, when Thea was sleeping on the bed next to him, all his and his alone. And if, for a change, they had not quarrelled beforehand, his happiness was complete. He tried to put everything else out of his mind from an unconscious desire for self-preservation. After all, it may all have been a pack of lies and slander . . . there were no eye-witnesses were there? As for his own doubts and suspicions — they could certainly not serve as the basis for anything . . . And in the final analysis — he would sometimes say to himself: it's a question of temperament and she's not responsible, a person's temperament can't be changed or restrained. And anyway, was she his private property? Did anyone have the right to subjugate another human being in any way whatsoever? Everyone was free to do as they wished, and nobody had the right to dominate anybody else. And what did he have to complain about? What? Especially when there was nothing definite to accuse her of . . . All women lusted after men. It was part of their very nature, a basic characteristic that couldn't be changed. And if they didn't act on their impulses — it was only because they were ugly or hypocritical or simply because they didn't dare. And why should Thea be an exception to the rule? At least it was better to be open and above board about it.

This train of thought always calmed Gurdweill down. Especially when Thea happened to be at home at the time, a kind of living refutation of all the suspicions and slanders.

All these speculations are futile, a waste of time, he reflected complacently. The whole thing is utterly unimportant. Especially now, now . . .

With tremendous pleasure he sucked on his pipe. The warm smoke of the cheap tobacco which burnt his tongue and tickled his tonsils seemed perfectly delicious to him. As if avid for even greater pleasure, he placed the stem of his pipe next to his nostrils and breathed in the bitter, pungent smell of the nicotine as if it were some reviving scent.

To be perfectly honest, he went on musing, he really had nothing to complain about. On the contrary: he had plenty of reasons to be very well satisfied. What more could he ask for? Even his work had been going well recently. Yes, you could say it was bearing fruit. True, he was still very far from perfection. Of that he was well aware. But nevertheless! He hoped that he was now on the right path. The main thing, in the last analysis, was to express himself and his world honestly, in the simplest, most immediate and most direct way possible. He felt quite clearly that he was making great strides towards this goal — and what else could he want? And now it was a holiday too! The afternoon free, and the whole of tomorrow and the day after tomorrow too!

"You'd better begin making dinner, rabbit!" said Thea.

Gurdweill glanced at his watch:

"But it's still early — only seven o'clock. Perhaps we could wait an hour? Of course," he immediately retracted, "if you're hungry, we can eat now."

Thea buried her head in her book again without answering. Gurdweill stood up, went over to the window, drew the curtain aside, and looked out. The snow was coming down in thick flakes, giving rise to a feeling of downy silence. There was no one to be seen in the little alley below. The snow fell by itself, with nothing to disturb it, falling softly and secretly. A desire which had been with him since childhood to wallow in the soft, deep snow reawoke in Gurdweill. And together with it he saw a picture of himself sinking his little body in a pile of eiderdowns heaped up on some bed. But this picture did

206

not stem from any actual memory and after hovering for a moment in his imagination it immediately gave way to another scene. Gurdweill saw a broad plain covered with deep snow, and a sack full of grain or flour or salt falling on to the snow with a soft, dull thud. And not one but many sacks, innumerable sacks, falling on to the snow from above. This scene gave him inexplicable pleasure and brought a smile to his lips. At that moment two men emerged from the hotel opposite and turned in the direction of the railway station. They were walking fast, and Gurdweill imagined that they were probably hurrying to catch a train and that after a journey of half an hour or an hour they would get off at some silent, snow-covered village and go into their houses where their wives and children were waiting for them, and the Christmas tree was standing in all its glory, and a tantalizing smell of cooking was coming from the kitchen, and a cat was stretching lazily. A pleasant warmth seeped through Gurdweill's body. He approached his wife and stood beside her, resting his right hand on the back of her chair. Thea gave him an inquiring look.

"You know," he said, "I think a cat would be nice . . . If not a dog then at least a cat . . . With a cat the room's not so empty . . ."

Thea burst out laughing loudly: "It seems to me that you're turning into an old maid!"

"No," he stammered uncertainly, "I just thought . . . especially later on . . . babies like pets . . ."

"What babies?!"

"You know . . . later on . . . the baby . . ."

"There's no baby!" Thea interrupted him firmly. "Nothing's certain yet!" From the day she met Gurdweill she had felt an urge to hurt him, to make him miserable in any way she could. And this urge had not faded over the course of time, but had grown stronger and stronger the longer they lived together. His constant submission and resignation only provoked her further. She despised him for suffering in silence and invented all kinds of cruelties to torment him. Why didn't he shout, lose his temper, curse her, throw her out? Then perhaps she would have found it in her heart to love him a little, in so far as her nature was capable of love at all. For to a certain extent she was attached to him even now. He was necessary to her and she could not have imagined her life without him. But Gurdweill accepted everything without protest, and this provoked her unendurably. She could not believe, not for a moment, that he was a coward. She knew very well that he was no such thing. Then why was he so long-suffering with regard to her? Perhaps she was even a little offended by his behaviour. She knew that every thrust of hers, however superficial, made him wince, that his silence did not stem from insensitivity. With her woman's instinct she soon discovered his vulnerable spots and aimed directly for them — but Gurdweill bowed his head and held his tongue.

"You're not so bad," he said looking straight into her eyes, "I know that you're not so bad ... And you'll love the baby as much as I do, even more than I do, I know it ..."

"You don't know anything! As for the baby — we'll see! If I want to! And it's got nothing to do with you! I've already told you — it's none of your business!"

But Gurdweill was sure that she would have the baby. If nothing untoward happened, she would have the baby. And all her threats could not spoil his good mood.

"What do you think," he changed the subject, "is there time for me to shave first, or should I put it off until tomorrow? If you're hungry and you want to eat now, then of course ..."

He passed his fingers over the stubble of his beard, which had not been shaved for two days now and made a faint brushing sound as he stroked it against the direction of the growth.

Thea wanted to go on reading and gave him permission to shave.

"In that case I need some light. I can't see."

"And what do you want me to do about it?"

"I only meant," he said carefully, "that if you sat here, on the couch, and we put the lamp on the table, we could both see."

"No! Move the table and you'll be able to see. The lamp stays here!"

Gurdweill accordingly set the table lengthwise between the couch and the bed and sat on the opposite end, next to the door. The little mirror he set up in front of him was too far from the light for him to see his face properly in it, and in the end he gave up looking at it and shaved himself by touch. As always the scraping of the razor gave him a curious, inexplicable pleasure, and he went on longer than necessary.

"Why are you taking so long about it, rabbit?" said his wife in a tone of mild rebuke, without raising her head.

"In a minute," said Gurdweill. "I'll be finished soon."

He returned the table to its place, washed his face, and began preparations for dinner. He opened the tin of sprats and emptied it into a dish. Then he cooked the rice, with Thea's help, and they sat down to eat. Thea ate without appetite, until she remembered the brandy.

"Where's the brandy? Why are you hiding it, you fool?"

Gurdweill got up unwillingly and fetched the brandy.

"I wasn't hiding it," he mumbled, "I simply forgot."

He poured himself a glass as well.

Suddenly Thea remarked: "It's been some time since we saw Perczik. He hasn't been coming to the café. Do you know how he is?"

"How should I know? Why do you need Perczik?"

"I just wondered. I heard some long story or other. Ulrich said that you knew all about it."

"It's not particularly interesting. Vrubiczek's son beat him up and now he's sick in bed. I warned him, the cad. I told him to look out but he took no notice. And now, he's got what he deserved."

"A pretty business!" laughed Thea. "He must have given it to him good and proper! And his wife?"

"Whose wife?"

"Young Vrubiczek's."

"They made it up."

"And you have to interfere in everybody's business, rabbit!"

"What do you mean interfere? All I did was warn him

for his own good. Johann asked me to talk to him. He can be grateful that he got off so lightly. He was lucky. It could have been a lot worse."

"Do you think he'll take him to court?"

"No. I don't think he'd be such a fool. He won't want a public scandal. Besides, he's probably afraid of his wife. He must have told her some cock-and-bull story."

"And how did it all come out?"

"Johann told me and I told Ulrich. Why should Perczik get away with being such a bastard?"

"When did it happen?"

"About two weeks ago."

"In the evening?"

"Yes. Johann followed his wife to her date with Perczik. When they turned into a dark alley, he attacked him. His wife ran away."

Thea was obviously delighted by the story. She questioned him closely about all the details, laughed a lot, and wanted to know everything exactly. But Gurdweill was sick of the whole affair, and in the end he said that he didn't know anything else about it.

After the meal, which lasted longer than usual, was over, Gurdweill went to warm up the coffee and they drank it laced with brandy. Thea was in high spirits; she had already resigned herself to the boring, empty evening. With a cigarette in her mouth she capered about the room, pinching and scratching her husband as she passed him.

"If you like," said Gurdweill suddenly, "I'll read to you from the New Testament."

"Wonderful! A wonderful idea!"

He cleared the table, took out the New Testament, a little book in a typical black cover, and began to read in a low, pleasant voice from St. Matthew's Gospel about the birth of Jesus Christ. He read for about half an hour, while his wife sat opposite him, her head resting on her hands, smoking without a pause. When he finished he went on sitting for a while without moving. A strange, eerie silence descended. The upper half of the room was shrouded in semi-darkness, as before. A feeling something like shame welled up in Gurdweill, and he could not understand what it meant. Suddenly what he had read seemed utterly naïve to him, insipid and lacking in any poetic spirit. All that was left was the unpleasant aftertaste of over-masticated chewing-gum . . .

"All this," he began in a whisper, as if talking to himself, "once had an attraction for me that was both fascinating and terrifying. Everything, I mean, that took place on the other side of the boundary between Jews and Christians. I was still a child, of course. The women passing me on their way to church on Sundays and holidays for some reason attracted me. And the church itself, which was situated not far from our house, gave me no peace. People seemed to be divided into two separate species, utterly different from each other, as different as cats and dogs. In a little village, unlike a city, religion still plays an important role in life. The boundaries are well-defined: Jews are Jews and Christians are Christians. You can't possibly confuse the two. Especially in the little settlements of Galicia and Poland. My parents weren't Orthodox but nevertheless they had nothing to do with Christians. In short: the Christians fascinated me in their strangeness. When I grew a little older, I would hang around the church on their holidays, moved and excited, waiting for something. The singing of the choir, threatening and obscure, would come pouring out into the fresh summer air like a slow stream of thick black tar. By then I already knew about the Inquisition, the Crusades, the persecution of the Jews, and I was constantly afraid that they would suddenly seize me and drag me inside and force me to do something terrible. And yet I kept on hanging around outside the church. You might say that in the depths of my soul I was even eager for the thing to happen. If they abducted me, I thought, and forced me to do something (I didn't know exactly what!) it wouldn't help them. I would suffer all the tortures of hell and I wouldn't do their bidding. Once I dared to approach the door and look inside, I saw nothing but dense darkness, dotted with weak candle flames. I could see people kneeling, too. From that day on, whenever I thought about Christians I would see something dark with flickering candles . ."

211

"And didn't you ever go inside?" asked Thea. "If you had gone inside, all the magic would have disappeared . . ."

"Not there," said Gurdweill. "Later on, of course, I went into all kinds of churches in different towns, but not there. If I ever go back to my native town, I'll go in. Not because it interests me now, but just for the sake of it."

"Why don't you ever tell me about the first time you knew a woman?" said Thea suddenly. "I'd be interested to hear about it."

"There's not much to tell!" replied Gurdweill, lighting a cigarette. "A banal affair with a maidservant."

"I'd still like to hear it, rabbit."

"I was fifteen at the time," said Gurdweill quietly, "but everyone thought I was twelve, because I was so small and thin. I was very naïve too, which also makes you look younger. I had no friends, either in school or out of it. The boys didn't like me, or at any rate, that's how it seemed to me, and since I was shy by nature and at the same time proud, I made no effort to make friends with them. I took no part in their games and pranks, I kept apart, as though I was in an invisible cage. During breaks I would sometimes see them whispering to each other with strange expressions on their faces, as if they were conspiring to commit some terrible crime. Sometimes I would accidentally overhear some enigmatic phrase, which I sensed contained a secret that somehow, although I did not understand it, affected me too. I would rack my brains for hours over such phrases, turning them over and over until I was exhausted. Needless to say, it never occurred to me to ask one of them what it meant. I felt obscurely that I would make a fool of myself by questioning them.

"During this period I was extremely nervous and irritable. I never had a moment's peace. I was always looking for something hidden; everything seemed to me to be shrouded in mystery; I was alert to everything happening around me and at the same time I felt ill. I was waiting for something to be revealed, in a state of constant suspense and anxiety in case I missed the moment of the revelation. I remember that I lost my appetite and looked so haggard that my mother began to worry about me. I sank into a peculiar kind of apathy regarding everyday affairs. I began to neglect my studies and could not even summon up the energy to read. And then suddenly I would bury myself in some book and devour it passionately, not stopping until my head started to spin. At night I couldn't fall asleep. From time to time I would be flooded by a wave of such terrible heat that I had to fling off my bedclothes. Then I would fall into a nervous, restless sleep, and have strange, terrifying dreams, and wake up the next morning worn out and depressed without the least desire for anything. Often I would wander aimlessly about in byways and alleys where I had never been before, straying and searching for something undefinable, until it grew dark and I had to go home. At that time I was once attacked by a gang of Christian boys. I fought desperately, as if I was fighting for my life. But I was alone and I was defeated. When I came home battered and beaten, I felt a curious satisfaction, a kind of content and peace of mind. Once I was hit by a stone — here, you see?" — Gurdweill pointed to his left temple, next to the ear — "There's still a little scar. You can feel it with your fingers. In the course of time, when they saw that I wasn't afraid of them and knew how to use my fists, they left me alone. And I remember, too, that I once took a thick darning needle I found at home, and rolled up my sleeve and stuck it into the flesh above my wrist, slowly, half a centimetre deep, in two or three places, and as I did so I felt a strange pleasure, and a kind of revenge. Then I washed away the blood and stuck some of my father's cigarette papers on the wounds. I only did this three times, by the way. The sight of the blood made me nauseous, I felt giddy and faint, and I stopped. I threw the needle away and adopted a new, bloodless, means of torture. I would light a match and burn the tip of my little finger, I don't know why precisely that one, burn it until I couldn't stand the pain. Then I would dip my charred finger in ink: a popular remedy for burns.

"At that time my parents' situation was somewhat improved. My sister, who had emigrated to America with her husband, began sending money every month, enough for us to live on. There were only the three of us at home: my

213

mother, my father and I, and we didn't need much. My father earned something occasionally too, and we made ends meet. And then that winter my mother fell ill and took to her bed. She had rheumatic pains in her right leg. She wasn't seriously ill, but she couldn't move. At first my father was going to write to his sister in the neighbouring town, and ask her to send her daughter to stay with us and help in the house for a while. We were staying in a large apartment with a number of rooms, in our old house which had remained in our possession after my father came down in the world, and which he stubbornly refused to sell. 'I'll never sell the roof over my head,' he would argue, 'a man who owns his house is still a man, but as soon as he sells his house he's no better than a beggar.' Now that my mother was ill, we needed someone to take care of the house and especially to do the cooking. After thinking it over, my parents decided to hire a maid."

Gurdweill lit another cigarette.

"Zushka, the maid, was short, dark, and rather dumpy, and she was about twenty-five years old. She had glittering eyes, and sharp, shining, little teeth like an animal's. Her upper lip was rather short, and her teeth were always exposed, as in a smile. Despite her clumsy body she was light on her feet. Mother said that she was a hard worker, too. Zushka knew a lot of Polish songs and she always sang when she was working. I loved to listen to her singing in her melodious voice: the folk-songs full of feeling would waft down the long corridor from the kitchen, rather muffled when they reached my bedroom and moving me to tears. For a long time I didn't know that it was Zushka singing: the voice seemed to be coming from very far away. I only found out later, quite by chance, that it was her, and it made no difference to me at all. All that mattered was the singing. To the maid herself I paid no attention. You might almost say that I didn't know exactly what she looked like; to me she was a kind of abstract idea — a maidservant in the house and that was all. After a few weeks I grew conscious of her presence. Suddenly she was there and the house was full of Zushka. I don't know if it was intentional or not: wherever I turned I encountered

214

her. Wherever I happened to be, she had something urgent to do. When I was in my room, she would always appear with a duster or a broom. She couldn't find any other time to clean the windows, dust the furniture or make the bed. Not only that, but she always squeezed herself so close to me that I could almost feel the heat of her body and hear her breath. And at the same time she would look directly at me with a strange smile, as if I were something ridiculous, until I felt extremely uncomfortable and my heart pounded. I felt shy of her without knowing why, and the minute she left I would run straight to the mirror to see if I had a smut on my nose or something of the kind. She behaved like this for several days, perhaps a week.

"One night, it was almost midnight, I was lying on the couch in my room and reading a book. My parents were asleep in their bedroom, three rooms away. The book was very gripping, I had almost reached the end, and I was still fully dressed, unwilling to waste any time on taking off my clothes. Suddenly the door opened soundlessly and Zushka appeared. She stood in the doorway looking at me and said with a smile: 'You have so many nice books, Master Rudolf, and I couldn't fall asleep, and so I thought to myself: why not go and ask Master Rudolf to lend you a good book . . .' And she smiled her strange smile. Only now I saw that she was wearing nothing but her bodice and petticoats, and her arms were bare to the shoulders. I took all this in with one brief glance and immediately felt dizzy. I jumped up, averting my eyes from her, and went over to the bookcase with my legs trembling to take a book. Zushka followed me and pressed up against me, as if there was no space for her in the room. My hands were shaking and the book fell on the floor. Zushka bent down and picked it up. I didn't even know which book it was, I had taken the first one I laid my hands on. I didn't dare utter a word, my whole body was trembling feverishly. I was afraid to turn my head towards her. I stood where I was. If I move now, I thought, something dreadful will happen, something unimaginable. But Zushka grabbed my hand, led me to the couch and sat me down like a little baby.

215

She remained standing in front of me. She said nothing and I sat there in a daze, with my head bowed. Suddenly she said: 'Have you ever seen a naked woman, you silly boy?'. . . 'What?' I blurted out stupidly. Without thinking I looked up and saw that her bodice was undone and that the whole upper half of her body was completely naked. I immediately dropped my eyes. I thought that I was going to faint. Zushka gave a smothered little giggle: 'If you're not silly, you'll see a lot more, a lot more, my little lad . . .' Suddenly she was sitting next to me on the couch. She took my hand and placed it on her chest. I felt her warm breast moving like a separate, living creature. Zushka was already lying on top of me with all the weight of her body, almost smothering me. Then she put my head between her naked breasts. She kept whispering: 'My little lad, don't be afraid, my little lad,' while she guided my hand over her body, which was suddenly quite naked. And at that moment I felt a strange hand, blazing hot and quivering, moving over my skin, underneath my clothes . . ."

Gurdweill fell silent. He was breathing heavily and unevenly, reliving the event as he had experienced it then. His last words had been spoken in a barely audible whisper, his eyes lowered to the table, as if in shame. Thea said nothing for a moment. Then she burst into loud, uninhibited laughter. Gurdweill stared at her in bewilderment, as if her presence in the room surprised him. Then he too smiled.

"Well done! Well done!" Thea cried approvingly. "Here you are rabbit, take this!" she offered him a cigarette as if conferring a prize. "Go on — what happened afterwards?"

"Afterwards? Afterwards I was miserable. I fell asleep with my clothes on, on the couch, and when I woke up the next morning, I felt as if something terrible had happened to me. I felt as if I had lost the most precious thing in the world, and lost it irretrievably. And then I cried. I cried for a long time. I was ashamed to leave my room. I was sure that everything was written on my face . . . And when I went into the kitchen to wash, I couldn't look at Zushka. But she said, as if nothing had happened: 'Did you sleep well, Master Rudolf? It's a lovely day today!'

216

. . . And afterwards, when I went into my parents' room, I lowered my eyes and blushed. I was sure that they knew everything. Soon they would begin scolding me. What were they waiting for? Why were they torturing me? I could not endure their silence and waited in great agitation for them to begin. But they said nothing. Then I told them that I had a headache and that I wasn't going to go to school. I was afraid to show my face outside and I was ashamed before my school fellows. For a long time after that I blushed whenever anyone looked at me."

"And was it only that one time?" asked Thea curiously.

"No, lots of times. That same day, in the afternoon, she came again. And in the course of time I grew accustomed to it and I no longer saw anything wrong in it. I even began going to her, in the kitchen. I went at night, when I knew that my parents were asleep. I was very attracted to her. She wasn't ugly at all. And three months later, when she left, I was very sorry indeed. But a few months after that, I left my parents' home myself."

Thea stood up and stretched. She went over to the window and looked outside. In the shaft of light from the streetlamp the snowflakes, which were much lighter than before, looked as if they were flying upwards. Apart from two windows on the fourth floor and one on the second, all the windows in the hotel were dark. It was obviously late. From the nearby railway station a short whistle suddenly pierced the quiet, snowy night, first one and after a while another, and in the end a third: long and wailing. In Thea's imagination a strange station flew past, the station of a remote little village where she had perhaps never set foot in her life, with an old priest standing in front of her in the line to buy a ticket. She moved away from the window and went up to her husband, who was still sitting in the same posture as before.

"It's getting chilly. Put on some more coal, rabbit."

She bent over and scratched his nose as a sign of affection. Then she yawned lengthily and began to get undressed.

"Come along, little rabbit, take off my stockings."

Gurdweill shut the door of the stove after throwing in

217

two shovelsful of coal, and went to take off her stockings. Thea lay across the bed and thrust her foot towards her husband, who knelt down on the floor. He pressed his lips to her thigh.

"Hurry up!" said Thea. "It's cold."

And then, as if to herself:

"It must be interesting to seduce a little boy . . ."

"What?" The same stupid "What?" escaped Gurdweill's lips as on that first evening with Zushka.

"Get undressed quickly, rabbit! You're permitted to sleep with me tonight," said Thea and slipped under the covers. "Bring me the cigarettes and matches!"

Gurdweill took his pile of bedclothes from the bed, set it down on the chair, and began to make up his bed on the couch. He spread his coat over the red, stain-spotted quilt, so that he would not be cold at night. Then he took off his clothes, put out the lamp, and got into his wife's bed.

19

Gurdweill moved over to the couch and lay flat on his back, as he always did before going to sleep. The nocturnal silence enveloped him like something tangible. Thea was already sleeping. Gurdweill felt a mild, agreeable tingling in his limbs, as after a lukewarm bath, and a vein pulsed secretly and sluggishly somewhere in his body. It was difficult to determine the exact place where this vein began: if he listened to his leg, it pulsed in his leg, if he listened to his head, it pulsed in his head, very slowly and apparently without meaning any harm. "Well," thought Gurdweill, "you can't worry about that now if you want to go to sleep . . . But who said that you want to go to sleep? There's plenty of time for sleeping. Tomorrow is another day! And what about that other thing inside you, that special, happy thing, that's there too. It's a pity you can't remember now exactly what it is . . ." It must be very late. Ages ago, an eternity ago, it was midnight! No, he wasn't going to look at his watch now — too much work. To get up, strike a match — no! But if some clock should take it into its head to strike the hour, for example! Never mind, it made no difference. The main thing was, that there was a point of happiness somewhere inside him. He had no desire to know exactly what it was. Over there, for example, on the left (where the bed stood), everything was fine! No complaints in that quarter — on the contrary, this evening had really been a peaceful, contented one . . . Little things didn't count! No need to pay any attention to them!

"What about 'seducing a little boy,' for example?" asked someone inside him.

"It doesn't mean a thing. A slip of the tongue, not worth considering," replied Gurdweill nonchalantly. "There are more important things, and we don't take any notice of them either . . ."

"Exactly what I wanted to ask. Why don't we take any notice of them?"

"It's late," Gurdweill tried to evade the issue. "Time to go to sleep."

But the other refused to be silenced:

"But we already decided before that tomorrow's a holiday, and we can sleep as late as we like, if only they let us . . ."

"Who won't let us?" Gurdweill fell into the trap.

"They won't let us," replied the other without elaborating. "You're a clever chap, when you want to be. Do you really want me to name names? You know very well, who . . ."

"Nonsense!" said Gurdweill dismissively. "What kind of nonsense is that? You know very well that nobody tells me what to do."

"Come, come!" smiled the second ironically. "That's not exactly so! There's room for doubt there."

"Stop hinting and beating around the bush!" Gurdweill began to get excited. "You know I can't stand that kind of thing! Just come right out with it!"

"I think it's quite clear. You're the one who likes mysteries around here. Do you really want me to call things by their true name? Fear, for example."

"What fear?" shouted Gurdweill. "There's no fear! The idea of fear is completely out of place here!"

"If you're so sure that everything is all right, why are you so upset?"

"That's enough!" announced Gurdweill. "I don't want to talk about it any more! I'd rather smoke a pipe."

"A pipe can't change the facts," insisted the other. "I'm talking about the childish fear of seeing things as they really are . . . Not to mention that other, of which we are both well aware . . ."

"Donkey! Idiot!" Thea's familiar words of abuse rose uncontrollably to Gurdweill's lips. He forgot all about the pipe. "I've already told you before, that I don't want to hear that word again! He takes hold of some silly word

220

and doesn't want to let it go! 'Fear, fear!' Fear of whom? Is that how well you know me? A coward? Prove it! Let's hear some facts! I could quote a few incidents that prove just the opposite! For example — but I really don't want to get into an argument with a fool like you!"

"First of all, my friend, keep calm. I've already told you that your excitement looks suspicious to me ... but let's leave it alone. You wanted to smoke a pipe, didn't you? Go ahead! We've got plenty of time, haven't we? As for the rest — that's the whole point! It's precisely the fact that you're not a coward by nature that makes the whole thing so astonishing! That a woman — well, never mind! Light your pipe first ..."

Gurdweill reached out in the darkness for the chair next to the couch, where he hung his clothes and placed his watch and smoking gear. After fumbling about a bit he found the tobacco and pipe and began stuffing it.

"A pipe is an agreeable thing, I admit," whispered the other again, "but when it's the only thing a man has in the world, it's not very much, is it?"

"What do you mean, the only thing? What a lie! There are quite a few other things, I'd say! There's the child and there's Thea ... and there's ..."

"Wait a minute! The child, you said. Good! But has the child been born yet? So how can you say you have it? Not, God forbid, that I want to wish you ill! But a lot of things can happen before a child is born ... Can anyone predict them? And besides, what if Thea really decides to 'get rid of it' as she said? She's quite capable of it, you know! Who's going to stop her? You, perhaps?"

"She won't get rid of it," Gurdweill said quickly, in a panic. "Don't say things like that! She wants it too, just as much as I do ... The truth is that she's not a cruel woman at all ..."

"That's not the subject under discussion, if she's a cruel woman or not! I'm not prepared to discuss it with you. But you'll admit yourself that she's subject to all kinds of uncontrollable impulses, caprices, call them what you will ... And if, for example, she suddenly gets it into her head that pregnancy and birth will spoil her looks, do you really think she'll take any notice of you and your protests?! She's not afraid of operations, that we already know! On the contrary, she's only too happy at the excuse for an operation! Did she really need that operation on her breasts three months ago? And the other operations she's had since you've known her — were they necessary? Three operations in a few months! It's really grotesque when you come to think of it, and it's hardly something you can ignore. And now, with such a wonderful opportunity for another operation!"

"She'll never get a doctor to do it! There's no medical reason for it! She's perfectly healthy . . ."

"Are you really sure she won't?" scoffed the other. "I never imagined you were so naïve! She'll find a doctor to do it all right — for money! There are plenty of doctors who make a living from it!"

"Enough, stop torturing me! I'm tired to death."

A wave of heat flooded him, a disagreeable, annoying, feverish heat. Inside his temples his pulse beat like a sledgehammer, and at the base of his skull there was a dull, empty pain, as if his brain had been drained away. There was a vile dryness in his mouth and the bitter taste of the pipe smoke. Irritably he pushed the bedclothes down to his belly.

"In any case," the other began again, "it's a possibility that has to be taken into account. It's not as inconceivable as you think! A woman like her . . ."

"What do you mean 'a woman like her'?" Gurdweill was by now boiling with rage. "You really are a hopeless idiot! She's no worse than other women!"

"You think so? Lotte Bondheim, do you think she resembles Thea, for example? Or Jenny Koppler, or any other woman you like? No, no, my friend — you can't pull the wool over my eyes!"

"I admit that she's different from them, and that's the reason I love her."

"You love her, you say. Don't make me laugh! It would be more correct to say — but you'll only get upset again . . ."

"Go on, say it! I'm interested to hear."

222

"I would say — fear . . ."

"Oh no, not again!" groaned Gurdweill. "That damned word again! That idiotic word! If you don't stop I'll . . . I'll go out of my mind."

"Come, come, calm down. It's not so easy you know. I promise you: you won't go out of your mind. You know what you need? You need a little courage, and that's all."

"What do I need courage for? I've got enough already! And another thing: I don't want to fight anybody . . . I want peace and quiet!"

"That's exactly the problem! You think it will help you, but you're only putting it off — in the end you'll have to fight! And the longer you wait the harder it will be . . ."

"I tell you I won't fight, and I won't fight! And anyway, there's nobody for me to fight! Do you hear? I don't want to! I don't want to! And now let me go to sleep, to sleep, to sleep!"

Gurdweill turned over on his side and began repeating the words "to sleep" over and over to himself. His thoughts began to slip away, as if they were gradually evaporating from his mind; he became lighter and lighter, he floated up and glided through the air, to the other side, the other side . . . Only the words "to sleep" went on smouldering in his mind, like a dull, exhausted ember. Suddenly the silence was broken by the explosive sound of dry wood cracking. Gurdweill started violently and sat up in bed. He imagined that he had fallen from a great height. He listened to the silence through every pore of his body and heard nothing. After a moment he realized that it had only been some dry piece of furniture snapping. He even remembered that he had definitely heard the explosion at the moment of its occurrence, which calmed him somewhat. But on the other hand he was filled with rage against the landlady and her "horrible furniture." We'll have to look for another room — he said to himself — it's impossible to sleep here! He lay down again and was obliged to begin everything from the beginning, since by now he was wide awake. Now I'll have to count to a thousand, he thought, sometimes that helps too. Somewhere in the distance a clock struck three. But there was no knowing if it was three quarters of an hour or three o'clock. No, he would not look at his watch! It made no difference one way or the other.

Gurdweill began to count. When he reached ten, he was suddenly seized by a wish to know whether the snow had stopped falling outside or not. If it froze over a little, it would be a fine winter day tomorrow . . . twelve, thirteen, nonsense! Everything was perfectly all right! How could he have bothered his head over such nonsense? When was it, today or a long time ago? . . . Twenty, twenty-one, twenty-two, Zushka . . . If his parents had known then! A nice bit of jam, there was no denying . . . Perhaps he should change the end of the story he'd finished yesterday . . . She doesn't only leave her husband, but her lover too — the pair of them together . . . especially the lover . . . He would have to think about it . . . Fifty-six, fifty-seven, fifty-eight — "Do you think about me, Herr Gurdweill? I think about you a lot, aie-aie-aie!" — he heard the old landlady saying. And right afterwards: "You've got a fine wife, Herr Gurdweill! A very fine wife, psss!"

"Hee-hee! Very fine indeed! . . . Exemplary, no less! . . . Ho-ho! Time will tell just how exemplary she is!"

"No, no! I can't stand any more, eighty-five, eighty-six . . ."

"Naturally! When you haven't got the guts to look the truth in the face! Why don't you pay some attention to the hints your best friends drop? And what about that idiot Dr. Kreindel's sarcastic remarks? Is it all, all smoke without fire? . . . But you know the truth yourself . . . You pretend not to know because it's more convenient for you that way, because you prefer a false, illusory peace of mind to the truth. But you know yourself that things can't go on like this any longer!"

Gurdweill thought that he would go mad. A cold sweat broke out on his forehead. He sat up with a jerk and began searching frenziedly for the matches on the chair. He lit one and glanced at his watch. Five to four. He held the burning match until it seared the tips of his fingers, and then lit another and another. For the first time in his life he was afraid of the dark and his own frantic thoughts. He glanced at the bed next to him. Thea was sleeping with her face turned away from him, towards the window. If he listened intently, he could hear her quiet, rhythmic breathing. Apart from that, nothing stirred. The stillness was dense and juicy, full of her alien sleep. And the little flame flared and flickered and faded like a mirage, faded and flared again as he hastily lit another match. Gurdweill was suddenly swept by a terrible rage against this woman next to him, as if she were the sole reason for all his suffering, from the day that he was born. The child vanished from his thoughts. It was all one to him now. All he saw was this tall woman, sweeping him up in her arms and capering round the room with him. He felt a terrible insult, an insult which shook him to the foundations of his being and at that moment he hated her with a deadly hatred. He could easily have risen from the couch, dressed himself and gone away, far, far away, never to return. It was all one to him! He didn't need anyone, anything! But at the same time he felt quite clearly that he would never, never be capable of doing it; that he was enslaved to this woman forever, in life and in death; that his fate was chained to hers, irrevocably. And then he remembered the child again and he said to himself: Nonsense! I love her in spite of everything. It's amazing how one sleepless night can drive a man out of his mind! No wonder crimes are committed at night! When a man can't sleep he's capable of anything. The mad are unable to sleep, and the sick too. "The night is bloody with crime and madness" — he recalled a line from some poem. Gurdweill lay down again with a resolute air, as if he had resigned himself to his fate. But no sooner had he given up all hope of sleep than his tension relaxed, and overcome with weariness he fell asleep within a couple of minutes.

In the morning Thea sat up in bed.

"Rabbit, rabbit, aren't we going to get any coffee today?"

There was a drowsy, contented note in her voice, as after a sound night's sleep.

The smell of a pipe gone cold and stale human breath hung in the air. The idea of the cold, hostile stove was enough to banish any desire to get out of bed.

225

Thea's voice stole faintly into Gurdweill's slumbers as if it had nothing to do with him. He stirred slightly and went on sleeping. After a moment he was hit by a second, more energetic volley.

"Well, Rudolfus, are you planning to sleep all day?"

A light flashed on in his brain. The voice definitely meant him. His body felt as battered as if he had been mercilessly beaten all night long. He would have given the rest of his life for a few more minutes of sleep. He grunted:

"In a minute, in a minute, Thea!"

Hoping for a few moments' grace he went on dozing. But it was a nervous, agitated sleep now, a sleep which had been broken into and saturated with the fear of the inevitable, imminent awakening. Not the private fortress of before, where no stranger could penetrate. He felt as if his blankets had been stripped off him and he was now sleeping absolutely naked, exposed to the eyes of strangers. When the next rousing cry was aimed at him from the bed he recoiled as if he had been bitten and sat up with a start. His hair stood wildly on end and his pale, crumpled face, with a bright pink mark from the crease in the pillow running down the left cheek like a scar, looked like the face of someone dangerously ill. His bewildered eyes gazed round the room as if he were seeing it for the first time, until he encountered the stare of his wife, who was busy lighting a cigarette, and the memory of the sleepless night and its terrors came back to him in a flash. Gurdweill smiled, happy in the knowledge that it was all over, that it was now the next day, and that everything was the same as usual: the room, the furniture, Thea. He looked at his watch lying on the chair: ten o'clock, not too late!

"Why are you staring at me like that, rabbit, as if you'd just fallen from the moon? This is Vienna, Kleine Stadtgutgasse, Frau Fischer's house. It's the twenty-fifth of December, Christmas, and now hurry up and make some coffee for your wife Thea, Baroness von Takow by birth, and presently married to yourself, Rudolfus Gurdweill, also called Rabbit, in a ceremony performed according to

226

the law of Moses of Egypt and the Jewish congregation of Vienna. Understood?"

Gurdweill smiled. She had woken up in a good mood.

"If you don't mind," he said boldly, "throw me a cigarette. I'll smoke it and get up in a minute. It's only ten o'clock."

The cigarette hit him in the face and fell on the floor. Gurdweill picked it up, lit it and lay back again.

"We're going to Baron von Takow's for lunch!" announced Thea. "Excellent!"

If only she was always like this, he thought, his happiness would be complete! He discovered to his delight that he was not in the least tired, despite his lack of sleep.

"Well, what about breakfast?"

He got up, dressed quickly, and hurried to the kitchen, without washing first, to make the coffee.

After a while he came back with boiling hot coffee, bread and butter, and the sprats left over from the day before, and served his wife breakfast in bed. Thea ate voraciously, as if after a hard day's work, to the delight of her husband, who kept glancing at her from the table, where he was taking his own meal.

"You must eat a lot, dearest, don't forget you're eating for two now."

Thea did not hear, or pretended not to hear. When he went up to her bed afterwards to take away the tray, he bent over her with sudden fervour and pressed his lips to her hand. "The hand that hit," he thought and felt an indescribable pleasure. Thea pulled her hand away, giving her husband a look full of contempt and disgust as she did so — a look which escaped his notice. After carrying the tray to the table he approached his wife again. His face was radiant with joy.

"You don't know how m-much . . ." he stammered with downcast eyes, "how m-much you mean to me . . . I would be prepared to take anything from you . . . that is . . . just don't harm the . . ."

With an impatient gesture Thea pushed him away: "Stop it, I want to get up!" and she jumped out of bed. Submissively Gurdweill sat next to the table and watched

227

his naked wife washing from a distance. No, he thought sadly, I can't win her heart, whatever I do. He saw the milky light flowing through the windows into the cold, untidy room and his sadness grew even more profound. When Thea turned as she sponged herself, and his eyes fell on her belly, it seemed to him that it was a little more curved than before, and this immediately gave him back his equanimity. Thea, as if she had read his thoughts, said:

"Father doesn't know yet. Don't say anything, you hear? It's my business!"

"Will you tell him today? He'll be very happy."

"Not yet!" she smiled spitefully. "If I decide to keep it, I'll tell him in my own good time. And you, don't interfere!"

In fact, she did not have the slightest intention of aborting the baby. She wanted it for some reason which was not clear even to herself. Not out of an excessive love of children, at any rate. She only said what she said in order to make Gurdweill miserable and see him tremble. She knew how he longed for a baby and wanted to hurt him as much as she could with the threat of an abortion. Later on, when this threat was no longer valid, she would find something else for him. It would be interesting to see how much he was prepared to suffer in silence . . .

Thea dressed herself with the deliberate, rhythmic movements which were so familiar and agreeable to Gurdweill. An independent, forceful character, he thought, a vitality that can almost be measured mathematically, that in her nature expresses itself explicitly, directly . . .

"Why so down in the mouth, rabbit? Get dressed and let's go!"

Gurdweill went over to the window. Yesterday's snow had already melted. The street was wet and slushy. Dirty, blackening lumps of snow had collected in the gutters at the sides of the pavements. Gurdweill would willingly have stayed at home. His need for rest and solitude was overpowering. He wanted to be by himself and felt unfit for human company. At his father-in-law's house he would be obliged to talk, to be sociable — and he simply did not feel up to it.

"Perhaps you could go alone, Thea? I don't feel up to it. I hardly slept all night."

But this time Thea was not prepared to do without him.

"You have to come with me! I promised that we would come together. They're expecting us. It's all fixed!"

And after a minute:

"I have to go somewhere this afternoon anyway. You can come home then."

And so Gurdweill went to wash. The cold water revived him somewhat and his heavy, dazed mind cleared a little. He took off his shirt and washed his body, too — his skinny, underdeveloped, almost hairless, boyish body, white with a gleaming whiteness. Thea was now dressed in a white silk blouse and a brown skirt. She sat at the table, smoking and staring at her husband, who was scrubbing his back with a cloth, as if she wanted to penetrate to the secrets of the soul concealed behind his white, pampered skin. Gurdweill sensed her eyes on his back and began to feel uncomfortable. He was rather ashamed of his undeveloped body, especially before his wife, whom he suspected of despising him for it. He slipped behind her and quickly put on his shirt.

As they were about to leave Ulrich knocked on the door.

"Ah, you're going out!" he cried in the doorway. "In that case I won't disturb you. But if you're on your way to a restaurant I'll come along."

"We're off to the old Baron for lunch," said Thea, "but do come in anyway. We've got a little time left."

Ulrich came in and sat on the edge of the couch without removing his coat.

"I honestly don't feel like it," said Gurdweill, his tongue loosened a little in the presence of a third person. "But Thea's promised and they're expecting us. What's up with you, Ulrich?"

"Nothing's up with me, as you know. One does one's best to enjoy one's heaven-sent idleness without complaining. I haven't seen you around for a few days and was afraid

229

that something had happened to you. And what about you, Thea? How did you spend the 'Holy Night'?"

"In deadly boredom, my friend. Holiness is always boring, it's a well-known fact . . ."

"You may be right," said Ulrich. "I also thought I'd go out of my mind with boredom last night. But for the snow, I would certainly have hanged myself."

"The snow? What do you mean?" laughed Thea. "If I wanted to hang myself, the snow wouldn't have stopped me."

"Yes, the snow! When I saw the white street, I changed my mind . . . I thought I might as well take a last stroll in the first snow. And I did and I was saved. Because after the stroll I didn't feel like doing it any more. I simply went to sleep. And you were at home, were you? If I'd known, I would have dropped in."

Ulrich stood up: "Well, I won't keep you any longer. Perhaps you'll be in the café later on this afternoon?"

"Not me!" said Thea. "I have to go somewhere. Maybe later, about sixish. How about you, Rudolfus?"

"I don't know yet. Probably yes, but I can't say for sure."

They went down to the street. Gurdweill and Thea set off for the Praterstern to take a tram, and Ulrich accompanied them. The cold was damp and penetrating. Gurdweill felt as if it were directed specifically against him. He raised his collar and huddled into his shabby coat. It's an inner cold, he thought to himself, the coals are burnt out . . . What does Dr. Astel always say? "Human beings should be well-heated and oiled . . ." Yes, Dr. Astel! He hadn't seen him for ages. Nor Lotte either.

"Have you seen Dr. Astel lately?" he asked Ulrich, who was talking to Thea. "What's he up to?"

"Nothing! His friend Bloch has come from Berlin for the holidays. I expect he'll be in the café this afternoon."

At the tram stop they found Dr. Kreindel, wrapped in a fine fur coat and smoking a cigar. He saw them coming in the distance and took a few steps towards them.

"What a lucky coincidence!" he cried in affected happiness and kissed Thea on her hand.

"Something told me this would happen. I had some

business nearby, and afterwards I wondered whether to take a cab, but nothing came past and I decided to take a tram. And now I see that I have no reason for regret! I haven't yet had the honour, young man —" he turned to Ulrich.

The latter introduced himself.

"And so, Herr Ulrich," Dr. Kreindel continued, "a friend of Herr Gurdwein's, presumably?" he gave Thea a sidelong glance. "And presumably a writer, too, eh? Have I guessed right? Obviously!" He confirmed to himself. "What else? And the *Gnädige* Frau, well, I trust?"

"Very well, Herr Doktor," smiled Thea.

Dr. Kreindel smiled too, exposing his gold teeth.

"Delighted to hear it, *Gnädige* Frau! As long as you've got your health and your appetite, hee-hee . . ."

Him of all people! — Gurdweill thought with suppressed rage — on my one holiday I have to meet him too!

"And Herr Ulrich," Dr. Kreindel turned to Ulrich, "does he also write fiction like our friend Herr Gurdweill, or is it philosophy, perhaps, if I may be permitted to inquire?"

"Neither the one nor the other," Ulrich made haste to reply, "quite the contrary!"

"And what is quite the contrary, if I may ask?"

"The contrary is, that I don't write at all. Except for letters, and that too very seldom."

"In that case, you're not a writer at all, by your own account! What a pity! So my eyes deceived me! And I was sure that any friend of Herr Gurdweill's had to be — in the words of Mörike: 'a soul which finds its mate,' etc. . . And what is your profession, sir, permit me to ask, since I have already guessed wrong once . . ."

"I," said Ulrich, "am a chicken-plucker by profession . . ."

"Ha ha ha!" Dr. Kreindel laughed heartily. "How could I have missed it? Excellent, excellent! You really look like a — what did you say — chicken-plucker . . . When I first set eyes on you I couldn't make up my mind between a chicken-plucker and a philosophical writer and I chose the second — what a mistake, hee-hee-hee! And tell me, is your profession profitable?"

231

"Very!"

"That's the main thing, my friend. What does Schiller say: 'A man's honour is his work, since . . .' and so on. What a shame that I have no time to spare. Here's my tram coming. But it was a great pleasure, a true intellectual pleasure . . . I hope we'll meet again. We must have a long talk, my friend. Goodbye!"

He shook hands hastily and jumped onto the tram, which was already moving. As it receded he waved and flashed his gold teeth.

"What a character!" said Ulrich. "I'll have to get to the bottom of him one day."

"You won't find that so easy," Gurdweill assured him. "He can twist a dozen like you around his little finger. I can promise you that these few minutes were enough for him to know you inside out. But if he interests you, why don't you come to fetch me from work one day, at about six."

"Come on, rabbit! Here's our tram!" Thea tugged at his sleeve.

And they rode off to have lunch with the old Baron.

20

THE weather isn't fit for a dog!" The old Baron greeted them as he opened the door.

"Yes, it's freezing," Gurdweill agreed.

In the salon Poldy, the eldest brother, lay sprawled on the sofa. He was reading the newspaper, smoking a cigarette in a long brown holder, and the grey and white striped cat was purring as it dozed on his lap. Without getting up or taking his eyes from the paper he held out his hand to the newcomers.

Freddy was pacing up and down the room with his hands in his pockets. He waited for Thea to go to the mirror to tidy her hair, and asked Gurdweill in a whisper if he had any money. He asked this question in a tone of indifference, as if it were some trivial matter which had nothing to do with him, without interrupting his pacing. The negative reply made no apparent impression on him. He went on pacing on his long legs, like some exotic bird, and humming a tune through his nose.

The room was steeped in an atmosphere of profound, oppressive boredom which immediately seized hold of Gurdweill in all its intensity. He felt as if he had been lying ill in that room for days on end, and that its walls and furniture exuded the smell unique to sickrooms. He had an impulse to hurry over to the windows and fling them open. He looked around the room as if he was seeing it for the first time, wondering at the hybrid furniture, some of which was old, dark, and heavy, presumably family heirlooms, and some of which was new, cheap and mass-produced. A feeling of general and absolute futility suddenly descended on Gurdweill, hitting him in the face like something tangible and making his heart contract. But he immediately recovered. Nonsense! — he said to himself

— all you need is a good night's sleep. He went up to examine the portrait of the Baron, as he had already done many times before. It was an oil painting, not very large, hanging between four other ancestral portaits. The Baron was shown in a Major's uniform, a middle-aged man with a beard trimmed in the style of the Emperor Franz-Josef. Gurdweill found his expression silly. Those tiny, watery-blue eyes, staring fixedly ahead, said absolutely nothing. They could have been rubbed out without affecting the rest of the face. The nose was well-developed, strong, full of energy, and the chin between the two prongs of the forked beard, prominent and athletic. There was no resemblance between this face and Thea's, and no one would have imagined that she was his daughter. Both sons, on the other hand, resembled their father. Especially the elder, Poldy.

Thea pulled up a chair to the head of the sofa and glanced at Poldy's newspaper. He was reading the continuation of a serialized adventure story.

"Phoo, Poldy!" she exclaimed. "How can you read such rubbish?"

And she snatched the paper from his hands. The abruptness of the movement made the cat on his lap wake up, raise its head and stare with round, dazed eyes.

"Give it back, Thea!"

But he went on lying down without moving.

"Leave that nonsense now!" said Thea, and she threw the paper into a corner. "Will you be seeing Richard today?"

"I don't know. Maybe. Why?"

"If you see him, tell him that I couldn't make it to the café then. He'll know. And to phone me at the office after the holiday. You won't forget?"

"I won't forget."

Gurdweill wasn't listening, but the name Richard pierced him like a spear. Without knowing who Richard was and what he meant to Thea, the name itself disturbed him. He even felt a kind of anger against this Richard, although he was no more than an abstract idea to him. But the next moment he came to his senses — what on earth did it

234

have to do with him? It didn't interest him in the least!
. . . He kept an ear open in his wife's direction, however.
He also made an instinctive movement to get up from his
chair, but then he changed his mind and sat down again.

Thea asked Poldy:

"And Reizi, how's she?"

"I haven't seen her," replied Poldy apathetically.

"What? Is it all over between you?"

"Almost. Enough!"

"You're a fine one, Poldy!" said Thea with a certain
satisfaction. "By the way, I knew it was a passing thing.
She's a nice girl, Reizi, but she doesn't know how to keep
a man: she lacks intelligence. And who have you got your
eye on now?"

"I wouldn't dream of telling you," Poldy sniggered.
"It's a secret!"

"You sly creature!" His sister tickled him under the
arm. "You just want to make me curious! Is she blonde?"

"I'm not saying! Not now. Maybe some other time."

Freddy was still pacing gloomily up and down the room,
as if he were waiting for a train that was late. The conversation between Thea and Poldy began to bore Gurdweill.
The lewd tone annoyed him, too. It was a quarter to one;
there was still some time to spare before lunch. The Baron
was in the next room and the Baroness was busy in the
kitchen. Gurdweill picked the newspaper up from the
floor and began reading it. But he kept one ear open
in the direction of his wife and brother-in-law.

All of a sudden Freddy stopped next to him and said:

"Do you like cats, Rudolf? I don't. Neither cats, dogs,
nor any other kind of pet. I can't understand what Father
sees in them. A cat, for example, always gives you the
impression that he's waiting to catch you out. Look at
him. He seems to be sleeping, right? But you can never be
sure that he's really asleep. At this very moment he might
be listening . . . and he hears everything! I'm sure of it!
He hears your innermost thoughts! Even the ones that
you yourself are unaware of, that don't penetrate your
conciousness! . . . And it's not very pleasant! Sometimes,
when I'm alone in the room with the cat, I feel like killing

235

him. I can't bear the idea of someone watching me all the time and looking inside me. Not that I've got anything to hide, but just because it's a nasty feeling . . . People, now — that's different! They don't see anything! You can be with them and at the same time you can be with yourself and think whatever thoughts come into your head. They won't notice a thing. But not animals, not cats or dogs . . ."

Gurdweill sat and looked at him in amazement. He would never have suspected his brother-in-law of harbouring such thoughts. This long, skinny fellow, who seemed about to bend and break into two at any moment with a dry, brittle snap, had always seemed to Gurdweill to be completely hollow, like a dry stalk. He had never exchanged more than a few pointless remarks with him in his life.

Freddy drew up a chair, sat down next to Gurdweill, and continued calmly:

"This cat of ours knows very well that I can't stand him. He hides away from me . . . He always keeps his distance . . . He never comes near me. And it goes without saying that it would never enter his head to jump into my lap, or rub himself against my leg. He knows . . . He goes up to everyone but me . . . And you should know that I've never done him any harm yet. Except for looking at him from time to time. But he knows what I'm thinking and he's afraid . . . He probably also knows that I once strangled a cat when I was a boy and he's afraid . . ."

"You're exaggerating," said Gurdweill, who was beginning, for some reason, to feel uneasy, "they don't know anything!"

Freddy was oblivious.

"It didn't happen here. We were on vacation in Salzkammergut. I was about nine years old. And there was a cat there. Not ours. Perhaps it belonged to our neighbour, I don't know. There was a litle villa not far from us that belonged to some Professor from Vienna. In any case, the cat had a habit of wandering around our garden. Whenever I went into the garden I would find it there, walking around as if it owned the place, or standing still and turning its head from side to side and listening. It wasn't a big cat, and it had black and orange patches on its coat. A couple of times I even caught it coming down the corridor, perfectly cool and collected, without the slightest sign of fear. Its impertinence began to annoy me. A cat should be frightened and run away, but this one wasn't frightened in the least. In the end it really upset me, but I went on waiting. Once or twice I tried to approach it. I would approach very slowly and it never ran away. When I was close enough to touch it, it would simply walk calmly away . . . This disdainful contempt infuriated me more and more. I could hardly think of anything else, and it preoccupied me even in my sleep. One night I dreamt that the cat came into my room, the room I shared with Poldy, and approached my bed with its calm, unhurried walk and at the foot of the bed raised its head to look at me. In my dream I was asleep and I didn't want to wake up for the sake of this impertinent cat. I thought that I would wait and see what it wanted. Because it was standing and looking at me as if it was making up its mind about something. I saw that its eyes were a reddish-brown and they had a sharp glint in them. Before then, when I was awake, I hadn't noticed its eyes. In short: I lay and looked at it and it looked at me and I knew for certain that it was planning to do me some harm. After standing there for a while, it jumped on to my bed, at my feet, and began walking slowly over my body, towards my head. I didn't move. Close to my head it stopped, paused for a moment, looked at me with its red-brown eyes, which at close range were unnaturally big and round. Then it slowly coiled itself around my neck. I felt a slight, almost pleasant, pressure, and an intense warmth on my neck. But the pressure increased, it became difficult to breathe, and I suddenly realized that it intended to strangle me. I whipped my hand out of the blanket and grabbed it by the neck. With a great effort I managed to pull it off me. I shook it in front of my eyes, with my hand round its neck and its body hanging and dangling down. But I immediately realized that its neck was hard as iron, and the harder I squeezed the more it hurt my hand. I looked intently at its head again, and found that its eyes had completely

237

disappeared. And its head, too, was no longer the head of a cat, but some strange thing, more like an inanimate object than an animal. I flung it on to the floor with all my strength. It fell with a noise like a heavy metal object. I looked at the place where it had fallen, at the foot of the bed, and to my amazement I saw that the cat, the very same cat, was getting up, stretching itself as if after a pleasant doze, and raising its head to look at me. Then it jumped up on to the bed again, and the whole thing repeated itself in every detail over and over again.

"The next day I watched and waited all day long, seeking the cat in the garden and everywhere else, in vain. It was nowhere to be found. That night it did not appear in my dreams either. But the day after I saw it emerging from the corridor again, taking its time as usual. I followed stealthily at a distance. It went into the garden, came to a halt under the big pear tree on the lawn, and waited . . . I began to approach, it didn't move. I drew very close, bent down and stroked its back — it purred and began to rub itself against my leg. Then I dropped onto the cool lawn, still damp from the dew, and took the cat on to my lap. It let me. I stroked it again and again and looked into its eyes, which were now, unlike my dream, light blue and transparent as glass. As I stroked, my fingers crept closer and closer to its neck, and suddenly I wrapped them round it, the fingers of both hands, and began to squeeze, harder and harder. The cat uttered one brief wail, and was silent. It twitched and jerked, trying to reach my face, but I held it at arm's length. I squeezed harder and harder, its eyes grew very round and protruded from its head, and in the end it stopped twitching. A long, narrow tongue, like a pink ribbon, poked out at me. It seemed to me that it was still moving, and I went on squeezing. In the end I threw it down in disgust. It fell on to the lawn with a dull thud and lay still, with its legs outspread. I jumped up. It had to be hidden, but the idea of touching it filled me with revulsion. However, I had no choice. I gripped it by the tip of its tail and carried it to the raspberry bushes next to the fence and hid it there. That evening I removed it and threw it into the river."

There was a short pause. Then Gurdweill said:

"A strange, nasty story . . . very nasty indeed . . ."

Unconsciously he turned to look at the cat, which was still lying on Poldy's lap. He felt vaguely ashamed and was unable to look Freddy in the eye. The latter had dwelt on the details with a strange, sadistic enjoyment, he thought. No doubt this cat, too, would come to the same sticky end . . . Gurdweill was horrified by his own thoughts, which he suddenly suspected Freddy of being able to read without the intervention of words. He tried to think of something to say to distract Freddy's attention, but his mind was a blank. Thea was still talking to Poldy. When would they sit down to eat? For a moment he imagined that he felt an emptiness in his stomach. At any rate he wanted to get the meal over and leave. Suddenly he heard himself saying:

"I can manage half a schilling, if that's any help to you."

Freddy did not reply immediately. After a moment he said simply:

"All right, let's have it!"

He took the coin and dropped it disdainfully into his inside jacket pocket, without looking at Gurdweill. The impression which his story had made on his brother-in-law gave him obvious satisfaction. As he stood up he whispered into his ear, smiling strangely:

"You'll see, his end will come too — that one there, I mean . . ."

"No, why?" Gurdweill protested in alarm. "Don't do it, Freddy! It's ugly!"

In his mind's eye he saw Freddy squeezing the cat's neck with his bony fingers, and an inexpressible disgust welled up in him. But Freddy was already walking round the room again, his hands in his trouser pockets, his head bent and slightly tilted to one side, as if he were pondering some complex problem.

The Baroness then appeared with the Baron behind her. The latter announced:

"We're going to eat, children!"

The meal dragged on interminably. Gurdweill felt irritable and impatient. He was sitting next to Freddy and could not avoid thinking of what he had told him, with the

239

result that he lost his appetite completely. The old Baron ate heartily, his face flushed with pleasure and exertion, praising the food and the Baroness, who for lack of a maid was obliged to keep running back and forth to the kitchen, holding forth on politics and the grave economic situation, and from time to time asking Gurdweill respectfully for his opinion. Immediately after coffee, when the Baron reclined on the sofa to smoke his customary cigar, Thea and Gurdweill took their leave. Outside Thea said that she was late for her appointment and hurried off.

21

GURDWEILL began walking towards the city centre. He had no idea as yet of where he was going, but he was glad to be alone again. The penetrating cold of the morning had grown somewhat milder. There was a faint wind blowing too, which seemed to give off an imperceptible whiff of spring. Without hurrying, pausing frequently, he strolled down Währinger Strasse, which was steeped in a holiday atmosphere, passed the Old People's Home, where the clock said a quarter to three, reached the Schottentor, and turned right into the Ring, without any definite destination in mind. His spirits suddenly lifted, as if all the obstacles in his path had been swept away; his step quickened of its own accord. Whichever way you looked at it, everything was as it should be, from every point of view . . . what, pray, did he lack? Why, you might almost say that he was a man to be envied — without any exaggeration! . . . And if, God forbid, everything were lost, everything — he would still have himself, he himself, Gurdweill, with all his five senses intact. Five senses in good working order should be quite enough for anyone, no? The whole world was his!

Outside the Parliament building he hesitated unconsciously for a moment, like a hypnotized subject in a theatre-show the moment before he points at the person holding the hidden object in his hand, and turned into the side street. After taking a few steps he realized that he was in Lerchenfelder Strasse, and came to a halt. What was he looking for here? The moment the question crossed his mind it occurred to him that he was standing next to Lotte Bondheim's house. If this is what my feet command, he said facetiously to himself, I must obey them. They know best . . . And he took the elevator up to the second floor.

The maid left him in the lobby for a moment, and then she came back and led him into the drawing-room which was already familiar to him.

"Please wait here, sir. Fräulein Lotte will be with you in a moment."

He sat down in a brown leather armchair, and before long Lotte came in wearing her kimono and gave him her hand without showing any sign of surprise, as if she had been expecting him.

"I had a premonition that I would see you today. But I didn't know that you would actually honour me with a visit. I was about to get dressed and drop into the café. I have an appointment with Dr. Astel, but not until half past five. In any case, it's a good thing you came."

She drew up a chair, sat down, and gave Gurdweill a penetrating look.

"And where has Thea gone?" she asked suddenly.

"Thea's gone . . . she had to go somewhere . . ."

Lotte smiled ironically.

"If you have a cigarette," he added, "I'd be grateful. I forgot to buy any."

"Perhaps you'd prefer a cigar? Daddy smokes the best."

She slipped into the next room and returned with a fat cigar.

"See what it feels like for once to be Herr Bondheim, Director of the Agricultural Bank."

"Or Dr. Kreindel, who gives me my daily bread," joked Gurdweill, too.

And after taking a couple of puffs:

"Not bad at all! The rich know how to live!"

Lotte was paler than usual. Her pallor was conspicuous against the dark colours of her robe.

"I don't like Sundays and holidays," she said. "They're so boring."

She stood up and opened the door to the passage a crack, and called out to the maid to make tea.

A person at home is like a fruit without its skin, reflected Gurdweill. His slightest gesture reveals some intimate little secret. The tone, for instance, commanding and pleading at once, in which she called the maid . . .

242

Lotte returned and sat opposite her guest, tucking her robe around her knees. She took a cigarette from the box she had previously placed on the table next to her, lit it carelessly, and began blowing reddish-blue smoke-rings, one after the other. The short winter's day was growing increasingly darker. A bleak silence filled the house, as if there were nobody living there.

"Aren't your parents at home?"

"No, they went out to 'enjoy themselves.' It's the same every holiday. They go to a café together and sit there for an hour or two. Papa reads the newspapers and mama leafs through the magazines and fashion journals. My mother, I must tell you, is even more of a slave to fashion than I am. She's always nagging me about not being smartly enough dressed, and sending me to the dressmaker or to buy a new hat. When they've done with the papers, they begin discussing how to marry me off. It's their favourite topic of conversation. Finding me a husband is their main aim in life. After that, if the weather's fine, they go for half an hour's stroll, and then they come home. If I'm at home when they return, papa tells me that it's time for us to have 'an important talk.' Always with the same portentous expression on his face, as if it was some historical occasion. He points commandingly to a chair, probably with the same gesture he uses with his clerks in his private office at the bank. My mother is usually present at these sessions, too. I sit and wait and so does my father. After a short silence he asks me, always the same two words: 'Well, Lotte?' I pretend I don't understand. 'When are you going to invite us to your wedding?' ... Me: 'I don't know yet. I haven't got anyone to marry. Nobody wants me.' 'That's not so, Lotte,' says my father solemnly. And my mother chimes in: 'No, it's not true, Lotte. You're the one who doesn't want anybody.' At this, everyone falls silent. After a moment papa says, as if he's just been struck by a brilliant idea: 'What about Dr. Astel, for instance? He wants you.' ... And he darts a penetrating look in my direction to see how I react. 'We'll have to wait and see,' I say ... A pause. After this there are a few more short, stiff questions on the same subject, and the 'important talk'

243

is over. The same conversation takes place about once a week, always according to exactly the same formula, and always on Sundays or holidays. On the other days of the week we talk about everything under the sun, but never about that."

The maid brought in tea and a selection of sweetmeats.

"How old is your mother, Lotte?"

"Forty-five."

"I'd never have guessed. She looks younger. By six or seven years at least."

Lotte stood up and switched on the electric light, which filled the room with a dense, brilliant, orange light. As she poured the tea, Gurdweill watched her graceful, rounded movements and thought: she really is a wonderful girl, this Lotte. A "thoroughbred." She really deserves to be loved . . . if I didn't love . . . What a strange nightmare I had last night . . . By daylight things take on their proper proportions, their true colours . . . A nightmare like that can make a man desperate. Thank God nights like last night come to an end.

"What lovely hands you've got, Lotte," he found himself saying.

"Have you only noticed now? A little late in the day . . ."

"No, not only now. I've known it for a long time. They have a life of their own . . ."

He took her hand and examined it:

"They're like two kind, beautiful little living creatures. You could look at them forever without getting tired."

"Very nice!" said Lotte, a pleased, excited blush covering her face. "And now let's have our tea."

She stirred her tea, gripped the handle of the tea cup between her thumb and forefinger, and with her other fingers daintily curled and fanned out, began taking little sips with her full lips pursed and protruding slightly towards the rim of the cup. Soft sucking sounds trembled intimately in the air, giving rise to an indefinable happiness . . .

Lotte put her cup down. Her grey eyes were suddenly overcast with a sadness which was not lost on Gurdweill. She must have remembered something sad, he said to

244

himself, and sensed a faint melancholy welling up in him, too. And suddenly something wonderful happened to him: he saw a vision, a kind of daydream, which lasted no more than three or four minutes, but was so vivid in all its details that its reality could not be denied. He saw her, Lotte, as a little girl, with her auburn hair curling wildly round her head. She was wearing a light, knee-length, pure white dress, for it was summer, perhaps a summer afternoon. She was standing all alone in a broad, grassy meadow. Then she took a few hesitant steps, changed her mind and stood still again. She raised her hand to shade her eyes against the sun, and gazed intently into the distance. After a moment a man much taller than her and wearing a straw hat appeared and approached her from the side (Gurdweill only saw him when he was right next to her), bent down and said something to her. Lotte turned to face him, examined him from top to toe, and took a step away from him. But the man stretched out both his hands, as if to embrace her, and his cane fell to the ground. Lotte began to run, to run as fast as she could, her hair waving in the wind. At first the man made a movement as if to pursue her. But he immediately changed his mind and bent down to pick up his stick, which he brandished in the air as he stood and watched her flee. Lotte was already far away from the man, but she went on running through the meadow without looking behind her. Suddenly she stumbled and fell. She tried to get up, but was unable to do so. She remained on the ground, lying on her side, her face distorted with pain and tears. The man, who had seen her fall from where he stood, ran up to her, picked her up, and carried her for some distance until he reached a house which he entered through a green, latticed gate. Afterwards Gurdweill saw Lotte lying in bed, her face pale and her eyes closed, with a number of people standing around her, among them the man who had brought her there. And here the vision ended.

"Did you ever fall as a child and have to stay in bed afterwards?"

"Yes. As a matter of fact, I was just thinking about it. How did you know?"

245

"I just saw it. And who was the man in the straw hat who carried you home?"

Lotte stared at him, petrified.

"But how do you know? I never told you about it."

"I know. I just saw it. It was in a broad meadow, in the summer. You were wearing a white dress and standing by yourself . . ."

"Yes, that's right. The man was my uncle. He was staying with us in our holiday cottage. He died three years ago."

She reflected for a moment, her eyes downcast, and then added:

"I felt a sudden fear. He took me by surprise. And there was something in his tone, not his words, that held a hidden threat."

"Strange," grunted Gurdweill to himself, his eyes fixed on Lotte, who was sitting leaning back in her chair, playing with a box of matches.

He put the empty tea cup down and said enthusiastically:

"Isn't it wonderful, in spite of everything, to be alive, even to suffer?"

"To suffer?" repeated Lotte with sudden annoyance, "That's a matter of taste. To my taste — no!"

She stood up. Gurdweill made to follow her example.

"Wait. I'm going to get dressed and then we'll go out together."

After taking two or three steps towards the door, she turned around and returned to Gurdweill, saying in a low, hesitant voice:

"My nerves are getting worse . . . I haven't been able to sleep for ages . . . God knows where it will end . . ."

Without thinking she sat down again. There was an expression of profound sorrow on her face, at the sight of which Gurdweill felt his heart contract. He wanted to say something but could not find the words. Silently he took her hand and pressed it gently.

"Sometimes you feel," said Lotte in a voice which shook slightly, "that you're rolling like a ball down a very steep hill, rushing into some abyss with terrible speed . . . You can actually feel the speed . . . And you're overcome by

246

despair at your utter helplessness ... At that moment, simply in order to defy the blind force controlling you, simply in order to assert your own individual will — however minutely, against the coercion of Nature, against the world, against yourself — you're capable of anything, anything ... You refuse to resign yourself to your fate ... You lie there in the middle of the night, abandoned to all kinds of strange ideas, which go in and out of your mind at will, as if it were public property. And then your face is suddenly revealed to you as in a distorting mirror: a grotesque, horrifying face, not yours and yet — inescapably yours ... As if you've been stirred round and turned upside down ... And the night's black and smooth, like a huge, menacing beast, biding its time. And over there, in the room next door, your parents are sleeping. I don't think of them at all but I know they're there, as surely as if they were part of my own body, and I choke on the knowledge ... And what if — the insane idea suddenly flashes into my mind — what if I were to get up now, steal into their bedroom on tiptoe and beat in their skulls with a hammer, first my father's and then my mother's? ... And I suddenly know, with the clarity of a vision, exactly where the wooden mallet is kept in the kitchen, although I have never used it in my life and never seen it more than once, and I can even hear, quite distinctly, the dull thud as the two hard objects meet ... And I feel a cramp and a strange tingling in my fingers, and then a hidden pain, which I cannot at first locate. And suddenly I realize that my nails have dug so deeply into my thigh that it's bleeding ...

"And all this," Lotte began again, after panting for breath as if she were choking, "not because I have some grudge against my parents. Not at all — you could even say I loved them. Papa, and mama, too. True, not the blind, animal love you sometimes come across between children and their parents. I'm perfectly well-aware of their absurdities — they stick up like humps on the flat surface of their boring little lives. But I'm attached to them nevertheless. And all of a sudden in the middle of the night, to have an idea like that ..."

Lotte breathed heavily, her bosom heaving. Suddenly

she stared straight at Gurdweill until he dropped his eyes in confusion. With an evident effort, she said:

"Perhaps . . . perhaps it doesn't have to be this way . . ."

Gurdweill was afraid that she was about to say something even more terrible than what she had already said, something that would in some way involve him, too, and he prepared himself inwardly. But Lotte said no more. She stood where she was for a moment longer, then stood up and turned to leave the room. In a state of shock Gurdweill watched her feet in their silken slippers, step after step being swallowed up in the soft Persian rug. The whole house suddenly seemed to him to be full of dread, as if a murdered body were hidden there. He too stood up and began walking round the room, full of pity for Lotte, who seemed to him a desperately ill woman. He went over to the window and drew the curtain aside. The asphalt on the short, deserted street gleamed blackly and wetly. It seemed that no one would ever stray into this desolate street, and that the lamps cast their dim light into it in vain. Gurdweill's heart contracted, as if squeezed by an invisible hand. The gnawing sadness of the empty street settled into his soul and made him forget everything else. It seemed to him that he had been standing there for many years, and that he was tasting the very essence of life. And it occurred to him that he had once stood like this before, next to a window overlooking a short, empty street on a rainy evening, wrapped in the same mood as now, but he could not remember where and when it had been. Perhaps it had only been in a dream or in his imagination, something once fleetingly perceived and now superimposed on the present scene, together with the traumatic feelings associated with it, as sometimes happens to sensitive people . . . Gurdweill went on standing there, unconscious of the passing of time or the fact that Lotte had entered the room, until her clear voice broke into his reverie. He started violently, as if waking from a deep sleep, and stared blankly at Lotte, who was standing next to him wearing a hat and wrapped in a black fur, ready to go out. He suddenly remembered what she had told him before, and he shuddered.

"I didn't know that you could dress so quickly," he said,

taking his coat from the sofa where he had left it when he came in.

And as if deliberating with himself he suddenly said: "The best thing to do, it seems to me, is to consult a doctor . . . and without delay . . . there are drugs for insomnia . . ."

In a sudden, incomprehensible burst of anger, Lotte exclaimed, her face flushed:

"What are you talking about, a doctor? You really are an imbecile!"

She immediately controlled herself and continued, more calmly:

"Let's go. I always dress quickly. Half an hour at the most." And she opened the door with a hard little laugh, which for some reason tore at Gurdweill's heart like a cry of pain.

In the Café Herrenhof they found Ulrich sitting with Dr. Astel and his friend from Berlin, a shy man with a timid expression in his eyes, whose age and occupation were difficult to guess. When Dr. Astel introduced him as Herr Bloch, he smiled in embarrassment, as if being called Bloch and being there made him guilty of some kind of crime. After the introduction he remained standing, making vague, unfinished gestures as if to indicate that he would be happy to give up his seat to Fräulein Lotte. But she had taken Ulrich's seat. When everyone was safely seated he dropped into his chair with all the relief of a man who has finally completed some arduous task.

Lotte, who was sitting diagonally opposite him, inquired:

"Herr Bloch comes from Berlin, I understand?"

"Yes," replied Bloch, blushing faintly, "that is to say, I live in Berlin."

"I was there once," said Lotte. "I didn't like it. It's like something written in copperplate, without any signs of individuality. Herr Bloch lives in Kurfürstendamm, I presume?"

"No. I suppose I should have lived there . . . but I happen to live in Freiburg Strasse."

"Why on earth should you have lived in Kurfürstendamm?" Dr. Astel laughed.

249

"I don't know," said Bloch in confusion, "I just feel I should . . . Presumably because I don't like it in the least, and since one is usually obliged to live under conditions which are the opposite of one's true inclinations . . ."

"Not everyone!" pronounced Dr. Astel.

"And how do you like Vienna?" inquired Lotte. "First impressions are always interesting."

"A city with a heart, in my opinion. One could grow fond of such a city, I imagine. But I can't say anything definite yet. I've only been here for three days."

For a while they spoke of different cities, and then the conversation turned to the German nation. Gurdweill took no part. The café was full of holiday visitors, unfamiliar faces never to be seen here on ordinary weekdays. It was very hot and stuffy, the air was so thick you could cut it with a knife. A place to be avoided by anyone susceptible to headaches. At the table to the right of them sat a corpulent man with a pale, plump face like a eunuch's, blowing his cigar smoke right into Gurdweill's face without taking any notice of the angry looks the latter darted in his direction. In the end Gurdweill said to him:

"Pardon me, sir, do you think you could blow your smoke in another direction and not straight into my face?"

The man looked at him insolently for a moment and said in a plump, self-satisfied voice:

"Certainly, sir," — blowing another cloud of smoke into Gurdweill's face as he spoke.

Gurdweill moved his chair noisily and turned his back on the man.

"What a swine!" he muttered to himself, but loudly enough to be overheard.

"What? What did you say, sir?" His neighbour tapped him on the shoulder with his knuckles as if knocking on a door. "Please repeat what you just said!"

Gurdweill jumped up, his face burning.

"I must ask you to leave me alone, just leave me alone!" he repeated in a trembling voice, bending down and thrusting his face into the other's.

The man apparently took fright and said in a conciliatory tone:

"Calm youself, sir, I beg you, nobody's trying to provoke you. Your nerves must be very poor."

"My nerves are nothing to do with you! Mind your own business!"

The whole exchange took place in whispers and was over in a moment, without attracting any particular attention. It seemed that the two of them were acquainted, and having met by chance, were taking the opportunity to exchange a few casual remarks. Only Lotte noticed that something was amiss.

Gurdweill resumed his seat at the table. His anger disappeared, as if swept away by a storm. When he raised his eyes, he saw Lotte looking at him and began smiling for no apparent reason. She leaned towards him over the table and whispered:

"You taught him a lesson, that fat pig!"

If only he was capable of treating his wife in the same way, she thought, how different everything would be!

"Will you join us for supper, Gurdweill?" said Dr. Astel.

He could not say. He was waiting for Thea to arrive.

When was he expecting her?

"At about six."

"Well it's nearly seven now. We'll wait another half an hour. If she comes, we'll all go together."

At that moment Thea appeared.

"Here comes Thea!" cried Lotte, who was sitting facing the door.

"You're rather pale, my dear," said Thea to Lotte, after greeting them all and sitting down on her husband's chair, "it's a long time since I saw you last. The winter seems to have disagreed with you." She suppressed a spiteful smile. "Let's hope that summer will restore you . . ."

Lotte did not reply.

"Why don't you drop in to visit us one day, my dear? You know our address, I think."

"You're always so busy . . . even in the middle of the night . . . the time never seems right to pay you a visit . . ."

"The middle of the night!" Thea laughed. "I am very busy, it's true. And not with nonsense either, my dear . . . But for you I'm prepared to put everything else aside.

251

Just say when it's convenient for you, and I'll be at your disposal. Besides, Rudolfus is home every night. Isn't he worth anything in your eyes?"

"On the contrary," replied Lotte gravely, "in my opinion he's worth a great deal, more than a thousand others . . ."

"Come, come, let's not exaggerate. If I didn't know better, I'd think that you were in love with him, ha ha . . . But you really are exaggerating, my dear. Here I can claim superior knowledge, I think . . ."

The men were engaged in a conversation of their own and paid no attention to their whispers. Gurdweill was now sitting at the other end of the table, too far away to overhear them. But he sensed that Thea was talking about him, and this made him feel uneasy. The room suddenly seemed unbearably hot. He longed to go outside for a breath of fresh air. It's a crime to come into this place on a holiday, he said to himself — the ugly faces, the stuffiness, the heat . . !

Lotte suddenly flared up and interrupted Thea in a furious whisper:

"You should be ashamed of yourself! Yes, ashamed to talk about your husband like that! I happen to know him very well indeed! I knew him before you did! Shame on you!"

"Why are you so excited, my dear," said Thea with affected calm, "there's no reason for you to excite yourself . . . In a minute I really will think that you're madly in love with him . . ."

"What if I am?" cried Lotte, hostile sparks shooting from her eyes, "what if I am? You can think what you like — who cares what you think? But I'll tell you one thing: all the men that you, that you go around with, aren't worth his little finger! They're not worth the dust on his shoes!"

"Please don't exaggerate, child," sneered Thea. "What do you understand about men? There, there, baby!"

"What you understand about men doesn't interest me in the least! I don't want your kind of understanding! Your men are nothing to me! Nothing! I don't need to take whatever comes to hand! I can pick and choose! I'm young enough and pretty enough for the pick of the bunch!"

"For Rudolfus, in other words?" Thea laughed cattily. "No, my little one! You won't get him! Not because I need him. But you won't get him! I've got him exactly where I want him and I won't let him go! I can do what I like with him — I even hit him, and often! How do you like that? I hit him as much as I like, for my own private pleasure — and he'll never leave me! As long as I don't kick him out, he'll never leave me! I could kick him out whenever I felt like it, I don't need him in the least. But I won't do it! And you won't get him! I'll torment him to death, to death I tell you, because it gives me pleasure — and still he won't leave me of his own free will!"

"You snake! You wicked bitch! Women like you should be flogged, whipped like dogs! Put in jail! You should be . . . you'll see! You'll come to a bad end! You'd better look out!"

"Is that a threat or a prophesy, my beauty? Perhaps you would be kind enough to tell me?"

Lotte was silent. Her heart was beating fit to burst. She felt as if her head were trapped inside a blazing furnace. She exerted all her self-control in order not to fall on the woman next to her and choke the breath out of her body. She would have given her life for the pleasure of doing it! She had never felt such hatred for another human being before. A hatred which could drive a person insane.

"You really are angry with me, aren't you, my dear? Why don't we forget all about it . . . It would be a shame to let such nonsense spoil our friendship, don't you think?"

And with a conciliatory gesture she placed her hand on Lotte's, which was resting on the table. Lotte shook it off with an expression of revulsion, as if some loathsome insect had settled on her hand.

"Leave me alone!" she said. "There's no friendship between us! I don't make friends with fishwives!"

"Dear me! What a little snob she is! Who would have thought it? How amusing! We must have a long talk one day . . . You interest me, my dear . . ."

"But you don't interest me!"

Lotte turned to Dr. Astel and suggested that they make

a move: the heat was terrible. He beckoned to the waiter, who seemed in no hurry to bring their bill.

"Will you be staying in Vienna long, Herr Bloch?" Thea inquired.

"I don't know yet. Two or three weeks."

Thea gave him an appraising look. She remembered what Dr. Astel had once told them about him and decided to have a little fun at his expense.

"And how do you like Viennese women?" she asked with a smile. "Are they prettier than the women in Berlin?"

"I . . . I don't . . . I haven't had a chance . . . I haven't really thought about it yet . . ."

"What's there to think about? Here you are — just have a look!" She made a sweeping gesture round the café. "As many women as you like! You can make up your mind in a minute! Take Fräulein Lotte, for example — isn't she pretty?"

"Indeed she is! Fräulein Bondheim is very pretty! You'd have to go a long way to find such a pretty girl."

He spoke with great solemnity, even reverence, keeping his eyes lowered to the table. "You see, sir! Beauties wherever you look!" Thea laughed. And turning to Lotte:

"There you are, my dear — men compliment you thanks to me, and you're not in the least grateful!"

There was so much cynicism in her tone that everyone began to feel uncomfortable. For a moment there was an uneasy silence, and Gurdweill for some reason felt himself to blame, but as always in similar circumstances, this time, too, he found nothing to say. It was the diligent Dr. Astel once again who broke the uncomfortable silence:

"Well, gentlemen, are we going to have supper together or aren't we?"

In the lobby Thea found the right moment to exchange a few friendly words with Bloch and make an appointment with him for the following afternoon.

22

ON the red and blue trams masses of human beings were carted to their day's labour from the suburbs to the city centre, and from there to the suburbs again. They were mainly young people of both sexes, torn from the sweetest part of their slumbers by the necessity of earning their daily bread, and busy now, as they stood shoulder to shoulder in the crowded coach, demolishing the remnants of buttered rolls wrapped in grey, transparent paper. The interval between sleep and work was very short, barely sufficient for the journey itself, with the result that the one often invaded the territory of the other, to the annoyance of their employers. But a new day, a forerunner of spring, was rising in the carefree, abandoned city of Vienna, whether the people crowded in the noisy, rattling trams saw it or not. The streets seemed clearer, more spacious, more polished, like a picture-postcard of some other, distant, unknown city. These handsome streets were close at hand, you trod them underfoot, but nevertheless your heart longed for them with all its might, and you felt a strange urge to get into a train and travel a few hours in order to reach them . . Others, wiser and more prescient, had risen early to greet the glorious day, as if they had known in advance of its coming. They, too, had eaten hastily and hurried outside, where you could see them now with their dogs — that long, slender pointer, for example, standing on three legs next to the first lamppost and thrusting his alert head into the crisp morning air.

Yes, it was a day to gladden the heart and arouse new hope. And since he had risen early in the morning, Gurdweill decided to walk to work. His coat had grown very shabby during the winter months, the edges of the sleeves and pockets were frayed, and in the light of the young spring day it looked even more worn than it was. But Gurdweill did not notice. As he strolled along Praterstrasse there was a rebellious springiness in his step. On a day like this it was even harder than usual to have to go to the office and spend eight hours in the company of Dr. Kreindel. Even the posters outside the Karlstheater, advertising *The Merry Widow* in huge red letters, upon which Gurdweill never bestowed a glance, now compelled his attention as part of the other, free life, so completely different from that in the back room of the bookshop.

It was still rather chilly; a delicate layer of frost on the pavement had not yet altogether melted. But it would certainly be very warm in two or three hours' time, and in the fields the farmers would doubtlessly be sowing the newly-tilled soil.

A smell of burnt coffee beans wafted out of one of the houses, and as Gurdweill entered its ambience something black and shapeless flashed into his mind, trailing behind it, beyond his reach, another black, that of the previous night, with the exchange between himself and Thea which had begun in the light of the oil-lamp and continued after it had been extinguished, from bed to bed. Money, money, money! — Gurdweill groaned — but where to get it? True, she needed extra nourishment now for the unborn baby, but what more could he give her? He was already living on a subsistence diet, and sometimes he went without even that! And what she had said — no! It simply wasn't true! A slip of the tongue, that was all, to provoke him. If it had been true, would she have said it — even in a rage? Inconceivable! And she hadn't said whose it was either . . . "The child isn't even yours!" . . . Out of the blue! No! She was angry, that was all, and she lashed out with whatever came into her head. She always liked teasing him. Like the way she had kept on threatening to "get rid" of it — and look what happened in the end! And now she had invented this new lie for him. And if it was really true? Unconsciously he stopped walking. Well . . . then . . . A baby was a baby . . . Since it was hers it would be his anyway . . . It was his child and nothing else mattered a damn! If it came to that — there wasn't a father in the world who could swear that his child was really his! Who could be sure? And why should he, Rudolf Gurdweill, be an exception to the rule? No, he had to stop bothering himself with idle speculation. The child was his, and that was that!

But Gurdweill's good mood was spoilt nevertheless. The spring morning already seemed alien, not for him. The thought of all the days to come, which he would have to spend with Dr. Kreindel or some other Dr. Kreindel, weighed heavily on him. Suddenly he felt old and tired. He huddled deep down into his coat, like a man locking his doors and drawing his blinds in the middle of the day, and bowed his head in submission to necessity.

In the bookshop he greeted his colleagues curtly and immediately retired to the back room. Dr. Kreindel had not yet arrived. He took off his coat and sat down at his desk. He found a few cigarette stubs and a paper in his jacket pocket and began rolling a new cigarette with the used tobacco. Should he ask him for a few schillings in advance? Yes. Only a small sum — ten schillings! Somewhat reassured by this idea, he removed the black oilcloth cover from his typewriter and began typing a letter, the cigarette stuck to his lower lip.

Soon afterwards Dr. Kreindel appeared and greeted him with a hearty "Good morning!"

"A lovely day, eh?" he said as he took off his coat. "A day for poets! On a day like this you would prefer to wander round the streets, or take a trip out of town, wouldn't you my dear Herr Gurdweill? Don't deny it! I understand you only too well! Don't I belong to that exalted family of poets and artists myself? Ha ha, you know I do . . ."

Gurdweill went on typing and pretended not to hear.

"What? Did you say something?" he asked.

"And if I did? Of course I said something, something worth its weight in gold! But great men never listen to anyone but themselves . . . In the words of Gottfried Keller: 'The word of genius is spoken by one individual to an entire generation' . . . etc."

He settled himself into his chair behind his desk and began reading the morning's mail. He disfigures everything, reflected Gurdweill as he went on typing. On the

257

wall opposite, in the courtyard, there was a vivid triangle of sunlight, which lay there for some time without changing its shape. For about an hour and a half the rapid clattering of the typewriter and the rustle of paper filled the office. Then Gurdweill collected the pile of letters and took them over to his employer for his signature. Dr. Kreindel handed him the morning's correspondence, told him how to reply, and asked him to examine the accounts from the beginning of March as well, since it seemed to him that there was a mistake somewhere. Gurdweill took the letters and the ledger and retured to his desk.

"How would you like a good cigar?" Dr. Kreindel suddenly asked.

"A bad sign!" thought Gurdweill and went up to take the cigar. At the same time he took the opportunity of asking for the ten schillings advance.

"Of course I'll let you have it, my dear sir! With pleasure! Remind me to give it to you later."

As Gurdweill turned away he struck a match and offered it to him to light his cigar.

"Yes," he added, "I wanted to ask you how your work was getting on. It's a long time since we discussed it . . . I mean your real work, of course, the work which will make you immortal, not the work you do here, which is quite irrelevant as far as intellectuals like us are concerned . . ." He bared his gold teeth in a twisted smile. "You see, sir, great minds think alike: when I say 'work' you may be sure that I mean the work you do at home, your literary work, which is 'done in the dark and spreads its light from one end of the world to the other' — in the words of the great Goethe himself!"

"If it's 'done in the dark,' it can hardly be discussed in public," Gurdweill laughed.

"In public! Of course not in public! I agree with you that it can't be discussed with any Tom, Dick or Harry! Nobody knows that better than me . . . in public — no! But to me, your friend and fellow writer, surely you need have nothing to hide from me . . . And good advice is not to be despised either! And who can give better, more discriminating advice than me? An expert is another

matter entirely! 'If only we left it to the experts . . .' —
who said that? It's slipped my mind for the moment.
In any case, whoever said it knew what he was talking
about . . ."

Gurdweill returned to his desk and sat down, facing Dr.
Kreindel. The aromatic cigar relaxed him and immunized
him, as it were, to the latter's sarcasms. He even derived a
certain pleasure from his prattle, as if it were concerned
with someone else entirely.

Dr. Kreindel continued:

"And that I am an expert on literature, my friend, you
have surely realized by now . . . Especially with regard to
your own writing — precisely because it's so deep . . . I'm
not interested in superficialities. 'A good swimmer needs a
deep river' — as the proverb says."

"But what if I don't need any advice?" smiled Gurdweill.

"So everything's going smoothly, is it? Well, that's a
different matter, of course! Nevertheless, good advice
from an expert can always come in handy!"

"Perhaps we can change the subject? This one's becoming boring."

"Change the subject? Oho, my friend, if only you knew!
Changing the subject would be even more boring . . . boring and unpleasant . . . As Kleist says: 'There is always
worse to come . . .' Unfortunately, that's the way of the
world . . . 'Change the subject!' If only I thought that it
would be more agreeable, I would change it immediately,
believe me. As you yourself know, my friend, the only sub-
jects I enjoy discussing are noble, exalted ones — simple,
mundane matters I like to get over as quickly as possible.
Because they are invariably unpleasant, and a fastidious
mind shrinks from dwelling on them. For example, if I
were obliged to inform you that you were being dismissed
from your post, let's say, that you were being given one
month's notice as of today — would you find this 'change
of subject' less boring?"

"It's all up!" said Gurdweill to himself. "This is the
swine's way of giving me the sack!" A torrent of conflicting
feelings engulfed him and sent the blood rushing to his
head. He even felt a sense of satisfaction, which struggled

to push all his other feelings aside and rule in their stead. Suddenly he realized that his cigar had gone out. With a vigorous flick of his finger he knocked off the ash and lit it again. One more month — and then . . ! But what would Thea say? Something thick and hard rose up inside him and stuck in his gorge. He tried to swallow it down again and swallowed a mouthful of bitter cigar smoke, which made him want to retch. Mechanically he took out his handkerchief and spat into it, hawking noisily two or three times.

Dr. Kreindel continued in a portentous tone:

"With people of our calibre, of course, one can never be sure. There are always surprises. Something which may seem unpleasant from the vulgar, material point of view, may give rise in us, for some mysterious reason, to precisely the opposite of the expected reaction. Precisely the opposite. As the Persian saying goes, 'it's an ill wind, etc. . .' Aren't I right, my dear Herr Gurdweill? In the above circumstances one of us might well say to himself: 'What, from such and such a day we'll be unemployed? Exactly what we were hoping for! From now on we'll be free to work unimpeded at our true vocation, which is the only thing that counts . . . isn't that so? As for eating and drinking and so on — what do people like us care about such things?' . . . You see, my friend, I know this line of thought inside out — at first hand, you might say, since my nature is exactly the same. I've already told you, I think, that you and I are almost twins — twins in the spiritual, intellectual sense of course, which is the only sense that matters to people like us!"

"In short," said Gurdweill, making a strenuous effort to speak in a normal tone of voice, "I take it that you're giving me a month's notice from today?"

"Can there be any doubt about it, my friend? To my regret, to my regret! Business is bad, I have no choice. But who will suffer from it most? Certainly not you. As I say, you're probably delighted. From now on you can abandon yourself to your literary labours and forget the rest of the world — but what about me? Who will make up to me for the loss of your precious company? You'll forget

260

Dr. Kreindel in a jiffy, I promise you, from the hair on his head to the boil on his bum, in the words of the popular saying, hee hee ... Vanished into the blue, as far as you're concerned! But it will be a long, long time before I forget the inspiration of the profound intellectual discussions we held in this office, believe me! Drawing on that well-spring of divine abundance ... etc., etc ... who said it? Schiller, I believe ... I can't remember at the moment. You see, the strength of my emotions is affecting my memory ... Yes. To get back to the subject, I have to praise you to your face, my dear Herr Gurdweill: there isn't another man in the world to whom I could speak so frankly, so intimately, as you. Can you deny it?! Intelligent people don't grow on trees, you know. One or two in a generation — and that's it! Intelligent, I mean, like you and me ... Imagine my sorrow at the thought of losing you ... "

"And how long, for example, my noble, intellectual friend, can you go on ... talking like this?"

"Me? As long as you can go on ... keeping quiet like this, hee hee! Friends have to express their feelings before they part, you know, and if the one is too modest to say anything, the other is obliged to speak for both ... When you stop working here, you won't want to waste your precious time on coming here to have a little chat with poor Dr. Kreindel, will you? Admit it! And when will I ever have the chance to enjoy your charming company again? Only now, when the hour of parting approaches, can I begin to estimate the depths of my attachment to you ... As for yours to me — it's scarcely the same thing, is it? Don't deny it, one feels such things immediately! Why, it's just like an unhappy love affair, with one party dying of love and the other smiling scornfully, feeling nothing but pity and impatience. In our case, I'm afraid, the unhappy lover is me ... "

Gurdweill suddenly stood up and began walking slowly towards Dr. Kreindel. There was a wild expression on his face, which was very pale. Dr. Kreindel broke off abruptly and followed Gurdweill's every move as if he were watching a wild animal about to pounce on him at any moment. Gurdweill reached the desk and stood facing Dr. Kreindel.

261

For a moment he glared at him in silence, and then he said in a slightly hoarse whisper, measuring every word:

"You, Dr. Kreindel, do you want me to finish the letters this morning? Yes or no? If the answer is yes, then shut up! Just shut up!"

Suddenly the face opposite him looked like that of some unimaginably repulsive insect, and his rage changed instantly into a feeling of terrible nausea. His legs felt weak and exhausted, as if they had dissolved into water. Without waiting for an answer, he turned round and returned to his desk.

"Is that all, my dear?" sniggered Dr. Kreindel. "You needn't have troubled yourself to get up for that, hee-hee . . . Am I deaf? I can hear from a distance too, you know, especially words of yours, which are worth their weight in gold . . . You really shouldn't have bothered! As for the letters — what's the rush? If they're ready this afternoon it won't be a tragedy either! What are letters? When we have such important matters to discuss! Are we such gross materialists? This unique friendship of ours has nothing to do with such pettiness — you know it as well as I do. Us two — and letters! That's all for outward show, for small minds . . . But the true relationship between us is one of the spirit, the intellect . . . twin souls . . ."

Gurdweill flung the remnants of the cigar on to the floor in disgust, put a fresh sheet of paper into the typewriter, and began typing with a furious clatter which silenced Dr. Kreindel, who smiled smugly to himself. It was nearly midday, and the wall opposite was completely illuminated by the sun, which had already covered half the courtyard in its orange glow. "If only it were now!" — the thought snaked through the lines of the letter covering the paper in the typewriter — "Come what may, but now, right now! In the middle of a day like this. Another month — I can't stand it . . ." He heard Dr. Kreindel going into the shop and felt as if a current of fresh air had entered the room. If he had to wait another month — he continued the thread of his thought — the first, strong taste of happiness would be lost. Little by little he would get used to the certainty, and in the end he might even go to the other extreme and

262

regret the loss of his job. He removed the completed letter and glanced at his watch. It was time to go to lunch. And the ten schillings? No, he had better forget about it. He couldn't face the thought of asking Dr. Kreindel again. As he was about to leave, Dr. Kreindel came into the room.

"Ah, you asked me for ten schillings, didn't you? Here you are!" And he handed him the banknote. "*Bon appétit,* my dear friend!"

23

WHEN Gurdweill returned from work that evening, he did not find his wife at home. She came and went as the fancy took her: sometimes she didn't come home until after midnight. Gurdweill began lighting the stove, and as always when he was alone in the house, he soon succeeded. The stove was as capricious as an hysterical woman: sometimes it obstinately refused to burn and nothing helped, and sometimes it responded in a moment — one match was enough. Gurdweill made himself black coffee, a commodity of which they never ran short, and ate a slice of the delicious fresh bread which he had brought with him from the shop. After this meal he took his copybook from the suitcase where he kept his manuscripts hidden from Thea, and sat down to continue the story he had already begun, but on no account could he concentrate. His feelings were in a turmoil. If only Thea would come home early today, so that he could unburden himself of the news of his dismissal! He could already imagine the scene and hear his wife's abuse. Not only that, but he could also feel the guilt which he would no doubt feel later towards his furious wife. Two cigarettes, one after the other, did nothing to help him to concentrate his thoughts. Full of rage against some unknown person, he locked his copybook away, put on his coat and went out.

He had it in mind to take a short stroll along the Hauptallee. To this end he had to turn left when he came out of the gate, in the direction of Nordbahnstrasse, but his feet bore him to the right instead, and by the time he realized what was happening he was already at the corner of Kleine Stadtgutgasse and Heinestrasse. In that case, he said to himself, I might as well go this way and see what's going on in Praterstrasse. He therefore crossed the road, and continued along it until turning into Novaragasse, which ended in Praterstrasse. When he reached the end of the street he suddenly saw Thea at a distance of five paces, parting from a man he did not know. Gurdweill stood as if turned to stone. He wanted to run, so that Thea would not see him, but his feet refused to obey him, as in a nightmare. The strange man kissed her hand and Gurdweill heard him say: "Until tomorrow, then!" before jumping on to a passing tram. Thea turned towards Novaragasse and saw her husband. She walked straight up to him. Her anger was already full-blown, as if she kept it inside her, ready and waiting to be whipped out the moment the opportunity presented itself.

"Wha-at?! You dare to spy on me? Wait for me!"

Gurdweill did not move.

"Come on!" She reached him and pulled him hard. "You're coming home with me!"

Gurdweill silently obeyed, and went with her as if he were under arrest. As they approached the house he recovered and mumbled:

"But all I wanted was to go for a little walk. It was pure coincidence . . . I don't want to go home yet . . ."

Thea said nothing and Gurdweill went upstairs with her. They entered the room.

"Light the lamp!" ordered Thea.

"Take that!" she cried and slapped him on the cheek with all her strength the moment the lamp was lit.

"What, are you mad?" Gurdweill blurted out, bending down to pick his hat up from the floor.

"And if you ever dare to spy on me again — I'll kick you out of the house like a dog! Like a dog, do you hear? It's none of your business where I go or who I meet! And just for your information, if it's of any interest to you, I go to bed with as many men as I like — as many as I like! Including all your friends!"

Gurdweill stood and watched her. His mind was suddenly quite clear, as if the slap had sobered him up after many days of drunkenness. At this moment he felt no rage. But for the first time since he had met her he saw now, as if in the light of some inner illumination, that she was ugly, and what she had said about going to bed with as many men as she liked seemed ridiculous to him, impossible, an empty boast. He remembered the child. His child, who was going to be born in five months' time, if the doctors were right, and a pulse of happiness began to throb inside him. He went and sat down on the couch, just as he was, with his coat still on and his hat in his hand. But then he remembered that he wanted to go for a walk and he straightened up again. Thea was washing her hands at the basin. And suddenly Gurdweill said quietly, as if nothing had happened between them:

"Listen, Thea, Dr. Kreindel gave me the sack today. With one month's notice."

Thea turned her head and looked at him for a moment in silence.

"It's true. Business is bad, he says, and he has no choice but to let me go."

"You sound as if you were pleased about it," said Thea, and to his astonishment there was not a trace of the former rage in her voice. "I don't care where you get the money from — as long as you bring it!"

And she went back to scrubbing her hands.

"Or perhaps you imagine that I'm going to work to support you?"

"I don't imagine anything. What am I supposed to do? It's not my fault. I'll try to find money. I can give you five schillings now — I took it in advance."

"Good! Put it on the table. And the rest doesn't interest me! You know that I have to eat properly now because of the baby. Just don't forget it!"

" Of course I won't — how could I forget it?"

The fact that she had mentioned the baby now, and in connection with him too, made him blissfully happy. It meant that what she had said yesterday in so many words, and all the other hints she had been dropping lately, were nothing but a joke to tease and torment him. Only what she had just come out with, in all innocence, only that was true . . . and there was no more room for fruitless speculation! All at once all desire to go for a walk left him. He began taking off his coat, and changed his mind in the middle.

"Perhaps you'd like to go with me to the café?" He said, and added humorously: "Once a year it might be interesting to go with your husband for a change . . ."

He was sure she would refuse. But for some reason she consented, stipulating only that he make her a cup of coffee first. After drinking the coffee and lighting a cigarette, she called her husband and sat him on her lap.

"You're not really a coward at all, or are you, rabbit?"

"A coward? I don't know. Why?"

"I'm just curious. Who knows, one dark night I might take it into my head to strangle you in your sleep . . . Ha ha . . . Aren't you afraid?"

"I'm not afraid. You're not capable of it. Why should you do such a thing? And even if you did strangle me — I wouldn't care . . ."

Thea laughed. And as if trying it out, she put her hands around his neck and squeezed lightly.

"Like this, for example!" She laughed nastily and squeezed harder.

Gurdweill parted her hands. A sharp fear ran through his body like an electric current.

"You said when I was asleep, not when I was awake," he gave a forced smile.

Sitting on her lap began to make him feel uncomfortable. Thea suddenly seemed alien and terrifying, and for a moment he saw her as really capable of committing the act. For some reason he remembered his old fear as a child when, at night, he had to pass the only brothel in the little town. The building stood on a small hill on the edge of the town, set apart, and a dull reddish light shone through the red curtains on its narrow windows. Soldiers would sway drunkenly in front of it, and every time the door opened to let them in or out a gust of abandoned laughter, mingled with a loud banging on the piano, would be released into the street. Gurdweill was then fourteen years old, and had no idea of the true nature of the place, but he sensed that something special and extraordinary was going on inside it. He imagined some kind of robbers' den. That old fear of houses of prostitution had remained with him to the present day, and for some reason he remembered

267

it now. He jumped off his wife's lap, while she went on smoking reflectively, her eyes lowered. There was a heavy, disturbing atmosphere in the room. It seemed to Gurdweill that the light of the oil-lamp had dimmed, and he raised the wick.

"Well, do you want to go out or not?"

A few minutes later they were walking silently down Heinestrasse, arm-in-arm like a pair of lovers. After a while they turned left into Taborstrasse. It was chilly, but with the chilliness of the first evenings of spring, whose sting has already been blunted and through which you imagine that you can already smell the violets and the bursting lilac buds. Gurdweill was tingling with a quiet, buoyant expectation of something which was undefined but wonderful beyond measure. He believed that it was the general expectation of spring pervading all of nature now and welling up secretly in his own soul too, despite the barrier of the city and its agitations. And the fact that he still preserved the ability to sense the upheavals in nature in spite of everything, filled him with joy. The inner connection between himself and nature, which had been so strong before, in the small town of his birth, and even when he first came to the city, and which had grown weaker and weaker during the course of the years, especially the past year — this connection was still there, it had not been broken off completely, which meant that his instincts were still healthy and had not yet degenerated owing to the influence of city life. And this meant that he must still possess the youth and freshness which made it possible to create. At this moment Gurdweill felt instinctively that he was destined to write something tremendous and extraordinary, original from beginning to end, unlike anything the human spirit had ever conceived before. A great need came over him to tell someone about this feeling, a feeling which was the fullest expression of his true self, but he could not tell Thea. He knew only too well that she would greet any such confession with mocking laughter. From the moment he had become aware of her frivolous, contemptuous attitude towards this, essential, side of his nature, he had set aside a special compartment in his soul where Thea could not intrude. He kept her out. It would have been easier for him to reveal this corner to Lotte, for instance, than to his wife.

On the corner of Obere Augartenstrasse they were suddenly accosted by Franzl Heidelberger, who greeted them with a hearty laugh as usual, and barred their way.

"Ho ho, what an unexpected meeting! Very glad to see you! You're avoiding us, Herr Doktor! And the *Gnädige* Frau has not honoured us at all! No, your lady wife must pay us a visit — I insist! I won't take no for an answer! It would be an insult to our hospitality, isn't that so? And Herr Doktor himself! I always say to Gustl: 'Gustl,' I say, 'what's happened to our Herr Doktor, where has he disappeared to? Perhaps we didn't treat him with the proper respect? Or perhaps you offended him in some way? What did you do to him, to make him avoid our humble home?' 'Me?' says Gustl, 'I know nothing about it! I never did any harm to the Herr Doktor!' So there you are!"

Since that Sunday at the end of last summer, Gurdweill had not visited their home. Uneasily, he remembered what had happened between himself and Gustl on that occasion. He felt embarrassed and somewhat ashamed and wanted to get away from Heidelberger as quickly as possible.

"I was busy, my dear Herr Heidelberger," said Gurdweill, and immediately regretted "my dear," which seemed to him obsequious and also a kind of payment for services rendered, "so many troubles and cares."

"Who isn't busy? But where there's a will there's a way, I say — isn't that so, Frau Gurdweill? This very minute, for example, while we're standing here and chatting, we could just as well go up to my place. On condition, of course, that you have nothing more pressing to do! We jump on to a tram and we're there in ten minutes, believe me. What do you say?"

"It's late. Some other time — with pleasure. But why don't you come with us? We're going to sit in a café for a while."

"With the greatest of pleasure! If I can't make you change your minds!"

When they started walking, Heidelberger said:

269

"What an evening! A true spring evening! In the day-time a man is worse than a beast. Work and more work! Cows and pigs are better off than men! They get their food for nothing, at least, but we have to kill ourselves with work for a measly bit of bread. It isn't fair, I tell you. Not that I'm a Bolshevik! No sir, Heidelberger Franzl isn't such a fool! A Social-Democrat and proud of it! Yes indeed! A registered party member! But a Bolshevik — no siree! I don't need it! What for? Don't they work there under the Bolsheviks eight hours a day? So there you are! Man is worse off than a beast — here, in Russia and America — all over the world! There's no difference!"

They passed a tavern and Heidelberger pressed them to come in with him. They could go to the café later. Thea had no objections and they went in. "Today you're my guests, of course. What will you drink? A good old wine? Or perhaps a new one?"

When the waiter brought the wine Heidelberger poured it out with obvious enjoyment, and they touched glasses. After taking a gulp of wine and wiping his moustache with his hand, he continued:

"The evening is something else again! Here a man feels like a man, isn't that so? In the evening and at night — every man to his own pleasure. Cards, women, even theatres and books and so on — each to his own taste. I don't know how it is with you, Herr Doktor and Frau Baroness. (How did he know that she was a Baroness? Gurdweill wondered.) As for me, I can tell you one thing: cards — never! Cards don't mean a thing to me! For that you won't find me at home! Here you'll have to look for somebody else!"

"And what about women?" asked Thea slyly.

"Women are something else entirely! Here I won't say no! Thank God for women! But, I always say, you have to be careful. There are women and women! If you draw a bitch — pardon me for the expression, Baroness — she'll never give you a minute's peace! Heidelberger Franzl knows what he's talking about! Believe me! Here's to you, Herr Doktor and Frau Baroness! The wine's not bad, eh? A bit of wine beats everything, aren't I right? Not too

270

much, mind: half a litre or a litre is enough to make you happy."

"Have you got any children, Herr Heidelberger?"

"No, madam, not yet. But it won't be long now! A man must have a son! Otherwise his wife gets bored. And Gustl wants one too. And Heidelberger Franzl can afford the pleasure! I earn a pretty penny I can tell you!" He added proudly: "Foreman at a big machine factory — one rung below Engineer Schmidt himself! That's something!"

Gurdweill no longer wanted any wine, and he particularly wanted to prevent Thea from drinking, as he was afraid it might harm the baby. Apart from which, he now found himself for some unknown reason unable to bear Franzl Heidelberger's company, especially in Thea's presence. He was full of tense expectation, and his heart shrank from something unpleasant which he knew with absolute certainty was about to happen. He wanted to get away immediately, and pressed Thea to leave.

"What's your hurry, my friends?" said Heidelberger. "Why not have another drink? We meet so seldom! Gustl is always asking about you, Herr Doktor!" he added, giving Gurdweill a meaningful smile. "I'd say she was missing you, Herr Doktor! An excellent woman, don't you agree?"

Thea gave her husband a mocking, sidelong glance which cast him into confusion. He said nothing.

"Well, when will you come, Herr Doktor? What shall I tell Gustl? And the Baroness?" Heidelberger urged.

They promised to drop in when they had a chance, and rose to leave. Heidelberger was still "thirsty" and he remained behind. It was already half past ten, but they decided to go on to the café nevertheless.

"What kind of a woman is this Gustl?" asked Thea casually.

"A simple woman," said Gurdweill evasively, feeling rather uncomfortable, "there isn't much to say about her."

"But you seem to have had a big success with her. How strange . . ."

Gurdweill said nothing. How sharp their senses are! he reflected. She caught on immediately!

"That Heidelberger isn't half as much of a fool as he

looks. I'd like to get to the bottom of him one day . . .
What would you say, for instance, to a little swop?"

Gurdweill pretended he didn't know what she was talking about.

"It would be interesting . . ."

What could possibly be so interesting about it?

Gurdweill wanted to protest. But he restrained himself in time. Better to hold his tongue and not fan the flame of her lust by open resistance. If he kept quiet she might forget all about it. He hated the idea of Heidelberger touching his wife. Him especially . . . and with his own approval too! Never mind the others! He didn't know them and he didn't really know if it was true. But to have it out in the open, with a licence from him — no! If she had to, then let her do it in secret, without his knowledge . . . His consent was out of the question. If only her pregnancy were already over! When the baby came, everything would change for the better. Then nothing would matter. Then he would be able to bear everything easily.

Not a trace of his previous good mood remained. The old melancholy, which seemed to have become a permanent part of his personality, began to gnaw at his heart again. He no longer paid any attention to the evening air caressing his face with its cool, reviving touch, or noticed the rattling trams dashing to and fro in the spacious Schottenring. Perhaps it would have been better if he had gone for a walk by himself, as he had originally intended.

In the café they found Ulrich and Perczik exhuding an air of ancient boredom. They sat without talking, as if they had already said everything there was to be said to each other. Gurdweill was reminded of the attic in his parents' house, which they went up to once a year, their hands shrinking from contact with the dusty old junk collected there. They're worn out, thought Gurdweill, obsolete. Everything that they were capable of doing or saying to the end of their days was known to him in advance, and for a moment he tasted the quintessential boredom of it all. No, there was no room for surprises here! He would have liked to leave immediately, or, at least, to sit at a different table. But Thea made straight for their table. Both their faces lit up, as if an unexpected salvation was at hand. With much ado they raised themselves from their seats to greet the newcomers. For a while they chatted of this and that, without Gurdweill participating. Then Perczik told them something he had read in an American newspaper, about a beautiful young woman (he added these two adjectives himself, to create more of an impression), who had lost her right ear in a motorcar accident, and who had advertised in the newspaper that she was willing to pay five thousand dollars to anyone who would sell her a right ear . . . the ear had to be five and a half centimetres long, exactly. And in another edition of the paper he had read of the offer of a woman from Willington, who had an ear of the correct measurements for sale, but who was not prepared to part with it for under ten thousand dollars.

Ulrich fingered his ear with admiring affection, as if he had just discovered that a little stone which had been lying around in his house for years was actually a precious gem.

"I wouldn't sell it for anything!" he announced.

"And you, Perczik?" intervened Gurdweill. "You would, I bet! Just think: ten thousand dollars! And afterwards you could always find another, cheaper ear. Here in Europe you could probably pick up a good ear for two thousand . . . Add another thousand for the operation — and you're left with a clear profit of seven thousand dollars!"

"If you'll sell me your ear for two thousand, I'll sell mine for ten."

"I wouldn't sell mine for a million! I have nothing for sale! I need everything for myself! And anyway I don't need money."

"Nevertheless," laughed Thea, "if anyone wants to buy them I would suggest you sell them both, rabbit. Ten thousand dollars aren't to be sneezed at! But who would want to buy them?"

Perczik twisted his mouth into a spiteful smile. Gurdweill imagined an amputated ear, like the ones in illustrated ABC's for children, neatly wrapped in cotton wool and mailed to America in a little box . . . He felt a distinct

273

surge of nausea, as if he had eaten something too fatty to stomach. He pushed his unfinished coffee aside. But the disturbing picture, having once invaded his imagination, could not be banished. It grew of its own accord and took on a life of its own. In vain he tried to distract himself by playing with the coffee spoon. Now the important thing was for the ear to reach its destination safely. The hold at the bottom of the ship where they kept the mail must be swarming with rats ... And what if the box reached America empty? Some other means would have to be found ... The people in charge of such things presumably had tried and tested means at their disposal ... Imagine if such a thing happened to him, if his ear was eaten by rats! Gurdweill felt a kind of tickling in his ears, as if they were crawling with ants. Phoo! he said to himself. What nonsense!

"Rudolfus seems to have fallen asleep," he heard Thea say. "Did you drop off, rabbit? Let's go home."

Ulrich and Perczik stood up to go too. They'd been sitting in the café long enough, they said, as if they felt the need to apologize. But a walk in the fresh air would be nice, and they would be happy to accompany Gurdweill and Thea. On a night like this it would be a pity to go home so early.

And they all set off together, in spite of Gurdweill's sulky expression. Perczik's company was particularly unwelcome to him.

"You'll miss the last tram, Perczik, and you'll have to walk home," he said.

But Perczik was dauntless. "Then I'll walk!" he said. "Tonight it will be a pleasure!"

There was no way of getting rid of him.

They passed Tuchlauben, which was quiet at this hour, and turned into Graben as into a spacious, brightly lit drawing-room. The street was full of movement. Here amusement seekers and party-goers went from pleasure to pleasure. Cars drew up outside brightly-lit doorways, while others moved away. The smell of perfumed bodies mingled with the stench of the petrol fumes; dinner-jackets and magnificent evening gowns; Negro music and

274

wailing saxophones; stiff-backed doormen at the building entrances like red signposts. But a little further on, at the approach to Kärntner Strasse, everything was dominated by the silent, lofty St. Stephen's Cathedral, transported here directly from the Middle Ages with the dust of the journey still clinging to its ancient limbs. Its Gothic spires, like bony fingers, touched the night itself, the real night in the sky above, undisturbed by the puny city lights. It was a kind of go-between, thought Gurdweill, a mediator between the night above and the night below. A flower-seller and a hawker of oranges and bananas, two old ladies wrapped in layers of shawls, were still sitting behind their wares in front of the Cathedral, leaning against the wall as motionless as if they were part of the building itself, like the other statues decorating its façade. It was five to twelve by the Cathedral clock. Perczik changed his mind and said:

"I'm off to Schottentor. I can still catch the tram if I hurry!"

"How can you spend an entire evening with that man?" Gurdweill asked Ulrich when Perczik was some distance away. "You need the patience of a saint."

"I don't know what you've got against him," said Thea. "I can't see that he's worse than anyone else."

"He's worse! And a small-minded bore into the bargain."

"Too true!" agreed Ulrich. "But if he comes and sits down next to you, you can hardly chase him away."

Next to the canal Ulrich parted from them and set off down the Kai, his slow footsteps thudding hollowly on the pavement. Gurdweill looked lingeringly after him. A feeling of pity suddenly stirred in him for this man, whose life for some reason seemed to him utterly empty and forlorn. He felt a momentary impulse to catch up with his friend, say something kind and consoling to him and accompany him home, for it was unthinkable to leave him alone in such a state. At that moment Gurdweill saw himself as a happy man in comparison to Ulrich, a lucky man. He was all right — any way you cared to look at it! And if there were one or two little flaws, they were too insignificant to count . . . Not like Ulrich . . .

"How pathetic people really are. You see a man who

275

looks young and healthy, even high-spirited and everything seems fine. And suddenly an unconscious look, a
gesture, betrays his hidden wounds more clearly than any
long confession. There isn't enough pity in the world. Not
the crude, officious kind, but the mute, modest com-
passion that flows straight from one soul to another, without a word or even a gesture, and which alone is capable of
giving comfort and encouragement ... Perhaps this pity
will save the world ..."

Gurdweill, who thought he had been talking to himself,
was surprised to hear Thea's voice:

"The wishful thinking of the weak! They themselves
are pitiful and preach pity to the rest of the world! But
the world doesn't need pity. The world belongs to the
brave and the only hope for the weak is to hurry up
and get out of it as quickly as possible! There's no need
to prolong their agony ... or to worry about saving the
world either! The world can look after itself — it will go
on existing according to its own fixed, immutable laws!
Thanks to the strong, the elect, who operate according
to the same iron laws! Unknowingly, not of their own
volition, impelled by an imperative inner force. Thanks
to them, because of them, the world exists!"

"Nietzsche said the same thing and he was wrong. Since
the world is composed mainly of the weak — and the
heroes themselves are weak too — it obviously needs
them! And anyway, who are we to say who's needed here
and who isn't? How can we know the hidden intention
behind things? Everything in the world is self-evidently
needed and necessary ... Philosophical systems are only
hypotheses and there is always room for counter-hypo-
theses to contradict the old ones. The fact that someone or something exists is in itself its justification for
existing, and it doesn't need a special licence from anyone ..."

"In any case," said Thea, "as far as I'm concerned,
I can do without pity. I don't need it! And I don't pity
any creature in the world either. It's one feeling I lack
completely, thank God!"

"That's your nature, and there's room for a nature like

276

yours too . . . And who knows if you're not in need of pity yourself . . ."

At these words Thea burst into loud, abandoned laughter in the middle of Praterstrasse, giving rise to curious looks from a number of passers-by.

As soon as they arrived home they got undressed and went to bed. Gurdweill had a strange dream, in which Perczik wanted to eat Ulrich's liver, which looked like one of Dr. Kreindel's cigars, and Ulrich cried and pleaded until Thea came and announced that Perczik would have to pay Ulrich two thousand dollars and also provide him with a new liver, from an American factory . . .

Part IV: The Baby

24

THEA gave birth prematurely, in her seventh month of pregnancy, to a snub-nosed son. The doctors said the baby would survive. Thea lay in the maternity ward of the General Hospital, pale to the point of transparency. She was in high spirits, as always when in hospital, and treated her husband kindly. The child was already eight days old, and his name was Martin, Martin Gurdweill. Gurdweill came to the hospital every afternoon. He would wait for the visiting hour all the other hours of the day and night, which fed on it like parasites. But this precious hour, it soon transpired, was far shorter than an ordinary hour, two-thirds shorter at least, and no sooner had you entered the first ward, walked down the aisle between the two long rows of beds on either side, and gained the ward next to it, where Thea was lying — than the sing-song voice rose from the bottom of the courtyard crying: "The vi-si-ting hour is ov-er!" and once again you had not had time to feast your eyes properly on your son.

It was the beginning of July. Dry, orange-blue days. The pavements perspired, oozing black asphalt. Golden beer, cold and frothy, was the order of the day. Your clothes hung heavily as mill-stones, your shirt stuck to your chest and back. When you crossed the bridges over the canal, you were drawn to the water below as irresistibly as a suicide. You envied the naked bodies wallowing in the sand next to the bathing-booths on the river banks, and sometimes even the half-naked labourers working high on the scaffolding of some new building. It was two months since Gurdweill had stopped working for Dr. Kreindel, and for all that time he had been unemployed. It was hard to find another job, especially now, during the summer vacation. He worked on his own writing, and occasionally received small sums from publishers. He filled in the gaps with loans, hoping that in the long run he would be able to make a living from his writing. From the day his son was born he was extremely harassed. The birth had taken him by surprise, and not only because it had taken place before the expected time. He had to get used to the new situation which had come into being with the birth of the child, and although he had thought of scarcely nothing else during Thea's pregnancy, he was still not really ready for it. He felt like a man come to a foreign country without knowing its customs or language. With the baby a new era had begun in his life. It was a watershed. Now everything else had to take second place to the baby. Even Thea seemed unimportant. When all the old disturbing thoughts connected with her came into his mind, he was able to push them aside easily: the boy made up for everything. And the letter signed "a faithful friend" which he had received the morning before and which had agitated him all day — even that could not distract him for long. Such things meant nothing and did not deserve to have any notice taken of them, said Gurdweill to himself. What value could the words of some benighted trouble-maker possibly possess? For this mysterious "friend" was certainly not an honourable man! No decent man wrote anonymous letters! It was nothing but malicious gossip! And how did he know that Dr. Ostwald, of all people, was the father? Was he standing at the foot of the bed? Did he have any proof? Just because she worked for him? If it was true that she was unfaithful to her husband, then it wasn't only with Dr. Ostwald, but with quite a few others as well — so how could the letter-writer possibly know that Dr. Ostwald was definitely the father? Perhaps it was because Dr. Ostwald had sent her a present in honour of the baby's birth? But that meant nothing at all! It was a very common custom. She'd been working for him for over three years, after all — so why shouldn't he send her a present if he could afford it? On the contrary — if he were really guilty, he would never have sent a present, especially not something like a pram, to attract suspicion to himself. But this last proof failed to satisfy Gurdweill. "No!" — he

282

said to himself — "that's no proof! He might have sent it precisely in order not to attract suspicion to himself!" But the truth was that it made no difference one way or the other, and he had wasted the whole of yesterday on worrying about it for nothing. In the last analysis the father could just as easily be him, Gurdweill himself . . . It was him she had lived with, after all. That, at least, nobody could deny! And why should the father be someone else and not him? At any rate, it wasn't Dr. Ostwald — of that he was almost certain. As for what Thea herself had said on more than one occasion, there was no need to take that too seriously. She only said it to annoy him. Besides, she had never actually mentioned Dr. Ostwald by name! Never! Only that the baby wasn't his, Gurdweill's — and that didn't mean a thing . . . And now — he interrupted himself — there's an end to the matter! And he decided to put the whole thing out of his mind and never to let it trouble him again.

Gurdweill was sitting on a bench in the Volksgarten. The sun was entangled in the tree-tops, touching the upper half of the Parliament building, which was visible above the iron fence, with an orange glow. Most of the afternoon was already over, and the little children in the park were worn out with running and playing. Flushed and hungry they returned to their mothers and nannies and gobbled down what was left of the food they had brought with them. The avenue below was deep in shade, but the air was still warm and hazy. Not far off, the park band was playing, and the tune united with the rattling of the trams and the hooters of the cars outside to form a curious medley of noises and sounds. By concentrating intently on the music it was possible to weed out the foreign elements and return it, with a strenuous effort, to its pristine state. But Gurdweill actually preferred it the way it was, with the pulse of the life of the city beating inside it. Thus he imagined the music of a band playing on a ship at sea, and absorbing into itself the pounding of the mighty waves. Suddenly he felt a surge of great joy at being alive in this city, at being a part of all this vast, varied movement. At that moment he loved everything. All the people around him were related to

283

him; all the children were his kin. He smiled affectionately at the children standing next to the bench; a little girl in a blue dress and two little boys with grubby knees, and he was filled with joy when they returned his smile. It would not be long before his Martin, too, would be a little rascal with flushed cheeks and bare, dusty knees. Everything was so beautiful that it would be niggardly to complain. It was true, of course, that there was a lot of sorrow in the world, but at this moment he, Gurdweill, was incapable of feeling a jot of it. It did not touch him at all. How could he help it if the cigarette he was smoking was exceptionally good today, better than he had ever tasted before? How could he help it if the carnations and the narcissi in the round flower-bed opposite him were imperceptibly invading his soul with the exquisite delicacy of their colours? And how could he help it if he now had a son, a real son, whose name was Martin and whose present address was the white cot number 26, in the General Hospital of Vienna? Perhaps at this very minute he was crying in his thin, weak voice — but that was nothing to worry about. He was only getting rid of his surplus energy. And the day itself, which was declining into evening as he sat there! Everyone who lived a single day tasted the whole of eternity, of that there could be no doubt. Happy the man who was privileged to live one single day!

"And what's your name?" he asked the little girl standing next to him and looking at him as she nibbled a bar of chocolate.

The little girl laughed and did not reply.

"Why don't you answer the gentleman, you rude little girl?" said her nanny, a young and not unattractive girl, who was sitting next to Gurdweill and reading a book, preening herself as if this attention paid to her charge was a compliment actually intended for her.

"I shan't say," the little girl tossed her head. "Let him guess!"

Gurdweill began reeling off a list of names, while the little girl, so delighted by the game that she forgot her chocolate, cried "No, no!" Then he began making up names, strange names which sounded like the primitive

284

language of some tribe in the jungles of Africa, and conjured up a picture of naked Negroes and exotic trees with heavy fruits hanging from their boughs. "Bootoomi," he said, "Kashiloo, Moo, Aroozi, Memhooroo, Bizimi . . ."

"No, no!" cried the little girl, convulsed with laughter, exposing sharp, tiny teeth smeared with chocolate. "There aren't any names like that!"

The nanny too smiled in amusement.

"Then your name must be Suzi! Yes, that must be it! Because you look like Suzi and you're as big as she is too . . ."

"Not true!" protested the child. "I'm bigger than she is! Suzi's still a baby! She's only so big" — she held her hand about six inches from the ground — "and she won't go to school next year even, but I'm going to school this winter! Aren't I, Fräulein?"

"Yes, dear."

The nanny closed her book and put it down on the bench next to her, evidently anticipating more amusement from the conversation than the book.

"In that case," Gurdweill resumed, "if you're going to school soon, you really are a big girl. And a big girl like you must have a name!"

"Of course I have! Should I tell him, Fräulein?"

"Yes of course you should."

"Well then, my name's Tini. Tini Mertel."

And after a second's pause:

"And what's your name? You must say your name too!"

"Don't be so cheeky, Tini!" the nanny rebuked her.

"I'll tell you with pleasure, little missy. My name's Rudolf."

"Like my uncle! Like Uncle Rudolf!" the little girl cried in delight. "And what's your other name?"

"Gurdweill."

"Gurdweill," she repeated in a disappointed voice. "But Uncle Rudolf's surname is the same as ours. Mertel. And he's got a big car! He always takes me for a ride in it! Once he took me all the way to Grinzing. And mummy was there too. Have you got a car?"

"No, little missy," smiled Gurdweill, "I haven't got a

285

car. But I have got a little boy, and his name is Martin."

"And what class is he going to?"

"No class at all! He's still in a cot. He's only so big —" he showed her with his hands.

"Ooh!" the little girl pursed her mouth in disdain. (I'll bet her mother does the same — the thought flashed through Gurdweill's mind.) "So small! I don't like such little boys! They're so stupid!"

"And haven't you got a little brother that size?"

"No! I don't need one! They scream all day long!"

"But my Martin doesn't scream," said Gurdweill. "He only laughs!"

"No!" the child insisted, as if she were about to be presented with a baby brother against her will. Then she repented and added immediately:

"But you can bring him here one day to show me. And if he doesn't scream, he can come with me once in Uncle Rudolf's car. I'll tell Uncle Rudolf to let him come. But only once, and that's all! Right, Fräulein? We can let the baby come in the car once. But if he shouts, then he can't come any more!"

"No, wait!" she changed her mind again. "He can't come now. Bring him another time. When we come back from our holiday. We're leaving in two days' time. Or maybe you're going to Ischl too?"

"No, I'm not going to Ischl. Probably somewhere else . . ."

For a moment he saw a little village nestling between towering mountains in his mind's eye, and a quiet, gentle longing stirred in him to be there now with Thea and his son Martin, to live in peace, safe from any threat of trouble, steeped in this afternoon's loveliness forever.

"Have you ever been to Ischl before?" he asked.

"Poo!" cried the child boastfully. "Lots of times! Last year we went there too! It takes a whole day in the train to get there. You go over three awfully high bridges! And I'm allowed to look out of the window too! Mummy lets me look. It's awfully deep down there, but I'm not afraid! Not even a tiny little bit! There are tiny little houses down there and cows as small as flies, but they're real live cows. They stand and eat with their necks stuck out and their heads on the ground. And there's one black one, black all over like Herr Messerschmidt's dog. I don't like the black one — foo, the ugly thing! Then comes a long, long tunnel. All of a sudden it gets so dark, you can't see a thing. Not even mummy. And we quickly close all the windows so nobody can fall out in the dark. But I'm not one bit afraid. And suddenly it's light again. And the sun's shining. Then we open the windows again. Then comes another tunnel, even longer. And it's night again. And then we come to Ischl. The train goes: trr- ta! trr-ta! And then it hoots and then we're already in Ischl. Your little boy would be afraid! All those little boys are so stupid! But I'm not afraid, not one little bit. Has he ever been in a train, your little boy?"

"No," replied Gurdweill with a smile.

"You see, it's because he's afraid."

"But, Tini, he's not afraid at all!" said Gurdweill, affectionately stroking her flaxen curls. "He's a brave little fellow and soon he'll be going to school too. And I'll buy him a little car. A real car, green, with two seats and a spare wheel at the back. And then you can both ride in it together."

"Good!" Tini agreed. "But who's going to drive?"

"You'll both take turns. First you, then Martin."

At that moment he caught sight of Dr. Astel and Lotte in the distance. They had already seen him and were coming closer. He stood up and gave the little girl his hand:

"Well, Tini, I have to go now. But we'll meet again, won't we?"

He nodded at the nanny and walked towards his friends.

"Well, well, look who's here!" said Dr. Astel. "Ever since you became a father nobody's set eyes on you."

Gurdweill blushed, and felt furious at himself for doing so.

"And how is the son and heir? Everything all right? From the way you disappeared anyone might have thought you were the one giving birth!"

"I haven't reached that stage yet," said Gurdweill in an attempt at a joke.

Lotte, who had been scrutinizing him with an appraising look, finally asked:

"And what is his name?"

"Martin," replied Gurdweill, staring at Lotte, whose voice sounded dead and dull, as if she were in the depths of depression. But there was no sign of this in her face.

They moved off and began strolling silently down the avenue. They walked between the two rows of chairs, as far as the kiosk which sold cold drinks, turned right next to the fence, circled back, and landed up on the other side of the round flower-bed. The oppressive heat had begun to lift; the evening would be cool and pleasant. And Gurdweill's mood, too, grew light and airy. He was filled with a feeling of great, pure happiness. Young girls just past adolescence were sitting and reading romances in the middle of the park, marvelling at the astonishing similarity between themselves and the mysterious, refined heroines of their books. So absorbed were they that they did not even notice the young men passing them for the umpteenth time, devouring with their eyes their nubile freshness, blooming even more tenderly in the passionate absorption of their reading. There were young matrons, too, sitting on the hired chairs and apparently waiting for their husbands to meet them on their way home from work. They were knitting or embroidering, and some of them were reading too, but with less innocent abandon than their younger sisters, half an eye open for any male glances that came their way. There were men of every sort, some of whose working lives were over: retired military men whose civilian clothes did nothing to obscure their former rank, and who bore their commanding white moustaches as proudly as medals won on the battlefield; retired businessmen in funny, old-fashioned hats and suits made to measure fifteen years before. Others whose working lives had not yet begun: high school pupils and university students. And others, who belonged to neither of the above categories and were spending their holidays sitting in the park because they could not afford the expense of going to a country or seaside resort. But outside, behind the wire netting of the fence, the city surged and roared, trams dashed to and fro, cars hooted, heavy carts rumbled, people hurried God knew where, newspaper-sellers yelled, and crippled soldiers begged for alms. The evening advanced steadily, its approach more clearly sensed inside the park than in the busy streets outside. Gurdweill said to his companions:

"What do you say to spending the evening somewhere out of town, Cobenzl, for example?"

Dr. Astel and Lotte had no objections.

"Why not?" said Lotte. Especially since she did not have to be home for supper. In the summer their domestic arrangements were different. Besides which, she was going on holiday in a few days' time, and that called for a farewell celebration, didn't it?

On the way to the tram stop Gurdweill asked her where she was thinking of going this year.

She had not made up her mind yet. But probably to Achensee or Zell am See. In any case — to the Tyrol. Yes, this year she pined for the Tyrol. As for the rest — she always made up her mind at the last minute, when she bought her ticket, leaving her exact destination in the lap of the gods. Who knows, she might not go to either of the places she had mentioned, but to Zillertal, or Mayrhofen, for example — it would all become clear at the last minute.

Something warm stirred in Gurdweill's heart as she spoke of her approaching trip. He suddenly realized that Lotte was very dear to him, and that she would be a part of his soul forever. He would not have been able to give her up easily if she were going away for long. True, he did not see her very often, but the certainty that she was somewhere close at hand, kind and caring, and that he could see her whenever he wanted to, had a reassuring effect on him. And what if she were suddenly to die . . . the thought came unexpectedly into his head, as if it had crawled through some crack into his consciousness, and he was so horrified that he came to a standstill. Why should he think of death now, and in connection with Lotte of all people, who was young and apparently perfectly healthy? Appalled, he tried to banish the thought from his mind by dwelling on the pleasure of strolling through Cobenzl on such a wonderful evening, as one tries to mask a bad odour by spraying scented water in the room — but he was unable to recover his balance. The thought of Lotte's death retreated into a corner of his mind, and went on spreading its secret poison through his soul. Gurdweill's mood was spoilt.

"Why so glum all of a sudden, Gurdweill?" asked Lotte, who had noticed the sombre expression on his face.

"On the contrary, I'm not glum at all!" replied Gurdweill, and tried to smile.

"No wonder he's worried! He's a father now!" Dr. Astel joked.

A tram with three empty coaches stopped right in front of them, and filled up in an instant. In half an hour they arrived in Grinzing, and decided to ascend the mountain first and have supper there. To their delight, they managed to find places in a motorcoach for Cobenzl immediately, and drove up the fine, broad road lined with villas surrounded by gardens, woods, meadows and vineyards. The woods were already dark but otherwise the air was steeped in the rosy glow of sunset. A light breeze wafted towards the huge coach charging up the mountainside. There must have been birds warbling in the tree-tops, and crickets chirping — but their voices were silenced by the roar of the coach. When it reached its destination and stopped, the silence seemed absolute and even slightly disturbing. Then the passengers began to alight. They were standing in front of the broad, open terrace of the big "Cobenzl Café-Restaurant," which was rather crowded. Gurdweill and his companions preferred something less ostentatious, and entered one of the little cafés nearby. From the edge of the café terrace they could see the city spread out over a vast area below them, with dark church spires sticking up like silhouettes here and there against the background of the light evening sky. Far in the distance loomed the giant Ferris wheel, which for some reason was illuminated despite the fact that it was still daylight. The whole scene seemed taken from some fairy-tale world, and it was hard to believe that it was populated by people living perfectly ordinary lives.

Lotte said:

"It was a good idea to come here. One feels as if one has laid down a heavy burden, and can breathe freely at last."

They ordered wine with their meal. Lotte ate without appetite and left half the omelet she had ordered untouched. Gurdweill glanced at her and saw that her face had grown even paler and thinner than usual, and there were dark rings under her eyes. He felt a pang. What was the matter with her? — he asked himself. A high-spirited girl like her! One year ago she had been a different person! He would have to have a talk with her one day — when she came back from the Tyrol. In any case, his own appetite suddenly vanished too, and his roast meat seemed completely tasteless.

The twilight was seeping steadily into the sky, colouring it a greenish-greyish blue. There was something indefinable in the air, which infiltrated the soul and made it tender and a little melancholy, susceptible to all kinds of subtle, delicate, and barely perceptible agitations. In a meadow not far off, a small animal hopped rapidly through the grass. Probably a rabbit, thought Gurdweill tenderly, as of a beloved little brother. In the city below innumerable lights went on, from horizon to horizon. Far, far to the left was a swaying, moving chain of orange lights.

"Look, look over there!" Lotte pointed to the left. "It must be a train!"

And they all strained their eyes to pick out the slowly crawling train from among all the other lights.

"I see it!" said Dr. Astel. "Over there, next to the Ferris wheel."

But there was no longer anything to see. The train had disappeared.

The electric lights were lit on the café terrace, too. There were now fewer customers. The three waiters in their spotless white jackets stood huddled together next to the railing with nothing to do. So pitiful did they appear in their inactivity that Gurdweill felt an urge to order something and rouse them from their melancholy.

291

"Let's pay and go for a little walk," suggested Dr. Astel. "Or do you want to go on sitting here?"

Nobody wanted to go on sitting there, and they stood up and left. Lotte gave Dr. Astel her purse to carry and linked arms with her companions, one on either side. Gurdweill felt the warmth of her arm through his clothes, and a quiet, happy sense of security welled up inside him. They were walking along a rough, narrow path between two rows of rose-bushes, which occasionally brushed against their legs in the darkness. A fresh, dewy smell of new-mown hay was borne towards them from somewhere in the distance. Once in a while a low, subdued murmur escaped from the branches of the surrounding trees, lasted a second, and stopped. Then silence reigned again, interrupted only by the sound of their uneven footsteps. Nobody felt any need to speak. If only a clear, female voice would break into song now, from somewhere behind the trees, a song neither too happy nor too sad, pouring out as if from the throat of the evening itself — how perfect it would be, thought Gurdweill. He remembered a summer evening long ago, before the war, when everything was still so simple, clear and comprehensible. He was walking along the road near Meidling with Ilse Rubin when she suddenly said: "Happiness and misfortune don't come from outside, but from inside our own hearts." She was right. He had known even then that she was right. She was a strange girl. She knew how to find a positive side to everything, and the least little thing made her happy. And how simple the world seemed to her! She was the only person he had ever met who could never, under any circumstances, be pitied. It was impossible to feel pity for Ilse Rubin. Because even in the worst conditions, she was still happier than anybody else, thanks to her great love of the world. Where could she be now?

Dr. Astel began humming a tune which for some reason annoyed Lotte.

"Stop it!" she said.

"What, are we going down already?" he said immediately, as if to justify himself. "But it's still early! And this path leads straight to Sievering."

292

"There isn't any other way down!"

"Well then, we can go back up and walk round Cobenzl until eleven, and then go down to Grinzing in time to catch the last tram."

"No, we'll go on walking here!" said Lotte. "Right, Gurdweill?"

He didn't mind. Whatever they wanted was fine with him.

"All right then! We'll go back up!" said Lotte angrily.

On their way back the same path was less attractive than before, as if they had somehow spoilt its beauty by walking along it.

Lotte suddenly asked:

"I suppose you love him very much, your son?"

"Yes, I love him very much," replied Gurdweill simply.

"Was he born with hair?"

"With blond hair."

"Hmm . . . blond hair . . . I suppose we'll get engaged soon . . . in a few months' time . . . Perhaps in the autumn . . ."

She burst into nervous laughter.

"I'll be an old maid if I don't hurry up, won't I, ha ha . . . And my parents are getting hysterical too. You'll have me, won't you, Mark? You haven't changed your mind about marrying me, have you?" And in an affected, imploring tone: "Please, darling, don't change your mind . . ."

"But Lotte, I'm ready the minute you are!" said Dr. Astel, half in earnest and half joking. "I'm only waiting for your consent!"

"Really? Are you sure you haven't changed your mind? I only asked you to wait a little longer. Just a few more months. So you're not sick of me yet? You hear, Gurdweill, he's not sick of me yet! And then my name will be: Frau Doktor Mark Astel — how fine that sounds! You deserve a kiss for it!"

And she freed herself from their arms and kissed Dr. Astel quickly on the mouth.

"There you are, darling! That's on account. And how many children do you want, Herr Doktor Astel? Five? Six? With blond hair too, eh?"

Suddenly her voice grew hoarse. "Or perhaps you don't want any at all? A modern marriage? With each partner going his own way? Perhaps in his own apartment too? Separate tables and seperate beds?! Our friend Gurdweill wouldn't agree to a marriage like that, I know! He loves children, our friend Gurdweill, ha ha! And he won't be satisfied with one, or even five, will he, Rudolfus?"

"Why are you talking like this, Lotte?" said Gurdweill in a whisper full of pity. "It's not true, you know it's not like that at all . . ."

Every word she said cut his heart like a knife and caused him great pain. He wanted to comfort her in some way, and he took her hand and pressed it warmly. But Lotte pulled her hand away. The brilliantly-illuminated café terrace appeared before them again. Lotte was trembling convulsively, but she controlled herself with a tremendous effort. She took her purse from Dr. Astel and fished out a handkerchief. Under the pretext of blowing her nose she stealthily wiped her eyes. No one spoke. After a moment, when they had reached the "Cobenzl Café-Restaurant," Dr. Astel glanced at his watch. He said in a whisper, as if he were afraid of waking someone from their sleep:

"It's only a quarter past ten. If you like we can go in here and have something to drink. We've still got plenty of time."

"Good!" said Lotte, her voice quite different now. "I'm thirsty."

When they sat down next to the balustrade Gurdweill found himself opposite Lotte, and he saw that her face was even paler than before and her eyes were burning feverishly. Lotte wanted beer and they ordered three glasses and cigarettes. She drank about a third of her glass and pushed it to the middle of the table. Then she said with a faint smile:

"Why don't you say anything?"

She took off her light-blue straw hat, a plain cloche, and her short, thick, curly hair sprang up round her face, making it seem even paler. She had a pretty, feminine brow, soft and not too high. She took a white comb out of her purse and fixed her hair. Dr. Astel watched her every movement with a melancholy air, blowing thick smoke rings which the playful breeze snatched from his mouth, buffeted about until they were shapeless, and flung into the night. Two leaves from a nearby chestnut tree suddenly flew on to the pink and blue checked tablecloth, and landed next to Gurdweill's glass. He picked one of them up, raised it to his eyes, and examined it intently. Upon discovering a small yellow patch on one side of the leaf he tore it off, and began absent-mindedly chewing the rest in the intervals between puffs on his cigarette, thinking of Lotte and the explosion of misery he had just witnessed. He did not know how to help her, and sadness gnawed at his heart. He threw the leaf away and turned his head towards the sea of flickering lights below. The hidden city now seemed alien and hostile, and a feeling of anxiety welled up in him for his son and his wife, alone and unprotected somewhere down there. Nobody spoke. Even Dr. Astel's customary good humour seemed to have deserted him, for he maintained a stubborn, uncharacteristic silence. In his disconsolate silence he made Gurdweill think uneasily of a cheerful, high-spirited boy who had suddenly and inexplicably begun to cry. Lotte returned the comb to her purse. Gurdweill, who felt responsible, as usual, for the gloom which had settled on his companions, said to Dr. Astel:

"And where will you spend your holiday this year? Not in the Tyrol?"

"I don't know. Perhaps I'll go to Vorarlberg. But not before the end of the month."

After a moment he added:

"I'd be happy to invite you to join me for a week or two, if you liked."

Lotte sent Dr. Astel a grateful look. In spite of everything he was a good man, she thought, and a good friend!

"I wish I could. But now, with the baby, it's impossible. I can't leave him alone."

"Why should you have to look after him?" Lotte interrupted. "What about Thea? And her parents? Surely you can go away for one week?"

"No, it's impossible. At any other time I'd be delighted,

but not now. Besides, I don't need a vacation. I feel as fit as a fiddle. But I wish I could send Thea somewhere. She's the one who'll need a vacation when she comes out of hospital."

Lotte pulled a face and exchanged a meaningful look with Dr. Astel, but Gurdweill did not notice. Whenever he mentioned Thea's name in company he felt uncomfortable, and tried to cover up his embarrassment by changing the subject as quickly as possible. He took a big gulp of beer, as if to swallow his discomfort. Again there was a tense, uneasy silence between the three friends. The customers in the café were leaving one by one. Some of them got into the cars waiting like a pack of expectant animals on the empty lot outside the terrace, hooted, and roared off into the night; others set off on foot, punctuating the darkness with bursts of laughter and occasional snatches of song. Lotte wanted to leave, too. Her spirits had unaccountably risen, leading to an improvement in the mood of her companions as well. When they had left the buildings behind them and the lights had disappeared behind the trees, she began to run gaily down the smooth, steep road, obliging the other two to chase her, which they did with a will. Laughing in a high, clear voice, Lotte ran with small, rapid, drumming steps, while Dr. Astel let her get ahead before bounding after her on his long, stilt-like legs and catching up with her immediately as she panted for breath, her bosom heaving. After this race had been repeated several times, Lotte said:

"Gurdweill can't run for toffee! Come and catch me!"

Gurdweill chased her and caught her. He was small, but quick and agile. She rested her head wearily on his shoulder and let it stay there until Dr. Astel approached.

"I'm tired out, children! I can't walk any more. You'll have to carry me!"

The two men locked arms and made a seat for Lotte, who climbed on to it and put her arms around their necks. They carried her in this way for about fifty yards, while she rocked back and forth in time to their steps, as if she were riding a horse.

"This is the old Lotte again!" said Gurdweill to himself.

"This is the way I remember her a year and a half ago!" But nevertheless his heart feared for her.

"We can carry you like this all the way home!" cried Dr. Astel gaily. "You're as light as a feather!"

At that Lotte decided to get down. She was no longer in the least tired. And besides, she was afraid that "poor Gurdweill" would collapse under the strain.

Gurdweill assured her that she had nothing to worry about on his account. He could go on carrying her for hours! He would prove it to her! And Dr. Astel, for his part, was prepared to carry her all by himself, all the way back to town. He would be delighted to do it!

But she wouldn't have it. She wasn't as tired as all that! As long as they didn't walk too fast.

A car came racing furiously down the road behind them and forced them to step aside. Its headlamps cast a blinding, orange glare in front of it. From now on they kept to the side of the road. Lotte said:

"Summer nights! Sometimes you can feel them like the body of an ardent young woman! Haven't you ever felt it? There's a fragrance about them, it doesn't matter if they're mild or sultry, they always smell like a young woman's body. No wonder nights like this drive some men mad with lust. I can understand it. Especially in the countryside. A black night like this — can't you feel it breathing and speaking? And how tender and caressing it is, how passionate!"

They began to sense clearly the tender passion of the night. And mingling with it the tender, supple, fragrant flesh of Lotte herself, who had awoken their senses into a stunned awareness of the night and of her own body. They felt hot, intoxicatingly light-headed, and their mouths were dry. For the first time that night they felt tired. No one spoke. They went on walking down the hill. No cars passed them. The road was deserted and the trees made a wall to their left and their right. The leaves rustled very faintly, almost inaudibly. In the distance a train engine hooted and then was silent. Only their footsteps knocked against the night: tap, tap, tap, the footsteps of Lotte, Dr. Astel and Gurdweill. At that moment none of them would have dreamt of saying a word. No, the night had to be preserved, at least for a while, intact, round and dense, innocent of words. And perhaps these three people would remember it all their lives long, and return to it in their thoughts twenty or thirty years hence, with the sadness of delicate, lingering memories.

And then Lotte let out a smothered little laugh, as if concluding some secret thought. The others started as if woken from a heavy sleep, and for some reason looked embarrassed.

"Give us a cigarette!" said Gurdweill.

And all three lit cigarettes.

The road took a sudden bend to the left, revealing a number of isolated houses in the distance. The lights were on in the windows of the houses, and lighted streetlamps began to appear at long intervals. Behind the fence of one of the villas a dog began to bark at their approach, perhaps the same dog they had heard barking before.

"We must be coming to Grinzing!" cried Dr. Astel.

He looked at his watch in the light of the streetlamp:

"Ten past eleven! We can still make it! In ten minutes we'll be at the tram stop."

This was where the city began, but it began in the country. As if it were keeping a foot in both camps until it finally made up its mind. Low, country cottages lined the road with, here and there, a looming terraced house several storeys high. The city was like a musician trying out his instrument, striking false, faltering notes until he hit on the right tone and began to play. The streets were deserted and dimly lit. In most of the little houses the people had already gone to sleep. The snow-white curtains which could be seen inside some of the windows gave one the feeling of sweet, sound sleep and sheltering maternal wings. Somewhere a baby began to cry, and immediately stopped again. A limping dog came towards them at a lolloping run, stopped to sniff, and turned round to watch them from behind. At the entrance to a dark alley, on a bench hidden in the shadow of a tree, a couple sat locked in an embrace. Then the street opened up into a large, well-lit square, and the tram terminus was before them.

At that moment a tram emerged from the terminus and set off for the city, its bell clamouring loudly. Although it was not the last tram, the three of them all broke into a frantic run, as if at some signal agreed in advance.

"We're catching up, we're catching up!" cried Dr. Astel as he ran.

And they jumped on to the last coach and went on running until they reached the front seats, where they sat down. Then they looked at each other as if they had not seen one another for a long time, like people who have been sitting together in the dark when the lights suddenly go on in the room.

The coach was almost empty. Two workers in dirty blue overalls sat huddled in opposite corners, getting ready to enjoy a nap, as if the journey were going to last all night. Apart from them the only other passengers were a poor woman with a little boy and a covered basket, out of which poked the head of a dead rabbit. The boy kept on putting out his hand to touch the rabbit and the woman scolded him and slapped his hand, but he only laughed. In the end she took the basket and put it under the seat, where the head of the rabbit went on sticking out into the aisle. With hardly any passengers to weigh it down the tram hurtled ahead, making a deafening noise and bumping and jolting so violently that it seemed to have come off the tracks and to be careening over the paving stones. It rushed past the stations without stopping. When the conductor came to take the money for their fares he seemed unwilling to wake the sleeping workers, and appeared to be half-asleep himself.

Public places, thought Gurdweill, which were intended for crowds of people, were very depressing when they were empty and deserted, littered with the debris of lives that had moved on, such as squashed cigarette stubs, used tickets, crumpled newspapers, etc. They gave rise to a feeling of pity and horror at once. The same thing applied to the Post Office at night, cinema halls, cafés, theatres, circuses, and so on.

Above the opposite windows he read advertisements for the spring exhibition at the Sezession, which was already

299

over, for the Sixth Vienna Fair, which was to take place in the autumn, for Suchard chocolate and Gillette razor blades, for the great new star of the theatre, Roneggar, for a fantastic new sewing machine, for the biggest "mobile house" in the world, for *Der Tag* — "Buy it and read it!," etc. He needed none of these things. He read absent-mindedly, taking in only enough to absorb the boredom behind the words. Some of the advertisements had come unstuck and flapped irritatingly against the window-panes.

Gurdweill stole a sidelong look at Lotte, who was sitting next to him. She seemed tired and relaxed. He remembered the idea of her possible death which had come into his mind several hours before, and felt the same horror as then. But he immediately recovered and told himself that his fears were silly and irrational. If one were to take every passing notion of the kind seriously, there would be no end to it! Still, it would be a good thing if she were to marry Dr. Astel! Married life, when you got right down to it, settled people's minds. The little everyday worries did something to fill the void! He felt the need to say something to Lotte to efface the bad impression which he was certain that he had made on her. But at the same time he was afraid of blurting out some idiotic remark that would spoil everything, as he had sometimes done in the past. And as soon as the fear had entered his mind, he knew that he was doomed to say something he would regret. And he knew exactly what it was too. Precisely the thing which it was forbidden to say now. For a moment he tried to struggle with himself, although he knew it was in vain. He could not sit still and began to fidget about on his seat. He moved away from Lotte and crossed his legs. In the end he could control himself no longer. He moved abruptly back to Lotte and blurted out with a strange haste, as if eager to rid himself of something vile:

"Are you afraid of death, Lotte?"

He smiled stupidly and looked down at the floor. There, I've done it! he thought in relief. The answer no longer mattered at all. All that mattered was the question which he now justified to himself as a kind of warning, to alert her to the danger. Nevertheless her silence began to disturb him. He raised his eyes and saw that she was still sitting as before, with her head slightly averted and her eyes on the window opposite. A nagging doubt crept into his mind: had he asked his question aloud, or only thought it? Alarmed by the latter possibility, he asked again, this time loudly enough for Dr. Astel, too, to hear:

"Are you afraid of death, Lotte?"

She gave him a hostile look and said irritably:

"Do you have to know right away? Can't we put it off to some other time?"

"Gurdweill's in a philosophical mood," Dr. Astel said with a smile.

"Oh never mind, it's not important!" said Gurdweill.

Two stops before Nussdorfer Strasse the woman with the little boy and the rabbit got off. A big, heavy man with a broad, red face, a long, brown Virginia cigar stuck in his mouth and a bowler hat on his head, got in, dragging a skinny little woman behind him. They sat down directly opposite Gurdweill and his friends. The big man blew out puffs of delicate, almost invisible smoke and stared fixedly at Lotte. Suddenly he addressed his wife in a voice loud enough for the whole coach to hear:

"These Poles, you can't get away from them!"

The three friends pretended not to hear. Lotte sat there petrified. She felt that something was going to happen and wanted to tell her companions to get off the tram. But she said nothing. The man, seeing that his words had missed their aim, now addressed them directly:

"Yes, yes, I mean you!" he said in a Viennese accent and a voice as coarse as a butcher's. "Why are you staring at me? I mean Jews! You're Jews aren't you?"

Dr. Astel and Gurdweill jumped up together. The blood rushed to Gurdweill's head and his face went red and then white.

"You, you —" spluttered Dr. Astel furiously, waving his fist in the fat man's face, "you shut your mouth! Or else I'll throw you off the tram!"

"Who? You'll throw me off the tram?" growled the man, jumping to his feet. "Me? A Viennese? You go back to

301

Galicia where you came from! Me he wants to throw off the tram!" He turned to the two workers, who were suddenly wide awake, staring open-eyed at the combatants.

The conductor stuck his head in through the door and called:

"Gentlemen, stop fighting at once, or I'll put the lot of you off!"

"What? I paid for my ticket! Put the Jews off!"

The woman, who had been tugging at his sleeve all this time and repeating, "Stop it, Schurl, stop it," now stood up:

"Come on, Schurl, we have to change trams. Here we are at Nussdorf already."

"Shut up, you old bag! I don't need you to tell me where to change!"

They got off, and Gurdweill and Dr. Astel resumed their seats. The conductor said apologetically: "The man was completely drunk," and went away. The two workers went back to sleep. New passengers got in and the tension died down. Dr. Astel, whose anger had vanished in an instant, said with satisfaction, as if he had just won a decisive victory:

"What a swine! Guzzling beer like a pig and then coming to sling mud at the Jews!" No one replied. Gurdweill, for some reason, felt ashamed, as if he had been the cause of the quarrel. He sensed vaguely that he had missed the chance to do something he should have done, and was seized by a feeling of dissatisfaction with himself. He looked out of the window at the half-empty streets, which seemed to him alien and unwelcoming. He did not dare to look at Lotte, as if he had in some way offended her. When they finally reached Schottentor, he felt saved. It was midnight. Dr. Astel and Lotte had to change to the Ring tram and he had to go in the opposite direction. When they parted Lotte said:

"Well, Gurdweill, we probably won't see each other before I leave. Unless you feel like dropping in tomorrow or the day after in the afternoon."

To his regret, he would not be able to make it. The afternoons were particularly difficult for him.

At which she remembered that she, too, would be busy. There were still a number of things to see to before her trip. Some shopping she had to do. They had better say goodbye now. But she promised to send him a picture postcard . . . perhaps even a letter . . .

"Of course, of course!" said Gurdweill eagerly, taking no notice of her sarcastic tone. "Please do write, and I'll write and tell you how I am, and Martin too. Only if you're interested, naturally."

"Interested isn't the word!" replied Lotte with a hint of mockery. "I wish you well until we meet again!"

25

For a while Gurdweill stood and watched the tram receding into the distance with Dr. Astel and Lotte, and then he turned away. Since he had plenty of time to spare, he decided to walk home. The bedbugs can wait! — he joked to himself. Suddenly he felt liberated, as if some weight had been lifted from his shoulders, and he strolled at his ease. A delicate sweetness flooded his heart as he remembered his conversation with the little girl in the park. When Martin was her age — and it wasn't so far away — what a source of happiness he would be! The years would fly past before he could turn around. And in the meantime he would look after him himself, cherish him as the apple of his eye! And Lotte would be fine too . . . everything would come right in the end . . . her nerves, that is . . . Deliberately Gurdweill forced his thoughts in this less dangerous direction, for he felt his previous terror beginning to well up in him again like a dark shapeless lump, and he preferred to blame everything on the state of her nerves, the treatment of which would surely restore her to health and happiness.

The Kai was deserted. An abandoned newspaper lay crumpled on one of the benches. Here and there a dilatory couple sat on a bench in the shadows. Two people joined together, who looked from a distance like one. From time to time a policeman popped out of the dark and cast his eye over the boulevard — the guardian of public morality. Ah yes — making love on a dark bench in Franz-Josefs-Kai was against the law, and whenever a policeman appeared the couple would separate instantly into two, two people who had sat down to rest on the same bench by chance. Resting was not against the law. Every now and then some poor creature, one of the homeless people who made the city itself their home, loomed up out of the dark as if emerging from the bowels of the earth, and stumbled slowly, in uncertain zigzags, in the light. Sometimes something hidden and nocturnal stirred in the bushes at the sides of the boulevard. Once in a great while a car drove down the deserted street.

When dawn approached the bedbugs lost their power, reflected Gurdweill. Besides, he could sleep as long as he liked in the morning, until ten or even twelve. But the bench on which he was sitting was damp with dew, and after a few minutes he stood up and continued on his way. The clock on the wall of the Hotel Metropol said ten to one. By the time he reached home and got into bed it would be two o'clock. And by then the danger would not be so bad! Nevertheless, he would have to speak to the old lady tomorrow about the dirt. Now that the dog-days were beginning, life would be unbearable unless she kept the place clean. The trouble was that she kept insisting there wasn't "the ghost of a bedbug" in the house — and how could he prove the contrary? A profound disgust seized hold of him at the thought of the broken couch, which seemed to him at this moment to be entirely composed of the loathsome vermin. No, tomorrow she would have to clean the couch!

On the bridge he glanced down at the black water, and remembered someone telling him that a dip in cold water before going to bed was a good cure for bedbugs. He would do it! Then he thought about how frightening the river was at night, and at the same time how seductive, almost compelling you to throw yourself into it . . . This thought seemed to him silly, and he dismissed it as due to the weariness of which he was now clearly aware. All of a sudden, by some strange mental leap, he found himself recalling Lotte again. And now he was rivetted by one external detail: he could not remember if she had been wearing ordinary shoes today, or the new woven sandals she had bought a few weeks before. An open weave like that was very impractical, thought Gurdweill. If you were caught in a sudden shower, they would fill with water in a moment . . . and it would be even worse at night . . . If only she had consulted him beforehand, he would never have advised her to buy shoes so full of holes. But the main thing, of course, was her nerves . . .

His head slightly lowered and his eyes on the ground, almost rubbing against the walls of the buildings, he made his way slowly down Praterstrasse, and did not notice the girl coming towards him until she actually accosted him. With a shudder he raised his eyes and looked into the raddled, painted face under the red hat. His old fear of women of her kind clutched at his heart, and he tried to turn away. But the girl, evidently under the impression that he did not find her sufficiently attractive, began to plead with him in a sick, wheedling voice. He would see how satisfied he would be. She knew all the ways of love, and if he wasn't satisfied she wouldn't take a penny. The hotel was very close, two steps away. She put her hand on his cheek and caressed him. Gurdweill thought that he would choke on the sickening smell of her cheap powder. He shook off her hand and said that he was sorry but he couldn't go with her now. He was tired and he had to get up early in the morning, besides which he didn't have enough money on him. He said all this very simply, and concluded solemnly: at the moment it was out of the question, perhaps some other time. But if she needed money, he had two schillings which he would lend her with pleasure. The girl was insulted and refused. She wasn't asking for charity, Herr Doktor, she worked for her money! He had better keep his two schillings for himself — she didn't need them. On the contrary — she could give him another two, and then he would have four. But she was prepared to accept a cigarette if he had one. Gurdweill gave her a cigarette and a light. And then for some reason he offered her his hand, said "Goodbye," and hurried away with a disagreeable feeling of oppression. He could not overcome his disgust, and was angry with himself because of it. They were poor, miserable creatures, and there was no reason to be disgusted by them, he said to himself. But it did not help. This was the first time he had ever spoken to a woman of the streets. Whenever one of them accosted him he would mumble something unintelligible even to him and hurry

306

past. Or he would make a wide detour when he saw them in the distance. His boyhood fear had never left him, and needless to say, they never gave rise in him to the faintest stirring of desire. As far as he was concerned, they scarcely belonged to the female sex. And although he had made up his mind on a number of occasions in the past to go with one of them — both because his attitude seemed to him unmanly, morbid, and childish, and because he believed it his duty as a writer to penetrate every corner of life — as soon as he was about to take the plunge he found some excuse to put it off.

Gurdweill entered his room and lit the sooty oil-lamp. The room seemed very empty in the silence of the night. He walked around for a while and then started to make up his bed on the couch. It never occurred to him to sleep on the bed, even though it was certainly cleaner. He was, to some extent, a creature of habit, and since he had grown accustomed to sleeping on the couch, he could see no reason to change his bed. For a few days it wasn't worth the trouble. And besides, the couch had grown accustomed to him, too, adapting itself to the curves of his body like a mould, so that whenever drowsiness overcame him far from home it was this old couch that he saw beckoning to him in his imagination. But in the heat of the summer he felt a secret resentment towards it, too, as if it were an unfaithful lover conspiring against him with the hated bedbugs.

Gurdweill washed the upper half of his body, laid out his smoking gear on a chair, together with a candle, "just in case," and went to put out the lamp. It was already half past two, and he breathed a sigh of relief: the danger was past! In another hour it would be dawn! Just to be on the safe side, he opened both windows wide to let in whatever coolness the night afforded, and got into bed as cautiously as if he were afraid of waking up someone. Then he remembered that he had forgotten to examine the sheet. Resolutely he got out of bed again, lit the candle and scrutinized the sheet without discovering anything suspicious. Then he lay down, his fears at rest, and blew out the candle. He felt as dazed as if he had been drinking, and looked forward confidently to a long, pleasant sleep. But he forced himself to stay awake a little while longer, and lay there alertly, holding his breath like a hunter in an ambush. No! Not a sign of them! He had got the better of them this time, he gloated. He began to lose consciousness, the last vestiges of his thoughts floated vaguely into the distance, like wasps smoked out of a hive. When suddenly he felt a sharp sting in the region of his right foot, which shot through his sluggish body like an electric shock, and then another one, on the ankle of the same foot, and then a third, on the other foot this time. Gurdweill shuddered convulsively. He began kicking his feet about under the blanket. Wide awake now, he was filled with a terrible, undirected rage. The figure of the old landlady immediately took shape before him and his fury attached itself to her, as if she were the one biting him. He stretched out his legs again and lay waiting. Now he felt nothing. Perhaps his nerves had deceived him, he thought, slipping back into sleep, that was probably it. Because the time of danger was already past! He was just about to fall asleep again — when something dropped on to the tip of his nose, as softly and quietly as a crumb. So faint was its touch that it might have been a slight shrinking of the skin, an inner twitch without any external cause. But immediately afterwards Gurdweill felt something crawling down the side of his cheek, as lightly as a hair tickling, and a bad smell — a penetrating, revolting smell, with which he was only too familiar. God, one of them had parachuted straight from the ceiling on to his nose! That was just like them! For a moment he lay motionless, intending to take it by surprise. The bug was crawling down his neck, his shoulder, hurrying as if it were running away. Very carefully, Gurdweill began to raise his hand — and at the same moment he felt several bites in different places on his body — on his chest, his thighs, his back, his calves — as if the parachutist himself had commanded his troops to attack the enemy on all fronts! Gurdweill leapt out of bed like a madman, utterly routed. He lit the candle and began searching frantically all over the sheet, throwing the pillow aside and looking underneath it — no, nothing here! He spread the blanket over the couch and began again, the candle in his hand. And then he saw a big one lying at the foot of the couch without moving, pretending to be dead. But Gurdweill was not deceived. He set the candle carefully on the chair, took a match, and was just about to give it a poke when it began running frantically down the sheet hanging over the side of the couch. "Aha!" — said Gurdweill aloud — "this time you won't get away! I've got you now!" And he squashed it vindictively with the match, overwhelmed by revulsion. His rage abated somewhat. He took off his nightshirt and shook it out of the window. Then he did the same with the sheet and blanket and made up his bed again. But he hesitated before lying down. His watch said ten past three. He lit a cigarette and paced up and down the room naked for five minutes or so. In the end he grew tired. Things couldn't go on like this! He lay down again and concentrated on falling asleep. Everything seemed quiet enough — they must have declared a truce. He felt a faint bite on one of his raised knees, but he decided to take no notice. He would ignore the pain and make an effort to fall asleep, and then he would have some peace at last. But all his good intentions were in vain. The pain grew sharper, unbearable. And it was immediately followed by a concerted attack, all over his body at once, as if every inch of him were swarming with the loathsome creatures. Gurdweill jumped out of bed again and ran straight to the window. He was in despair. He suddenly felt a strange need to shout at the top of his voice, to wake up everyone in the house, and summon them to his aid. This time he did not bother to light the candle. What good would it do? He stood at the window, worn out and trembling slightly from the faint chill in the air and from his own agitation, afraid of the couch on the other side of the room, afraid of thinking of it, overcome with disgust. For a moment he considered making up a bed on the floor, next to the window, but he dismissed the idea immediately. Who was to say they wouldn't come here, too? No, there was nothing for it. He would have to stand here the whole night long. And tomorrow — God help her if she didn't clean the couch!

A baby started crying. In the distance a policeman blew his whistle with a note as spiralling as a corkscrew, and Gurdweill was reassured. He did not feel so alone. The night was cool, and not very dark. He heard the sound of brisk, even footsteps not far away. Heinestrasse — thought Gurdweill. He went on standing by the window, leaning his elbows on the sill. He was so tired that he no longer felt his limbs. In the end he gave in and returned with stumbling steps, half asleep on his feet, to the couch. Soon it would be light, soon it would be light, he comforted himself. The dead rabbit in the tram was really quite grotesque — one last thought flickered through his mind — and Lotte would have to buy herself another pair of shoes without delay, so that she wouldn't catch cold . . . Red shoes like the girl in Praterstrasse . . . Gurdweill wanted to take off and fly to the other side of the Danube, where Martin, his son Martin, was standing and waving to him. But he could on no account rise from the ground, which filled him with an inhuman sorrow. When he looked down to ascertain the reason, he discovered to his astonishment that one of his feet was chained to a peg fixed in the ground, and this chain — whose painful pressure he now felt just above his ankle — was preventing him from flying. Martin went on beckoning and calling and Lotte, too, was suddenly standing next to him, waving something like a signal. At first Gurdweill could not make out what it was, but then he saw that it was a very large open-weave shoe, which she had taken off her head like a hat . . . Suddenly they were surrounded by a throng of people who were all calling him, waving their hats, beckoning with their hands — and he couldn't move. Then he gathered all his strength and pulled himself away. The force of the pull tore his chained leg in half, and he felt a great pain in his knee as he splashed into the canal. Ah, now everything was lost! How could he swim with one leg? He tried to cry out for help, but the water got into his mouth and he began to suffocate, and to sink into the depths with terrifying speed.

Bathed in a cold sweat, he woke up. Damn it all! His heart pounded violently and his breath came in rapid pants. He began scratching his knee until it bled. Outside

310

the sky was already turning blue. Somewhere in the distance a bird began its early morning song. In the room next door a bed creaked. Gurdweill turned over and sank instantly into a deep, dreamless sleep.

At eleven o'clock the next morning he woke up, feeling drowsy but refreshed. From the top of the window a slanting shaft of golden, dancing dust penetrated the room, making a pool of sunlight underneath the table. A woman in a dressing-gown leant out of the hotel window opposite, and for a moment she seemed about to throw herself into the street. Gurdweill wanted to see her face, but she was in no hurry to lift her head and he soon gave up. Down below carts rumbled, a tram bell rang in the distance, cars hooted, a whip cracked, a loud, shrill voice called: "Frau Voi-tik!" and a rag-and-bone-man cried in a hollow, monotonous voice: "Rags and bones, rags and bones!" Gurdweill found himself thrust into the middle of the hustle and bustle of the day, which did not lack a touch of poetry. He examined his soul and found it full of joy and contentment. Only one little corner sounded a discordant note. He wanted to ignore it, but it refused to be ignored and demanded his attention. He began to seek the reason, passing all his personal affairs in review through his mind; everything seemed in order. A sleepless night, tormented by bedbugs — no, that was all in the past now, a nightmare which was over and done with! That wasn't the reason! So what was? On no account could he locate the source of his uneasiness, and in the end he dismissed it from his mind.

The woman opposite had disappeared from the window, to Gurdweill's regret. Thinking that she had taken something of the charm of the morning away with her, he jumped out of bed, pulled on his trousers, and began to shave. From the corridor he heard the landlady's endless shuffle. The afternoon post arrived and Gurdweill's name was called with the loud confidence peculiar to postmen, who seem to think that every house they enter in the course of their work belongs to them. Gurdweill quickly finished shaving and hurried into the corridor to seize his letter before the landlady could begin pawing it all over to take

311

the edge off her curiosity. It was not an important letter. The editor asked him to send the story he had promised them for their next number as quickly as possible, etc. The landlady followed him into his room, eager to hear the latest news. Gurdweill, the letter still in his hands, nodded towards the couch and cried:

"Bedbugs! Bedbugs! You have to clean! I can't sleep!"

He realized that he had spoken in her tone and exclamatory style, and a smile crossed his face. He was obliged to repeat himself several times until she understood. In the end she said in her usual way: "Herr Gurdweill is mistaken . . . he's imagining it! There are no bedbugs here . . . Ten years I've been living in this house, ten years, aie, aie, aie, and I haven't seen the ghost of a bedbug! In other houses — you have no idea! Hundreds, thousands, psss! You can't shut an eye! The way they bite, it's something shocking! Tfu! The dirty things! But my house is clean, thank God! Very clean, everybody knows!"

Gurdweill was beside himself. He thought of the previous night and its horrors and gave the landlady an annihilating look. He rushed over to the couch and pulled the blanket off in a fury.

"And what's this? And this? And this?" he screamed, pointing at the suspect spots on the sheet. "Is that what you call clean?! You have to clean properly!"

The old woman approached, bent down and studied the sheet.

"Aie, aie, aie!" she whispered, shaking her head. "That'll be one of them fleas, Herr Gurdweill . . . Give the bedclothes a good shake — that'll do the trick. The main thing is — no bedbugs! Bedbugs are something else — disgusting, psss! But a flea isn't so terrible. They have them in the best families! The cinema, that's where you pick them up . . . The number of fleas in the cinema — psss! Herr Gurdweill probably likes to go to the cinema and brought one back with him . . . It's not so terrible! I like the cinema myself, aie, aie, aie! The things you can see there! Not long ago I saw . . ."

"It's got nothing to do with the cinema!" said Gurdweill through clenched teeth, flushed with anger. "I tell you it's not fleas! It's bedbugs! Bedbugs! You have to clean right away!"

The old woman inclined her head and bent her ear with her hand.

"I can't hear too well, Herr Gurdweill, it's old age does it, aie, aie, aie!"

"Bloody old bitch!" hissed Gurdweill under his breath. And he yelled right into her ear:

"Clean! Clean!"

The old woman recoiled.

"You don't have to yell! I can hear you all right. Of course we'll clean! Don't we clean every day? My house is always clean, thank God. Not like other houses . . ."

With a bony finger she scratched her scant grey hair, which was scraped back into a little bun, and added:

"You can rest easy, Herr Gurdweill. Everything necessary will be done. I can't abide dirt. You have no idea! My dear departed husband, the second one that is, may he rest in peace, even used to scold me about it. I like everything around me to be clean as a whistle — you can see for yourself! And he would always say: 'Why wear yourself out with unnecessary work? Enough!' Yes, those were his very words, aie, aie, aie! And how is your son, Herr Gurdweill? Will he be coming home soon?"

Gurdweill nodded. Of the cleaning he had already despaired. What could you do with a deaf old woman who was not right in her head into the bargain? He would try to have a word with her daughter, Siedl. Maybe that would help. For some reason, he didn't like the old woman asking him about his son.

"A fine, handsome child, I expect — just like his father! I'm that curious to see him, psss!" She shook her hand emphatically opposite the new pram shining with black laquer standing between the bed and the window. "And what a fine pram you've got waiting for him! A very handsome pram, psss! It must have cost a pretty penny!"

Gurdweill went up to the pram and pushed it further away from the bed. That's all that was needed — for the pram to be infested with bedbugs too! Dr. Ostwald's gift was a fine one indeed, the most expensive pram to be

313

bought, but Gurdweill, for some reason, did not like it. From the moment it had arrived it had been a thorn in his flesh. Every minute he found another imaginary fault in it. In the first place it was too heavy . . . it would be difficult to get it up and down the stairs when they began to take the baby for walks . . . And it was too big too, in his opinion, big enough for twins, it took up the whole room . . . Altogether it didn't suit Martin . . . And as he stood contemplating it, a wonderful idea came into his head: he would try to change it for another pram, a good one! It was so obvious — he couldn't imagine why he hadn't thought of it before! Thea hadn't seen it yet and she wouldn't know . . . He would borrow a little money from someone and add to the price, if necessary. This pram wasn't for Martin . . . Yes, this very day, after visiting the hospital, he would go straight to the furniture shop and get it over with. Perhaps he wouldn't even have to add anything. Prams like this one cost a fortune, even though they were worth nothing . . . This decision lifted a weight from his heart, his spirits soared, and the bedbugs ceased to have any importance at all.

The landlady, who had left the room in the meantime, now returned with a broom, which she leaned against the table. She began dusting the sides of the cupboard and the backs of the chairs and the bed with a very industrious air, as if to underline the cleanliness of which she had previously boasted.

Gurdweill went to the kitchen to warm up the dregs of the black coffee left over from yesterday's breakfast. The gas flame began humming intimately to itself, lapping the sooty bottom of the coffee-pot with tiny blue tongues. The kitchen was shrouded in semi-darkness. The big, square window on to the corridor was made of rough, opaque glass. The heat of the sweltering summer day outside was only dimly felt in here. Somewhere a clock struck twelve. Sitting on a chair next to the gas burner, Gurdweill listened with great enjoyment to its steady hiss. A cosy hiss, he reflected, calling to mind placid, capable housewives and domestic peace . . . A benevolent smile appeared on his lips and remained there for a moment or two. Then

314

the coffee was heated, he switched off the gas, and the hiss stopped as abruptly as if the soul of the kitchen had suddenly flown out of the door. Now the semi-darkness seemed heavier and more oppressive.

The old woman had finished tidying the bed and was now busy sweeping the floor. Naturally, she had not lifted a finger to clean the couch, and it was clear to Gurdweill that she had no intention of doing so. But he could not bring himself to begin arguing with her again. When all was said and done, she was an old, tired woman — he excused her to himself. As soon as he had a chance he would buy a bottle of lysol and smear it over the couch himself, after washing it first with boiling water. He drank his coffee, finished getting dressed, and half an hour later he took his stick and left the room.

26

OUTSIDE, the sultry yellow heat lay heavily over everything. There was a lassitude in the air, and even the traffic seemed to be moving more slowly than usual. The dogs' tongues were hanging out of their mouths, long and quivering, like pink ribbons; their ribs heaved in and out as they panted for breath, and the heat seemed to increase at the very sight of them, as if it were pouring straight out of their jaws.

Gurdweill hesitated for a moment, wondering whether he should go somewhere for a bite to eat. He was not in the least hungry. In the end he went into a little restaurant in Nordbahnstrasse and ordered roast beef and beer. Then he took a tram to the hospital, where he arrived half an hour after the visiting hour had begun.

There were thirty white cots in the newborn babies' ward, a long room with a lot of windows, which were all wide open. Some of the babies were sleeping and others were wailing in weak little voices. Nurses went in and out. Through the windows you could see green trees, square mown lawns, gravel paths, and green-painted benches. A tall, blonde nurse who already knew Gurdweill, led him to number 26, took Martin out of his cot and gave him to his father with the words: "He's a good boy, he never cries!" adding immediately, as she did every day: "No kissing, and don't touch his mouth!" She stood and watched as Gurdweill held the baby wrapped in white swaddling clothes, and smiled at him with a feeling of happiness that knew no bounds. The tiny face, which had been almost featureless at birth, was developing from day to day, and Gurdweill rejoiced.

"Well, my lad," he said aloud, "so we've got a nose, and a chin too, and a smiling mouth, just like a proper man. Like Goethe, for instance, or Kant. And that's the main thing, right? And it won't be long before we'll be walking too. And until then we'll carry you wherever you want to go, I promise you."

He became aware of the nurse standing next to him and felt a little silly. He smiled in embarrassment and said:

"So he's a good little chap, is he, and he doesn't cry. I'm delighted to hear it!"

At that moment the baby pursed up his mouth and began to wail. Gurdweill rocked him in his arms. He suddenly felt a strange desire to throw him up in the air like a ball, and catch him, but he controlled himself immediately. He clucked his tongue at him, but the baby went on crying. The nurse took him away and returned him to his cot.

"That's enough! We mustn't tire him."

It was time for Gurdweill to go, but before leaving he bent over the cot and said, as if the baby could understand him:

"Really, sir, you're making yourself ridiculous! What a way to behave! But if you must — then by all means go ahead! A little crying never hurt anyone. Daddy's going to buy you a beautiful pram soon, just wait and see! A proper palace for his majesty!"

The baby suddenly stopped crying, as if consoled by the idea of the pram.

"That's better!" said Gurdweill, and started walking away backwards, waving goodbye. He walked down the long corridor and went to see his wife. Thea was sitting up in bed and talking to her neighbour. Gurdweill glanced at the temperature chart hanging at the foot of her bed and found it to his satisfaction.

"And how are you, rabbit?" Thea interrupted her conversation to ask. "Have you seen the little one?"

"Yes. He cried a bit but he's stopped now."

Gurdweill sat down on a chair and began playing with his stick.

Thea said: "I've decided to go to my father when I come out of hospital. It will be easier there at the beginning.

317

Mother will help me until I've got my strength back. I've got leave for another three weeks. I'll stay there for a week or two, as long as I think necessary. Father's due for a visit at any minute, and I'll talk to him about it. I can't understand why he isn't here yet. And then you can take the pram and whatever else is necessary over there — I'll tell you what later."

Gurdweill did not say a word. He knew that it was the right thing to do, for a number of reasons, but he felt uneasy about it nevertheless. He couldn't trust Thea to take her responsibilities seriously enough. He was afraid of what might happen to the baby if it was not under his constant supervision. But since he had no choice in the matter, he decided to make the best of it and spend as much time at Thea's parents' house as possible.

His father-in-law did not come, but Freddy came instead. He sat down on the edge of the bed, and stretched out his long legs, which reached right up to the next bed. During the entire visit he hardly opened his mouth, apart from asking his sister how she felt and how the "infant" was doing. After that he sat and smiled to himself, as if contemplating some agreeable secret. From time to time he fixed his expressionless little eyes on Gurdweill, who was sitting opposite him, and tried to catch his eye, as if he wanted to remind him of something. Gurdweill, for some reason, found his brother-in-law's looks disagreeable. He suddenly remembered the story about the cat, which the latter had told him some months before, and his thoughts jumped unconsciously to his son, Martin, who would soon be living under the same roof as Freddy. He shuddered in horror. But he immediately dismissed his vague dread as groundless and insubstantial. And in order to appear frank and fearless, and especially to banish his insubstantial fears from his own heart, he said to Thea, raising his voice so that her brother, too, would hear:

"Your father will probably come tomorrow. And after you speak to him I'll move the pram and whatever else you need. You're right, it will be better for you to spend a week at your parents' place. Better for you and better for the baby!"

318

As he spoke he looked at Freddy out of the corner of his eye, to see how he reacted to this news. But Freddy went on smiling to himself, as if he were not even listening. After a moment or two he woke up.

"So! The infant will be moving in with us. There'll be fun and games . . ."

Gurdweill looked right at him.

"What do you mean — fun and games?" he demanded belligerently.

"Just what I say — fun and games. There's nothing these infants like better than screaming their lungs out — as if you wanted to hurt them . . . Ha, ha!"

Gurdweill felt a powerful urge to punch his brother-in-law in the jaw, and wipe the insolent, infuriating grin off his face. Every word he said seemed to have a secret, malevolent significance hiding behind its apparent innocence. Gurdweill began to feel uncomfortable and he stood up. He wanted to run away from the man sitting opposite him, but instead of doing so he immediately sat down again. I have to be on my guard against him, he thought.

"And what do you do with yourself all day long, Freddy?" he asked with affected indifference, looking straight into his eyes.

"There's nothing to do. And one sweats so in this heat. What can a person do without a job, without a penny in his pocket? Sometimes I go for a swim."

Gurdweill looked down and his eyes encountered his brother-in-law's shoes, which were covered with a thick layer of dust, as if he had walked a long way. The sight of these dusty shoes for some reason restored Gurdweill's equanimity. And only now he became aware of the over-powering smell of iodine and carbolic in the air, the smell common to all hospitals, as if you were smelling their very souls, which always had an upsetting effect on him. He glanced around the long room and saw that some of the visitors standing between the white-painted, iron beds were getting ready to leave. His watch said twenty to four. Gurdweill stood up; he wanted to peep at Martin again before he left. Thea was still sitting on the bed with her feet

319

in the grey hospital slippers on the floor. He suggested that she lie down again, in order not to tire herself unduly, but she took no notice of him. He kissed her and left, followed by Freddy. In the corridor he began to say goodbye.

"No, I'm coming with you. I want to see him too."

Gurdweill could not prevent him, but this time he only stayed next to the baby for a few moments. Freddy stood a little way off from the cot, bending his long, thin body towards the sleeping baby, the secretive smile once more hovering on his lips. The way he was standing made Gurdweill think of a bird of prey crouching over its victim. He said:

"That's it! Let's go!"

In the courtyard Freddy asked:

"Are you free now? We might spend a couple of hours together."

"I have to go to Mariahilfer Strasse to attend to something. And after that I have to go to a few other places too."

"Good! I'll come with you. I've got plenty of time. Have you got any money on you?"

"No. Only the tram fare."

Gurdweill very much regretted his lack of cash. Otherwise he might have been able to get rid of this pest by offering him a loan. As it was, Freddy had enough for his own tram fare and was ready to accompany him wherever he went. There was no way to get rid of him. In vain Gurdweill deliberately walked in the heat of the sun, hoping that his companion would get tired and go home. But the heat made no impression on Freddy. With his long legs he easily kept pace with Gurdweill, who was not much more than half his size, and never said a word. Gurdweill himself began to feel the heat and wiped his sweating forehead with a handkerchief. He resigned himself to his fate, and crossed to the shade, accompanied by his brother-in-law. The newspaper vendors advertised *Der Tag, Die Zeit, Der Abend*, etc. Their voices grated on the nerves and increased the torments of the heat wave. What a despicable way to earn a living — selling newspapers! — reflected Gurdweill rather incoherently as he stepped on to the tram. Freddy maintained his silence throughout the journey. He waited outside when Gurdweill went into the furniture shop. The negotiations took about twenty minutes; Gurdweill prolonged them on purpose. He wanted a fine pram for his son — the finest pram they had. In the end he chose the one that seemed to him the best in the shop, unaware of the fact that it was exactly the same as Dr. Ostwald's pram at home, except for the colour which was navy-blue instead of black. He tried to lift it and found that it was as light as a feather, not like the other one which was as heavy as a truck, so heavy you couldn't move it an inch . . . He agreed to pay an extra ten schillings and to bring the other pram with the money the next day at half past five, when he would tell them where to send the new one — which would enable him to have it sent directly to his parents-in-law, and save himself unnecessary trouble. With the deal closed to the satisfaction of both parties, Gurdweill left the shop in a joyful mood. In an instant all his doubts about his fatherhood seemed to have been dispelled — as if it had now been verified and confirmed by incontrovertible proof . . . Everything was now his: the baby, the pram, Thea — there was no doubt about it! He was radiant with happiness. In the meantime he had forgotten all about his brother-in-law. But Freddy was still waiting. Leaning against a lamppost, he was standing diagonally opposite, keeping watch on the door like a private detective. His company no longer bothered Gurdweill. On the contrary, from a certain point of view he was even pleased to have him there, as a witness to the proof of his paternity . . . He went straight up to him.

Freddy said in a slightly plaintive tone:

"It took you a long time. But never mind. I haven't got anything else to do."

Gurdweill now had to go to Dr. Astel to borrow money. But since there was no chance of finding him at home before six, there was no reason to hurry, and they approached the Ring at a leisurely stroll. After taking a few steps in silence, Freddy suddenly said:

"Actually, what do you want a baby for?"

Gurdweill stopped short and gazed at him in astonishment, as if he had gone out of his mind.

Freddy explained:

"What I mean to say is — how can a person feel love for such an insignificant little thing? It's neither flesh nor spirit — it's nothing at all! . . . A matter for foolish women. And to think that people devote their lives to it, even before it comes into the world — it's incomprehensible!"

"It seems to me that you're not quite sane. You can't understand the simplest, most natural things."

Freddy took two cigarettes from the upper pocket of his jacket, one for himself and one for Gurdweill, lit them and continued as he walked:

"It's got nothing to do with nature! As far as men are concerned nothing could be more unnatural . . . What I say is: women, I can understand. It's their job! But men! Where does this love come from? I'm not at all sure that it's not an affectation pure and simple. What can one possibly feel for such a little nothing? As for me, I can't say I'm too fond of the little creatures myself."

"Don't worry, you'll feel differently one day. When you reach middle age."

"No, I don't think so," replied Freddy calmly, with his peculiar smile. "By the way, I don't intend getting married either. What for? There are plenty of women around without getting married. And in any case, after half an hour I've had enough of them. Let's go and have a beer. I've got a few groschen left . . . After that they bore me to death. And if you say — what about love? I say: fiddlesticks! There's no such thing! Why fall in love with this one rather than that one? No, you can count me out! It makes no difference to me — they're all the same!"

They were passing a little tavern and Freddy dragged Gurdweill in. They sat down at a wooden table and a waiter brought them two tankards of cold beer covered with snow-white foam.

"Thank God for beer," said Freddy after slaking his thirst. "Where would we be without it?"

After a moment he resumed his theme:

"Let's take you, for example. Why did you take it into your head to marry Thea? What do you need her for? She would have gone to bed with you anyway, I can guarantee!

She may be my sister, but what do I care about that? But I'm really surprised at you, after all you're not a fool — what do you need to get married for? You go to bed with her once, twice — enough! Is there any lack of women in the world? They're as common as dirt! If I were you I wouldn't stay with her for one single day!"

"Come, come! You're a real woman-hater!" laughed Gurdweill. "I had no idea you were so hostile to women."

"Woman-hater! I'm not a woman-hater. I neither hate them nor love them. All I want is peace and quiet. Give up my peace of mind for a pinafore? — Never! Especially when I can get what I want at a reasonable price and without any obligations! And the boredom, how can you stand the boredom? What on earth is a person supposed to do with them afterwards?" He took a sip of beer and concluded firmly: "No sir! You can count me out!"

"But not everyone is like you. There are other people who feel quite differently."

"Too bad for them! Their heads aren't in the right place, poor devils . . . They get what they deserve and that's all there is to be said on the subject."

There was a brief silence.

"You know what, Rudolf, why don't we leave all this old junk behind us and go abroad together? To France, America, Brazil — the devil knows where! I'm sick of everything — the city, the people, my parents — the lot! We can get hold of the money somewhere . . . What do you need Thea and that little worm for? Leave them for God's sake! You'll find better, believe me! At least we'll see the world, since we have to live in it whether we like it or not! Different people, different ways of life, a bit of movement, adventure! You can die of boredom here! And I'll find the money. Enough for me, and maybe even for you. We don't need much. We can go to France first, to Paris, and after that we'll see."

"No!" said Gurdweill. "I'm not going anywhere. I don't suffer from boredom here either. I feel fine."

In the depths of his heart he knew that he was not telling the whole truth, and that he did not always feel so fine. But Freddy's proposal, although there was no

323

doubting its sincerity, seemed so childish, so bizarre — as if he had told him to fly to the moon, or to commit suicide.

"No," he repeated. "If you really want to go abroad, you'll have to go by yourself. For me the time for such adventures has passed. If I ever have the money for it I might go abroad, but under different conditions."

"It's only because you're tied to Thea's apron-strings, I know it. Since when are you such a solid citizen that you can't go anywhere without a wagon-lit? Well, let's leave it at that!"

He emptied his glass angrily: as far as he was concerned, Gurdweill was a lost case.

"I'll go alone! I'll find a way!"

Suddenly Gurdweill found himself feeling sorry for this young man, whose cynical smile had disappeared, leaving a grim, suffering expression on his face, which seemed that of a far older man. He didn't get much satisfaction out of life, he reflected. Compared to him, he, Gurdweill, was a happy man with a hold on life . . . He felt slightly ashamed of his happiness in front of Freddy. The hostility he had felt towards his brother-in-law in the hospital had vanished without a trace. "He'll come to a bad end" — the thought flashed through his mind with the force of a sudden revelation, and as if to comfort him for something, he said:

"Would you like to come with me? I have to pay a call to Dr. Astel in Karlsgasse. He usually comes home from the office after six."

Freddy rose silently to his feet and followed him out of the tavern. He walked with him to the corner of the street, where he suddenly stopped and announced:

"No, I'm not coming with you! It's boring."

The cynical smile reappeared on his face. "By the way, our cat's disappeared . . . three days ago, hee- hee . . ." He stared straight into Gurdweill's eyes. "Father's in despair, the old fool! I think he must be getting senile to make such a fuss over a revolting old cat."

Gurdweill paled.

"You killed him yourself, you monster! And you're not even ashamed!"

Freddy went on smiling without saying a word. Then he turned away and strode off, stooping slightly.

Dr. Astel was not at home, and Gurdweill descended the stairs again and stood next to the entrance to wait for him. He could not get out of his mind the cat which Freddy had killed. In vivid detail, he imagined the cruel scene. He saw Freddy holding the tabby cat by the neck, while it twitched and twitched. Gradually the twitching grew weaker until it stopped — the cat was dead. The scene filled him with inexpressible disgust, but he could not dismiss it from his sight, and was forced to watch to the bitter end. The deed had been done at dusk, of this Gurdweill was certain, when there was nobody at home. Afterwards the murderer had taken an empty suitcase — the smooth, brown, calfskin case with yellowing labels saying Budapest, Bruck, Graz, etc., stuck on its sides, which Gurdweill had often seen in his in-laws' house — placed the body inside it, and carried it to the Danube. He himself, in similar circumstances, would have thrown the evidence of his crime into the Danube, Gurdweill reflected, and was horrified at the thought. He began pacing agitatedly to and fro in the deserted street . . . Of course, he could also have thrown it behind some nearby fence. Firstly, because he didn't want to carry it all the way to the canal, and secondly, because he was pressed for time. Someone could come home at any minute and surprise him when he returned with the suitcase — and then it would all come out . . . No, he couldn't take it to the canal, it was too risky . . . But what has the whole disgusting business got to do with me? he interrupted himself impatiently.

He took out his watch: it was half past six. Dr. Astel was late today. Perhaps he wasn't coming home at all? He would wait until half past seven at the latest. Sometimes Astel stopped somewhere on his way home. If he hadn't shown up by then — he would have to look for him in the café in the evening, or go to his office in the morning, or perhaps find someone else to borrow the money from . . . He went through all his acquaintances in his mind, and seized on Vrubiczek the shoemaker. Yes, he would certainly be at home. As for the others — he doubted it.

325

The street was now steeped in shade, which did nothing to reduce the heat. Someone nearby was practising scales on the piano, up and down, up and down, endlessly and tediously, over and over again with maddening monotony. On the opposite pavement a nursemaid passed with a small child who was pulling a grey plush elephant on a string, turning his head every now and then to make sure that no harm had come to his toy. A red-headed girl stuck her head out of a window on the top floor of a building at the end of the street, looked around for a while and disappeared inside again. A young telegram deliverer rode up on a bicycle, which he leant against the wall of the building opposite before running up the steps, his trouser cuffs secured by bicycle-clips. In a moment he was back again, springing energetically on to his bicycle and riding off rapidly. A light, barely perceptible breeze wafted the tantalizing smell of roasting meat into Gurdweill's nostrils. He sensed a tickling on his palate and swallowed his saliva.

No! — he began brooding on the same subject again — it would have been impossible to throw it into the Danube ... So he must have left it somewhere near the house, perhaps in some garden. If they looked for it, they would be sure to find it ... But why should anyone look for it? A dead cat — tfu! And afterwards? Afterwards he simply went home with the empty suitcase, with the old labels of different railway stations stuck on its sides. His parents were still out and nobody saw him return. He put the suitcase away and lit a cigarette to smoke at his ease. And when his parents came home — what did he know about anything? To be on the safe side he probably opened the kitchen window first, and left it open: "The cat must have escaped through the window" ... Ah, if the old man only knew that Freddy had killed it! He would have thrown him out of the house! And now Martin was going to stay in that very house! ... A shudder ran down Gurdweill's spine at the thought. He felt a sudden cramp in his stomach and stopped pacing. What? — he immediately came to his senses. Have you gone out of your mind? He would never do anything to the baby! That's insane! I'll kill him if he

326

touches it! The devil knows what's wrong with me today! It's pure madness!

He took out his pipe as if to reassure himself and began searching feverishly through his pockets for his tobacco pouch. He must have forgotten it at home. At that moment Dr. Astel tapped him on the shoulder.

"Have you been waiting long? It's only by chance that I came home at all. I have to leave again right away. Anyway, come upstairs with me for a moment."

As soon as he entered the apartment he rolled up the drawing room blinds, which had been down all day to protect the furniture from the sun, and went into his bedroom to change. Gurdweill sprawled out on the soft sofa, which was covered with green velvet whose touch made him think of hair cut with a barber's clippers. Suddenly he felt free of his previous distressing thoughts, as if he had shed them like a skin in the street outside. His fears now seemed bizarre, the product of a morbid, hyper-active imagination. The pleasant coolness of the room revived him; he puffed on the cigarette he had taken from Dr. Astel and listened to the splashing of the water in the kitchen, where his friend was washing, with the joy of a blind man whose sight has been restored by a successful operation. How could such an idea have entered his head? A baby wasn't a cat, after all! And who said he had actually killed the cat in the first place? Maybe he was only boasting . . . It was perfectly possible that the cat had really run away, as cats sometimes did — through that very same kitchen window, which somebody had forgotten to close . . . And perhaps it would come home again, perhaps it had already come home in the meantime! And if it didn't come home, there were all kinds of other possibilities — it might have been run over by a car, or a cart, or a tram . . . He himself had seen a dog run over by a tram, and killed instantly. And if it hadn't been run over, it might have been stolen . . . There were people who stole cats . . . It was a handsome cat, you had to admit, why shouldn't somebody steal it? And anyway, what on earth did his father-in-law's cat have to do with his, Gurdweill's, son? To hell with the cat! He was suddenly filled with such rage against this cat

which kept intruding on his thoughts, without so much as
a by-your-leave, that if it had been within his reach he
might easily have strangled it himself! As for Freddy —
from this day forth he refused to listen to his nonsense
any more! He wasn't interested and that was the end of
it! Angrily he threw the fag end of his cigarette on to the
floor, but immediately came to his senses and picked it up
again and put it out in the ashtray on the smoking table in
the corner. Then he lay down on the sofa again. Without
noticing the hidden association between his thoughts, he
suddenly remembered Franzi Mitteldorfer, whom he had
gone to visit more than six months ago at Steinhof, and
whose mother, whom he had met by chance in the street
in the spring, had told him that she was feeling better and
would soon be sent home. She must be cured and home
by now. Gurdweill decided to go and visit her that very
evening, since Dr. Astel was engaged. In a few days' time,
when Thea came out of the hospital, he would be far too
busy to go and see her.

Dr. Astel came into the room dressed in a new grey
suit, ready to go out. With a carefree gesture he handed
Gurdweill the fifteen schillings which the latter had requested.

"Here you are. I'm sorry I can't spend the evening with
you. As it is, I have to hurry. Are you free on Saturday
night? Good, at seven then, at the Herrenhof! And now
let's be on our way."

They walked over to Karlsplatz, where Dr. Astel hailed
a passing cab and drove off.

Gurdweill felt hungry and went to have something to
eat in a little bourgeois restaurant in the Wiedner Hauptstrasse. Half an hour later he was sitting in an almost empty
tram, whose windows suddenly flamed, as it swerved left,
in the rosy glow of the sun setting somewhere in the
distance, somewhere far beyond the city or any human
habitation. An agreeable, complacent feeling stole over
Gurdweill, which may have had something to do with the
tasty, filling meal he had just eaten. The heat of the day
was fading, and it was easier to breathe. A draught blew
through the empty coach, touching his face and ruffling

328

his hair. Suddenly he remembered Lotte and he was overwhelmed by a desire to see her again before she left the city. What a pity that he had not asked Dr. Astel when she was leaving. He was sure to know. When she came back Martin would be a big baby. He would invite her to his house, to see him. He knew that she would like him ... What a strange girl she was! Why didn't she marry Dr. Astel? She should have a baby ... Thea wasn't really a natural mother, even though she loved Martin, you could see that at a glance ...

Immersed in these, and other, similar reflections, which welled up in him as mildly as the quiet evening twilight, he reached his destination. Franzi herself opened the door, and at first he did not recognize her, partly because of the dim light in the corridor, but also because of the roundness and healthiness of her face, in contrast to the last time he had seen her in Steinhof. He took a step backwards: for a moment he wondered if he had come to the wrong door. But the young woman recognized him immediately and cried with undisguised joy:

"Oh, Herr Gurdweill! What a surprise! Mother, come and see who's here!"

She led him into the room he remembered from the year before, which was still quite light. Nothing had changed during the course of the year, as if the months had passed somewhere outside, far away, while here, inside the room, time had stood still, and all was exactly as before, except for the sound of hammering which no longer disturbed the quiet as it had done then. Suddenly Gurdweill knew, with utter certainty, that deep within himself the inner core of his own being, too, had remained intact, and that it could never be changed by the passing of time and external circumstances of life — which gave rise in him to a fleeting sense of the eternity of the universe. He said:

"I'm so glad, Frau Mitteldorfer, glad from the bottom of my heart, to see you looking well and healthy!"

Her mother came into the room and almost fell round Gurdweill's neck, so great was her joy at seeing him. So welcome, so dear a guest! She would go and put the coffee on at once. It would be ready in a second. Herr Gurdweill had come at just the right time, for Franzi was about to go to the cinema in Gumpendorfer Strasse. If he had come fifteen minutes later he would have missed her. And now, if Herr Gurdweill wished, he could go with her. Poor baby, she deserved a little fun after what she had been through these past months — wasn't that so? They could go straight after coffee. She would bring it in a jiffy.

The old woman hurried out of the room.

"Mother seems intent on chasing you out of the house," said Franzi with a smile. "But it's really not necessary. I can easily give up the cinema today, I'm so glad to see you."

"Not at all," said Gurdweill. She was on no account to change her plans for him. He would accompany her with pleasure, if she so wished. But in that case they had better hurry if they didn't want to miss the beginning of the film.

"The cinema's only a few steps away. We won't be late — they only start after nine."

Gurdweill was careful not to refer to her illness in case it embarrassed her. But the young woman immediately referred to his visit to Steinhof herself, with a frankness which disconcerted him.

"You must pardon me," she said, "if I didn't behave properly when you came to see me. I expect I was over-excited. Imagine — a place like that! If you only knew how people suffered there! It's awful! The nurses behave like tyrants, and complaining to the doctors doesn't get you anywhere. They don't believe you. They seem to think that a person who's mentally ill is no better than a wild animal. And you're afraid to complain, too. The nurses bully the patients, they hit them whenever they feel like it, I think they actually enjoy it. You can't get any justice there. It's worse than the Inquisition! And the patients themselves! Oh, it makes your hair stand on end! It's something you can never forget as long as you live! Even now I often wake up in horror in the middle of the night, and it takes me a long time before I realize that I'm not there any more and calm down a little. The really insane don't feel it so much, but anyone who has periods of lucidity can go mad there! One day I'll tell you about it in detail. You're a writer, Herr Gurdweill, and someone

330

should tell the world the truth about what goes on inside that place."

She fell silent.

His head lowered, his back to the window, Gurdweill sat and listened to Franzi. The visit to Steinhof rose up before him in vivid detail and he relived all its fears and torments. Unintentionally he stole a glance at her legs and saw that her stockings were now smooth and tight, and her feet were shod in new, brown shoes. "She's learnt to put on her stockings properly again," the absurd thought crossed his mind, and he was furious with himself for thinking anything so stupid.

"You know," she went on, "even now, although I've been home for two months, whenever I touch on the subject I feel a hidden fear that the nurses will somehow find out and revenge themselves on me . . . Even though I immediately tell myself that it's ridiculous, that they've got no power over me any more and they can't harm me — in the depths of my heart I'm still afraid. I can't get rid of the terror they instilled in me."

"The fear is understandable," said Gurdweill in a whisper, as if talking to himself, "but it will grow weaker in time, until in the end it disappears. Try not to think about it too much, to distract your mind with other things, and you'll gradually forget about it."

Franzi's mother brought in the coffee.

"If you want to go — you'd better drink up!"

She climbed on to a chair and lit the gas. They drank their coffee, hardly speaking. The gas flame began to sing in its soft, monotonous hiss, and was immediately joined by the drowsy buzzing of a fly. Someone nearby began to whistle the popular tune:

"Wer hast denn dei-ne schoenen,
blauen Au-u-u-gen her,
so traut . . ."

Franzi left the room and came back after a moment with a straw hat on her head.

Outside a light breeze was blowing, setting a few scraps of grey cloud to flight. There was a smell of approaching rain in the air.

331

Gurdweill said:

"You know, ten days ago my wife gave birth to a son."

"Really? I didn't even know that you were married."

She turned to face him and added:

"You don't seem like a married man."

"Nevertheless I've been married for over a year now. I have a wife, a son, a father-in-law and a mother-in-law, and . . . a brother-in-law as well . . . two, as a matter of fact . . . all present and correct!"

"I suppose you must be very happy about your son. And his mother even more so! She must be beside herself with joy! For a woman there's nothing else like it in the world! When my Fritzi was born — how happy I was! And even now — but for him I don't know where I would have found the strength to withstand all that suffering."

"Yes," Gurdweill agreed, "you're quite right!"

Tomorrow he would change the pram and then everything would be his: the woman, the baby, the pram — everything. If only she wasn't going to stay with her father . . . but that would soon pass too . . . He felt an urge to tell Franzi about it and he said:

"They're still in hospital — my wife and the baby, that is. But afterwards they're going to stay with my in-laws. Only for a week or two. I decided that it would be for the best . . . her mother will be able to help her with the baby — that's very important! Especially at the beginning, don't you agree?"

"Of course!" said Franzi, and Gurdweill felt a certain relief. It was on the tip of his tongue to add: "But one of my brothers-in-law likes strangling cats . . ." but he caught himself in time. "This is getting beyond a joke!" he said furiously to himself. "You're letting your thoughts run away with you again!"

Then they arrived at the cinema and he stood in the queue to buy tickets for the film.

27

AUTUMN announced itself with blustering winds, chillier nights, and leaves as broad and golden as tobacco leaves, which lay scattered under the trees lining the streets, blew boldly on to the pavements, and made a crunching sound like sugar under the feet of the passers-by.

It was the end of September. Every day Thea went to Dr. Ostwald's office while Gurdweill looked after Martin, who was now three months old. He weighed eleven pounds, his development was satisfactory, his skin was slightly tanned, and he had his mother's flaxen hair. Gurdweill would bathe him and dry him, change his nappies, soothe him when he cried, put him to sleep, and take him out for walks in his pram — all with tender love and devotion. He even washed the nappies himself and performed all the other necessary chores. Thea hardly helped at all, apart from breastfeeding Martin, which obliged her, to her resentment, to hurry home during her lunch-break. Towards evening, when she came home from work, after feeding the baby and having something to eat, she would usually go out again, without Gurdweill knowing where she was going, and return at midnight, or even later. Gurdweill had his hands full. His face was drawn and hollow, but he did not care. He would have given his life for Martin. Every now and then he would transfer the baby, at his wife's command, to his in-laws' house, pushing the pram through a fair slice of the city to Schulgasse. Martin would remain there for a few days, and Thea would sleep there too. (The old Baron adored his grandson, although he was still inconsolable about the mysterious disappearance of his cat. And Freddy, who was busy preparing for his trip abroad, would twist the knife by saying, with his cynical smile: "Why worry, the cat will come back in the end —

it must have gone to the country for a rest . . .") Although Gurdweill had more time to himself when the baby was at the Baron's house, the vague fear that some harm would come to his son there in his absence poisoned his mind and gave him no peace. Sitting with friends in the café, he was liable to jump up abruptly and rush out to take the first tram to Schulgasse, only to find Martin sleeping peacefully in his pram. He could not bear the child to be out of his sight. During this whole period he did hardly any work on his writing, apart from an occasional evening when Thea was out and Martin was sleeping.

What he liked best was sitting on a bench in the Prater Hauptallee on a fine afternoon, with Martin in his pram beside him, among all the nursemaids and young mothers who already knew him and often offered him a helping hand. Among themselves they referred to him jokingly as "the young mother," but they pitied him too, and were glad to help him.

"The poor, pathetic creature!" they said. "What does a man know about such a little baby? A baby needs a woman — that's obvious! It's a law of nature!"

"And where's the mother?"

"She must have died giving birth."

"Ah, the poor little chick!"

"Or perhaps she didn't die at all. Perhaps she's only ill."

"Yes, perhaps she's ill."

"But isn't there a grandmother? Or some other female relation?"

"Evidently not."

"Then why don't they put him in the municipal crèche? At least they've got expert nurses there!"

"Yes, he'd be better off there than like this."

"Who knows? I for one wouldn't put my baby in the crèche!"

"But the baby looks well, you must admit. He's quite healthy."

"Yes, there's nothing wrong with his development."

"And he's a bonny baby, too. A sight for sore eyes."

"Yes, but poor little worm — he was born under an

unlucky star! He hasn't got much of a chance, and that's a fact."

"It'll be a miracle if he lasts out the year. In ninety-nine out of a hundred cases they die after a few months. And what's the wonder, poor motherless mites!"

"But he seems so nice!"

"Who?"

"The father!"

"Yes, he's a nice man."

"And well-educated too! I'll bet he's a professor or someone like that. You can tell from his face."

"But not very rich by the looks of things. Otherwise he would have taken a nursemaid. Professors aren't too well off since the war. Lots of them are starving."

"And those that aren't professors aren't starving perhaps? Who isn't starving today apart from a few crooks and war-profiteers?"

Thus they chatted on a fine, early autumn afternoon, with the mild sunshine spreading over the yellowing grass and the trees, whose branches were now interspersed with large patches of sky, while the city's roar created a murmuring wall to their right.

One day one of these women was bold enough to address Gurdweill directly:

"A baby needs a woman to look after it, don't you think?"

Gurdweill said nothing.

But the young woman was not to be deterred. She began again, this time going straight to the point:

"Please don't be offended, sir, but we wondered, because we never see the mother taking him for a walk, poor little mite! I don't want to interfere in your private affairs, God forbid, but it really breaks a person's heart to see a child without a mother to look after him!"

"His mother can't!" Gurdweill said shortly.

"Ah, she can't. In that case, it's another matter, of course. I suppose she's ill, poor soul. What a tragedy!"

"She isn't ill, but nevertheless she can't do it."

"Indeed? She isn't even ill! That I can't understand! A mother who's not ill and who doesn't take care of her

335

own baby! There are all kinds of mothers in the world, it seems!"

Gurdweill said nothing. How was she supposed to know that Thea worked all day long? And besides, what difference did it make who looked after him? The main thing was that he was healthy and developed well. He lacks for nothing under my care. I look after him better than any woman. I wouldn't trust Thea to take care of him even if she wanted to.

"You can't say that he's not a healthy baby," he said in the end, pointing to Martin who was sleeping in his pram.

"No, nobody could deny that he's healthy. But nevertheless it's not a job for a man, in my opinion."

"But if I tell you that his mother can't do it!" By now there was a note of annoyance in Gurdweill's voice. "She simply can't do it, I tell you!"

He took out his watch. It was nearly half past five: time to go home. He said goodbye to his neighbour on the bench, and began walking away, pushing the pram carefully in front of him. Women were really stupid! he reflected. You could tell them something a thousand times and they simply refused to get it into their heads!

He negotiated the busy Praterstern, with the age-blackened Tegetthoff monument looming up commandingly in the middle of it, and immediately reached his own street, which was now deep in shade and so quiet that the silence hit him in the face like something tangible. He left the pram in the vestibule and carried the baby up to the room, where he put him down on the bed, and went downstairs again to bring up the pram. Meanwhile the baby woke up and let out a shrill, despairing wail, as if somebody was about to kill him. Gurdweill rocked him in the pram and spoke to him in a reasonable tone of voice:

"I'm ashamed of you! A big boy like you, crying like a woman! Mother will be here soon to give you your supper, you'll see!"

The child fell silent for a moment, but immediately began again. Gurdweill took him out of the pram and began walking up and down the room bouncing him in his arms, just like Thea used to do to him when she felt like a romp. Martin refused to stop crying.

"I never knew you were such a silly boy!" said Gurdweill. "You never told me so before. You know very well that Daddy's busy now. He hasn't got even an ounce of time to spare! For instance, he has to wash your smoking jacket for the cocktail party tomorrow! A modern young man like you can't go to a cocktail party in a soiled smoking jacket! What would the pretty girls say? All the conquests you've made up to now would come to nothing! The least little sloppiness in a gentleman's attire can ruin everything — as you know very well yourself! And Daddy's got a pile of other work to do besides — all for your personal benefit! No-o! So you're stubborn as well! A nasty fault! I really thought you were more intelligent. And if you don't stop now, our ways are parting! You're going right back to your pram and I'm not saying another word! Stubbornness is one thing I won't countenance!"

Thea opened the door and came in without Gurdweill hearing her.

"Why is he screaming like that? Why don't you make him keep quiet?!"

"He's screaming because he's hungry. Take him and feed him."

"Wha-at?! Because you don't know how to handle him! Let him wait a while, he won't starve! Shut him up! I can't stand the noise!"

"You can see that it's useless. Feed him and he'll calm down."

Thea shot her husband an annihilating look and began unhurriedly taking off her coat and hat. Then she took a cigarette out of her purse and lit it. Slowly she sat down on the sofa, the burning cigarette between her lips, and began baring her breast.

"Give him here!" she commanded.

The moment his lips touched the nipple the baby stopped crying.

"You see, he was hungry, poor little thing!"

And after a moment:

"Don't you think that ... that you should take the

337

cigarette out of your mouth when you're feeding him? The smoke's getting in his eyes."

"What? What's it got to do with you?"

"You can smoke as much as you like afterwards," Gurdweill stood his ground, "it doesn't take so long, after all!"

He approached her and said coaxingly:

"Give it to me, dearest, there's a good girl, control yourself for a few minutes."

With her free hand she pushed him away roughly.

"It's none of your business! I'll do whatever I like!"

"But you're harming the baby! Why should you harm him for nothing?"

"Why do you take such an interest in him?" she said viciously. "Haven't I told you already a thousand times that the baby's mine and mine only — mine and . . . In any case you've got nothing to do with him . . ."

"I don't care!" Gurdweill interrupted her. "It makes no difference! A baby is a baby! Even if he was a complete stranger you wouldn't have the right to ruin his eyes with smoke! It's simply gratuitous cruelty!"

"That's enough! I don't want to hear another word! Go downstairs and buy something for supper! I have to go out soon!"

For a moment he felt an urge to snatch the baby out of her hands and never let her touch him again — come what may! He wasn't going to abandon his child to her caprices! But he controlled himself. At that moment he hated his wife, but he was no match for her. He consoled himself with the thought that he still needed her now, but the moment the child was weaned he would take him away from her! Nothing would stop him! He sent her a look full of suppressed hostility, which she did not notice, and left the room.

When he came back, Martin was lying in his pram.

"We have to bathe him first. We can eat later, after he's gone to sleep."

"No, we'll eat first! I told you I have to go out! You can bathe him yourself, or ask the old woman to help you."

As soon as they had finished eating she got dressed and left. In the depths of his heart Gurdweill was glad.

338

He could cope better by himself, without shouting and arguments. He cleared the table and brought in the little tin tub from the kitchen, put it on a chair, set out a clean nappy and bath towels, and went back to the kitchen to heat up a big kettle of water. The old landlady was happy to help him, as she had already done many times before. And a few minutes later the baby was splashing his tiny limbs in the lukewarm water, to his vast and evident delight. He laughed all over his face and Gurdweill laughed joyfully with him, as he scrubbed his smooth little body with a yellow sponge.

"Aie, aie, aie!" exclaimed Frau Fischer, holding the baby in the water. "A baby is a blessing in the house! A woman feels it more than a man. Especially a bonny baby like Martin! A real ray of sunshine, God save him, psss!"

Gurdweill smiled at her gratefully. "She's a kind-hearted old creature in spite of everything!" he said to himself.

The landlady went on whispering:

"He's just like his mother. Alike as two peas in a pod. A person can see it in the dark! He doesn't look like Herr Gurdweill at all! — Siedl says the same. But he certainly takes after Herr Gurdweill in his character, so quiet and honest, just like his father, psss! But I do say, and so does Siedl, that his mother doesn't spend enough time with him, aie, aie, aie! A fine woman, Herr Gurdweill's wife, a very fine woman! But she's got no time, no time at all, that poor mother!"

Gurdweill wrapped Martin in the towel and dried him, put him down on the bed, and struggled to push the tiny clenched fist, which his son insisted on putting in his mouth, into the swaddling clothes. The twilight gathered in the room. Stooping slightly, her skinny arms hanging in front of her withered body, like some four-legged animal standing on its hind legs, the old woman stood and watched Gurdweill's every movement.

"Herr Gurdweill does it very well," she chattered on. "Everything just as it should be, psss! Better than a real woman, even . . . Well, a clever man can put his hand to anything. As my dear husband, may he rest in peace, used to say. If not for Herr Gurdweill, what would become of him, the poor little mite, aie, aie, aie! Seeing as his mother has got so little time for him! What a piece of luck, I must say, that Herr Gurdweill is such a clever, handy man! Golden hands, psss!"

Gurdweill finished swaddling the baby and put him down in the pram. He put his finger to his lips to request silence, and began rocking the pram and humming an old tune whose origins he had long forgotten. Frau Fischer went out of the room.

Half an hour later he was standing in his rolled-up shirtsleeves bent over the tub, which he had pushed against the door in order not to wake the baby, and wringing out the already washed white swaddling clothes. The oil-lamp gave off a dim light. Through the half-open windows the evening streamed in, with the muffled city roar filtered, as it were, by the distance it had travelled, and purified of base materials. Gurdweill liked this dim, distant roar; a familiar mood, compounded of contentment and the desired degree of lofty melancholy, stirred inside him without quite taking hold. From time to time he straightened his back, which was beginning to hurt. Something urged him to break into song, but he repressed this urge with a vague feeling that it was impossible to give way to it now. Immediately he remembered the sleeping Martin, and the reason for the prohibition. But as if to spite him the desire to sing grew stronger and stronger, until he could barely restrain himself. "Idiot!" he exclaimed aloud.

A loud, ringing peal of female laughter rose from the street below, and stopped abruptly. Gurdweill smiled benevolently and placed the wrung-out swaddling clothes neatly on the chair.

"Yes, go ahead and laugh," he said silently to the invisible woman, "it's a pleasure to hear you laugh!" He did not hear a door opening and footsteps coming down the corridor. Now there was a knock at the door of the room, two hesitant taps, apparently with a single finger. Gurdweill put out his hand and opened the door.

"Oh!" he cried in surprise.

"I'm disturbing you," said Lotte. "I've come at an inconvenient time."

340

"Not at all! On the contrary!"

Only now he realized that he was without a collar or jacket, and he blushed slightly.

"Excuse me, Lotte, for my, er, appearance . . ." he stammered in embarrassment. "I'll get rid of all this in a minute. But please sit down, on the couch! I'm so glad! That you came now, I mean. I can't tell you how glad I am! I'll be free in a minute."

He began hastily taking the laundry off the chair but then he changed his mind and put it back and took hold of the half-full tub. Lotte watched him in silence.

"Pardon the mess. During the day there's no time, and now that the baby's asleep . . ."

Lotte opened the door and he went out with the tub. From somewhere in the corridor came the sound of water splashing and gurgling and then the banging of the tin tub against a wall, or something of the kind. And a moment later he was back to take the laundry.

"And you do all that yourself!" said Lotte with a mocking note in her voice, nodding at the laundered swaddling clothes.

"Yes, why not?"

"Hmm, I should have thought that sort of thing was more suitable for a woman than a man . . ."

"Old-fashioned prejudices, Lotte," said Gurdweill with a forced smile, "in our day and age roles aren't so well-defined."

After hanging the laundry in the kitchen, on a line stretching from the window to the opposite wall, he returned to the room and put on his collar and jacket. Lotte sat on the couch in her coat and hat, playing nervously with her purse. She declined the tea or coffee which Gurdweill offered. There was no need for him to trouble himself, she really didn't feel like anything to drink. Gurdweill drew up a chair and sat down next to her.

"How did you enjoy yourself in the Tyrol? I heard from Ulrich that you came back six days ago. I wanted to see you with all my heart but I simply couldn't manage. As you see, I'm busy even in the evenings. The baby can't be left alone."

341

Lotte said ironically:

"And I suppose Thea's busy at the office in the evenings too . . ."

"No," mumbled Gurdweill, "she's not busy at the office. But she likes to go out for a while in the evenings. After a whole day at work she deserves it. She really can't be expected to sit at home and look after the baby after working so hard all day."

"No, of course not," said Lotte sarcastically, "how could you possibly expect such self-sacrifice . . ."

"I don't think you've seen my Martin yet," Gurdweill changed the subject. "Would you like . . . if you're interested, that is . . ."

Lotte gave him an enigmatic look and stood up. She did not want to hurt her host, whose appearance for some reason seemed to her profoundly pathetic. She went up to the pram, bent over the peacefully-sleeping baby, and looked at him unsympathetically for a while in the light of the oil-lamp which Gurdweill had taken off the table. Standing there with the lamp in his hands Gurdweill was suddenly overcome by the strangest feeling – a feeling which froze his blood and sent a shiver down his spine. It suddenly seemed to him that Lotte was only looking at Martin in order to ascertain if he was still alive . . . There was something about the way she was looking at him . . . Gurdweill bent over the other side of the pram, with his head almost touching Lotte's, and tried to hear the baby's breathing. But he couldn't hear anything, and he was seized by a terrible dread. His heart stopped beating. He put the lamp down on the floor next to the pram, and threw himself on his son in such violent agitation that the child woke up screaming. The whole thing took no more than a second. Then he lifted the oil-lamp from the floor and put it back on the table. He was as pale as death.

Lotte cried anxiously: "What's the matter? What's wrong, Gurdweill?"

"Oh, nothing! It's nothing!"

His breath came in short, laborious pants.

"It was only my imagination . . ."

And he began mechanically rocking the baby, whose

screams immediately stopped. For a moment Lotte went on standing and staring at him, and then she sat down on the couch again. There was a silence broken only by the faint sound of the rubber wheels on the floor. At the bottom of the street someone shouted in a rough, unpleasant voice: "Throw it down! Go on, throw it! I'll catch it for sure!" And right after that came the sound of footsteps disappearing into the distance. The darkness closed up again like still waters over a stone. Gurdweill came and sat down beside Lotte again, smiling shamefacedly, as if he had been caught red-handed.

"He's fallen asleep again," he grunted in embarrassment and stole an anxious look at Lotte, eager for her judgement as an artist who had just displayed his paintings.

"Yes, he seems a healthy baby. He looks exactly like Thea, her nose, her hair . . . And are you going to be busy with him all the time from now on? Until he grows up?"

"Not all the time. Sometimes he spends a few days at my father-in-law's house. Then I've got more time to myself, naturally. You know, my brother-in-law Freddy's planning to go abroad soon . . . for a long time . . . You know him, don't you? No? Well, it doesn't matter!"

"Who cares? Will it make any difference to the world if your brother-in-law goes abroad or not?"

"No, you're right, it's not in the least important . . . I just mentioned it . . ."

And a moment later:

"And how are you, my dear? Did you recover your strength in the Tyrol?"

"There was nothing wrong with me in the first place, as far as I know!"

"No, no, of course not! But your nerves were a little upset. The city has a detrimental effect on sensitive people."

"My nerves aren't in the least upset!" Lotte flared up inexplicably. "They never were and they aren't now! You had better worry about your own nerves!"

Gurdweill suddenly knew that whatever he said to Lotte

343

this evening would make no sense and would only annoy her, and that nevertheless he would not be able to stop himself. This inner certainty gave rise in him to an exaggerated excitement and an uncontrollable desire to say everything he had to say immediately, and get it over with. At the same time, he was suddenly flooded by a feeling of immense fatigue, as in anticipation of imminent corporal punishment. As always when he was upset, he began to search for cigarettes, pushing his hand unthinkingly into the same pocket again and again. He found nothing, although he was sure that he still had several left. Lotte opened her purse and offered him a cigarette. He took it, and even before lighting it he heard himself say:

"Well, and what about Dr. Astel? You said you were going to marry him in the autumn, didn't you?"

He felt a certain relief.

Lotte stared at him in astonishment without replying. After a moment she said:

"What on earth has it got to do with you? You're not very polite, I must say! I never knew you so ill-bred!"

And she added:

"I'll marry him when I feel like it! And perhaps I'll never marry him at all! Haven't you got anything else to worry about?"

"All I want is to see you happy." He took hold of her hand. "You have no idea how dear you are to me and how important your happiness is to me!"

Lotte withdrew her hand, stood up and went over to the open window. For a moment she looked down, and then she returned to the couch and sat down again.

"And happiness lies in being Dr. Astel's wife?"

"I don't know if that's where your happiness lies. I don't know how you feel about him. It's only because of what you said before you went away, about getting married to him, that I thought . . . In the last resort our happiness comes from within ourselves, not from outside."

"And who told you that I wasn't happy now, just as I am? Ha, ha, ha! What an outburst! Look here, my friend, you see the mote in another's eye without seeing the beam in your own . . ."

"I don't understand what you're getting at."

"There's no need for explanations! It's perfectly obvious!"

In the next room Siedl's ugly, rasping voice gabbled something rapidly, swallowing half the words, so that what she said was completely unintelligible to them.

"Who's croaking there like that?" said Lotte with a shudder.

"That's Siedl. Her voice is really unpleasant."

"And who's Siedl?"

"Oh, don't you know? She's my landlady's daughter, an old maid."

The light from the oil-lamp fell directly on Lotte's face, which was thin and drawn, despite the superficial tan from the sharp mountain air, and upon which a new line of suffering was stamped. Her big, wonderful, grey eyes were surrounded by dark circles which made them look even bigger, and quite black. It occurred to Gurdweill that she was probably suffering from insomnia, and for some reason this seemed to him terrible. What did she lack, this Lotte? — he asked himself.

"Perhaps you should take off your hat," he said compassionately, "otherwise it will give you a headache."

Lotte said nothing. She may not even have heard him. With her head tilted slightly to the left she sat without moving, staring straight in front of her. She appeared to be sunk in sombre, sorrowful reflections. In the room next door Siedl's voice fell silent, and down in the street, too, all was quiet. The silence began to oppress Gurdweill. In Lotte's frozen stillness, she who was so vivacious by nature, there was something very painful, unnatural and frightening. It grieved him to see her like this, and he wanted to say something, however trivial, to break the silence and distract her. He pressed her hand and said:

"You still haven't told me how you spent your time in the Tyrol. If you had pleasant company."

Lotte started as if from a dream.

"Pleasant company? What pleasant company?"

"In the Tyrol?"

"No! I didn't go there to look for company!"

"Weren't there any other Viennese there?"

"Yes, there were. Bank clerks and so on. Nobody interesting."

She shivered slightly, as if she felt cold.

"Should I close the window? Are you cold?"

"No, I'm not cold. That is, I am a little cold. You can close the window if you like."

When he sat down again he said:

"Well, and were there a lot of goats there?"

"Goats? Why goats?"

"I don't know, no special reason."

"Ha, ha — a nice association of ideas! Goats and bank clerks! Actually, there are some goats there. I saw a few. But mainly there are a lot of cows — fat cows. In the evening the air is full of the tinkling of their bells when they come home from the pastures. A hail of bells all over the village. But they're only a fraction of the herds. Most of them stay up in the alps all summer long and only come down in the autumn. And their owners greet them like long-lost children. In the evenings, after work, the cows are the main topic of conversation in the church square. They come down with garlands of mountain flowers on their heads and heavy bells hanging round their necks. Every prosperous farmer has a few cows on the alps."

"It must be very interesting — life in a village in the Tyrol. People like them must still be living as they did three hundred years ago."

"Almost. At least the old ones. The younger generation is already a little spoilt by the spirit of the times. They've been in the war, in prison camps, and their original colours have been a little blurred. But in a couple of years it will all be forgotten. Everything will go back to what it used to be. The mountains conquer people, stamp them with their own special stamp, force them to submit to their own way of life. Life is hard there, grim and depressing. No wonder that the mountain people are all so godfearing and superstitious."

Martin began to cry and Gurdweill hurried over to rock the pram. Lotte, too, rose to her feet and came to stand next to Gurdweill and look at the baby — which

346

gave Gurdweill an uneasy feeling, like an echo of what he had felt before.

"I don't know what the matter is with him today. He always sleeps through the evening and only wakes up at about four o'clock in the morning."

"Does Thea breastfeed him?"

"Of course! What did you think?"

"I thought that you . . . Ha, ha, ha! Since you do everything else."

Gurdweill forced a smile.

"You should have taken a nursemaid for him," she said with a sneer.

"I couldn't afford it," replied Gurdweill seriously. "But no! Even if I could I wouldn't have done it. You can't trust them. They don't take care of strange babies properly . . ."

"But taking care of strange babies is a nursemaid's job. They don't get paid for looking after their own babies, you know!"

"Yes, of course . . . But I . . . I've already grown accustomed to looking after him myself and it doesn't bother me a bit."

"I can work at my own writing too," he added, as if to justify himself. "In the evenings I can work as much as I like. And sometimes during the day as well. In fact, I love working while Martin sleeps. It gives me a special kind of peace of mind. In these last months I've been working far more than I did at the beginning of the summer. From that point of view he's been a real blessing."

He bent down to see if the baby had fallen asleep and motioned to Lotte with his head to return to the couch. It was now half past ten. Lotte announced that she would be leaving soon. However, she immediately resumed her former place on the couch.

"Would you mind if I opened the window a bit? Only if you're not cold, of course. I want to smoke, and the smoke is bad for him."

Lotte lit herself a cigarette, too, but immediately put it out again.

"You know," she said suddenly, "a man like you can

347

make one despair . . . I don't know if you're really a fool or if you only pretend to be one . . ."

"What do you mean?" he asked ingenuously. "I don't know what I've done to deserve such praise . . ."

Lotte went on in a whisper, as if she were talking to herself more than to Gurdweill.

"It can drive a person out of his mind . . . For a man to deceive himself into believing that everything is as it should be, when nothing at all is as it should be! Not the least little thing! A babe in arms can see it, a blind man can see it! . . ."

Gurdweill looked at her uncomprehendingly. He felt that her words related to him, and for some reason he even felt guilty, guilty towards Lotte, but he didn't know exactly how or why. He shrank from asking for an explanation, and began to examine his finger nails.

Lotte suddenly jumped to her feet.

"Well!" she said. "I'm sure you'll realize your mistake one day, but then it will be too late!"

And she put out her hand to say goodbye.

"I'm so sorry that I can't accompany you. I can't leave the baby. If only you would wait a while — Thea's due home at any moment now."

"I don't need Thea!" she burst out angrily. "You can keep your Thea for yourself! And I don't need you either, do you hear! Not in the least! And I never will either! So there! And I don't want you to accompany me, I don't want you to! You're all, all . . . Don't you dare acompany me, do you hear!"

Red in the face, she turned on her heel, and abruptly left the room. Gurdweill hurried to take the oil-lamp and followed her into the corridor to light her way. He heard the hasty drumming of her footsteps on the stairs, and he felt a sudden need to run after her, and stay with her until she calmed down. It was unthinkable to leave her alone in her present state! But he stayed where he was at the head of the stairs, with the lamp in his hand, and remained there for a while after the front door opened and closed and Lotte's footsteps disappeared into the night. Then he went back into the room and mechanically put the lamp down on the table. His heart contracted in a pain so immense that he could hardly breathe. He felt that a terrible wrong had been done to Lotte, and although he was not directly to blame, he had witnessed it without protesting. Suddenly he went up to the couch and fell on his knees before it. He buried his head in the place where Lotte had been sitting and stayed there for a long time, petrified with grief. When Thea came home half an hour later, she found him still kneeling motionless in front of the couch. And he did not stir until she poked him, like some inanimate object, with her foot.

28

ALL Gurdweill's devoted care and concern did not help. Two days after Lotte's visit the baby changed completely. He began to cry without stopping and to twitch convulsively. It was impossible to put him to sleep, and when he did finally drop off, he woke up again after a moment or two screaming. When Gurdweill saw that his screams did not stop, he telephoned a doctor he knew who lived in the neighbourhood and who had been to see the baby a number of times before. The doctor came early in the evening and found that Martin was suffering from a gastric complaint "common among infants at this age." He recommended immediate hospitalization, since the illness in question was "not to be taken lightly," he would be telling a lie if he said otherwise, and here at home he could not be taken care of properly. The child needed a doctor to look in on him several times a day, which would be quite impossible at home.

Gurdweill was thunderstruck. He stood helplessly before the doctor, his legs giving way beneath him. How could anyone ask him to part from his son? To hand him over to strangers, especially now, when he was sick, the poor little mite? On the other hand, he knew that it was necessary, that he had no choice in the matter. He looked at the doctor imploringly, as if willing him to come up with some other, more satisfactory solution, but the latter only twirled his moustache with a professional air and repeated:

"There's nothing for it, my dear Herr Gurdweill! It's the only alternative in such cases. This fear of hospitals is completely irrational. And besides: what other choice do we have? I'm sorry, but there it is!"

He patted Gurdweill on the back encouragingly:

"Be brave and try to keep calm. By the way, I work

350

there in the mornings and I'll keep an eye on him myself."

Thea arrived home from her office. She agreed with the doctor immediately:

"But of course! If he's sick, he has to go to the hospital! Who can look after him here?"

Adding that it was urgent and they should get him there without delay, the doctor said that he would go down and telephone the hospital at once to prepare a bed for him. Suddenly Gurdweill knew, with absolute certainty, that everything was irrevocably lost. He said no more. The doctor left and he took the baby, who had chosen just that moment to fall asleep, out of the pram, wrapped him in a blanket, and carried him out without a word to Thea, who lay back on the couch, smoking a cigarette.

He got on to the number 15 tram with Martin in his arms. An old woman got up to give him her seat, but he remained standing. Nothing made any difference to him now. It seemed to him that the baby was very light, he could hardly feel him on his arm — even though he weighed about twelve pounds, which was a very decent weight. No! — his thoughts jumped in a different direction — the way Thea had behaved! . . . What indifference! . . . She had not even looked at Martin when he left with him in his arms . . . How could anyone treat a baby like that? It was incomprehensible. Surely she couldn't be so hard-hearted!

The children's hospital was not far and they soon arrived. It was growing dark; the sky was overcast and a cold autumn wind tore through the streets, blowing dry leaves into people's faces. A stout nurse, her face beaming with kindliness, took Martin from him after they had written down the details of his birth and taken care of the other formalities in the hospital office, and gave him back the empty blanket. All this was done with a machine-like speed, before giving Gurdweill a chance to feast his eyes for one more minute on his darling son. Now he regretted having brought him here, especially since he had been sleeping peacefully all the time, as if there was nothing wrong with him. And perhaps the doctor had made a mistake? Perhaps there really was nothing wrong

351

with him . . ? He went on standing indecisively in the office, his eyes on the ground. And suddenly the certain knowledge came to him that he had just done something terrible, which could never be undone. How could he have listened to the doctor and brought him here? Had he lost his wits? And Thea? She had agreed without the flicker of an eyelash! With unpardonable indifference! He was flooded with hatred for Thea, as if she were personally responsible for the whole disaster. He was just about to tell the nurse that he had changed his mind about leaving the baby in the hospital when she said, without raising her eyes:

"Visiting hours are from ten to twelve in the morning, and two to six in the afternoon, for the mother. Other members of the family can only come in the afteroon, from two to four."

And Gurdweill folded the blanket, put it under his arm, and left the hospital.

Outside evening had taken hold. The gas lights flickered in the wind, which had grown stronger. Gurdweill suddenly felt very tired. But he did not want to go home — what would he do there now? For a while he walked to and fro in front of the wire fence surrounding the hospital grounds, stopping from time to time and trying to penetrate the double-storeyed white building hidden in the garden, but without success. Then he crossed to the opposite pavement, from which only the lighted windows and curtains of the second storey were visible. He strained his eyes to penetrate the spotless white curtains — in vain! It was impossible to see anything! A crowded tram drove past with a clatter. Ah, what he would have given to be permitted to go inside again and see him! Just to peep at him once and leave again. At that moment a baby began to scream somewhere. A cold shiver ran through him. He could have sworn that it was Martin's voice . . . it was exactly the way Martin cried! But he immediately told himself that it would have been impossible for his voice to carry over the grounds and across the street, and through the closed windows, too. Nevertheless, he went on standing there and listening with a breaking heart to the baby, and he did not calm down until it stopped crying, when he decided that it was time to go. He crossed the street again, and pressed his ear to the wire netting, but he could not hear a sound. After a few minutes he began walking slowly away, dragging his feet listlessly, but he soon changed his mind, retraced his footsteps, and put his ear to the fence again, alert and stealthy as an eavesdropper. But this time too he heard nothing suspicious. In the end he went away.

Not far off, on the little plaza in front of the Augarten, there were a few benches dotted with fallen autumn leaves. He went straight up to the first one and sat down. He picked up a newspaper lying at his feet, absent-mindedly read its title in the light of the streetlamp: *Neues Wiener Journal*, and threw it down again. Tomorrow morning at ten he would try to gain entry. Perhaps the nurse would make an exception in his case and let him in. Ah, the poor little mite! The newspaper at his feet rustled in the wind and Gurdweill bent down instinctively to pick it up again. There was a kind of hidden connection between himself and this morning paper, which had already, as it were, given up the ghost. He felt obscurely that he needed it, without knowing why — and this obscurity began to madden him. Suddenly it dawned on him: to wrap up the blanket, of course. No! — he instantly resolved — he would buy a new, clean newspaper for the blanket, not this crumpled old paper lying on the ground. He rose to his feet and was about to pick up the blanket when he suddenly saw that it was not there. He was seized by horror. This loss was a bad omen. He began searching the ground around the bench feverishly. There was nothing there. Then he set off to retrace his steps to the hospital, walking toe to heel and stooping to scan the ground in all directions. And before long he found it. He was overjoyed, as if he had been granted a sign that from now on everything would be all right. He folded it up small and from now on he held it in his hand, not under his arm as before. He walked slowly back, passed the bench on which he had been sitting a few moments before, and glanced at the newspaper which was still lying on the ground. What did he need this newspaper for? He was suddenly filled with inexplicable rage — he was going to buy a new one! But the nearby kiosk was closed, and at first he could not understand why. "It's not a holiday today! Closing shops on an ordinary weekday — what a nerve!" But then it occurred to him that the reason must be the lateness of the hour, and looking up at the illuminated clock on the Nordwestbahnhof, he saw that it was half past seven. "In that case, no wonder!" he said aloud, in explanation. And suddenly the full extent of his disaster came home to him, with the force of a revelation, and he felt as if a heavy object had struck him in the face. He turned around and began rushing back, as if he might still be in time to repair the damage if he hurried. But he did not run like this for long. Suddenly he stopped in his tracks, as if realizing the pointlessness of his haste. He looked around him and saw that he was standing right next to the same bench again. He bent down and picked up the newspaper, sat down on the bench, and began wrapping the blanket in it.

The wind had not died down. Gurdweill was not wearing a coat and he suddenly felt cold to the marrow of his bones. No! — he decided — he would leave it until tomorrow! Tomorrow he would fix everything. And he stood up and set off in the direction of Taborstrasse.

He walked slowly. He had plenty of time. It crossed his mind that here in Taborstrasse it was warmer, but he did not dwell too long on this idea. What difference did it make to him now? In any case he wouldn't freeze to death! The main thing was that he didn't know what to do with his time. It was only eight o'clock — there was a gap of fourteen hours, fourteen empty and unutterably oppressive hours, until ten o'clock the following day. He found himself in front of the Zentral cinema, from whose entrance a dense shaft of light emerged, reaching all the way to the opposite pavement. Out of habit, he stopped to look at the advertisements on either side of the door, without taking in a word. When he turned to go he suddenly saw Thea coming towards him with a strange man. His mind cleared immediately, and he felt a choking sensation rise in his throat. He stood rooted to the spot.

Thea, who recognized him from a distance, motioned him with her head to go away. Gurdweill did not move. As she walked past him she aimed such a vicious pinch at his arm that he almost cried out in pain. "Idiot!" she said under her breath and entered the cinema with her escort, who had not noticed anything.

His first outraged impulse was to run after her and shout in her face that the baby was mortally ill, and how dare she take it so lightly ... But he recovered himself in time and continued walking towards the city centre, utterly dejected and miserable. He was all alone, with nobody in the whole world to whom he could speak of his grinding sorrow. He had never in his life felt as lonely as he did now. He wandered aimlessly from street to street, a dull, animal pain seething inside him like a heavy poison. Without knowing how he got there, he suddenly found himself outside the Café Herrenhof. He went in. Dr. Astel and Ulrich were sitting together, deep in conversation. He accepted their invitation to join them, but after a few moments he stood up again.

"No!" he said. "I'm not staying here!"

And he went outside again. He could not stay still in one place. He had to keep on walking, and soothe his pain and loneliness by tiring himself out. And he went on walking, without noticing the streets he was passing. But he turned his back unconsciously on the well-lit, busy streets, because there was a heavy darkness in his soul, and he could not bear the light. After walking like this for about two hours, he arrived at the street where he lived. It was half past eleven. He opened the door to his room carefully and noiselessly, as usual, in order not to wake the baby, but as he did so he remembered that Martin was not at home and his caution was superfluous, and he slammed it angrily behind him. Thea was not there. He lit the oil-lamp automatically and sat down at the table, supporting his head, which was very heavy and at the same time empty of thoughts, on his hands. Silence reigned in the house, silence rose from the street and poured into the room from the open window. For a while Gurdweill remained sitting at the table, tired out with walking and numb with

355

grief. On the wall above the couch, just under the ceiling, an enormous spider stood without moving. On the paving stones of the street outside a tin object clattered with a clear, hollow sound, its fall impinging on to his consciousness only now, as if the noise signified its beginning instead of its end. Gurdweill suddenly stood up and walked over to the pram, which was in its usual place between the bed and the toilet table, bent down and looked inside it intently for a while, as if to ascertain whether the child was asleep. He saw that it was empty, just as he had left it several hours earlier. Then he went over to the couch, where he had placed the little blanket when he came in, removed the newspaper wrapping, and spread it over the pram, as he did when covering Martin. And suddenly, impelled by some irresistible force, he took hold of the handle and began rocking the pram to and fro. The next instant he let go, terrified out of his wits, and ran to the couch. His face was grey. Instinctively he looked round the room, to make sure that no one had caught him red-handed. "Ah!" — he groaned aloud — "I'm going out of my mind! What's to become of me?"

For a while he lay curled up tightly on the couch, still as a lump of dead matter. Then he jumped up abruptly and strode decisively to the open window. What's all the fuss about? he said to himself. In a few days' time he'll get better and come home! You ass! You're not the only person whose baby ever got sick! So what? He'll get better again!

Thea came in without his hearing her. When he turned his head and saw her, he recoiled. She gave him a mocking look and began taking off her coat, without saying a word. Then Gurdweill said, in a voice which seemed to him to belong to somebody else:

"You can go and visit him tomorrow morning, from ten to twelve, and from two to six in the afternoon."

He hesitated a moment and added:

"Take leave and go there tomorrow morning to feed him."

Thea gave a short, spiteful laugh.

"And if I don't obey your orders, my lord and master?"

"It's not an order," he replied calmly. "I only wanted to remind you. The child is gravely ill, as you know, and the least negligence on our part might have serious consequences. You heard the doctor yourself."

"It's my own business! I'll go to the hospital when I feel like it! And if I don't feel like it, I won't go at all! Go and shut the window! The cold's coming in!"

After doing her bidding he said:

"In any event, I'm asking you not to forget. It isn't a laughing matter."

Thea, who had begun taking off her dress, paused for a moment and looked at her husband in surprise. His firm tone was completely new to her. Aha! — she said to herself — so the little one's beginning to kick, is he! Suddenly the whole thing seemed supremely ridiculous to her, especially since she remembered how only half an hour ago she had been making fun of this husband of hers to her new lover, and telling him how he looked after her baby, which wasn't even his — of that she was quite sure — and how her lover had remarked that in that case her husband must be a "born nursemaid," and he would recommend him for a job as soon as the opportunity arose — which had redoubled their mirth.

She burst out laughing loudly. Gurdweill's blood rushed to his head at the sound of this reckless laughter. He was filled with such rage against her that it surprised him, since he was so used to her behaviour that at any other time he would hardly have noticed it. But he controlled himself immediately, and only said, in a trembling voice:

"I don't understand! What's there to laugh about? There's nothing funny about the situation as far as I can see."

"How do you know that there's nothing to laugh about? Come here, have a cigarette! You amuse me greatly, my little man!"

Gurdweill did not respond. He went to the bed, gathered up his bedclothes and began making his bed on the couch. Provoked by this open defiance, Thea approached him in her petticoat, put her arm around his waist, and pushed a cigarette into his mouth.

"What's this, rabbit, won't you take a cigarette from me?"
And she added:

"They're the best! Take it from me! I've just been given them as a gift!"

The cigarette made Gurdweill's gorge rise in nausea, and he spat it out on to the bed.

"I don't feel like smoking now. What do you want of me? I'll smoke later . . ."

"Not later, but right now!" insisted Thea. "So my cigarettes disgust you, do they? Things have come to a pretty pass, I must say! Come along, let's sit down and smoke together."

He was obliged to submit to her will and overcome his nausea. He could not begin a quarrel now, at midnight, and he gave in again, as usual. Thea sat him on her knees, and watched to see that he smoked properly. The fact that he was smoking a cigarette that she had just received from her lover, filled her with an extraordinary, perverse delight, especially since she knew that he, her husband, knew very well where it came from, and was smoking it against his will.

"Well, and how does it taste to you? Good, eh? I knew you'd like it!"

Gurdweill sat on her lap and stared at the wall. He was suddenly overcome with great sadness and infinite despair, squeezing his heart as in a vice. He wished he were a thousand miles away, in a different country, among strange people, with Martin, of course, a place where everything was clear and simple, and where nobody forced you to smoke such awful cigarettes . . . a place where there was no need to smoke at all . . . But at the same time he knew that there was no escape, and that he would never be able to free himself from Thea's clutches. Because he loved her . . . yes, he loved her in spite of everything . . !
His eyes fell on the spider, which was still in the same place, just under the ceiling, huge and black. It's sleeping now, concluded Gurdweill, and realized that he himself was very tired. He threw away the cigarette end, and was about to jump off his wife's knees. But she stopped him.

"What, don't you want to be nice to me? . . ."

358

"I . . . not now . . . some other time . . . I'm tired . . ."
mumbled Gurdweill.

"So! You don't love me any more!"

"Yes, but . . ."

Suddenly he clutched her neck with both hands and pressed his lips to her mouth, as if he were casting himself into a deep abyss. Thea picked him up at once and carried him to the couch.

Afterwards Gurdweill was ashamed. Over there the baby was lying sick, perhaps at this very moment screaming in pain — and here he was making love!

"You'll be able to go and feed him tomorrow, won't you, dearest?"

"I've already told you not to interfere in things that are no concern of yours! If I feel like it I'll go, and if not I won't!"

She was lying on her back on the couch, both hands under her head, and Gurdweill was sitting next to her.

"Go and fetch my cigarettes!"

When he sat down beside her again, she suddenly said:

"What would you say if you knew that today, only an hour ago, or even less, I was with someone else? Only an hour before you?!"

There was a cruel expression on her face, and her eyes were fixed on her husband's face, to see how he reacted. But he was used to it. She wants to make me angry again, he thought. A piece of gratuitous cruelty!

"I don't believe it," he said firmly.

"Is that so? You don't believe it! And the man I went to the cinema with, I suppose you think I played tiddlywinks with him, do you? Ha, ha, ha! I can tell you the details if you like."

"It isn't true!" he stood his ground. "And anyway, I'm not in the least interested. I don't want to know."

He wanted to get up, but Thea grabbed his arm.

"Sit still, my little man! So, you don't believe it? Very well . . ."

And she began to tell him, in cynical detail, everyhing that had happened between herself and the strange man, holding his arm so that he couldn't escape. From

359

time to time she interrupted her account with a short, spiteful laugh, and then she continued again with evident enjoyment. Gurdweill listened unwillingly, in an agony of revulsion, breathing heavily and bathed in sweat. But at the same time, and without his being clearly aware of it, the story also gave him a curious, painful pleasure — the perverse pleasure which is inherent in suffering — and it was no longer possible to say with certainty that he was listening only because he was being forced to . . . When Thea concluded, he said nothing for a while. In the end he stood up as if he was shaking off a bad dream. He went up to the table and sat down next to it.

"It still isn't true!" he suddenly blurted out, as if to himself. "A lie from beginning to end . . ."

"Idiot!" exclaimed his wife.

That evening no more was said.

It was now half past one and they lay down to sleep. Too upset by everything that had happened during the day to fall asleep, Gurdweill lay on his back, staring into the night. One window was open, the evening wind having died down, and a vague chill, compounded of both winter and summer at once, seeped soundlessly into the room, touching Gurdweill's face so lightly that he did not even feel it. He was exhausted, his limbs were crushed with weariness, and his head felt heavy, drowsy, and feverish, as full of fragments of thoughts as a pot full of peas. Ah, if only he could fall asleep! The ridiculous notion came to him, that if only he could fall asleep here at home, Martin would fall asleep there, in the hospital, and be cured . . . And now he himself was hindering the cure . . . He closed his eyes and lay absolutely still, willing himself to fall asleep. And suddenly something like a cold wind blew through his skull, just under the forehead, from right to left — an acute nervous pain which caused him to open his eyes again . . . The doctor had ordered hospitalization and presumably he knew best . . . And the hospital had made a good impression . . . The stout nurse had smiled at Martin kindly — a sign that she — no it wasn't a sign of anything at all. It didn't mean a thing! Well, he would see in the morning. And if he didn't like what he saw, there was nothing to prevent him from taking the child straight home! No one to look after him at home? — And he, Gurdweill, where was he?! And if a doctor's supervision was necessary — then let the doctor come twice a day! He would find the money! Yes, tomorrow it would be decided, one way or the other, according to the situation. But that newspaper under the bench — what a nuisance it had made of itself! It didn't give him a moment's peace! What was to stop him carrying the blanket without making it into a parcel? There was no need for the newspaper at all . . . But what had he done with it in the end? He had brought it home, he remembered, and put it down on the couch, but afterwards — had he removed it or not? Perhaps he had spread out his sheet without removing the newspaper first? Gurdweill began moving his feet cautiously about at the foot of the couch, and listening for the rustle of paper, but he couldn't hear a thing. Stop this nonsense! — he said to himself — It makes no difference anyway!

He turned on to his side, with his face to the window, determined to fall asleep. And Thea? — a new thought rose to the surface of his mind — no, there wasn't a word of truth in her story . . . He absolutely refused to believe it! She had simply made the whole thing up . . . She took a perverse delight in teasing him and so she invented all kinds of things . . . But he would not fall into her trap . . . What did he care? But if it was really true . . ? What if everything she said was actually true? Well, then . . . even then it didn't make any difference to him . . . in other words, it was none of his business . . . What did he lose by it . . ? But the whole thing was a lie from beginning to end — it was obvious! Just like that other lie: the one about Martin not being his son . . . He really couldn't be bothered with such nonsense . . .

Now he began to feel an intense, irritating heat stealing unpleasantly over his body. Ah, there's no end to it! he groaned in despair. At this rate I'll never fall asleep!

At that moment someone walked past in the street. Gurdweill strained his hearing to the utmost, listening to the footsteps as if his life depended on it, and following them as they were swallowed up in the night and vanished

361

without a trace. Now there was nothing but their abstract echo, which went on pulsing in Gurdweill's ears for a while until it, too, faded away. The silence closed in again, heavy and palpable, and Gurdweill for some reason regretted the footsteps which had disappeared.

"And the pram, what's going to happen to the pram?" The question took him unawares, piercing him before he could arm himself against it.

In a terror which struck to the roots of his being, he began frantically scratching his thigh, in order to distract himself. But although he scratched until he bled, it did not help. The thought came clearly through the pain:

"You can't just ignore it, you know . . . The pram can't go on standing in the room afterwards . . ."

A cold sweat broke out all over his body and he sat up abruptly.

"There's no such thing as afterwards!" he almost shouted aloud. "There's no such thing as afterwards! . . . The pram's for the baby, for Martin!"

Unconsciously he lay down again.

"The pram's only a means . . . Be honest with yourself . . . What use is a pram to anyone?"

"What use?" retorted Gurdweill furiously. "Everyone knows that a baby can't do without a pram!"

"As long as there's a baby . . . But when . . ."

"Tomorrow Martin's coming home! There's no need for the hospital! The doctor doesn't know what he's talking about! He'll be fine at home!"

"You have to face the truth! The baby's sick, you know that yourself. There's no getting away from it. And a sick baby can also . . ."

"The truth is that there's nothing wrong with him! I gave him to the hospital for nothing! An upset stomach in a child . . ."

"But that's just it! With babies it's a dangerous disease! You've read about it yourself! Only a small percentage get well, and the rest . . ."

"I don't want to, I don't want to — and finished! . . . All I want to do is sleep!"

Gurdweill felt as if he was about to suffocate. A vein

pounded in his temples like a sledgehammer, and his whole body burnt as if on fire. The blanket was very heavy and he threw it off angrily and lay there naked for a while. Then he jumped off the couch and went over to the open window. The cold penetrated obliquely, like a slanting shaft of light, seizing him by the legs and thighs and giving him gooseflesh. I can't afford to catch cold now — he thought — I have to be well! As he turned away from the window, he glanced at the pram, whose white blanket shone in the darkness of the room. He averted his eyes immediately, and went back to the couch. Suddenly it occurred to him to look and see if the newspaper had remained underneath the sheet when he made his bed. He pulled it up, and found nothing. Then he searched the floor, both at the foot and the head of the couch, groping in the dark with his hands and bare feet, and in the end he moved the couch cautiously away from the wall and pushed his hand into the gap — the newspaper was nowhere to be found. Suddenly the insanity of this search struck him and he was filled with rage against himself. You idiot! he scolded himself. What on earth do you need that damned newspaper for? He went up to the table to take a cigarette. There was a newspaper lying there. Yes, it was the same newspaper! It had to be, there was no other newspaper in the room. Or perhaps Thea had brought one home with her? To make sure he went to the window again and read the name in the light of the streetlamp below. In a sudden fit of rage he threw the newspaper out of the window. As he did so he felt a twinge of regret, as if he had thrown away something precious. He even leant over the sill and looked down, but he couldn't see anything, even though the pavement below was quite well lit by the streetlamp. There was nothing lying there, that was clear. Where had the newspaper disappeared to? It began to worry him. He looked up and down, until in the end he caught sight of it entangled in the branches of the only tree on the street, to the left of the window. The nerve of it! — said Gurdweill to himself — if only he had a stick, or something of the sort, he would get it down before it knew what had hit it! For some reason, he felt cheated

363

. . . In the end he turned away from the window, and quite forgetting that he had wanted to smoke a cigarette, lay down on the couch and covered himself with the blanket. For a while there was silence. Then a distant clock struck three. Is that all! thought Gurdweill. In that case, it's not so terrible! And soon afterwards he thought that the film showing at the Zentral this evening wasn't particularly interesting . . . otherwise he would have gone inside . . . that is, of course he wouldn't have gone inside! . . .

"Of course not!" the inner voice echoed him mockingly. "The circumstances weren't exactly propitious . . ."

Gurdweill pretended not to hear.

"With the blanket under your arm!" the voice continued ironically.

"It isn't unheard of to go into the cinema with a blanket, you know. I went into the café with it didn't I? . . ."

"Ah, if only it were simply a question of the blanket! By the way, Thea seems completely unaffected by the whole thing . . . It's business as usual with her: the cinema, a lover . . ."

"It isn't true! There's no lover! He was only an acquaintance . . ."

"Let's assume you're right — after all, the important thing at the moment isn't whether she went to the cinema with a friend or a lover, but that she went to the cinema at all! Don't you agree? That says it all, about her character and her attitude to the child . . . You must admit, other mothers wouldn't behave that way . . ."

"What? Rubbish! Is it her fault the baby's ill? Why shouldn't she go to the cinema?"

"In any event, another mother wouldn't have let the baby go to hospital . . . She would have wanted the baby with her, at home, whatever happened . . . You know I'm right . . . Why should we deceive ourselves?"

"But she's at work all day long!"

"And so? Couldn't she ask for a few days off . . ? And tomorrow, do you really think she'll go and see him in the morning?"

"Of course she'll go!"

"Perhaps . . . but even if she does, it will only be on the

364

impulse of the moment, certainly not out of any great love for her child ... She's a bad, cruel woman; there isn't a drop of human feeling in her ... Enough pretending and covering up for her morning, noon and night! ... You'll see afterwards ... She won't be too sorry afterwards, you'll see ..."

"The same old story again!" Gurdweill jumped up. "There's no end to it tonight!"

"There won't be a second child in a hurry ... You should prepare yourself for the ..."

"Now I'm really going to smoke a cigarette!" declared Gurdweill furiously. "Since a person can't get any sleep around here ..." And he got out of bed, tired to death, and tottered unsteadily to the table.

"A cigarette!" the voice whispered mockingly. "You know who those cigarettes belong to, don't you? ... They're a present, a present! ... You didn't find them at all to your taste before ..."

"It doesn't matter! There aren't any others in the house!"

He lit a cigarette and went back to the couch. After taking a couple of puffs he threw it down. It really was a rotten cigarette!

"I knew it all along! But perhaps the cigarettes aren't really so bad ... Perhaps it's the source ..."

"Not at all!" protested Gurdweill. "They're rotten cigarettes!"

"Rotten! You yourself have smoked them often enough in the past, and enjoyed them too! Why deny it? Nile is an excellent brand! ... Admit it, it's the source that bothers you ... and very understandably too!"

"The ones I smoked were better! You can get good and bad cigarettes of the same brand! Sometimes you wind up with a box of bad ones ... The source doesn't interest me in the least! Not in the least ... Surely you don't take me for such a fool?"

"Nevertheless I think there's been a little substitution here, which you yourself are not even aware of ... Very common phenomenon! A slight case of substitution, or suggestion — call it what you will ... But why be so indignant about it? Why can't you simply admit it? There's

365

nothing dishonourable or dishonest about it! It's quite natural for a man not to want his wife to be . . ."

"But I've already told you that it's not true! And that I don't care! . . . I wouldn't hesitate to admit it if it were really so! But it isn't so!"

There was a dry, bitter taste in his mouth. He longed for a drink of water but he was too tired to get up. Besides, he thought, water's the worst thing for sleep, it wakes you up completely. At that moment an engine whistled in the nearby railway station, at first a short, cut-off blast, and then a long one. In the middle of the night they have to work, poor devils! He felt a rush of pity for the railway workers. Then he turned over on to his right side, facing the wall. There was a short pause. His senses grew numb and he sank into a kind of stupor. The night invaded him.

And the stout nurse from the hospital loomed up dimly out of the darkness and took on a definite shape. Yes, it was she, Gurdweill did not doubt it for a moment. And it did not surprise him in the least that instead of the usual white cap she was wearing a tall, grass-green hat, with a long red feather at its side. This curious hat, especially in combination with the white hospital gown, gave her the look of a bird, perhaps a white cock with a big red comb. Gurdweill knew that he had to beware of her, that for some unknown reason he must not go near her. Suddenly the reason became clear to him: the feather was excessively long, and if he came too close it would scratch his face with its sharp tip, and he would not be able to let Thea see him like that . . . He kept his distance and waited. The nurse was standing in front of a kind of music stand, three-quarters of her plump face turned towards Gurdweill, and her eyes on something that was lying on top of the stand, whose nature was not clear from a distance. They were alone in the room. The waiting began to grow irksome, Gurdweill was tired and thought that it would be nice if he could find a bench to sit on, like the ones in the garden outside. He looked around him for somewhere to sit down, but apart from the music stand the big room was bare. That's only natural, he immediately excused this to himself, offices are never furnished. He leant against the

366

wall, and looked out of the opposite window. There was a large apartment block there, with many storeys and numberless windows. Gurdweill was astonished. I never knew, he said to himself, that they'd started building skyscrapers like the ones in America in Vienna too! It must be a hospital, he concluded — everyone wants to go to hospital and they need a lot of space . . . Suddenly he remembered that he was in a hurry, he had no time to spare — how could he have forgotten it until now? Afraid of disturbing the nurse at her work, he tiptoed out through an immensely tall and broad doorway, like the entrance to a vast warehouse. The entrance needs to be wide for the railway carriages, when they come in to spend the night — said Gurdweill, confidently to himself, yes, it's very cleverly done!

Afterwards he found himself carrying a heavy box in an unfamiliar street full of people. He could neither force his way through the dense crowd nor turn aside, and was obliged to move forward step by step, held up by the crowds of people in front of him and pushed by those behind him, bathed in sweat because of the weight of his load. If only he could put the box down for a moment and rest! But there wasn't room for a pin. Why did he need such a big heavy box, he thought bitterly, a smaller and lighter one would have done just as well! As soon as he got away from this crowd, he would change it for another! The box was open, and Gurdweill was carrying it in front of him, the open end uppermost. Suddenly he had a good idea: why should he keep all the newspapers in the box? Especially since they were written in a foreign language he did not even know? If he could read them, at least, it might have been different. But as things were! No, he would get rid of them one by one, since the crush prevented him from overturning the box and getting rid of them all at once. And the box would gradually grow lighter. But now something amazing happened: no sooner had he thrown the newspapers out than they flew back into the box! They came flying from all directions, far more than he had thrown out, in their thousands and tens of thousands, falling straight into the box, and forcing Gurdweill to the ground as they fell. The box was already full, the newspapers were stacked high on top of it, and still they went on falling. There was no end to it.

Suddenly he was seized by a terrible despair. From behind the crowd pressed him forward, and from the front they stopped him from advancing. And now it was no longer newspapers that were falling, but flat white tiles, which stacked themselves as they fell into a tower reaching higher than his head, so that he could no longer see in front of him. Suddenly Gurdweill knew that the tiles were being thrown from the huge hospital, which the crowd had destroyed in order to build an even bigger one, since the old one did not have room for all the sick children. Just in time, reflected Gurdweill, since his own Martin was showing signs of illness and now he would be able to put him in the new hospital. But how was he going to carry all these tiles by himself? He felt that in another minute he would collapse under his burden, he simply would not have the strength left to go on. He looked imploringly from side to side, to the extent that the stack of tiles permitted, but nobody seemed to understand what he wanted. It did not occur to him to ask them for help in so many words. With the last of his strength he carried the box a few more steps, and then he let it go. And suddenly he saw that the street was completely empty, which did not suprise him in the least. The box stood at his feet, and it too was empty. Gurdweill remembered that he was tired, and was just about to sit down on the pavement, next to the box, when he changed his mind. Since the box was now empty, he could sit inside it and be sheltered from the wind! And so he did. At first he felt uncomfortable sitting in the box, which was not very large. He had to huddle up and fold his legs, one of which began to hurt, but after a moment he got used to it and even began to enjoy it. He sat and looked down the street, without seeing a soul. Oh yes, he recalled, today was a holiday — no wonder all the shops were shut! As he continued looking about him, he noticed something long lying on the pavement not far off.

Then he saw: it was the drowned girl who had been fished out of the Danube not long ago. And not a single policeman in the whole street to look after her! How could

368

they leave her all alone, poor girl! What if she needed something? But of course! A brilliant idea suddenly struck him — he would put her in the box! That was the best place for her! He got out of the box and bent over the girl. Yes, it was her, no doubt about it! But where was her nose? When he saw her then her nose had still been intact . . . She must have bumped into something, and her nose had fallen off . . . Never mind, she could do without it! The main thing was, that he had a box to put her in! When he picked her up he discovered that she wasn't at all heavy, in the usual way of corpses, and this surprised him greatly. After he had taken a few steps, something fell to the ground. He looked around and saw that it was one of the girl's arms, which had become detached from her shoulder and dropped off. Appalled, he bent down to pick it up — and the other arm dropped off too. Gurdweill stood there in despair. He did not want to put the girl down, but as long as he went on holding her, he could not pick up her arms from the ground . . . Ah, if only Thea were here, he reflected bitterly, she could have done something to help! But she was always at the cinema when you needed her!

At that moment the girl opened her mouth and said: "Don't worry about those old arms! They're not worth it! Leave them where they are. I've got other, better ones at home!"

"Nevertheless," ventured Gurdweill, "it seems a shame . . . I can manage, really I can! A little patience and everything will come right. It's better to have two pairs, after all . . ."

"No, it's not necessary! Try to hurry up, won't you! They're expecting me at home for dinner."

Gurdweill started off towards the box. On the way both her legs fell off, one after the other. Gurdweill heard them fall with a pang, but without being able to pick them up, and when he finally reached the box there was nothing left of her but her head and torso, which did not show any marks in the places where her limbs had broken off. She looked like one of those round, limbless dolls, which jump up again when you push them down. He put her in the

369

box. Loath to leave her arms and legs lying scattered in the street, he went back to pick them up. But the limbs were nowhere to be found. They had disappeared without a trace. Gurdweill searched everywhere in growing despair. He knew that she did not have any spare limbs at home, and she had only said so to save him unnecessary trouble. And what was he to do now? He couldn't leave things like this! Suddenly he remembered that the girl was already drowned, in other words — dead, and she really didn't need any arms and legs . . . And besides, he was sure that Thea must have picked them up, when she came out of the cinema, and hidden them somewhere to tease him . . . He would find them later!

When he returned to the box, he found the nurse from the hospital there. She was no longer stout, but tall and erect, and although she looked like Thea, Gurdweill knew that she was not Thea, but the nurse. At the same time, it occurred to him that in dreams one figure is often substituted for another, in a kind of sleight-of-hand, and this discovery filled him with happiness, because he knew that it was now of the utmost importance for him to be on his guard and alert to everything that happened. In the meantime darkness had descended. The box and the nurse at its side were illuminated by the light of a nearby streetlamp. The nurse suddenly held out a little bundle, which Gurdweill had not previously noticed in her hand. The little bundle was wrapped in a snow-white blanket (he recognized it immediately as Martin's), and she seemed very angry and in a great hurry. For a moment he wondered whether to take the bundle from her or not. But the nurse said angrily, and now it was clear to him that she really was Thea: "Take it, you fool, and put it in the box! Can't you see that it's Martin?!" But Gurdweill could not see anything, because the baby was completely wrapped up in the blanket. It's a good thing that he's so well wrapped up, he thought, otherwise he might catch cold.

He took the bundle and said: "Why in the box? If it's Martin, he's got a nice pram of his own! There's already someone lying in the box."

Thea laughed and said: "The pram's gone! I sold it

to Dr. Ostwald yesterday for the baby about to be born
... From now on he's going to have a new baby every
month and he needs a lot of prams..." And she went
on laughing wildly.

Gurdweill was filled with such terrible rage that he
thought he would die. "How could you do such a thing?
How could you sell it? You know the baby's only got one
pram and he needs it for himself!"

"He doesn't need it any more," Thea laughed venom-
ously. "Can't you see that he's dead? A dead baby doesn't
sleep in a pram, but in a box! Didn't I keep on telling you
that I don't need a baby? I've been wanting to kill him for
a long time ... In the end I gave him to Freddy. What an
expert! With one finger down his throat he finished him
off ... Hurry up and put him in the box! There's no time
to waste!"

Hoping against hope that Thea was joking as usual,
Gurdweill undid the bundle. Martin was dead. His eyes
were open, and he was smiling his babyish smile, with his
tiny fist next to his mouth — but he was dead nevertheless. Gurdweill knew this now with absolute certainty. He
was filled with despair, and a terrible rage against Thea,
who was to blame for everything — a rage deeper and
more painful than any he had ever experienced awake.
He threw the baby down and leapt on Thea and began
hitting her with his fists, on her face, her breasts, her belly.
But he quickly realized that his fists were encountering no
resistance, just as if he were hitting thin air, and he was
frightened to death. He stopped. Thea went on standing in
front of him and laughing. Then she suddenly took off her
hat, saying: "So, my little man! You think you can hit me,
do you?" And she seized hold of his throat with both hands
and began to throttle him. Gurdweill screamed with all his
might (there were already people standing round them)
but his voice was inaudible and the screams remained stuck
in his mouth. "This is the end," he thought, "nothing can
save me now!" And he felt an amazing pressure on his
heart, which was not at all unpleasant, and he stopped
breathing ...

When he opened his eyes it was still night. His body was

371

bathed in sweat, his heart pounded, and his breath came in short, heavy pants. For a moment he did not know if he was awake or dead, the dividing line between his dreaming and waking state was so flimsy and transparent. Nor did he remember when he had sat up, for he was now sitting on the couch. He felt his chest with his hand and came to the conclusion that he was alive, and awake. To make doubly sure, he tried to penetrate the darkness, and after straining his eyes for a moment he was able to make out the outlines of the bed and the two rectangles of the windows opposite. Now there was no longer any doubt: it was only a nightmare. But he could still see the dream in all its details, and he felt a certain regret at having woken up. It was possible, after all, for a man to die in his sleep . . . But he was awake, that was clear. And where was Martin? Only a moment ago he had held him in his arms! He jumped out of bed and ran to the pram. It was still empty, with the white blanket spread over it. So Thea hadn't really sold the pram to Dr. Ostwald! Despite this happy thought, however, he was still as furious with her as if everything she had said in the dream were true. He felt the blanket with his hand, and found, to his distress, that there was nothing underneath it. But he soon remembered that Martin was in hospital, and went back to bed, where he fell straight into a heavy, dreamless sleep.

29

THE next day Gurdweill was already waiting in front
of the hospital at half past nine in the morning. It
was a fine, clear, autumn day. The sun was shining and
the trams clattered to and fro. Gurdweill paced back and
forth in front of the gate to the hospital grounds and
smoked. He was barely aware of the fatigue resulting
from the morbid, nervous sleep of the night before, and
even felt a glimmering of hope that everything would
be all right in the end. But the waiting was hard to
endure. How slow time could be, how it could crawl and
congeal! Whereas sometimes it could be swift and elusive
as an arrow! When you watched it, when you followed its
course, it stood stubbornly still; half an hour could stretch
to an infinity. The preliminaries, reflected Gurdweill, were
usually longer than the main event ... The whole of life
was composed of these preliminaries and the rest lasted no
longer than a few short moments ...

After a while he decided to walk from one end of the
fence to the other twenty times with medium-sized steps
— this would probably take about twenty minutes, and by
then he would be able to go inside. He began pacing and
counting with his eyes lowered and his coat flapping in
the wind. A rag-and-bone-man with a bundle wrapped in
a bottle-green shawl hanging over his shoulder zigzagged
down the middle of the road, raising his eyes to the
windows and calling "Rags and bones!" in a loud, hoarse
voice. A baker's boy walked past with a basket full of rolls,
while a little black dog trotted frantically behind him at an
angle which made him look as if he were running sideways.
The little dog stopped in front of Gurdweill, turned to look
behind him for a moment, and then trotted off to catch up
with his master. A poor, bent woman emerged from a side

alley, where the hospital fence made a sharp right-angle, and shuffled hesitantly towards Gurdweill, waiting until he put his hand in his pocket before approaching him. Then she took the coin timidly from his hand and turned back into the alley.

Gurdweill was no longer counting: he had forgotten all about it. He must have paced the length of the fence thirty times by now, and he took out his watch and looked at it. It was four minutes to ten.

A different nurse, one he had not seen yesterday, assured him that the baby's condition had improved and said that she hoped he would be allowed to go home in two or three days' time. It was impossible to see him now, outside visiting hours. But where was the mother? The baby had to be fed! All Gurdweill's pleas to be allowed to see him were in vain. He went into the corridor and waited there for a while. Suddenly he saw the nurse from yesterday, and he went up to her and begged her to let him peep at the baby. The nurse took pity on him and led him into a room where about twenty cots were standing. As he followed in her footsteps his heart beat loudly and his stomach contracted in a kind of spasm. The baby was asleep, his face pale but tranquil, and his hand, which was clenched into a tiny fist, was sticking out of the blanket next to his mouth. Suddenly the scene from his dream rose before Gurdweill's eyes, and he felt faint with terror. His knees gave way beneath him and he gripped the back of the chair next to him.

"As you see," said the nurse, "he's sleeping quietly. Last night he had a bad time but he's better now. His fever has gone down too."

There was a sunbeam lying across the cot, and Gurdweill found himself thinking that it was a good thing, at least, that the sun was not beating directly on to his face and disturbing his sleep . . . Here and there a baby cried, and Gurdweill absorbed the sound unthinkingly. He stood quite still with his eyes fixed on the sleeping Martin. He seemed to have forgotten where he was, and that he had only been allowed in for a moment. Then the nurse told

374

him that he had to leave now, and he came to his senses and walked out of the hospital.

Outside he remembered that he should have straightened the blanket and covered the baby, since he was sure that he was not properly covered ... And this thought caused him considerable distress, as if the entire fate of his son depended on it. He stood still and wondered whether he should go back and fix the blanket; he was sure the nurse would let him in again, he would plead with her until she let him in. And precisely because he knew how ridiculous this wish was, and how impossible to realize, his longing increased until he would have given his life to be allowed to go in again and straighten the blanket. In the end, however, he continued on his way. If only his hand had not been clenched like that, at least! True, babies often clenched their fists, but still ... And if it was clenched, why did it have to be so close to his mouth, the way it had been there? Nonsense! he scolded himself — a dream's only a dream! How can you take it so seriously? But Thea was late! What of it, he tried to defend her to himself, perhaps she had been held up. She was probably on her way right now and would be arriving at any minute. Perhaps she had had to wait a long time for a tram. That was what always happened in Vienna: whenever you were in a hurry to get somewhere there was never a tram in sight. And not only in Vienna, it was the same all over the world ... And he felt a surge of rage at the trams for being against him. But he consoled himself with the thought that Martin was sleeping soundly now and Thea would have plenty of time to get there before he woke up.

He approached the same bench as the night before and dropped on to it without thinking. After a moment he realized where he was and jumped up, full of a fear which he himself did not fully understand, and began walking towards the city. He had time, all the time in the world. He could have afforded to donate some of it to quite a few of the people in the city, but none of them wanted to share his time with him. And so he walked on alone, aimlessly and without paying any attention to his surroundings, a prey to

375

troubled thoughts and struggling against the obscure sense
of doom trying to invade the frontiers of his consciousness.
The sun warmed him. The boughs of the trees projecting
over the Augarten fence into the quiet, narrow street were
already half-bare, criss-crossed with sky, and the leaves
scattered over the pavement rustled as they disintegrated
under his feet.

For three days the baby lay in the hospital and on the
fourth day, when Gurdweill came to visit him, they told
him that he had died in the night. Gurdweill heard the
news with terrifying equanimity. Just as a serious illness
reduces the gravity of death for the patient, filling him
little by little with minute doses of its poison, so that he
does not feel the inevitable end in all its intensity — so
Gurdweill had been prepared by the distress and inner
torment he had suffered during the baby's illness for his
death. He sank on to a chair in the hospital office and sat
there for a long time like a stone. He appeared to see and
hear nothing. His eyes were fixed on some point in the
remote distance, as if he were looking through the wall
and beyond it, and his hands lay limply on his knees. His
soft hat was tucked under his arm. It may be that during
these moments there was not the shadow of a thought in
his mind; it may be that he was afflicted by a kind of
general numbing of the senses, which transformed him
into something closely resembling an inanimate object.
From time to time the head nurse gave him a sidelong
glance; she was sorry for him and resolved to let him
go on sitting there as long as he wished. After a while
Gurdweill recovered and stood up. He approached the
desk, apparently wishing to say something. But no words
came out of his mouth. The nurse looked at him and
concentrated on his slack lips as if she were looking at a
dumb man and trying to read his wishes on his mouth. In
the end he said in a whisper, as if he had not spoken for
many days, that he would like to see him, the baby. For the
baby, after all, was his — he found it necessary for some
reason to explain — his own flesh and blood.

The head nurse rang a bell and immediately another
nurse appeared and led Gurdweill down the corridor,

376

turning right into another corridor, at the end of which she opened a door and took him into a smallish room, the morgue. There were a few little coffins standing on a kind of wooden shelf and a strong smell of carbolic acid in the air. She went up to one of the coffins and took off the lid. Before doing anything else, Gurdweill glanced around the room to see if there was a window in it. Because a window was very important . . . And he was not satisfied until he discovered a long slit in the wall, rather narrow, to be sure, but nevertheless sufficient to provide the room with as much daylight as necessary. Then he turned abruptly towards the open coffin, as if to take its occupant by surprise. The dead baby was lying there in his swaddling clothes. Gurdweill saw that the coffin was too long, with considerable space left over between the baby's feet and the end of the coffin, and this, for some reason, disturbed him. Then he fixed his eyes on the baby's face, which was yellowish, hollow, and much smaller than before. He went on examining it for a while, and suddenly he felt that this little corpse was completely strange to him; there was no relation at all between him and it. True, it had the same features, the same snub nose, the same hair as Martin — but nevertheless it was not he . . . Martin was different, alive, his own baby — whereas this lifeless corpse had nothing to do with him. He even felt a certain revulsion stirring in him at the sight of the small, dead body, and was obliged to avert his eyes. He couldn't bear the sight of him. And suddenly a strange thing happened: Gurdweill burst out laughing. He laughed secretly, making a gurgling sound in his throat, but it was clear that he was laughing. The laughter escaped against his will and he was unable to hold it in. The nurse turned grey with fear. She closed the lid, which she had been holding up all this time, with a loud bang, while Gurdweill went on shaking with laughter. Then he stopped abruptly, as if some seizure had suddenly left him, and turned and walked out of the morgue without a backward glance at the coffin or the nurse. He hurried down the corridor, almost running, bumping into another nurse and nearly knocking her down, and fled the hospital.

Outside he turned left, taking big, running strides, as if he were being pursued. At the end of Rauscherstrasse he turned into side alleys and reached Brigittenauer Bridge in a daze. His mind was a blank. Anyone who had seen him then — a short, thin man walking very fast, bare-headed and wild-haired, swinging both his arms (his hat had fallen from its place under his arm without his even noticing it), and his open coat flapping in the wind — might have thought him mad. A few people even stopped to stare after him in amazement as he hurried past. From time to time the sun peeped out of the clouds and immediately vanished again. A light wind pricked the skin on the Danube into goosepimples. The streets were full of traffic as people hurried home for lunch. Gurdweill continued walking rapidly. For the most part he kept to the pavement, and when he had to cross the street he did so with exaggerated caution, looking right and left at the rushing trams and cars. Sometimes he stopped dead in the middle of the pavement, his eyes on the ground as if lost in thought, and remained standing there for a few moments until he hurried on again. People saw him moving his lips and making curious gestures with his hands as if talking to himself. But Gurdweill was not talking at all. He was only singing an old tune to himself, without a sound or a thought in his head. Sometimes a smile would appear on his face and freeze there for a while, as if this were its permanent expression. Once or twice he dropped on to a bench and sat there for a few minutes before standing up and starting off again. Suddenly he found himself in Schulgasse, in front of his father-in-law's house, and for a moment something familiar hovered before his eyes, but only for a moment. His legs stopped for a second too, as if of their own accord, out of habit, but Gurdweill did not pause. There was a certain baffling question which now began throbbing insistently in his brain without his being able to find an answer to it. This question became clearer to him in Schulgasse, as if it pervaded the very air of the street, and from the moment it presented itself it nagged at him without stopping. Gurdweill could on no account understand why they needed a coffin when there

378

was a perfectly good pram, a pram which he himself had purchased .... And it wasn't a practical joke, it couldn't be, because Thea herself had said to him only recently that from now on the baby would sleep in a coffin and not in the pram, and Thea was not in the habit of making jokes ... And it was this which he could on no account understand. Especially the coffin itself! Hadn't he seen with his own eyes that the coffin was far too long for a baby of his size? A blind man could have seen it! Whereas the pram fitted him perfectly, as if it had been made to measure for him! And besides, how could they be compared at all? The pram was beautiful, he had chosen it himself, the finest pram in the shop — and the coffin was nothing but a few planks smoothed down and joined together! And how long was a thing like that capable of lasting? All you had to do was take hold of it to rock the child and it would fall apart on the spot. And you couldn't go out and buy a new one every day of the week! What a pity that he was too tired to go and look for Thea and stop her from selling the pram ... And the heat too, how terrible the heat was today! If only he had something to drink! That there was no one to give him a sip of cold water to drink on a day like this! ... Ah, his throat was parched with thirst!

Gurdweill's face was now as red as if it had been scalded. And there were two streams of perspiration sticking a few hairs across his forehead like threads and trickling down to his jaws. He was now walking slowly, swaying on his feet, along the Gürtel, near Westbahnhof. The sun had completely disappeared behind the clouds. The wind was colder now and there was a chill in the air. A train must have just arrived, since crowds of people were emerging from the station and crossing the square in front of him, some with suitcases or baskets in their hands and others with haversacks on their shoulders. It was half past three in the afternoon. There was a smell in the air of smoke and coal from an invisible engine. Gurdweill reached the park opposite the railway station and dropped on to a bench. For a while he sat there looking at the train passengers crossing the park on their way to the tram stop without seeing them. Suddenly his

379

teeth began to chatter and he got up and began walking again, shivering with cold. He crossed Mariahilfer Strasse and was almost run over by a speeding car, whose driver stuck his head out of the window to shower him with abuse when he reached the other side of the road. But none of this seemed to touch Gurdweill. Probably he did not even hear the driver's angry curses. A street opened up in front of him. Faint with weariness he dragged himself along it with the last of his strength. The thought that he had a room and a bed somewhere and that he could go home to them did not even cross his mind. He came out in Gumpendorfer Strasse and turned unthinkingly to the left, towards the city centre. After he had taken about a hundred steps down the street someone suddenly barred his way. Without raising his head he was about to step mechanically aside, when someone suddenly seized him by the arm.

"Good Lord!" cried Franzi Mitteldorfer in horror. "What's the matter with you?"

Gurdweill raised his bewildered, bloodshot eyes without appearing to recognize her. He said nothing.

"You have a high fever!" said the young woman. "You must go to bed right away. Come with me. You can lie down and rest at our place, and afterwards I'll take you home."

And she took his arm and led him away. Gurdweill followed her obediently. Although he recognized her he did not speak to her. He did not speak because of his great weariness and also because he had nothing to say. He climbed the stairs laboriously, supported by the young woman, and entered the house. She led him to the sofa.

"Here you are! Lie down and rest for a while, you poor thing! Put your feet up, don't worry — that's right!"

She helped him to get comfortable and stretch out his legs.

"And your hat — didn't you have a hat?"

"What, my hat?" He opened his mouth for the first time. "Never mind ... there's no need for a hat ... it's so hot. Something to drink! Has the whole town run out of water? Nobody gives you a drop to drink ..."

380

He spoke in a whisper, as if to himself. Franzi Mittel-dorfer stood and looked at him compassionately; she even had tears in her eyes.

"Please calm yourself. I'll bring you water right away."

She left the room and returned immediately with a glass of water, which Gurdweill emptied in a gulp.

"And now lie down and keep quiet," she said, as if she were coaxing a child, and wiped the perspiration from his brow with a clean white handkerchief. "My mother's taken the child out. As soon as she comes back I'll take you home."

Gurdweill lay on his back and looked out of the window opposite him, which appeared to have been set into the wall at an angle. This seemed to him very absurd. He tried to move his head, which felt as if it now weighed about a hundred pounds, but the window remained lopsided. It must be a modern style of building, he said to himself, but I prefer the old one. The old style looks better . . .

"Look here," he said aloud, "if I built myself a house I would never allow them to put the windows in crooked. In my opinion it's ugly and tasteless. And it's not functional either. You try to lean on the sill and you slide down to the corner! It's a joke! And the chimney of the house across the street is lopsided too . . . Our generation prefers the crooked — a symptom of decadence . . ."

And for some reason, he chuckled to himself.

"Listen," he said suddenly, "I have to go home now. The baby will wake up and begin to cry!"

He tried to get up but he didn't have the strength and fell back again.

The young woman sprang forward:

"Please lie down and rest! You'll go home soon!"

"Yes, that's right. I must rest first. I've been walking for a long time and I'm tired." He smiled guiltily. "I'll just rest for a minute and then I'll be able to go. But bring me a little water please! I'm thirsty!"

"I'll go and make some tea. Tea quenches the thirst better than water."

Suddenly it was night. Gurdweill peeped through a little window, which was actually more like a round hole

381

the size of the circumference of an ordinary glass, into a brightly-lit room. He looked through the peep-hole with one eye (there was no room for both), standing on tiptoe, because the hole was higher than he was. It cost him a great effort, but he did it nevertheless, because he knew that he was the sole witness and if he didn't see everything the deed would remain shrouded in darkness. Inside the room a man stood bending over a long, smooth bench (Gurdweill fixed this detail in his memory, since it seemed to him of the utmost importance). The man was standing with his back to him, but Gurdweill knew very well who he was. He thinks, the thought crossed his mind, that if he hides his face I won't know who he is! But I know very well: it's our tall doorman! He won't hide from me! The doorman was standing bent over the bench on which another man was lying, and hitting his skull rhythmically and deliberately with a stone, as if executing some procedure which demanded great precision. The man lying on the bench — although Gurdweill could not see his face he knew it was his brother-in-law Freddy — jerked his legs as if he wanted to kick the doorman, but the latter was standing at his head and also holding Freddy firmly with his other hand, so that his victim could neither free himself nor reach him with his kicks. In the meantime the doorman went on hitting him, and in the end Freddy lay still with his long legs stretched out in front of him. Gurdweill knew that he was now dead. And so it was. The doorman drew himself up to his full height and threw the stone into a corner. Then he rubbed his hands together two or three times as if well-pleased with what he had done, buttoned up his coat, and lit a cigarette. Gurdweill glanced at Freddy. The man was obviously dead, although there were no signs of blood or wounds on his face. "The wounds are internal," he explained to himself, "because he killed him with a flat stone, which is the same as strangling" — and now he had to hurry in case the murderer escaped. Despite his terrible exhaustion he got on to the tram with Franzi Mitteldorfer and within minutes he found himself standing in front of the Comissioner of Police, who was sitting at a black-covered table and looking at him through

a pair of opera-glasses. Gurdweill opened his mouth to tell
him about the murder — when suddenly heavy iron cables
began coming out of his mouth and falling in a pile at his
feet, and with them a spurt of blood. He was unable to
close his mouth or to utter a sound. An inhuman fear
seized hold of him as he realized that these cables would
be his undoing. Ah, if only he could speak and prove the
justice of his case! He tried to make signs with his hands,
but they too refused to obey him. Besides, he knew that
signs were useless; he had to speak, to speak! And he
began to pull the cables out of his mouth, hoping that
they would soon come to an end and allow him to speak.
His hands were full of blood, but the cables kept on coming. There was a huge pile of cables surrounding him like
a wall. Suddenly the Comissioner threw the opera-glasses
down with a melodramatic gesture like that of a bad actor,
and leapt to his feet.

"Look!" he pointed at Gurdweill. "Here's our murderer!
He was about to denounce the innocent doorman and now
see for yourselves the blood pouring out of his mouth!
What more proof could anyone want? The blood of the
murdered man, which he swallowed to hide his crime, now
bears witness against him!"

And he was immediately seized and dragged through
dark corridors and cellars. He could not even cry out, for
the cables were still coming endlessly out of his mouth.
Then he was thrown into a round room, and he knew
that it was a furnace and that he was going to be roasted
alive. But this is the Inquisition! he wanted to protest. The
Inquisition was abolished long ago! What you're doing to
me is against the law! But he could not utter a word. They
began to undress him and after all his clothes were gone the
heat increased unbearably, until he felt suffocated and the
heat seared his mouth and insides. He made a sign with his
hand, begging for something to drink, and they took pity
on him and brought him water. But when he drank the
water it turned to burning fire in his mouth, a thousand
times worse than the tortures of his thirst. Oh my God,
he groaned to himself, they're torturing me! Have mercy,
bring me a little ordinary water to drink! How can anyone

be so cruel? How can a man quench his thirst with boiling water? I'm dying of thirst!

"Here, drink this," said Franzi Mitteldorfer, holding out the glass to him. "A glass of tea will make you feel better."

"Ah, it's you!" said Gurdweill, coming to his senses. "Is the tea cold?"

"It's just right. Try it and see!"

In a semi-recumbent position he drank up all the tea. Then he said:

"Now I really must go."

"Right. I'll just write a note for my mother."

Afterwards she helped him to his feet, supporting him so that he would not fall, and led him with great difficulty down the stairs. She soon realized that it would be impossible to take him home by tram and hailed a passing cab. Throughout the journey Gurdweill did not say a word. He seemed asleep as he sat huddled in the corner of the seat like a dull, shapeless lump. It was already growing dark when Franzi Mitteldorfer took him up to his room.

"He's ill!" she said to the landlady who opened the apartment door. This time the old woman understood at once, and she accompanied them into the room and made up a bed on the couch while Gurdweill sat on a chair supported by Franzi.

"I knew it!" the old woman babbled as she made the bed. "I knew that he would make himself sick in the end! Working so hard, a fine man like him! And the baby dead too!"

The two women helped him to get undressed and lay him down on the couch. With utter indifference Gurdweill allowed them to do as they wished with him. Only from time to time a deep groan escaped his lips. The oil-lamp was lit and the old woman fetched a thermometer and stuck it in his armpit. Franzi Mitteldorfer moved about the room impatiently in her hat and coat. The thermometer showed a temperature of thirty-nine point eight degrees. Franzi Mitteldorfer told the old woman to call a doctor without delay. Herr Gurdweill was very ill, and to her regret she had to hurry home immediately. She would come back the next day to see how he was. And she said goodbye and left.

The doctor, who came two hours later, diagnosed a severe shock to the nervous system.

Part V: The End

30

THREE weeks had passed since Gurdweill rose from his sickbed. On the evening of the day that his sickness was discovered, his friends were sitting in the Café Herrenhof when Thea dropped in for a moment and informed them of the baby's death. Since they had not seen Gurdweill for some days and knew how attached he was to the child, they were concerned about him and they all got up immediately, Lotte, Dr. Astel and Ulrich, and took a tram to Kleine Stadtgutgasse. They arrived shortly after the doctor had left and found Gurdweill, whose fever in the meantime had risen even higher, lying unconscious on his back, his glassy eyes staring hollowly at the ceiling. Frau Fischer, who was busy soaking a towel for a cold compress to place on his head, told them everything, in detail and at length.

For eight days Gurdweill lay feverish and delirious, seeing visions alternately terrifying and blissful, in which the objects and people around him appeared in weird and fantastic combinations. He was taken care of by the old landlady and his friends, including Franzi Mitteldorfer, who came to see him every day and seemed to regard him as her own private patient. Thea went out to work and to meet her friends as usual, without making any concessions to his illness or lifting a finger to help him. Then the crisis came to an end and the doctor announced that the worst was over.

Utterly debilitated, too weak to move, he was obliged to stay in bed for an additional week after his fever had gone down. He did not mention the baby once during this period of recuperation, as if he had forgotten all about him. But sometimes, when his glance fell on the empty space between the bed and the window (Thea had sold the pram to a second-hand furniture shop while he was ill), it seemed to him that the whole room was empty, that the whole world was empty. However, the vital forces gradually returning to his body would not allow him to dwell on anything that might upset his equilibrium. He was in that state of happy, animal calm which comes to every dangerously-ill person when the danger is past and he is on the road to recovery. Lying supported on pillows, still too weak to speak, he would often smile, sometimes for no reason at all, at Lotte, who came to see him twice a day, or take her hand and stroke it in wordless gratitude, as an angry, stormy autumn raged outside and rattled the dirty window-panes.

It was three weeks since he had first ventured out into the street. Life had returned to its usual routine. Gurdweill lived, on the face of things, as before: he visited friends, wandered the streets, chatted briefly to this one or that one — but nevertheless there was a change in him, invisible to a stranger, and even more so to himself. He was even quieter than before, spent much of his time deep in thought, as if there was some very important decision which he had to make, and often replied absent-mindedly and irrelevantly when spoken to. The obscure oppression which had weighed on his soul ever since he had grown to know Thea, and which he carefully avoided scrutinizing in the clear light of consciousness, now began to exert an intense and unendurable pressure and to demand a logical analysis of its cause, and even some kind of remedy. All his thoughts now came up against Thea — wherever they turned they always ended up with her; she was the obstacle, the barrier, the source of all evil. In vain he sometimes tried, even now, to struggle against his feelings. Everything inside him was in revolt, all his thoughts accused her. And at the same time he knew that he would never find the strength to free himself of her. If only she would leave him! Although it was clear to him that he would be sorry, he would accept it as out of his hands and resign himself to his fate. But it never occurred to Thea to leave him. His constant submission provoked and goaded her baser instincts, and her sadistic appetite, which

390

had grown even greater in the course of their life together, found in him an unlimited source of satisfaction. As soon as she saw how profoundly the baby's death had affected him, she found a new way of hurting him. In contradiction to her previous avowals, she now took every opportunity to assure him that the baby had been his . . . and the further he withdrew into silence, the more vehement she became.

Nowadays he spent hardly any time at home. The room became repugnant to him, it was empty and desolate and gave rise to unhappy thoughts. He hardly worked, either. He was up to his neck in debt and always short of money. But this, it must be said, did not trouble him unduly. The crux of the matter lay elsewhere. He also felt obscurely that some end was approaching, that something was about to change soon — what and how he did not know.

It was a Tuesday. Warmer than the preceding days, which had been unseasonably cold. Gurdweill had wandered about the city for a long time, and was now sitting in his room, next to the stove, from whose open door a tongue of light burst forth, quivering on the floor between the couch and the bed, and casting a pale reflection on the bottom of the opposite wall. It was evening, almost six o'clock. Gurdweill did not light the lamp, since he liked being in the dark. In the light — the idea crossed his mind — a man sees what is outside him, and in the dark he sees himself. And the inside of things too . . . He suddenly felt like a primeval man in a dark forest, sitting by a fire he had built to frighten away the wild animals. He imagined hearing a stealthy rustle in the surrounding bushes, and through thousands of generations the animal terror of unknown forces holding sway all around him was transmitted to his soul. He made an automatic defensive gesture in the dark, and found himself back in the reality of the present. At that moment a motorcar blew two sharp hoots on its horn. Gurdweill waited in suspense for the third hoot, which did not come. In spite of everything — he returned to his previous line of thought — we're better off today than primitive man. A house like this with a stove and a bed waiting for you . . . He remembered several nights a number of years before, when he had been obliged to wander the streets of this very Vienna for lack of lodgings or money, some of them when the autumn was quite well advanced, like now — and his warm room seemed doubly cosy and secure. That, at least, was impossible now! And pity welled up in him for those unfortunates, in Vienna as in the other great cities of the world, who were still outside, forced to spend their nights on a bench under the open sky, or under a bridge, or in the sewers. Society should see to it that every human being had somewhere to live and a bit of bread to eat — that at least!

He stood up and added a shovel of coal to the fire. The new coals choked the flame; there was a series of explosive little sounds and wisps of dark, reddish smoke escaped from the cracks. Crouching on the floor, Gurdweill waited for the flame to leap up again. Then he returned to his chair. Now the tongue of light came out slightly slantwise, and licked the side of the couch in its dark-orange canvas cover. The outline of the couch imprinted itself on Gurdweill's senses, and by an unconscious process of association a feeling of mild tiredness stirred inside him. But he did not give way to the desire to lie down which suddenly overcame him. No! He would wait a little longer, and then he would make his bed and go to sleep early. He did not feel like going out again tonight.

In the corridor a door opened and shut. Had someone come in or gone out, he wondered. If someone had gone out, he did not envy him. Although it was not very cold outside, he felt a particular pleasure in staying at home this evening. Yes, he remembered, Lotte was looking worse from day to day. While he was still sick in bed, she had seemed to be looking better, but the truth was that she was looking bad. Apart from which, she had grown very quiet, which was not like her at all. Or sometimes she broke out unexpectedly in exaggerated fits of high spirits, which were not natural either. If only he could help her . . .

For a while his thoughts went on weaving around Lotte, and in the end he fell asleep. When he woke up, the coals were hissing and the fire had lost some of its heat. Gurdweill shivered sightly. He threw more coals on the fire and then lit a match and looked at his watch. He must have slept for a long time — it was nearly ten o'clock. His head felt heavy and there was a pain in his right side and his neck, presumably from sleeping in an uncomfortable posture in the chair. He began walking up and down to stretch his muscles. In the next room all was quiet. They must already have gone to sleep, the old woman and Siedl. He saw no need to light the lamp: there was a faint light from the windows, enough to make out the outlines of the furniture.

The door opened and Thea came in. She was home earlier than usual. She saw her husband sitting in the dark, and was immediately filled with rage:

"Why don't you put on the light, you idiot!" she cried, even before she shut the door behind her.

Gurdweill made haste to light the lamp, which was ready on the table. He remained standing by the table, careful not to make a move. He saw that she was in a bad mood and wanted to avoid a quarrel, but his heart told him that tonight would not pass quietly. All of a sudden he felt a surge of anger against himself and his caution. What! How long was he going to go on submitting fearfully to her every caprice! He pushed the chair out of his way, scraping it noisily on the floor, and went to look out of the window.

Thea finished taking off her outer garments and said:

"What's there to eat?"

"Nothing!" said Gurdweill shortly, without turning away from the window.

Surprised by his reply, Thea turned her head to stare at his back. In a calm, ominous voice she said:

"What do you mean — nothing? Why didn't you see to it that there was something to eat in the house?"

Now Gurdweill turned to face his wife. He did not reply immediately; he looked directly at her. After a moment he said bravely:

"Why didn't I see to it? Because I haven't got any money. As you know very well. And besides: for once you can make yourself something to eat."

Thea was flabbergasted. Red in the face with rage, she started forward:

"Wh-at? How dare you?! In that case, what do I need you for? Do you imagine that you'll sit here like a prince and I'll get your meals for you?"

"Not for me, for yourself!" replied Gurdweill fearlessly.

"Get out!" she pointed to the door. And when Gurdweill did not move, she added:

"Get out at once, I tell you! At once! And don't you dare show your face here again! You hear me, don't you dare!"

"Have you gone mad?" ventured Gurdweill. But Thea was already at his side, seizing him and dragging him to the door and pushing him out into the corridor. Then she threw his coat and hat after him and bolted the door from inside. It was all over before Gurdweill could grasp what was happening. Stunned, he stood in the dark corridor and looked at the door and the thin line of light underneath it. Suddenly it crossed his mind that the whole thing was a joke, and he tried to open the door. But the door was locked. Then Gurdweill realized that it was not a joke at all. He lit a match, picked up his coat and hat, put them on, and went downstairs.

In the street he looked at his watch in the light of the lamp. For a moment he wondered what to do next. He could easily spend the night, and even several nights, at Dr. Astel's place, or Ulrich's, but he quickly dismissed this possibility. How would he explain it to them? He could scarcely tell them the truth, that Thea had thrown him out of the house! As this thought came into his mind, he felt a sudden desire to laugh. His agitation had now died down, and for some reason the whole thing seemed ridiculous in the extreme. At any rate, he thought, he had to find somewhere to sleep tonight, and tomorrow he would see.

All he had in his pocket was one schilling, and for even the cheapest hotel he would need at least three. To save the tram fare, he began walking quickly towards the city centre, hoping to find someone willing to lend him a few schillings in the café. Gurdweill was surprised at himself for not being more upset by what had happened. All he felt was a kind of annoyance at the situation in which he now found himself. His heart told him that there was no

394

need to take it too seriously. Her anger would subside and everything would blow over. He could not believe that this was the end, and the important thing now was to borrow some money and find a lodging for the night. To a certain extent, he was even pleased at this way out. Better to be thrown out of the house than remain there, a prey to her wrath.

It was not cold. A fine, warm rain began to fall, spraying its drops in his face; the asphalt grew blacker and glittered wetly. Almost empty, the trams rolled past; every now and then an electric cable suddenly flared up overhead in a pale blue ribbon of fire, making a crackling sound like the snapping of a dry straw, and died down again. All at once Gurdweill was flooded by a torrent of rage so violent that it made him stop dead in his tracks. The room was his as much as it was hers, even more! He had lived there before she did — and now she was throwing him out! He felt an urge to run back and force his way in. She had no right to throw him out of his room! But a moment later he recovered his composure and set off again in the same direction as before. There was really no point in creating an open scandal!

In the café he found no one he knew. After a short hesitation he decided to order a black coffee and wait: perhaps someone would come. But half an hour passed and no one came. It was already half past eleven. Gurdweill was becoming very angry. Now he had spent his last penny on the coffee! He tried to read the evening papers in order to distract himself, but he was unable to take in a word and put them down again. If only it had happened in summer, at least! But now! And it was raining too! To spend the whole night outside in this weather! Gurdweill felt exhausted at the very thought. Too bad, there's nothing you can do about it! he almost said aloud. He decided to go on sitting there until they shut the café, at half past one, and then go for a walk. He resigned himself to his fate.

When the waiter passed his table he asked him casually if any of his acquaintances had been there this evening.

Yes, said the waiter, they had been there earlier and left

before Gurdweill arrived. Herr Doktor Astel, with the lady and the other gentleman, the blond one. They had spent about an hour in the café and left together.

"I'm lost!" thought Gurdweill.

"Tell me," he asked the waiter, "do you live far from here?"

"Me? Quite far. Near Westbahnhof."

"And how do you get home after they shut the café? There aren't any trams at that hour!"

"By foot. It's an hour's walk. Sometimes I go to the Franz-Josefs-Bahnhof, about a fifteen minute walk, and take the train."

"It's hard work, eh?"

"I should say so! On your feet from three in the afternoon to two o'clock in the morning without a break!"

The waiter twirled his moustache and looked pleased at this opportunity to discuss his work, which suddenly took on an uncommon importance in his eyes.

"Everybody thinks," he went on, "that it's an easy job, but it isn't easy at all! And sometimes you work all day for nothing! All your profits gone because of some little mistake, and you don't even know where it was or how it happened. Last week something of the kind happened to me. I began to add up the accounts for the day, and I found that there were ten schillings missing. I had to make it up from my own pocket. That day I came out at a loss. Because don't imagine that we earn ten schillings a day in tips! Sometimes you don't make even half that!"

"Yes, yes!" Gurdweill nodded understandingly. His thoughts were already far away, and he had not even heard the waiter's last words.

"Have you got a family too? A wife and children, I mean?" he suddenly asked.

"Certainly I have! Two boys. The eldest is finishing primary school this year . . . Coming!" he said to a customer who wanted to settle his bill, and turned away.

Two boys . . . thought Gurdweill, darting an envious glance at the white-jacketed waiter, who took out a fat wallet bursting with banknotes. Perczik appeared in the door and made straight for his table. My last chance!

thought Gurdweill. I don't owe him a bean, but he's a stingy swine. If he sits down without an invitation, I'll get what I want, he decided. And if not — I haven't got a hope.

"You're still sitting here so late at night!" exclaimed Perczik. "It's not like you."

As always when he found himself alone with Gurdweill, there was a faint note of embarrassment in his voice, which Gurdweill was at a loss to understand. He smiled and sat down at the table next to him.

I have to strike now, thought Gurdweill. If he refuses, it will be even more embarrassing for him.

"Look here, Perczik," he said heartily, "I'm short of cash!"

"Who isn't short of cash nowadays? The whole world's short of cash!"

Carefully avoiding Gurdweill's eyes, he took out a packet of cigarettes and offered him one as if he wanted to bribe him. Gurdweill took the cigarette, but his heart did not soften.

"I need five schillings and I need it now! You have to lend it to me! No excuses!"

"Five schillings? Where am I going to get five schillings from? It's almost a whole dollar! I know you pay your debts! You're the only one who does! I'd lend you the money gladly, believe me! But where on earth am I to get it at this hour of night? Tomorrow's a different matter entirely! I have a ten dollar note — I'll change it and give you the money tomorrow."

"Stop looking for excuses, Perczik. Hand over the ten dollars and I'll get the waiter to change them. He'll change them without any problems. Don't try to get out of it."

"The waiter — that's impossible! He'll give you less than the going rate, and why should I lose money?"

"I'll make up the difference to you! We'll see what the rate is today and I'll pay you back the difference later. Wait, I've got a better idea: I'll pay it right away. You lend me five schillings less the difference now, and I'll owe you five without the deduction — what do you say?"

"Certainly not! I'm not a money-lender you know!"

397

"Have it your own way!" said Gurdweill, shrugging his shoulders.

Suddenly he felt a surge of disgust for Perczik and the whole ugly business. He drew on the cigarette, staring straight in front of him. All at once a profound sadness descended on him, a sadness which had nothing to do with his present situation. For what difference did it make to him if he had to walk the streets all night long, or sleep on a filthy bed in some cheap, sordid hotel? At the thought of this bed, which he could see vividly in his imagination, he shuddered in horror. Better to spend all night wandering the streets. The melancholy which had suddenly flooded his being came from some deeper source. Its roots had long been entwined in his very soul, and his present situation had not given birth to it, but only, perhaps, helped to raise it from the depths.

Suddenly Perczik said:

"But if you can make do with less — two or two and a half – with pleasure! I've got exactly that much on me, apart from the cost of the coffee I still want to order."

Gurdweill took the money mechanically and dropped it into his coat pocket. Suddenly he felt an overpowering need to talk to someone, to open his heart to somebody. And he began to talk to Perczik, with a feeling of loathing for himself and the man he was talking to — a man he had always hated, and whose every movement irritated him. He was, perhaps, the only person for whom Gurdweill had always felt, from the moment he met him, an inexplicable hostility. And it was to him of all people that Gurdweill spoke now, with feverish haste, as if the time was too short for everything he had to say, telling him all kinds of things about his childhood which he had never told anyone before. And although the feeling of loathing did not leave him for a moment, he could not stop himself. Perczik watched him closely, devouring every word, with all the avidity of a police interrogator who had been trying for months to extract a confession from a suspect without success — when suddenly the man had come to him and confessed of his own free will. Gurdweill had always aroused his curiosity, but had been a closed book to him

398

— and now his hour had come. He noted down and filed away everything he heard in the space in his mind he had already set aside for the information, not wanting to miss the slightest nuance. And although he had not intended staying more than quarter of an hour at the most, he now settled down in his seat without a thought of leaving. He even ordered two more glasses of beer, one for himself and one for Gurdweill, remarking that he had accidentally discovered some change in another pocket. But he was careful not to ask any questions, or interrupt him, for fear that he might stop altogether. His curiosity was not lost on Gurdweill, who was also well aware that he would use what he heard, distorted and ill-understood, in his crude, superficial writing — but he did not care.

Neither of them sensed the passing of time, and in the end they were the last customers left in the café. The waiter came to settle the bill: it was time to go.

"I'll accompany you for a while," said Gurdweill when they stepped outside. "I'm in no hurry to get home. I feel like a little walk."

He now felt a certain connection to this Perczik, who had beome his confidant. Not only that, but the latter suddenly seemed less repulsive to him, as if he had risen to his own level simply by virtue of the fact that he had become a party to a number of intimate details of his life. The clock on the Schottentor said ten past two. It was not cold. There were only a few passers-by in the brightly-lit, deserted streets, which now seemed far broader than they did during the day. Their footsteps knocked hollowly against the night in Währinger Strasse, bringing a few prositutes out of the sleeping alleys. Gurdweill accompanied Perczik to his front door, where he remained with him for another thirty minutes, talking all the time, until in the end the latter said goodbye and rang the bell. Now it was half past three. Gurdweill felt completely drained, with a flat, unpleasant taste in his mouth as if he were suffering from a hangover.

He walked a few steps away from Perczik's house and stood still in the middle of the street, trying to make up his mind where to go. He still had a few hours to fill in until morning. Tomorrow, when Thea went to work, he would go home and lie down to sleep. And why shouldn't he go home now? Just because Thea gave way to vicious caprices, did he have to spend all night wandering the streets? Actually, he didn't feel like sleeping at all . . . He wouldn't be able to sleep even if he were lying on his couch at this very minute — but nevertheless! He would go home right now and force his way into his room, and damn the consequences! But in his heart of hearts, Gurdweill knew that he would not force his way into his room.

He set off, walking slowly, like someone taking a leisurely stroll for his own enjoyment. His feeling of disgust at himself for behaving as he did with Perczik did not leave him for a moment: he felt polluted. He was now near the Währinger district, not far from the street where Thea's parents lived. He remembered another night in the same place, a spring night one and a half years before, and his heart contracted with pain for something irretrievably lost. How everything had changed since then! Through that night all the days and nights of the future had seemed to glow with an extraordinary radiance. At any rate, they had certainly not included a night like this one. Only a year and a half had passed since then — and this short time had transformed him into a broken reed. Gurdweill now realized, with shocking clarity and for the first time, the extent to which life with Thea had crushed him. He was a broken man, perhaps irredeemably so.

He passed a bench next to the Volksoper and dropped on to it, feeling tired to death — as if all the tiredness which had accumulated inside him during the past one and a half years had suddenly engulfed him. And the worst thing of all — he continued his previous train of thought — was that there was no way out. He was trapped in a vicious circle: life was impossible with her, and even more impossible without her . . . A cold shiver ran down his spine and he stood up and went on walking. He took out his watch: only twenty minutes had passed since he had left Perczik. Until nine o'clock in the morning an eternity yawned — what would he do until then? A bottomless despair suddenly filled his heart and a great fear of the long night ahead, and he began to hurry, almost to run, as if running would bring him more swiftly to his goal, to the end of the night. In front of the Old People's Home he stopped at the kiosk which sold hot sausages to buy cigarettes. The buxom woman with the coarse, suntanned face dozing behind the counter woke up and counted the cigarettes twice over. Gurdweill caught a glimpse of a red scar cutting diagonally across her left cheek, from her ear to the corner of her fleshy mouth. Something gnawing like hunger inside him made him buy a pair of sausages, too, which he devoured before continuing on his way. He reached the Schottentor again and turned in the direction of the Kai. As he walked along it, it occurred to him to go down to the banks of the canal and find a place to sleep under one of the bridges, but he dismissed the idea immediately. It was too easy to catch cold next to the water. He was walking very slowly now, wearily dragging his body along, and the idea of somewhere to lie down struck him as the greatest happiness in the world. If only he could lie down somewhere to rest! Even here, on the pavement! He was swaying like a drunk, or like someone who had just risen from a sickbed. He no longer thought of the reason for his wanderings — he only knew that he was sentenced to go on walking and walking, despite his terrible weariness. A pity he hadn't brought his cane with him . . . together with the regret he felt at this thought, he was struck by its absurdity.

"There's no rest for the wandering Jew!" he said to himself, and reflected that the theatres, cinemas, and so on, could easily be converted into shelters for the homeless at night, when they were empty anyway and no use to anyone. People could sleep on the floor! Many would be glad of the opportunity! It was shocking that people were forced to wander the streets all night long while these buildings stood empty!

His body drawn to the ground, as if labouring under a wearisome burden, his head sunk to his chest, as heavy as lead, he made his way along Praterstrasse. Tomorrow, he thought with relief, if he failed to obtain a loan, he would go to the almshouse. There he would find a bed, at least. He had been told that it wasn't at all bad there. This hope for the morrow gave him a certain courage, and his steps quickened of their own accord.

When he reached the Tegetthoff monument he turned left without thinking, out of force of habit, crossed Heinestrasse, and soon found himself in Kleine Stadtgutgasse. The street was empty and dimly lit. It seemed as strange to Gurdweill as if he were seeing it for the first time in his life. The rows of windows on either side were menacing in their darkness. It was impossible to imagine that behind these blind windows life still stirred dully. The street was dead. But suddenly the despairing wail of an invisible cat broke out, and Gurdweill shuddered in horror. The cat fell silent and immediately gave vent to a second wail, which sounded particularly heart-rending in the desolation of the surrounding silence. Standing opposite his house, in the middle of the street, Gurdweill stared up at the third-floor windows. The two middle ones — the others, on the left, belonged to the landlady. Now Thea was sleeping in the bed, and Gurdweill on the couch . . . But what nonsense! He was standing here, in the street! Standing there in the dead of night in front of the windows of his own room, Gurdweill had the eerie feeling that he was confronting his own divided self, one half of which was up there on the couch and the other down here . . . All at once the certain knowledge came to him that in a moment Thea would wake up, open the window, and ask him to come up to bed . . . He waited in suspense. For a minute he even imagined that he could discern a faint movement inside, a definite movement . . . but no! The cat let out another wail; the window did not open and Gurdweill dropped his eyes. Suddenly he was seized with fear: if a policeman happened to pass this way and see him standing still in the middle of the street, he would surely think him a burglar or something of the kind. Disappointed, he began walking slowly away, when a sudden apprehension that some neighbour of his acquaintance might come upon him by surprise, and tell the whole street of his disgrace, made him quicken his footsteps to a run.

He crossed Heinestrasse again and came out at the Praterstern. A number of cars were parked at the kerb,

402

their drivers chatting desultorily with a few prostitutes who had apparently given up hope of finding any more customers for the night. There was a sense of desolation in the air, of a dreary, futile, hopeless poverty, of a profound and permanent misery, which was hidden by day and now crawled out of its holes and exposed itself boldly in all its nakedness, breaking out of the silent houses and the wretched creatures left in the street, welling up from the very paving stones. The other side of life revealed itself, like the shabby lining of a garment which looked well enough on the outside. As he surveyed the deserted Praterstrasse it occurred to Gurdweill, as if for the first time, that it was late at night, and people should be at home asleep. A feeling of pity stirred in him for the wretched creatures — these drivers, for example — who were obliged to be out in the street at such an hour instead of tucked up in a warm bed at home. But this feeling flickered out again immediately in the stupor of his numbing fatigue. Without thinking he turned into the Hauptallee, in the vague hope of finding a bench to rest on. Somewhere nearby a clock began to strike, perhaps the railway station clock, and Gurdweill stood still to count the strokes although he had a watch in his pocket. It was five o'clock. Four more hours, four more hours! — the thought penetrated the fog in his mind as he passed under the bridge and entered the deserted avenue, dimly lit by very widely-spaced streetlamps. Heavily, with the last of his strength, he dragged his feet to the first bench looming out of the darkness and dropped on to it.

There were already three people sitting on the bench, two men and a woman. When he sat down, they all started fearfully and peered at him through the darkness, only to sink back immediately into their slumbers, each one with his head resting on the shoulder of his fellow. Gurdweill could not see their faces in the dark, only that the woman sitting next to him was bare-headed. Nor was he in the least interested. All he knew was that he had to be on his guard for the policeman who could pass by at any moment. The place was swarming with them, they popped up in front of you as if springing right out of the ground. The main

403

thing is not to close your eyes! he said to himself, making a strenuous effort to open them as wide as he could. But his eyelids dropped of their own accord. Ah, the poor woman — there was something of Thea herself about her — how cold she must be! Without a hat, poor thing! He would offer her his, it was sure to fit her! But his hat — he suddenly remembered — was lost, what a shame! When you had to push such a heavy pram with a baby what was the wonder that your hat got lost? If only the shops were open he would have gone to buy a new one straight away. There should be a law to keep them open all the time, at night too, because it was winter now and the present state of affairs was quite intolerable! But she could lean on him and that would warm her up a little. No, it would be better to invite her to go to his room with him, it was nice and warm there now with the stove on. But he immediately dismissed this idea. Of course, he hadn't paid the rent yet! And Thea wouldn't let him in without paying the rent! She might even call a policeman to put him in prison! Because not paying the rent was just like stealing . . . Horrified by this possibility, he opened his eyes.

The woman next to him said in a hoarse, masculine voice:

"Have you got a cigarette for a neighbour, sir?"

Ah, I must have fallen asleep! thought Gurdweill. He was not sure if the woman had been addressing him, but in any case he took out a cigarette and offered it to her. At that moment a policeman appeared right next to the bench, gave them a piercing look, and apparently having concluded that everything was in order and in compliance with the "law," disappeared again into the dark.

"Those pigs!" muttered the woman hoarsely to herself. "They don't give you a moment's rest!"

And to Gurdweill:

"Can you tell me what the time is?"

He lit a match and looked at his watch. It was half past five.

Gurdweill's limbs were frozen, his right leg was numb and full of pins and needles, and felt so heavy that he could hardly move it. He had the feeling that all his limbs

404

were dislocated, and that his whole body had stretched and expanded, overflowing its natural boundaries and invading the surrounding space, merging, as it were, into the darkness, which had for some reason become denser. He felt as if he had been travelling in a train for days and nights at a stretch without closing his eyes, even though he had just slept for about half an hour. His eyes hurt and his teeth chattered with cold.

One of the men on the bench got up and set off wordlessly into the darkness, swaying on his feet and treading as silently as if he had no shoes on. The woman had already finished smoking the cigarette and fallen asleep again on her neighbour's shoulder. Gurdweill stood up and began moving in the direction of the Praterstern, limping on his numb leg, which gave way beneath him like cotton-wool. As daybreak approached the cold increased, and a wind sprang up too, penetrating to the marrow of his bones. When had it all begun? He had the feeling that he had never been at home, that he had always been wandering thus, worn out and exhausted. One wish only flickered inside him: to sit down somewhere warm, to sit still and close his eyes.

He was close to a tram stop and without thinking about what he was doing, he came to a halt and stood there waiting. An empty tram drew up and he got on and huddled into a corner. The only other passengers in the car were two poor women and a working man. The cold did not leave Gurdweill. On the contrary, it seemed to him that it was even colder inside the tram than outside, and at the next station he got off again. For a moment he stood still, as if trying to make up his mind what to do next. But in truth he was not thinking of anything at all. His chest was burning as if smothered in a mustard plaster, although at the same time he felt cold. He huddled deeper into his coat, stuck his hands into his sleeves, and looked up at the sky, which seemed to him to be growing lighter as daybreak approached. Then he began dragging himself wearily back in the direction of the Praterstern, from which he had just come. After taking a few steps it occurred to him that the Norbahnhof was nearby, and

405

he could go there. People would think he was waiting for a train. It must be warm there.

Now that he had a goal his steps quickened of their own accord. It was a quarter past six. A suburban train must have just pulled in: a crowd of workers, little bundles tucked under their arms or held in their hands, came pouring out of the exit. At the sight of the hurrying workers Gurdweill felt a fleeting shame, shame at the grotesque and pointless reason for his own presence here at this early hour. It was clear to him that everyone knew immediately what had happened to him, that they could read it on his face. He shot a wrathful glance in the direction of Kleine Stadtgutgasse, and entered the railway station.

The station entrance was empty, and half-dark. Two railway workers were sweeping the floor, one on either side of the hall. On a bench at the side a man was sitting hunched over the old basket at his feet. Only one ticket booth was illuminated. Gurdweill seemed in his own eyes like someone who had arrived too early for a party, before the table had been laid. It was cold in the entrance hall, and he did not have the strength to go up to the waiting-room on the first floor. Pretending to be a passenger, he went up to the timetable stuck up on the wall, and studied it for a while without seeing a thing. Then he went up to the ticket booth and asked the clerk what time the train left for Aspang, God knows why.

The clerk replied with open annoyance, as if his honour had in some way been impugned:

"The trains to Aspang depart from Aspangbahn, in the Third District, not from here! This is Nordbahnhof!"

"And when does the train leave from there — if you would be kind enough to tell me?"

"They'll tell you there!"

Because of this silly mistake he could no longer remain here in the guise of a passenger waiting for his train. From now on the clerk would no doubt keep a strict watch on him. He even felt obliged, for a moment, to actually go to the other station, as if he really had to take a train to Aspang . . . In any case he turned away from the ticket booth and went straight to the door, as if to show the

406

clerk that he was obeying his instructions to the letter, and without a moment's delay.

Outside a grey, tired day was breaking. Something was growing lighter, filtering into the space trapped between the walls and pushing the darkness aside. One by one the streetlamps went out. The area around the railway station was beginning to come to life. And Gurdweill's mind too began to clear, and even to produce a good idea: the cafés were opening, he had a little money left — he would have a cup of coffee and warm himself at the same time. This encouraging idea gave him new strength and he crossed the road briskly in the direction of a small workmen's café. It was already nearly seven o'clock; there were only two hours left before Thea went to her office.

In the café he seated himself unobtrusively in a corner and ordered black coffee. Black coffee — he said to himself — would keep him awake. A few workmen were having breakfast. Not far from him sat a poor woman of about forty, with a sharp, red nose and rather thin, wispy, auburn hair. From time to time she raised her eyes from the rolls she was noisily and hungrily devouring to cast a glance at Gurdweill. Perhaps she was the woman who had shared his bench in the Hauptallee — the thought flashed through his mind. It was not at all improbable . . . Well, what difference did it make!

He sipped the boiling coffee and warmth began stealing through his limbs. But he was too exhausted to take in a word of the newspapers which the waiter offered him. He wanted one thing only — to sleep. The black coffee did not help much. His brain spun with fragments of disconnected thoughts. His head felt very heavy, too heavy to bear, and there was a sharp pain at the base of his skull, beating incessantly inwards like a hammer. Time seemed to stand still, indifferent to Gurdweill's agony. He was sure that at least an hour must have passed since he entered the café, but this watch said otherwise. He was in despair. What was he going to do? If time went on crawling like this, he would go mad! The entire night, it seemed to him, had been easier to endure than the two hours which were still before him. And at the same time, how idiotic and pointless the

407

whole thing was! All because of a caprice, of unreasonable spite! A wave of rage against Thea surged up in him, so that he could hardly breathe. If she had been here beside him, he might have done something stupid. Gurdweill was alarmed at the intensity of his anger, which he had not known he was capable of until now. She encouraged his evil instincts, thought Gurdweill bitterly, all the worse for her! He was actually trembling with helpless rage. He wanted to get up and go home immediately — come what may! But he stayed where he was. He lit a cigarette, picked up *Das Tagblatt* mechanically and tried to distract himself.

The woman at the next table finished her meal. She went on casting sidelong glances at Gurdweill until it began to make him feel uncomfortable. What did she want of him? He was filled with an insane rage against all the women in the world, without a single exception. And now she was standing up. She's coming here! — the certain intuition flashed through his mind. She took one or two steps towards the door, changed her mind, turned back and made straight for Gurdweill's table. He recoiled instinctively and looked at her inquiringly.

"Please be so kind, sir, as to let me have *Das Tagblatt* when you've finished with it."

"I'm reading it now myself!" said Gurdweill angrily.

"No, no: when you've finished, I meant." And she added apologetically: "It's for the advertisements, you know. Once in a while there's something it would be a pity to miss."

Gurdweill held out the newspaper without saying a word.

"No, please!" protested the woman. "You finish it first! I'll wait a while."

"Take it, please! I don't need it any more."

The woman took the newspaper and thanked him, but she did not leave. After a short pause, she said:

"Perhaps you could help me out, kind sir, with a little money? I haven't got the money to pay the waiter for my coffee." Gurdweill could not believe his ears. Nevertheless he took out his money, set aside what he needed to pay for his own coffee, and gave her the rest: sixty groschen.

"That's all I've got."

The woman smiled in satisfaction and returned immediately to her table, leaving the newspaper with Gurdweill. Full of a murderous rage Gurdweill leapt up, grabbed the newspaper and ran over to the woman.

"You wanted to read the advertisements, didn't you!" he said, flushed and almost shouting. "Here they are, look!"

And he tapped the last pages with his finger.

"What do you want, mister?" she said insolently. "I don't feel like reading the advertisements! You're not going to force me to read the advertisements if I don't want to!" And addressing the room at large she added: "Have you ever seen the like?"

"In that case . . . In that case you have no right to beg for charity either, do you understand?"

"Who's begging for charity? You're a beggar yourself! Have you ever heard such cheek in your lives?"

"If you don't return my sixty groschen this very minute, I'll call the police!"

"What sixty groschen? Who took sixty groschen from you? You're drunk, my friend! Do I need your money? I could give you sixty groschen! And more! I've got more money than you have!"

Gurdweill stood and looked at her in bewilderment. Her sharp, snub nose was even redder than before, and her tiny, rat-like eyes looked straight at him with open hostility. Suddenly his gorge rose in such loathing that he wanted to vomit and he turned away and returned to his table, the newspaper in his hand. From behind his back he heard the woman's abuse:

"Have you ever? A beggar like him, a madman like him, trying to force me to read the advertisements! You just wait, I'll catch you one day . . !"

Gurdweill hid behind the newspaper so as not to see her ugly face, but to no avail. Her nose poked through the pages and confronted him, her abuse rang in his ears. In the end he could bear it no longer. He called the waiter, paid his bill, and left the café.

It was now well into the morning. A cloudy, late-autumn morning. Gurdweill dragged himself wearily back into the

409

Hauptallee, sat down for a while on last night's bench, got up again and went for a walk in Praterstrasse, stopping from time to time outside the windows of the shops which were already open to look unseeingly at the goods on display — until nine o'clock came at last and he started walking home. To be on the safe side, he waited on the corner of the street until a quarter past nine, in order to avoid meeting his wife, and then he went up to his room. Thea was not there. It seemed to Gurdweill that he had not been there for many days. The room looked strange to him, alien. But he had no time to ponder this. He locked the door and threw himself on the pile of bedclothes on his couch, just as he was, fully dressed and shod. In a second he was asleep.

31

AT half past two in the afternoon Gurdweill woke
up with a headache and a foul, bitter taste in his
mouth. The memory of the previous night immediately
invaded his heart like an oppressive, shameful nightmare,
thoroughly disagreeable down to its last, ignominious detail. But there was no time to waste: he had to find lodging
for the coming night.

He jumped out of bed, threw off his coat and jacket,
and sat down to shave. As he did so, he wondered who
to ask for a loan. Most of his friends were out of the
question: some because he already owed them money,
and some because they themselves were as broke as he
was. He decided to try to talk to Frau Fischer. She would
not turn him away empty-handed, even though he owed
her a packet, too.

Shortly afterwards he stepped outside, armed with two
schillings and a gnawing hunger. He was in luck, and
despite the lateness of the hour he was able to obtain soup
and roast beef at a small restaurant in the neighourhood.
Being the only customer, he gobbled down his food in
haste, since eating alone in a public place always made
him feel ill at ease. Afterwards he walked in the grey,
chilly afternoon towards the city centre, brooding on his
peculiar situation. No! He could not go home until she
expressly invited him to do so. She had chased him out
— it was up to her to appease him! Crawling to her was
out of the question! Apart from which it wouldn't do him
any good. And this being the case, he thought miserably,
he had no alternative but to find a room for himself. In the
long run, this might prove to be the best solution. At least
he would have some peace and quiet. But in the midst of
these reflections Gurdweill felt that it would not be a good

solution at all, and that it would not even secure him the peace he longed for. Life itself cramped him, suffocated him. There was no air to breathe. Wherever he turned, there was no way out. Perhaps he could only extricate himself by some act of aggression, some sudden, decisive break — but he did not know how or what. Besides, he felt so weak, quite incapable of any decisive action. Once upon a time, before the past year and a half, he had been strong. Then he had been capable of shaping the course of events to his will. But now everything had changed. He was a crushed, broken man. And in this state his life was not worth living. He could not go on like this.

Sunk in these sombre reflections he reached the Café Herrenhof and went inside. He found none of his acquaintances there, which did not disappoint him in the least. He went out again and looked at his watch. It was a quarter to four: he had about half an hour left. He set off in the direction of the Volksgarten.

His mistake lay, perhaps — he caught up the thread of his thoughts again — in the fact that he had ever hoped for peace and quiet, for a placid, normal life like anybody else — and this was the source of all his disappointments. He should never have deceived himself in the first place! He, Gurdweill — and contentment! Some people were destined for suffering from birth and he was one of them! Nevertheless, however, even if he was fated to suffer, that did not make his sufferings any sweeter . . .

Gurdweill sat down on a bench in the empty Volksgarten. At the sight of a couple of solitary nursemaids pushing prams he felt a deep pain. He had not been in the Volksgarten since the summer, when Thea was in the hospital after giving birth to Martin. How different everything had been then. Even now — an inner voice called out to him — even now all is not lost! Something can still be saved . . . But Gurdweill did not listen. Through the bare branches he stared at the autumn sky and it came to him that he, Gurdweill, now lived not at this or that address, but in the city of Vienna as a whole: in the literal sense of the words, he lived in Vienna. For some reason this struck him as amusing, and he smiled.

He began to feel cold and he stood up and started walking down the garden paths, crunching the gravel underfoot. Then he decided not to wait any longer, but to go straight to the tram. By the time he got to the Meidling District . . ! And even when he got there, he would still have to ask the way! Besides, he had been told that the institution opened its doors at five. To tell the truth, the almshouse interested him in itself, and not only because he stood in need of it at the present moment. Otherwise he could surely have found the money for a hotel somewhere. He had been wanting to acquaint himself with such a place for a long time, and now his chance had come.

After a three-quarter hour journey on the tram, he got off at the last stop, when daylight was already fading. He found himself not far from a railway bridge, in a cold, open square, in a place where he had never been before. Many-storeyed new buildings were dotted here and there, apparently workers' tenements. There was hardly a soul to be seen. The few passengers, all from the lower classes, who had dismounted from the tram with him had hurried off in different directions.

Gurdweill took a few steps forward, along the railway embankment, and then stood waiting for some passer-by to show him the way. An old woman, when asked, hesitated for a minute and then said that she had no idea where the almshouse founded by the Emperor Franz-Josef might be. He walked on a little and saw a man dressed in rags carrying a bundle in his hand coming towards him. "He'll surely know!" said Gurdweill to himself. And indeed he did.

"Pass under this bridge, young man," he said. "You'll find a stairway on your right. Go up it and you'll see it right in front of you. It's the only building there."

Gurdweill retraced his steps, passed under the bridge, where a single lamp cast a dim light, and ascended the stairs. It was pitch dark. He came out at a big, empty lot; about a hundred paces from the railway tracks stood a single building, large and white, and four storeys high, illuminated by four lamps. "There it is!" said Gurdweill to himself, and made straight for the building.

413

He found himself outside the women's wing. On a dark porch stretching the length of the wall a crowd of women of all ages stood or knelt on the floor — a hundred women or more. A deathly silence reigned, as if they were waiting with bated breath for some significant event to happen. There was something mysterious about the scene, and Gurdweill felt as if he had accidentally stumbled upon a cabal of conspirators.

He walked round to the other side of the building. Here he found men standing all along the wall, rank after rank, like an army. A legion of benighted souls, sullen, ragged, unshaven, young and old, the likes of whom you never saw there, in the city, or only rarely, and one by one. Three and four to a row they stood, in silence or exchanging whispers with their neighbours, most of them stooping in an ape-like posture. Some were smoking cigarette stubs. It was dark. The light cast by the two lamps at the corners of the long building was insufficient to illuminate the entire area.

Gurdweill approached and stood at the rear, without anyone taking any notice of him. His heart quailed, as if weighed down by the burden of these masses. The heavy, dreadful silence was immediately transmitted to his soul, and he had the feeling that he had been standing there in this same silence for many years, ever since the day he was born. Unconsciously he, too, began to stoop until his posture resembled that of his neighbours in every detail. From time to time a figure separated itself from the darkness of the night and joined the line. They made no sound as they approached, for they trod softly, with an animal stealth. Gurdweill felt as if they had been lurking here in the dark for a very long time, right under his nose, and now, with a single step, they came up and stood behind him. With exaggerated caution, as if afraid of rousing someone, he fumbled in his pocket for a cigarette. The flame of the gas light flickered in the distance. And suddenly the heavy silence was broken by the shrill whistle of a train, sending a shudder through Gurdweill's flesh, as if this reckless whistle might bring some harm to himself and all these creatures. The man standing next to him, tall

414

and haggard and sparsely bearded, muttered to nobody in
particular:

"Five. The whistle blows at five. They'll open up in
a minute."

Slowly they began to shuffle in, one by one, never
breaking their silence. It took about twenty minutes for
Gurdweill to reach the door, which was guarded by two
stalwart men with moustaches and hard expressions on
their faces. Some of the poor showed little red cards,
and others received such cards now from the guards.
The sparsely bearded man, whom Gurdweill allowed to
go in before him, was stopped in the doorway.

"I know you," one of the guards berated him. "You've
been here eight days in a row. Stand aside, you scum!"

And he pushed him out.

"Next!"

Gurdweill entered a narrow passage, where two super-
visors stood at a gate and inspected the men to see if they
were clean. Those suspected of uncleanliness were led to
one side, to bathe and have their clothing disinfected.
Many requested baths themselves. Gurdweill followed the
others, who were already familiar with the procedures of
the place, deposited his watch in the safe-deposit locker
in the passage, and went with them to the long, narrow
bathroom, which had wide zinc troughs running along
both walls and a rail in the middle, upon which hung rough
towels, stiff as scouring brushes, as well as the clothes of
the bathers. "When in Rome do as the Romans do," said
Gurdweill to himself, and squeezed· in among the hairy
men with their naked torsos, washed himself like them
with hot and cold water, sticking his fingers as they did
in the mound of soft, squashy, glue-like yellow soap lying
next to each pair of taps. In a small, square room leading
off the bathroom there was a cracked mirror on the wall,
shining in patches with a pearly sheen, and before it a table
holding a few filthy combs with their teeth stuck together,
and here wet heads and beards were silently, diligently,
combed — and the people in their rags and tatters took on
a somewhat different, less savage appearance. From here a
door led into a large, spacious hall, with two rows of tables

and benches set along the walls, leaving a wide passage in the middle.

Washed and combed they seated themselves noise-lessly at the tables, like obedient children. They sat still and waited. Gurdweill did not know what they were waiting for, but refrained from asking, in order not to give the impression of a greenhorn, and also because speech seemed out of place here, unnatural. It was both strange and terrifying to see these sombre people sitting in silence, three hundred grown-up men not uttering a word.

Suddenly they all stood up at once, as if at some in-audible signal, whispered a brief prayer, which slipped through their ranks like a soft forest murmur, crossed themselves and sat down again. Then the two people seated at the end of each table stood up and walked to the end of the room, where a big hatch, unnoticed by Gurdweill before, was set in the wall, and after a few min-utes returned bearing big trays with twelve slices of black bread and twelve grey, metal bowls containing a brown liquid: a soup made of flour and caraway seeds. Hungrily the bread was devoured by three hundred mouths and the soup gulped directly from the bowls for lack of spoons. Overcoming his revulsion Gurdweill drank the tepid, taste-less soup; he did not want to set himself apart from the others, or to appear to think himself above them. He gulped it down like a medicine, closing his nostrils from the inside so as not to smell the unpleasant odour which reminded him of the slightly steamy smell of the Russian Baths in the Landstrasse.

The meal over and the dishes returned to the kitchen, a voice cried "To the dormitories!" and once more they stood in line in the passage next to the kitchen, facing a heavy, iron door, like the door of a prison. The newcomers were given green cards, with the numbers of their dormi-tory and bed, which were valid for five days. Gurdweill's dormitory was on the third floor, and his bed was number 212. The big dormitory hall, dully lit by a single naked bulb, held from fifty to sixty iron beds, standing side by side with only a narrow aisle between them. There were no mattresses on the beds. The sleeping surface consisted of a rather pliable wire mesh, and at the head of each bed lay three neatly folded dark brown blankets.

Gurdweill was lucky — his bed was in the corner, next to the wall. He examined the blankets as thoroughly as the weak light permitted, and found them sufficiently clean. His neighbour, a squat, bald man of about fifty, took a needle and thread from his pocket, removed his trousers, and sat down on his bed to mend them. He said to Gurdweill (here their powers of speech returned, as if a magic spell had suddenly been lifted):

"You have to hand it to them, they keep the place clean here. This is the best shelter in Vienna, you can believe me, but only five nights a month. They watch you like eagles, but you can still trick them sometimes. A few groschen can buy you a card for a couple of nights. There are lots of people ready to sell, believe me. Maybe you've got a bit of black thread for me, Herr neighbour? I've only got white, and it doesn't match my trousers."

Gurdweill had no thread.

"Well, there's nothing for it then!" said Gurdweill's neighbour, smiling at him like an old friend. "The main thing is to mend the holes."

"I see you're new at the game," he remarked, seeing Gurdweill struggling with his blankets, "this is the way to do it: one you spread out like a sheet, one you fold up and put under your head, and the third you cover yourself with. And you should hide your clothes and shoes, too. The best place is under your head. That's what I do." He lowered his voice confidentially: "There are all kinds of people here and it pays to be careful."

Gurdweill made up his bed in accordance with his neighbour's instructions, took off his coat and placed it at the head of the bed, where he asked the latter to keep an eye on it while he himself went to have a look around. The room led through an open doorway into another, and the second into a third — all equally large and full of beds. The men stood about talking in little groups, or sat alone on their beds, some sewing, others reading torn pages of newspapers, and a few taking off their rags and

417

lying down to sleep. It was not cold. There was even a kind of market going on. Little deals were offered. One man ran from bed to bed and room to room announcing in a whisper: "Trousers to change! I've got trousers to change!" Another advertised: "Cigarettes!" And a third: "Shoes polished here!" Someone wanted to sell a penknife, another suspenders, a waistcoat, and so on and so forth, while many offered sleeping-cards for two, three and even four nights. All this was advertised in hurried whispers. The time was short, inspection was at eight and by then everyone had to be in bed. Gurdweill went out into the passage to smoke. The passage was packed, the barter in full swing. People sat on the stairs polishing patched, broken shoes, things were bartered, bought and sold. Someone asked Gurdweill if he wanted to sell his jacket; he would give him two schillings for it and throw in his own jacket as well, which was also worth a couple of schillings. Then he asked him to change shoes with him. There were so many people besieging the lavatories that he had to wait a quarter of an hour for his turn.

Then he went back to his dormitory. His neighbour was still busy sewing.

"Didn't I tell you? Someone was circling like a vulture around your bed. But for me there would have been an empty hole where your coat is now . . . So be careful!"

Gurdweill thanked him and sat down on his bed. His neighbour soon finished his job and put the trousers down beside him.

"Now you return the favour and keep an eye on my trousers. I'm going out for a minute."

And he went out into the passage in his underpants.

Gurdweill took off his clothes, put them under the blanket folded at the top of his bed and lay down. The movement in the dormitory began to slowly subside. The weak light falling from the ceiling illuminated lumpy, elongated shapes on the beds, while leaving shadows in corners here and there. People were tired and the silence which would soon dominate everything began to gather in the room. The windows were pitch-black, and it was certainly better to be lying here on the wire mesh, which

418

was softer than it looked and made a kind of hollow nest for his body, than to be wandering in the streets like the night before. Gurdweill felt as if he were very far away from the city of Vienna and everything familiar to him, on some remote island among strange people with alien customs. It seemed a very long time since he had last seen Thea. What was she doing now? Various answers, each more painful than the other, were ready to spring up from the depths of his mind in reply to this question, but he quickly deflected his thoughts to another subject. Last night, when he stood waiting outside his room in the dark, in case she should open the window and call him, she had not come ... She had not sensed that he was standing outside in the empty street and waiting ... Another woman might perhaps have sensed it ...

He lay on his side, facing the interior of the room. Suddenly he heard a muffled but vigorous knocking, which seemed to come from very far away and at the same time from right under his bed. Gurdweill could not ascertain the cause of the sudden noise and was filled with apprehension. He raised himself on his elbows and looked around at the people in the other beds, wondering why none of them were taking any notice of the knocking. Could he be the only one to have heard it? His neighbour had not yet returned from the passage — where could he have disappeared? The knocking lasted for about two minutes and suddenly stopped. Now Gurdweill realized that it had come from the central heating pipes running along the walls close to the floor. It must be eight o'clock, and this was the order to lie down and stop talking. At that moment his neighbour returned on tiptoe and began hastily taking off his coat and jacket. He cast a glance at Gurdweill, and seeing that his eyes were open, said in a whisper:

"That's it: go to sleep and don't open your mouth! Shhhh! The rules are strict here and anyone who breaks them had better look out. I know what I'm talking about."

He covered himself with his blanket and kept quiet.

The next minute the supervisor came in from the adjoining room, stalked from bed to bed like the sole survivor among the fallen on a bloody battle field (the silence was

419

only broken now by an isolated snore), and went out again, with the self-satisfied air of a man who had brought some important enterprise to a successful conclusion.

"Well, the inspection's over," muttered Gurdweill's neighbour, "but I'm not sleepy yet. And by the looks of things, neither are you."

"It's still very early."

"Exactly! Mind you, you have to get up at the crack of dawn here. At half past four they start banging on the pipes, and you have to jump to it. They carry on as if it was a bloody army barracks, or a jail. You can ask me — I know them both. I wasn't born yesterday, believe me."

Gurdweill's interest was now aroused, and since he had no desire to go to sleep yet he asked him when he had been to jail and for what crime. "A man of my age, my friend," said the man, not without pride, "has already done and seen a thing or two in his life! Sitting in jail is nothing to get excited about, believe me. Step out of line just once — and you're inside! Poor people are particularly lucky in this respect. You might even say that the jails were constructed especially for them. The rich never get within a mile of a jail. And if they ever do get into trouble, you can trust them to get out of it pretty quick, believe me! As for me, I've been inside more than once, and I can tell you it's not half as bad as it's made out to be. In a hard winter you might even do something on purpose to be locked up. At least you'll have a roof over your head and something to put in your stomach.

"The first time I was still very young when I was caught. I was put away for four straight years. My youth and inexperience were to blame. My father was a tailor by profession, a first rate cutter. A suit he made was like a poem. You can take my word for it: he was head tailor for the Bergner family for years. But he didn't like the work. Some people aren't made for work. They'd do anything rather than sit and work for a set number of hours every day. And you can't do a thing about it! It's a question of temperament. In my opinion, human beings are divided into horses and riders, and my father wanted to be a rider. In addition to which he happened to be excessively fond

420

of jewellery, especially gold rings set with precious stones. Not to wear them, mind, he didn't care about that at all: he liked to feel them, to feast his eyes on them, to play with them like a child with his toys. Just holding them in his hands gave him tremendous pleasure. And one fine day he gave up tailoring and began trading in gold jewellery: he would buy some ring (there's a special bourse for gold, you know), feast his eyes on it for a few hours or even a day, and then sell it again at a small profit, sometimes even at a loss, and buy another one. But his main source of income at the time was cards. He had a Romanian friend: a certain Chornotescu. A striking-looking man, with impressive manners and dandyish clothes. I can still remember his appearance perfectly: tall and well-built, with a clean-cut, masculine, young-looking face although his thick hair was going grey. This grey hair in conjunction with his young face gave him an air of aristocratic distinction. And in fact he had a weakness for adding various titles to his name — once it would be Count Chornotescu, once Baron Chornotescu, and so forth. And I must tell you that everyone believed him. Otherwise it would have been impossible. People were actually astonished if someone said that he wasn't really a Count or a Baron. Even his foreign German accent had something aristocratic about it. He was fluent in a number of languages, by the way. Besides German and Romanian he spoke French and Italian and a little English. As far as I was concerned, at any rate, he was a symbol of manliness, elegance, and worldliness. In any case, this Chornotescu was a permanent fixture in the big cafés, the Bristol, the Ritz, and so on, where he sat and waited for his prey. His first choice was the young and the foreign. He would approach them, introduce himself, and get into conversation. He was never at a loss for a subject: there was nothing he couldn't discuss with intelligence and discrimination. He had lived in all the big cities of Europe and had even been in America for a while. Once he had studied his game and found him worthy of his attention, he would invite him to dine at some expensive restaurant and play a hand of cards with him afterwards. In the meantime he would let my

421

father know. And that evening, at a pre-arranged hour, my father would turn up in the gaming-room of the café in question as a perfect stranger, station himself behind the Romanian's opponent and observe his cards as if in idle curiosity, and convey the information to Chornotescu by means of signals agreed between them. You can imagine the results. The victim had no chance of winning and within a couple of hours he was usually cleaned out. And if he demanded a return game the next evening, Chornotescu would always find some excuse to get out of it. He never played twice with the same person. He was far too careful. Sometimes my father would be the one to find the victim — he was an expert at it, too. Then he would play while Chornotescu watched, and the results were the same. They also went to the famous spas, Carlsbad, Marienbad, Ishchl and so on. Each of them would put up at a different hotel, the best hotels, naturally, and the game would begin again. They usually raked in big profits, but their expenses were high too. Apart from which there was a "dead season" here too, just as in other professions, when they had to live off their cash and sometimes go short. My mother had died when I was a boy and I had no brothers and sisters. My father wanted to make me into a merchant, and after I finished school he apprenticed me to a big textile firm. But I only stayed there for a few months. Fifty crowns were lost and I was fired. I wasn't sorry — sticking to one thing was never my strong point. I did nothing for a while and then my father apprenticed me to another firm. I didn't last long there either, nor in the third, the fourth, or the fifth place — it was always the same story. At the time my father abandoned tailoring I was already eighteen years old, and had been working for a big export firm for six months. I was a bright, willing lad, I knew the job, and was earning a hundred crowns a month, not a bad salary, and my bosses were pleased with me. But I had other plans; I wasn't interested in small beer. I waited for the right opportunity — and I didn't have to wait long.

"One day in autumn my boss gave me two thousand crowns to send in the post. It was a quarter to twelve. Our lunchbreak was from twelve to two, which meant

422

that I would not have to bring him the receipt from the Post Office until two o'clock. I made all these calculations with the speed of lightning, and resolved to act. With a start of two hours I would be outside the firing range before they discovered that anything was wrong. I took the money, found a hansom cab, and told the driver to drive straight to Norbahnhof. As luck would have it, the express was departing at one o'clock; I had just enough time to buy a ticket and get on to the train, and the next day I was in Berlin. I got off the train without luggage, without a friend, free as a bird in the great foreign metropolis. Here, I was sure, they would never catch me! Like a Berliner born and bred I strode boldly out of the station, straight into the street yawning in front of me. I was hungry, but I had no German money on me. I made my way from street to street — all the banks were closed for lunch. In the end, after roaming around for an hour, I came across a small money-changer who was still open. I changed a hundred crown note (I was careful not to change it all in one place!) and another two hundred at two other banks. After that I had more than enough for my needs, for the time being at least. The first thing I did was to treat myself to a slap-up meal at a fancy restaurant. Then I bought an elegant suitcase, and thus equipped I rented a room from an old lady. I signed in under a false name, as a student from Munich. From now on my name was Karl Schtippter, a name which for some reason took my fancy.

"In the following days I provided myself with elegant clothes and underwear, and got ready to enjoy a life of leisure. After all my expenses I still had one thousand two hundred marks left, enough for several months. Now I began to observe my surroundings. An occasional little windfall came my way from time to time, but these pickings were too insignificant to count for anything in my eyes. I was waiting for something more serious. Needless to say, I made no attempt to contact my father. Much later I heard that he had come to an arrangement with my boss, compensating him for most of the damage, and kept the matter quiet. My father, of course, had pressing

reasons of his own for wanting to avoid a police inquiry —
otherwise he would never have behaved so generously. In
any case, the upshot was that I was left to my own devices,
free to pursue my own "inquiries" in Berlin without anyone to bother me. I found myself a young 'bride' who
brought something in as well . . . Her 'aunt', a stingy old
bitch, proved adept, among her other accomplishments,
at doing the 'disappearing trick.' A cunning matron with
respectable airs and a triple chin, fifty years old or more,
she was still set on ingratiating herself with the opposite
sex. I had a special place in her affections and could
always go to her for help in time of need. She lived
in a large apartment with a lot of rooms, in a terraced
house which belonged to her. All kinds of individuals
whose occupations were shrouded in mystery used to
gather there, frequently playing cards and drinking until
daybreak. I was not drawn to cards myself, taking no
pleasure in the game and showing no talent for it. I played
once, and that was enough for me, even though I didn't
lose. Nevertheless, I was a regular guest at Aunt Bertha's.
Thus four months passed without anything of significance
taking place.

"And then, one fine day I met a man in a big restaurant
on Kurfurstendamm (needless to say, I only ate at the
finest restaurants). I realized immediately that he was the
very person I had been waiting for. A man in his prime,
from an ancient line of fabulously wealthy aristocrats, with
vast estates in Westphalia. He spent his winters in Berlin,
in his villa, with his only daughter, who was eighteen years
old. He had no wife but, on the contrary, was attracted
to members of his own sex — a fact which I registered
at once. I decided to take advantage of this inclination;
I was far from ugly, if I say so myself, tastefully dressed,
and charming. I saw immediately that he had taken a fancy
to me. I told him neither my real name nor the name I
had adopted in Berlin. For him I produced a brand new
name and an invented address to go with it. At first we
met two or three times in the same restaurant, and he
showed himself far from mean. He invited me to cafés and
wine-cellars, gave me a diamond ring, and even took me to

the theatre, where he introduced me to his daughter as 'my young friend Von Mirten.' I did not, apparently, succeed in making a very good impression on the daughter, who treated me disdainfully, looked down on me from a vast height, and did not deign to exchange a single word with me. I did not take her behaviour to heart, however, and pretended not to notice. All I cared about at the moment was the fact that I had the old man in my pocket — the rest would come of its own accord. I had my plan of action ready. At any rate, he had not yet made me an indecent proposal; he was probably waiting for the relationship to ripen. After the evening at the theatre I accompanied him home in a hansom cab, and he invited me to dine there with him the next day. The following evening — there were five other dinner guests besides myself: an old couple with their daughter, his daughter's friend, and a young man — I noted the entrances and exits to the house and decided to carry out my plan two nights later, when my hosts were invited to spend the evening with the old couple and their daughter.

"When the appointed night came, I took my tools, which I always had ready to hand, and set out for the villa. I arrived at the gate at about ten. Through the wire fence I could see the first floor of the building, where the bedrooms of the old man and his daughter were situated. It was dark. The street was far from the centre of town, quiet and deserted — a rich, residential street. On a rainy night at the end of February there wasn't a soul to be seen. I knew the house well from outside; I had spent the past two days examining it from every angle. I leapt over the fence, which was not very high, and jumped into the garden. At that moment the door opened and somebody came out. I held my breath and waited. I recognized the manservant. (They had only one manservant and a cook.) He opened the garden gate and set off down the street. This is my chance, I said to myself, I musn't lose a minute. When his footsteps receded, I approached and peeped through the kitchen window. The cook, an elderly woman, was busy reading the newspaper. I went round to the front door, to see if the manservant had by any chance left it unlocked, and to my amazement I found it open. Quick as a flash I took off my shoes, hid them in the garden, tiptoed into the hall and with one bound reached the first floor. I had no trouble opening the door, my tools were the best that money could buy, and in a matter of seconds I was inside the room. From then on it was plain sailing. In fifteen minutes I had gone over every nook and cranny and been well rewarded for my efforts. Although I didn't find more than a few hundred marks in cash I did find what I was really looking for — the family jewel case. I let myself out as soundlessly as I had let myself in, and after an hour's walk (I avoided taking a carriage) I was safe at home. When I opened the box my eyes darkened: it contained a fortune. Pearls, rings, earrings, bracelets, some of them precious antiques, whose glitter filled the room. I was seized with terror at the sight of all this wealth. I found out later that they were worth about half a million marks. I put everything back, except for three rings which I placed in my pocket. I hid the box among my clothes in my suitcase, locked it, and took it that same night to Aunt Bertha's for safekeeping until the next day. For I had made up my mind to travel to Hamburg the following day and from there to sail on the first ship to New York. I spent about two hours at Aunt Bertha's, and then went home to sleep.

"The next day I succeeded in selling one of the rings to a little goldsmith for six hundred marks. I bought myself a ticket on the evening train. And then Satan tempted me to try and sell the other two rings as well. The new goldsmith, to whom I offered them, examined them from all sides, looked at the stones through a magnifying glass, and asked me how much I wanted for them. I asked for three thousand marks, not wanting to arouse his suspicions by quoting too low a price, and we agreed on two thousand and seven hundred. But he told me, the scoundrel, that he didn't have such a large sum on him at the moment, and asked me to come back at three o'clock in the afternoon. By then he would get hold of the money and we would be able to close the deal. And what do you think I did, fool that I was? I actually went back to the shop at three o'clock!

426

I was only a boy, full of pluck, but my head wasn't screwed on to my shoulders yet. And for that little mistake I paid dearly. I ran straight into the trap. The minute I stepped into the shop I was surrounded by three detectives: that shameless informer had betrayed me to the police. At least they didn't get their hands on the jewel box. I insisted that I had thrown it into the Spree, and they dragged the river for days on end without, of course, coming up with anything. But I was sentenced to four years anyway.

"And what about the box? I never saw it again, my friend. As if it had really vanished into the Spree. When I had served my sentence, they sent me back to Vienna. I didn't have the money to go straight back to Berlin, and then I was conscripted into the army. It was only a year later that I managed to get a month's leave and go back. Not a trace of the aunt or the suitcase! As if the earth had opened and swallowed them up! All my inquiries were in vain. Not a soul in the house or the street could tell me a thing about her — the old thief! She simply stole the jewels and made off with them! Oh, if only I could have laid my hands on her then! I would have cut her to pieces, the rotten old bitch! But I had to go back to the army, and that was the end of it."

Gurdweill's neighbour fell silent. The shapeless bundles on the rows of beds were barely visible in the dim light. Heavy snores, variously pitched, rose here and there in the room, interrupted from time to time by a groan, or some other human sound. A long time must have passed since eight o'clock, thought Gurdweill.

"And what happened to your father and Chornotescu?" he asked.

"When I came out of the army, Chornotescu fell ill. As a young man he had contracted syphilis, which he was cured of at the time. But syphilis is a devilish thing. You can never be sure, never. It stays in the blood, without any external symptoms or pain, and when a man reaches fifty or thereabouts, it breaks out again, and that's the end of him. Chornotescu was afflicted by what they call 'general paralysis of the insane', the final stage of the disease. He lay in the hospital for a few weeks, suffering the tortures of the damned, and then he died. And two years later my father died too. He left one ring, which I sold for three hundred crowns."

Gurdweill was tired and fell asleep immediately, to dream wild dreams in which his neighbour played a large part, in different metamorphoses and strange guises. Suddenly he woke up in alarm. There was someone standing over his head. His mind cleared and he recognized his neighbour, dressed only in his shirt. Gurdweill sat up.

"What are you doing here?"

"My stomach is upset, Herr neighbour, a shocking attack of diarrhoea."

"So what are you waiting for? Go the lavatory!"

And he reached out for his trousers, which he recognized in his neighbour's hands. The latter handed them over as graciously as if he were making Gurdweill a present of them:

"Here you are, Mein Herr. Please don't take it amiss."

He turned back to his bed, pulled his own trousers out from underneath the blanket and began to put them on. For some reason Gurdweill felt a pang of conscience, and he said apologetically:

"I . . . I need them myself, you know. They're the only pair I've got . . ."

"Of course, of course, I understand perfectly!" said his neighbour and went out into the passage.

Gurdweill checked his other garments and found them all where he had put them. He lay down again, but was unable to fall asleep. His neighbour came back immediately and lay down on his bed.

"What do you think the time is now?" asked Gurdweill.

"I've no idea," replied the latter curtly, in an offended tone, and turned his back on Gurdweill.

Gurdweill lay staring at the ceiling. Time trickled out slowly and soundlessly, monitored by distant watches scattered all over the world. There was no watch here, and no proof that time was not standing still, merging with the black night outside and the isolated snores rising here and there inside the room. Nor was there anything to show that

Gurdweill himself had been here only since the previous day. Who could guarantee it? He might have been here for centuries, and there was no one to prove the opposite. In any case, he felt in his bones that he was closely connected to the people sleeping around him, that he belonged among them. And the fact that they were there with him even made him feel protected and gave him a certain sense of security. They were poor, miserably poor, they had been brought very low and were capable of anything, but at the same time they deserved to be loved and pitied, and their love and pity, too, was not to be rejected. In the life of every human being there was at least one moment when he felt an inner kinship with his fellows, whoever and wherever they were, without a single exception. Whether he felt it clearly and consciously, or dimly and elusively, like a sudden revelation which dissolved when he was on the point of grasping it — such a moment came to every man.

And Gurdweill's thoughts passed unconsciously, without any obvious connection, to Lotte, Lotte who had such beautiful, gentle hands, and who was burdened with some hidden pain which was eating away the marrow of her life. His heart grew very tender at the thought of her. He vaguely sensed that there was some connection between his own situation and her suffering, but the nature of this connection escaped him. Then he thought of Thea, without bitterness, without anger, but on the contrary: with calm longing and complete reconciliation.

He glanced at the windows, which looked like black blots on the pale wall. Deep night still prevailed. I should try to sleep a little longer, he said to himself and closed his eyes. At that moment, however, the central heating pipes began to boom with the same knocking noise as on the previous evening, a noise which sounded particulary irritating and intrusive now, in the sleepy silence of the room. The men began to wake up, to the accompaniment of yawns and coughs. They all got dressed with surprising haste, as if they had not a moment to waste. Gurdweill's neighbour cast a covetous glance at his trousers, and asked him with no signs of embarrassment whatsoever if he had slept well.

429

Downstairs, after washing and breakfasting on a slice of bread and brown soup dotted with black caraway seeds, as the evening before, everyone was turned out into the dark and the cold, and each went his separate way. It was half past five. Gurdweill started strolling unhurriedly towards the city centre, and by the time he reached the Ring it was morning and the streets were full of commotion. By some miracle he found a forgotten schilling in one of his pockets, and hurried into a little café, glad as a traveller returning from foreign parts to be back home again. After sitting there for about an hour he was suddenly overcome by an inner restlessness which impelled him to leave the café, even though he had no idea of where to go. He turned into Kärntner Strasse, gazed disinterestedly into shop windows, saw on a clock in a watchmaker's shop that it was nine o'clock, and unthinkingly quickened his pace. At the entrance to Johannesgasse he stopped automatically, then came to again with a jerk, as if recovering from a hard slap on the back, but continued along the same pavement nevertheless, his head bowed and his hands in his coat pockets. Just as he was wondering whether to go home again as he had done the previous day, his way was barred. He raised his eyes and saw Thea standing in front of him and smiling. Covered with confusion, he tried to step aside, but she gripped him by the arm.

"What's the matter, rabbit?" she asked, as if nothing had happened between them. "Where did you disappear to? Why don't you come home?"

Gurdweill stammered, his eyes downcast:

"I ... I thought ... That's to say, I was just on my way ..."

A mocking expression appeared on her face. She stared at him without saying anything.

Gurdweill blurted out:

"Have you got a cigarette?"

Perhaps he meant it as a hint that he bore no resentment against her.

Thea opened her purse and handed him a cigarette.

"Come along, walk with me to Johannesgasse, and then you can go home."

Gurdweill obeyed. Small, confused, he walked next to his wife, his mind empty of thoughts. Then he turned away in the direction of Kleine Stadtgutgasse.

32

A few days later he received a note from Lotte, asking him to come and see her that afternoon, as she was suffering from a cold and was afraid of going out. At three o'clock he rang the doorbell. Lotte herself opened the door and showed him into the salon. Her face was pale and elongated, her big eyes seemed bigger than usual and glittered feverishly. She pointed him to an armchair and she herself lay down on the sofa, where she had evidently been reclining before he arrived.

"It's nothing!" she said with a weak smile. "A mild throat infection. Nothing dangerous. And a bad mood to boot . . ."

The room was warm, and steeped in a tender, vaguely sad tranquillity, like the mood pervading a room in which a beautiful young woman has just given birth. There was no sound from the street but for a dim, distant, insubstantial murmur, audible only to the sharpest senses. Outside a grey, rain-spotted day was drawing in, with a blustering wind stirring the air and turning everything upside down. Inside the room the dusk had already gathered, and an invisible worm began gnawing, for no particular reason, at his heart.

The outlines of Lotte's face were barely distinguishable. She lay without moving, as if sunk in gloomy thoughts. After a short silence she suddenly asked, raising her head slightly to look at him:

"What are you going to do now?"

Gurdweill looked at her for a moment uncomprehendingly.

"What do you mean?"

"I mean are you going to remain in Vienna, in your

432

old room?"

"I don't understand. I never intended to leave the city, or to change my room."

He looked at her inquiringly, wondering whether she was feverish. But Lotte pulled her blanket up as if she felt cold. She fell silent again. Her silence began to weigh on Gurdweill. In the mirror on the cupboard opposite him his own reflection, black, frozen, his hair on end, stared back at him, and for some reason stirred his heart. From the next room the faint, barely perceptible, ticking of a clock dripped into the silence. Life shrank to a single point, which flew invisibly around the room, impossible to locate.

Lotte asked him to put on the light. He would find the switch next to the door. When he returned to his chair, she lit a cigarette, and sat up on the sofa, dangling her slipper-shod feet. She had an expression of firm resolution on her face which was, at the same time, profoundly sad. Gurdweill looked at her intently and discovered, as if for the first time, that she was extraordinarily beautiful, a beauty not of this world.

With a vigorous gesture she passed her hand over her brow and cropped auburn curls, as if to remove some final barrier, and in a soft but determined voice she began to speak:

"I asked you to come, Rudolf (Gurdweill noticed that for the first time she called him by his given name), not because I have a cold, but because there's something I have to talk to you about. Everything depends on it now . . . I have to make one last attempt first. I have to have it out with you once and for all. I've seen that you don't understand. For two whole years you've been blind. All the hints, all the innuendoes that a baby would have understood were like water off a duck's back to you. Even though in other matters, you see right to the heart of things. The reason isn't clear to me. Perhaps it's because you simply didn't notice. However much this hurts my feminine pride, I'm forced to conclude that your feelings are so involved elsewhere that you simply can't see what's under your nose. Believe me, the day will come when you realize that you've been deluding yourself. I've thought about it a lot, for weeks, for months. You've been seeking your happiness in a place where it doesn't exist, where it can't exist . . . When all the time your happiness was right there waiting for you, and all you had to do was stretch out your hand to take it . . . but you never did. It's not too late yet. And that's why I asked you to come."

She took a deep breath, and lit her cigarette which had gone out. At that moment there was a sudden blast on a hooter from outside, which seemed to Gurdweill to come from another world. Lotte took a few puffs of her cigarette, one after the other, and flicked the ash into a blue pottery ashtray. Gurdweill followed her movements, his heart heavy. He sensed a terrible storm blowing up and he wanted to stop it, but did not know how. On the other hand, he felt a perverse desire to hear it all, although he knew that what was to come would be painful, and might expose things better left hidden. He sat still. Out of the corner of his right eye, he took in the name of the author of a book lying on the table: Arthur Lerchner, which for some reason he transformed to Arthur Merling, prompting him to read it again, letter by letter. This process of transformation took place quite unthinkingly, confining itself exclusively to the area of visual perception, and reaching his conscious mind only as a vague, elusive reflection. His eyes looked and read wrongly of their own accord, corrected themselves and read wrongly again, and then the whole process repeated itself once more.

Lotte began again, her fingers dancing nervously on the table top:

"For when are you waiting? For what? Haven't you realized yet that things aren't going to change? They can only change for the worse . . . Isn't two years long enough for you to see what she really is? Everyone else knows, they've known from the beginning! You can't be so blind! You think you love her, but you're deceiving yourself! It's clear as daylight that you're deceiving yourself! Anything else is impossible. Or are you really such a simpleton that you can't see what's right under your nose? Tell me

434

honestly, do you love her or don't you? Yes or no?"

Gurdweill was in no hurry to reply. Fear and confusion struggled on his face. He had never yet asked himself this question with such brutal clarity. He had always evaded it, hidden from it. Now the hour of reckoning had come. He gave Lotte an imploring look, but she only fixed him with glittering, imperious eyes.

"I . . . I can't . . . it's impossible to talk about it . . ."

"Why not?" goaded Lotte. "You don't dare! Are you afraid of bringing down the whole house of cards that you've built?"

Gurdweill remembered that someone had already said exactly the same thing to him, but he couldn't recall who it was. And in the meantime he heard himself say, in a voice that did not belong to him:

"I don't know . . . of course . . . naturally I love her . . ."

"That's not true! You don't love her! You're afraid of her!"

"You're hurting me very much," the words escaped him of their own accord. "You don't know how much you're hurting me."

"And you? You've been hurting me for the past two years, day and night, without a pause! Did you ever stop to think about it? Yes, you! It's all your fault! You're all innocence, you let Thea torture you — and all the time you're to blame for all my suffering! You, you!" And she actually pointed at him.

"But why me? What have I done to you?"

He looked at her with an expression of unutterable sorrow in his eyes. He had a momentary urge to fall on his knees before her and beg her to forgive him, but he restrained himself. He heard Lotte say:

"Thea, your Thea! Do you know that she goes to bed with all your friends, with anyone she picks up in the street, completely indiscriminately, like a common whore? Do you know, yes or no? Do you know that she was having an affair with her boss, Dr. Ostwald, when you met her and she's never stopped since? Do you know that she makes fun of you, in front of you and behind your back, that she brags of all her exploits in public, in the café, to all your friends? They know everything! Every detail of your lives together and her own intimate life — and from her own mouth! They know that she hits you, that the baby wasn't yours — everything! She sits there and exposes you to the world with a cynicism that has to be heard to be believed! I could have killed her without batting an eyelid! She's a monster! Tell me — where did you sleep a few nights ago?"

"I . . . I . . . at h-home . . ."

"At home? You're lying! You didn't sleep at home for two nights in a row! She threw you out of the house!"

"H-how do you k-know?"

"How do I know? Everybody knows! Your wife Thea told the story in the café! And she laughed in delight, your darling wife! You should be ashamed to the depths of your soul! It's a disgrace to exchange a single word with a woman like her!"

Gurdweill bowed his head, numb with shock. Every word that Lotte hurled at him was like a hammer blow on his skull. His heart beat loudly and his breath came in heavy, uneven pants. His pale face sagged hollowly, and he seemed to have aged by twenty years. Everything he had just heard was new to him, but nevertheless was as familiar as if it had been drawn up from the bottom of his own soul. Lotte had dragged it out and laid it ruthlessly before his eyes. He felt as if all his pores had opened up at once and his blood was pouring out and scalding his skin. A suffocating lump rose from his chest into his throat. Perhaps he should have wept then. But he swallowed his tears and did not weep. He sat like a stone. There was a deathly silence. He wanted Lotte to go on, and waited in fearful impatience for her to do so. Her words would have been easier to bear than this silence. But Lotte said nothing. A fly began to buzz, and he was surprised that there were still flies alive now, in the winter. Then he read the name on the book cover again: Arthur Merling, and immediately corrected himself: not Merling but Lerchner, Lerchner! Afterwards he raised his eyes absent-mindedly to look at Lotte opposite him, and saw to his surprise that she was crying quietly in the darkness. Why on earth was she crying now? Of course, she had a cold — she probably felt sick ... But what could he do to help her, now that he was feeling so weak himself? Nevertheless he rose mechanically to his feet and with stumbling, somnambulant steps approached the sofa and bent over her. He stroked her hair as if she were a child. He did not say a word. He could not have spoken then if he had been whipped for his silence. He saw Lotte taking a handkerchief from somewhere and wiping her eyes. Good — she must be feeling better! Gurdweill stood up and returned to his chair. He picked up the book and turned it over and put it down again. Everything, everything had been destroyed. He had nothing left. And Martin? Oh yes, Martin was dead. He had been dead for a long time now. And Lotte had been crying too. She had definitely cried, and now she had stopped. Which meant that she was feeling better — and that was a good thing. He thought he heard someone speak — perhaps they were speaking to him? He looked at Lotte, a long, cold look, as if he were seeing her for the first time, and saw that she had lit another cigarette. What a lot she smoked! Who else smoked a lot? Ah yes, Thea smoked a lot, and it was probably bad for the unborn child ... But he could do nothing to stop her, she would only mock him. And then she would go and tell his friends, and Lotte. Yes, she would tell Lotte everything and make her cry ... But why was he so tired? He wasn't ill any more! Thanks to Lotte, who had taken care of him so devotedly! He really should say something nice to her, but he felt so weak ... He would say it another time ...

Lotte was saying something in a soft, gentle voice. Perhaps she had been speaking for some time, but her words had to break through several barriers in order to penetrate his consciousness. Eventually he heard her say:

"... Things can't go on like this. It's impossible. I can't stand by and watch another woman, who's not worth your little finger, destroying you. I kept thinking that you would come of your own accord ... but you never came. Even though your place was here, you didn't understand and you never came. Now things have to be decided, one way or the other. I haven't got the strength to wait any more."

437

She paused for a moment. A delicate spiral of bluish smoke rose from the burning cigarette lying in the ashtray. Then she burst out, as if to herself:

"Two years! How much a person can suffer in two years! So many days, nights, hours, minutes! Every minute an abyss of misery! It's too much to bear. Even a stone wears away in the end. I can't go on any longer. There's only one way out: will you leave her and go with me to some other country? We could leave in three or four days. There's no need for big preparations. We'll have a little money too. Papa will give me some. I've thought it all out. He'll give me money to go to Italy. He loves me very much and he thinks I'm sick and the southern sunshine will do me good. We'll go and stay in some little town on the Italian or French Riviera. And then we'll see. Perhaps later on you'll be able to divorce her. And if not, I don't care. We don't need a licence from anyone. The main thing is that we love each other. And there's nothing to keep us in one place either. We can stay somewhere for a few months and then move on somewhere else. You'll be able to work in peace and forget everything she did to you."

Lotte fell silent. Her eyes were fixed on Gurdweill, awaiting his reply. But he sat with his head bowed and said nothing. Her words had pierced his heart with an electric spark of hope, shimmering scenes of lands of sun and sea had appeared before his eyes, different people, a new life, a life with Lotte, darling Lotte, who was like no one else in the world, who was as dear to him as his own soul. Everything was so clear, so simple, so wonderful. But it all died away again in the twinkling of an eye.

"Well, Rudolf? You must answer me. I want a definite reply."

With an effort Gurdweill blurted out:

"I . . . What can I say to you? You are dearer to me than anything in the world . . . But I can't . . . I'll never be able to . . ."

"What can't you do?" said Lotte, turning pale as death. "What?"

"I can't g-go away . . . Believe me . . . Even if my life depended on it . . ."

438

"Why not?"

"It's impossible, I can't leave her . . . I haven't got the strength . . ."

"But you don't even love her! I know you don't!"

"I don't know. Maybe I love her and maybe I don't. But I'm incapable of leaving her. I'll never be able to leave her. Never."

"And me? You're abandoning me completely? He's abandoning me!" She turned to some invisible third person. "He's abandoning me! He's staying with her, with her! All is lost! He's staying with her!"

An inhuman anguish pierced Gurdweill to the heart at the sight of Lotte staring straight ahead of her at some point in the distance, as she repeated the same words over and over again. He fell at her feet, stroking her and covering her hands with kisses, coaxing her with murmured, broken words:

"Please Lotte, dearest Lotte, I'd do anything for you. Anything . . . But not that, you can't ask that of me . . . You can see for yourself that it's impossible . . . What can I do? I haven't got the strength . . . Please understand . . ."

But Lotte seemed insensible to his pleas and caresses. She let him do what he would and sat there repeating automatically: "All is lost. He's staying with her . . ." Her eyes were dry and glittered dully with a wide, unseeing stare.

Gurdweill rose from his knees and sat down on the armchair. But he immediately stood up again. He took a step towards the middle of the room and returned to stand in front of Lotte, who was now sitting still with her head in her hands, as if a grief too great to bear had turned her to stone. He called "Lotte! Lotte!" as if to wake her from some sleep, but she did not move. He went on standing before her, how long he did not know, and in the end she raised her head, looked at him blankly for a moment, and made a gesture with her hand as if to brush him aside. She stretched out on the sofa, covered herself with the rug, and lay without moving, staring at the ceiling. She seemed mortally ill, like a person in a coma. Gurdweill went on standing there helplessly for a long time, not

439

daring to move. Then he sat down on his chair again and listened to the frozen silence in the room and a distant door opening and a faint voice calling something in the street and the echo repeating interminably inside him: "All is lost, all is lost forever!" Something had actually exploded inside him, burst to bits in this dense silence, the fragments were still there, scattered all over the place . . . Someone was to blame, neither him nor Lotte, someone else, a stranger who had broken in where he didn't belong and damaged them deliberately . . .

Afterwards Lotte turned her head towards him. He thought that she was calling him, and he sprang up and approached her. In a broken, unrecognizable voice, which sounded as if some chord had snapped inside it, she said laboriously: "Please go now. I want to be alone."

She stretched out her hand, but immediately took it back again, and hid it under the rug before he could grasp it. Her eyes were staring at the ceiling again. Gurdweill stole one last glance at her bloodless face, wanted to say something, thought better of it and left the room.

In the street he was overcome with remorse and felt that he must return to her immediately. He had behaved with unforgivable cruelty. How could he have gone and left her — her, Lotte — all by herself?

But Gurdweill did not go back. His feet bore him forwards in spite of himself, obeying the dictates of some force more powerful than he. In the days to come the picture of Lotte as he had left her lying on the sofa would return to haunt him, her oval face so thin and pale, her eyes staring at the ceiling as if it held the answer to all her perplexities.

33

AFTER a sleepless night full of nightmarish visions, Gurdweill spent the whole of the next day in a frantic search for Lotte, popping in and out of the Café Herrenhof and even going twice to her house, where something prevented him on both occasions from going upstairs. The whole day long he did not meet a single acquaintance, as if they had all entered into some conspiracy against him. And the day after that — a Thursday, stabbed by sharp needles of rain — he went into the café in the afternoon, and was just about to leave again when he bumped into Ulrich in the vestibule.

"Arsenic . . !" he blurted out in a choking voice which sounded more like the bellow of a slaughtered bull than a human voice. "The night before last!"

Gurdweill felt an icy coldness sliding down his spine. He knew the answer to his question before he asked it:

"Who? Who?"

"Lo-tte . . ! It was too late to save her . . ."

Gurdweill leant against the wall to stop himself from falling. Ulrich, who was standing in front of him with his head bowed, was suddenly transformed into a dark, shapeless clod; he grew huge, immense, blotting out the daylight. All at once it was black as night. The darkness lasted — who can tell how long it lasted! When daylight returned, Ulrich was still standing with his head bowed, as before. And only now something hit Gurdweill in the face like a bullet from a gun. The heart was torn from his body and fell into a deep pit, leaving him an empty husk. He saw Lotte lying on her back with her eyes on the ceiling. She was lying right there, between him and Ulrich, and they could not make her get up. People going in and out stole curious glances at the two men standing motionless

in the vestibule. Nothing made any difference, since Lotte
did not want to get up. Gurdweill wanted to scream, but
his voice was inaudible. Later Ulrich woke up, seized him
by the arm, and dragged him into the street. Shoulder to
shoulder they walked, lost and silent, for half an hour, an
hour, an hour and a half. The darkness advancing along
the streets was forced to submit to the lamps, which went
on just in time. Afterwards Gurdweill found himself alone
in one of the ancient, winding alleys in the city centre.
Ulrich was no longer with him. And Gurdweill remembered that he had informed him on parting that she would
be buried tomorrow, at ten o'clock in the morning, in the
Central Cemetery. It was very strange. Who on earth were
they going to bury? That Ulrich sometimes came out with
the most outlandish ideas! Ah, now he had no one! the
dreadful certainty struck him like a lightning bolt. He was
alone, all alone in the world! He stood still and looked
fearfully around him. The alley was ill-lit and there were
no shops in it. It was a short, deserted side-alley with very
old buildings, into which people seldom strayed. Suddenly alarmed by the desolation, Gurdweill began to hurry,
almost to run, to the end of the alley, and turned into
another, just as desolate, where he slowed down, as if
the danger had passed. About twenty paces ahead of him
there was a man with an open umbrella. So it was raining!
Gurdweill lifted his eyes to the misty sky and a few drops
fell on to his upturned face, giving him a rather pleasant
feeling. On a sign shrouded in darkness he made out the
letter "M" at the beginning of a name engraved in big
gold letters. And suddenly the picture of a brightly-lit
room flashed before his eyes, with a big mirror hanging
on the wall, and in it, at the side, a black silhouette. He
heard Lotte's voice: "All is lost! He's staying with her!" . . .
But it simply wasn't true . . . He couldn't stay with her! To
Lotte he could bare his heart: He hated her . . ! He was
ready to leave right away . . ! Italy — what a wonderful
idea! There was no need to make any preparations . . !
As long as she stopped lying there like that with her eyes
fixed on the ceiling . . ! Because he simply couldn't bear
it . . .

The rain began to come down a little harder and Gurdweill mechanically turned his coat collar up. He came out now into Schottenring, crossed the road and began walking along the iron fence of the Rathaus Park. A tram rang its bell and stopped; people crowded on to it; the tram started again, hooting hoarsely and vigorously ringing its bell — Gurdweill neither saw nor heard. The pavements gleamed wetly, dark-orange in the light of the streetlamps. Next to the railing of the bridge, under which the tracks of the metropolitan railway line shone in the darkness, he stopped for a moment, glanced down unseeingly, and immediately resumed walking. Without thinking he turned into the Hauptstrasse of the Landstrasse District, which was rather steep at this point, and walked past large warehouses, some of which were still open. But the bright lights of this main street seemed to bother him, for he immediately turned into the first side-alley.

When he said to her then, that woven shoes were not practical, and that you could easily catch cold in them in the rain, she didn't listen . . . and now — could anyone really blame him? He would have to write her a letter, since he couldn't go and visit her, and have it all out with her in detail! But she was dead, dead! The knowledge hit him with such force that for a moment it stopped his breath. He pressed his hand to his chest. He had to exert the remnants of his strength to keep his body upright, for the earth was pulling him down with all its strength. And tomorrow at ten o'clock, tomorrow at ten o'clock, she would be buried! Ah, what had he done, what had he done? If only he could put it right! He would have done anything now, he would have given his life to take it back, to wipe it out! A blind, bestial rage against Thea suddenly surged up in him, and his hands clenched into fists at his sides. It was all her fault! All her fault! Gurdweill thought he would go mad with helpless fury. He groaned aloud. And Lotte — why had she done it, why? She should have waited a while! In the course of time they could have worked things out! Didn't he himself want to be free? All he needed was a little time! He couldn't detach himself so

443

suddenly, from one day to the next! And now it was all for nothing!

The rain kept coming down and Gurdweill went on wandering from street to street, standing still from time to time as if trying to make up his mind about something, and immediately setting off again. He walked down streets in which he had never set foot before, without noticing their strangeness. On the corner of one of these streets he was accosted by a young girl making an early start. He stared at her in blank incomprehension for a moment, and then turned his back on her. Only after walking about a hundred yards did he realize what she wanted, and he was amazed that anyone could still regard him as a living human being when everything, as far as he was concerned, was over. He was tired but he took no notice. From now on there was no rest for him. Impelled by some secret wish to survive he pressed on relentlessly: he had to increase the distance between himself and what had happened — so that he would not collapse beneath the burden of the ghastly tragedy, so that he would be able to go on breathing a little longer — but the distance did not increase by a single jot. Even the extremity of his physical fatigue did not dull the sharpness of the pain.

It must have been about half past eight. It had stopped raining. The air was unseasonably warm. The network of suburban alleys brought to mind some dead provincial town. Gurdweill walked on. Suddenly, without knowing how he got there, he found himself in a large hall, apparently a restaurant, where a few people were sitting and eating. Blinded by the bright lights, he peered around the room for a moment as if looking for someone, and then dropped on to a chair next to a table near the entrance, without taking off his hat or coat. The waitress came to take his order.

What would he like to eat? Gurdweill stared at her stupidly. He didn't want anything to eat! He wasn't hungry at the moment.

"Something to drink, then?"

"Certainly not! That least of all!"

"But this is a restaurant, sir, you have to eat something!"

444

"And if I'm not in the least hungry?"

"Then you've come to the wrong place! Nobody comes here unless they want to eat!"

"Yes, you're quite right! I must have come to the wrong place by mistake." And he rose to his feet and walked out of the restaurant, to the astonishment of the waitress.

He began wandering the streets again in a daze, as if his senses had been stupefied by a shot of morphine. He had nowhere to go. The anguish of his feelings reached his conscious mind dimly, as if through a fog. From time to time he became aware of a need to go to Lotte and speak to her frankly — she had to be made to understand that it wasn't his fault . . . How could she blame him for even the fraction of a second? He wasn't to know how far things had gone . . . But now that he realized the seriousness of the situation — obviously, it went without saying — he was completely free to do whatever he felt like . . . And he had plenty of spare time too . . . He didn't have to look after Martin any more . . . He could go to Italy, or anywhere else . . . It was up to Lotte to choose . . . It was only a question of getting a passport and so on . . . He would leave Thea a note . . . Or perhaps he wouldn't leave anything . . . As long as she, Lotte, agreed to wait a few more days . . . only a few more days . . . And also: not to go on lying there like that . . . He begged her to stop lying there like that . . . She couldn't travel anywhere lying down — surely she could understand that for herself . . . Besides, she must have all kinds of things to do, to prepare herself for the trip . . . And Thea — ah, how sorry she would be when she saw that the bird had flown the cage, ha, ha, ha! Gurdweill stopped his distracted wandering for a moment and laughed aloud. He was standing on Radetzkyplatz, a fact of which he was quite unaware. Then he hurried off again, talking to himself and gesticulating as he walked. What an idiot that Ulrich was! Thinking he could pull the wool over his, Gurdweill's, eyes! That would be the day! When he was the only one who knew how matters really stood . . ! How astonished everyone would be: all of a sudden he would be gone! "Where's Gurdweill? He's gone to Italy . . ! Turned up trumps in the end, that Gurdweill!

We always knew he had something in him!" . . . And guess what, dearest, I've got a little money of my own as well! Yesterday my sister sent me something from America, and I'm expecting a cheque from my publisher as well! We can leave tomorrow! The money will be enough for our travelling expenses and after that we'll see . . . It's a pity Martin can't come with us, though! Dr. Ostwald won't allow it, I'm sure . . . But it doesn't matter a bit! We'll be able to come and visit him from time to time . . . It's not so far, after all . . !

Unthinkingly he entered a little café. He came back to reality with a jolt. Ah, what would he do, what would he do! He groaned in despair. He sat down at a table and supported his aching head in his hands, just as Lotte had done on that last afternoon.

"It's all one to me!" he replied to the waiter who asked him for his order.

"Coffee, beer?"

He nodded without looking at him.

The waiter went off and returned with a cup of coffee. For a long time he sat with his head in his hands without touching the coffee. The hour of midnight approached, closing time for cafés of this kind, and the waiter came to settle the bill.

Gurdweill went out into the night again. The streets were deserted. It was not raining, but the paving stones were still wet from the previous rain. Gurdweill crossed the Sophia Bridge. Suddenly it came home to him that what had happened was irreversible. He sensed something around him and inside him rushing with terrifying speed into a deep pit. No force in the world could stop it. And even if he had been able to stop it, he might not have wanted to. Dimly he saw something coming to an end in front of his eyes, but he did not know how or what. Only now he realized how much he needed Lotte, how attached he was to her. Without his being aware of it, she had been his last support; unconsciously he had been nourished by her, by the mere fact of her presence — and now the end had come. Lotte was no longer on earth and nothing had any value any more, and he himself had no value any

446

more. He wanted to shout at the top of his voice to all the world that Lotte was gone forever.

He walked slowly past the Praterstern, his head hunched between his shoulders. By force of habit his feet carried him home. In front of the door he paused for a moment, as if deliberating with himself. In the end he rang the bell. Thea was already asleep, the room was in darkness. Gurdweill did not light the lamp. He pushed the bedclothes piled on the couch to the wall and sat down. For a long time he sat still in the dark. Then he lay down without taking off his clothes or making his bed, and fell into a heavy sleep.

At eight o'clock Gurdweill woke and sat up with a start. The knowledge that Lotte was dead pierced him like lightning. In an instant he was wide awake, but at the same time he felt exhausted, as if he had not slept all night. A grey day streamed through the windows. Gurdweill cast a glance at the bed, and the sight of Thea lying open-eyed with her hands clasped behind her head renewed all his furious rage of the day before at this woman lying there so calmly, as if nothing had changed. She called out to him to get breakfast, and jumped out of bed herself and went to wash.

"Why are you sitting there like a dummy?" she scolded when he did not move. "Go and make the coffee!"

He stood up and went into the kitchen. When he returned with the coffee Thea was already dressed. He put the coffee pot on the table and went to wash.

"Well, why don't you pour it out?"

She sat down at the table and waited for Gurdweill to take out the dishes, spread the butter, pour the coffee and serve her breakfast. He did all this like a machine, without saying a word or looking at his wife. He himself took a gulp of coffee standing up and put his cup down again.

"Why don't you drink?" said Thea, provoked by his silence and his strange behaviour. "Sit down and drink your coffee like a human being!"

"I don't feel like it. Nobody can force me to. I don't feel like it."

"Idiot!"

447

She finished eating and went out. Soon afterwards Gurdweill left too, got on a tram and reached the cemetery a quarter of an hour early. None of his friends had yet arrived in the spacious and slightly chilly hall whose windows overlooked a forest of tombstones. There was another funeral first, and a few people were gathered in a corner. An old woman suddenly let out a shrill, piercing wail, and a young man with mourning bands around his hat and sleeve supported her as if she were ill. She was the only one who cried, and her wail merged into the singing of the cantor and the choir. In his dazed, almost demented state, Gurdweill suddenly wondered what he was doing here, in this vast, strange hall. He leant one shoulder against the wall and listened to the voice of the cantor, which sounded hoarse and discordant to him and irritated him beyond measure. But he stopped singing immediately, and the coffin-bearers in their uniforms and caps like upside-down boats lifted the coffin and carried it outside, dragging the mourners behind them like a train.

Ulrich arrived followed immediately by Dr. Astel, and they both joined Gurdweill and stood beside him without saying a word. The tall Dr. Astel seemed to have shrunk and his face looked very worn and old. Gurdweill saw through a mist that the latter was unshaven, a fact which made a great impression on him, since he had never seen Dr. Astel in such a state before. Something terrible must have happened, he reflected, otherwise he would have shaved his beard . . . And he felt great pity for Dr. Astel.

Then Lotte's parents came, Gurdweill recognized her mother, with a few other men and women carrying wreaths of white flowers. They stood not far from the three friends, keeping their eyes on the ground as if they were ashamed to look at each other. No one spoke. Her mother kept wiping her eyes and from time to time her body was convulsed with silent sobs, while a middle-aged man with a grey moustache speechlessly stroked her arm, which was linked in his. That's her father! — said Gurdweill matter-of-factly to himself — there's a certain resemblance in the features . . . But only a small part of him was occupied with these trivialities, while the rest of him was not there

448

at all. It's going on for a long time — he went on with his reflections — they should hurry it up a little. When the coffin was brought in, the poor mother fell on it with a strangled cry of: "Lotte! Lotte!" which sounded more like a plea than a lament. Dr. Astel and Ulrich, too, approached the coffin. Only Gurdweill did not move. There must be a special room here where they preserve them — someone inside him reflected — the question is whether it's really necessary to preserve them at all . . . that's the question! . . . In my opinion there's no need to preserve them at all . . . Suddenly he turned to face the wall, leant his head against it. He went on standing there, and from time to time a shudder ran down his back, as if he was feeling cold. The cantor raised his voice in song again and the choir responded. The singing reached his ears from a vast distance. He did not turn his head. This singing had some kind of connection to Gurdweill, but he could not say what it was. Some time ago a cantor had been singing too — but where? Oh, yes! It was in Seitenstettengasse, when he got married and his collar was as stiff as armour. And now, why was he singing now? Lotte's mother was crying — how strange. Women always liked crying when the cantor sang . . . He himself didn't find it sad in the least. And why didn't Lotte introduce him to her father? He wasn't wearing that funny shirt now, and there was no reason to be ashamed of him . . . It was only thoughtlessness on her part, not nastiness . . . Lotte wasn't nasty . . . But the cantor had suddenly stopped singing — what was wrong with him now?

Gurdweill turned his head and saw that the hall was now empty, with the two last people going through the door. He moved mechanically and went out after them. At a distance of twenty paces he trailed behind the funeral procession, between the rows of tombstones on either side, on the gravel crunching drearily beneath his feet. He kept the same distance all the time, as if separated from the others by some invisible barrier. Someone must have died — it suddenly occurred to him — they say it's Lotte. Perhaps it really was Lotte, since he hadn't seen her for some days now. But still, it was very strange that Lotte should

449

be dead! People didn't die just like that, simply to surprise their friends . . .

The funeral procession stopped and Gurdweill stopped with it, keeping the same distance as before. From time to time he stole a quick look at the group of people, and carefully averted his eyes. The sky covered the cemetery like a blanket, downy and silent. It's going on too long, he thought, and he had no time to waste . . . He had things to do first . . . before setting out on such a long journey . . ! He felt an overpowering desire to get away, but something held him back. He dropped on to the gravestone next to him, but he did not remain seated long: the touch of the cold stone, which he could feel through his clothes, brought him to his senses for a moment, and he leapt up in sudden horror. Lotte, Lotte who had been so close to him and who not so long ago had wept before him for some reason or other — perhaps she really was dead! And who would he go to Italy with now . . ? No, it wasn't settled yet! He would have to think about it later, whether she was dead or not — at the moment his head wasn't sufficiently clear, because of the cold . . . Yes, without a doubt, it was because of the cold. (He pulled his coat tightly around him and even raised the collar.) How quiet it was here . . . a good place for intellectual work, if not for the cold . . . The tombstones wouldn't get in the way . . . He glanced at the tombstone next to him and read the inscription in gold letters: Michael Schramek, born in 1881 and cut off in the flower of his youth, in 1921, etc. So he was really dead, this Schramek! Here you could be certain, at least! It was written in so many words . . . But you couldn't always be certain . . .

When the mourners turned back Gurdweill, for some reason, sprang behind the tombstone and hid until they had all gone past. Then he ran to the fresh grave, looked quickly at the mound of earth covered with flowers and the two spades plastered with chocolate-like mud at its side, and hurried to catch up with the receding mourners. He walked behind them, keeping his distance, his shoulders sagging, his eyes dull, staring fixedly in their sockets like those of a blind man.

450

Outside the vestibule he found his two friends waiting for him, and as he approached them Dr. Astel looked at him blankly for a moment, as if trying to remember something, and suddenly fell round his neck like an axed tree and began howling horribly, his shoulders heaving as the animal-like sounds burst out of him in a series of shuddering sobs which seemed to come straight from the pit of his stomach. His hat slipped off and fell to the ground, but nobody noticed, for Ulrich had averted his eyes from the scene. Gurdweill for some reason found Dr. Astel's sobbing offensive, and he wished that he would stop. But his hand kept patting his friend's back, with strange, quick pats, as if he were straightening out a crease, or brushing the dust from his overcoat. In the end Dr. Astel stopped crying. His shoulders heaved once or twice in a final, weak convulsion. He picked up his hat and the three of them walked together to the number 71 tram stop, without saying a word or looking at each other. After travelling in silence to Schwartzenbergplatz, the last stop, Gurdweill parted from his friends.

The city was suddenly empty and desolate. There was nothing in it to which he could momentarily attach his thoughts. A gnawing emptiness, as if he had been fasting for days on end, filled his stomach. Instead of taking another tram, he walked slowly along the Ring, putting his feet down with a peculiar caution, as if he were in danger of falling into some hidden hole. A sharp cold pricked the tips of his fingers, like needles. A few, isolated snowflakes drifted aimlessly through the air, at about the height of a man. An enigmatic smile froze on Gurdweill's lips ... If it transpired that he was guilty of something, and if anyone accused him — but how could anyone blame him ..? Wasn't he ready to go to Italy ..? And then again, who could prove that he was afraid of ... of Thea? He had never been afraid of her, and he certainly wasn't afraid of her now ..! No, the only difficulty was because of Lotte, because she was dead. This last word, which had stolen up on him and taken him, as it were, by surprise, suddenly crashed into his mind like a thunderbolt, and the pain was so terrible that he thought he would go mad. He

451

began to run, with someone inside him shouting at the top of his voice: "Dead, dead, dead!" He saw nothing in front of him, he took no notice of the passers-by who stopped to look at the strange man running with his open coat flapping at his sides, he did not feel it when he bumped into someone and was pushed violently aside, so that he almost fell to the ground — he saw and felt nothing but Lotte, his dearly beloved Lotte, who had been lying on the sofa a little while ago and who was now dead, dead and gone forever! He had seen her being buried with his own eyes! He had seen it, and so had Ulrich and Dr. Astel! And other people too! They could all bear witness! And she had died because he — of this, too, there could be no doubt — because he had refused to go with her to Italy! And now no one could bring her back! Because he had seen her being buried with his own eyes, in the Central Cemetery not far from Schramek!

The snow was falling faster now, in fragile flakes. The wind which had been raging in the streets before had disappeared around a corner. On either side of his running feet carpets of snow lay like scattered flour on the pavement, with a wet, black path running down the middle. Opposite the Urania building he crossed the road without looking right or left, and was almost run over by a tram, whose warning bell he did not hear, and whose driver only managed by a miracle to stop at the last minute. A crowd instantly collected round him. Someone cursed. Without understanding why these people were blocking his way, Gurdweill gazed dumbly around him. The policeman who popped up in front of him with a little notebook, asked him for his name.

"It's not my fault," muttered Gurdweill. "Really, it's not my fault . . . I'm ready to leave . . ."

His eyes begged the onlookers for help.

"Your name please, sir!" the law repeated sternly.

"Me? Gurdweill, of course. Rudolf Gurdweill."

"And your address?"

After writing everything down in his notebook, he offered him a piece of good advice:

"You must be careful when you cross the road!"

"Yes, that's right," said Gurdweill, as if to himself, and continued on his way.

It was two o'clock in the afternoon when he entered his room. He dropped on to the couch and held his head in his hands. For a long time he sat there in his hat and coat without moving. He looked as if he might have been asleep. But he was far from asleep. It was uncomfortably cold in the room. Their breakfast dishes were still on the table, Thea's cup empty and his full of the undrunk coffee of the morning, which had collected a brown skin on its surface from the milk. Gurdweill raised his head and gazed around the room with a puzzled look in his eyes: everything in it seemed strange and unconnected to him. The couch on which he was sitting, the bed opposite him, the other furniture in the room — none of it felt close to him. He wondered why he had only become aware of this feeling now, after two years and more. It seemed to him that he had only remained here, among this shabby furniture, for such a long time, because he was unconsciously hoping for something. Somewhere outside this room there was something for the sake of which it had been worthwhile to go on suffering until the right opportunity presented itself. But now, when . . . No! He was overcome by a feeling of irrepressible loathing for everything surrounding him. Unthinkingly he rose to his feet and went over to the table. At the sight of Thea's empty cup he was suddenly flooded by a host of miserable memories, of embarrassing situations which she had brought about, of humiliations and insults without number. And for these things he had ruined his life and perhaps been guilty of the death of another human being! As on a number of other occasions in the past few months he was suddenly overcome by a fit of blind rage against Thea, a rage which was capable of anything, the kind of rage which perhaps only a woman could arouse. He took the empty cup and hurled it to the floor with all his strength. "Good!" he said aloud, looking with a certain satisfaction at the fragments scattered in all directions. Then he bent down, gathered up the broken pieces, and placed them one by one on the table. The sound of the

453

shattering china still echoed in his ears. Absent-mindedly he took a sip of the cold coffee, and spat it out again immediately into the chamber pot. Then he stationed himself by the window and stood there for a long time watching the falling snowflakes. Inside him everything was as desolate as an abandoned ruin in a bleak mountain wilderness. There was nothing in the whole world which had any value or was capable of providing a crumb of comfort. All around and everywhere was despairing grief and loss and the proximity of death, and it was strange to see someone hurrying by in the street below, as if there was still anything left worth hurrying for.

Dusk descended, and the snowflakes grew increasingly invisible. Inside the room the darkness gathered and turned into a thick mass, swallowing up the couch and everything around it. Only on the table the empty cup and the little pile of broken china still gleamed palely. Mechanically Gurdweill turned away from the window and went back to sit on the couch. His hat was still on his head. He had not eaten anything all day, and although he did not actually feel hungry, something gnawed at him incessantly, as though his insides were being squeezed by an invisible hand. It crossed his mind that he should eat something, but he immediately forgot about it again. And once more he was overcome by the same catatonic stupor as before, and he sat without moving in the dark, his head hanging and his chin resting on his chest. Perhaps Thea would come and want something to eat, he thought hazily, she would be angry and scold him, but he didn't care any more. He would go away . . . there was nothing for him to do here any longer. He would go tomorrow, or the day after, or some other day. If only he knew where to go! There was no one in the world that he could go to. But what difference did it make? There was one thing he had to do first — that was clear. A pity he had forgotten what he had to do before he left. His head was so heavy, he couldn't get half a thought out of it. How awful Dr. Astel's scream had been — bursting out of him so unexpectedly and for no reason — No! That wasn't true! There may have been a reason after all! He himself had once known the reason

454

clearly, how strange that he had been so quick to forget it
... His memory had begun to fail him lately ... Once he
had had a good memory, just like ... like who again? Oh,
yes! Like Dr. Kreindel, who knew all those quotations by
heart ... Gurdweill smiled to himself in the dark. It was
a good thing that he didn't have to work for that Dr.
Kreindel any longer! For him a man had to have a memory
like a gramophone record, otherwise he didn't count ...
Well, thank God, he was going to Italy soon and he didn't
need Dr. Kreindel any more ... It was strange, though,
that Lotte was taking so long ... It was hard waiting all
this time ... Well, never mind! He could pack his things
in the meantime ..!

He stood up and lit the lamp. Then he took down the
suitcase, which was covered with a thick layer of dust, from
the top of the wardrobe, and wiped it with a dirty shirt.
He opened it, thrust his manuscripts in their yellowing
newspaper parcel to one side, and began pulling his underwear and collars out of the wardrobe and throwing them
higgeldy-piggeldy into the suitcase. Suddenly he stopped
and let the shirt he was holding fall to the floor. He
straightened up and clutched his head in his hands. "What
are you doing?" he groaned. "This is insanity!"

At that moment the door opened noiselessly and the
old landlady came in. She shuffled up to Gurdweill and
stood looking first at him, and then at the suitcase open
on the floor.

"Are you thinking of going abroad, Herr Gurdweill?"

He looked at her uncomprehendingly. After a moment
he whispered, as if to himself:

"Yes, yes, I'm going away somewhere ... Not right
away, that is ... I can put it off ... Certainly I can
put it off ... In fact, I have to put it off ..."

And as if to confirm his words, he bent down and shut
the suitcase with his clothes inside it, stood on a chair and
put it back on top of the wardrobe.

"Going abroad in this cold, Herr Gurdweill!" said the
old lady.

Gurdweill did not seem to hear. He dropped wearily
on to the chair.

"You're unhappy, Herr Gurdweill. Anyone can see it. I think about you a lot. I'm always thinking about you, psss! It's so cold, I thought, and I just happen to have a bit of hot coffee ready — what do you say to a cup of hot coffee, Herr Gurdweill?"

Gurdweill did not hear a word she said. But as if in response to some inner question, he nodded his head, which Frau Fischer took for assent. She went and and returned immediately with a steaming cup of coffee. Gurdweill sipped it mechanically, stopped, and sipped again, with the old lady standing beside him and watching him, as if she were supervising a small child or an invalid, until he had drunk it all up. Then she left the room, taking the shards of the broken cup from the table with her. For a while he went on sitting there in his hat and overcoat, and in the end he stood up, put out the lamp, and went down to the street.

It was about six o'clock. A delicate film of snow covered the pavement. It was cold, but the snow had stopped. Gurdweill stepped out briskly, as if in a hurry to get to some appointment in time. When he reached the Praterstern, he waited at the tram stop. Driven by some hidden force, he was impelled to go somewhere, he knew not where, and he got on to the first tram that arrived. He sat huddled in a corner, his head hunched between his shoulders and his coat collar raised. His face under the hat pulled down over his forehead was shrivelled, hollow, and covered with the stubble of a two-days-old beard; his glassy eyes stared fixedly at the legs of the passenger opposite him. With every nerve strained he listened to the the tram wheels skipping over the rails, to the slightest jar and jolt, to the staccato blasts of the conductor on his whistle. And as he did so he counted the stations: seven, up to now. Then he raised his eyes and with a great effort recognized Schwarzenbergplatz. He got off and walked automatically to the number 71 tram stop. He did not have to wait long, but there was a long way to go. One by one the passengers descended: the suburb came to an end and nobody needed to go any further. Now the coach sped deafeningly over the rails, swaying and jolting violently, and Gurdweill was the only passenger left, a fact of which he was quite unconscious. In the end the tram shuddered to a halt, rattling its window-panes. "Last stop!" cried the conductor, and Gurdweill jumped up and alighted in a deserted parking lot, fitfully illuminated by a few widely-spaced streetlamps. For a moment he stood still, as if trying to make up his mind which way to turn, and then continued walking straight ahead, in the direction of the tram. There was not a soul to be seen anywhere. An icy wind blew here unimpeded, churning up flimsy columns of snow. The city roar reached his ears from the distance, insubstantial as the driven snow, and nearer at hand the tram creaked once or twice before setting off on its way. And then there was the silence, which seemed to have a sound of its own. Gurdweill walked straight down the middle of the lot, swaying from time to time, just like the empty tram before. After about two hundred steps he found himself in front of the entrance to the Central Cemetery. The gate was closed and a stone wall, higher than a man, surrounded the graveyard: a vast, quiet city, inhabited by many sleeping generations. A single lamp cast a weak light over the semi-circular porch. Gurdweill tried to open the gate and the low wicket beside it and found them locked. Then he began pacing to and fro in front of the porch, in the vague hope that the gate might accidentally open. In the distance a dog began to howl, stopping and starting again at intervals. After walking up and down for about twenty minutes, he thought the better of it and set out to encompass the walls, in case he might find another opening. But the wall was interminable, and he soon realized that he would never have the strength to walk all the way round it. He retraced his steps and stood in front of the main entrance again. If anyone had asked him what he was waiting for he would surely not have known how to reply. It seemed that he did not even really know where he was. He had made the journey unconsciously, in a state verging on a hypnotic trance. He only knew that something terrible had happened to him in this place, and that the shadow it had cast on his soul burnt and cut him without stopping. Here, at the scene of the event, perhaps it might still be possible to mend matters, to erase, change, restore something to its previous state. And he waited for something that was about to happen, that was sure to happen in the next few minutes. But nothing happened. For an hour he waited and nothing happened. And suddenly, as if for the first time, he was pierced by the devastating certainty that it was no longer possible to mend anything, neither now nor in the future, that Lotte was really dead and that she had been buried here, this morning, and that from now on all was lost, hopelessly and irretrievably. An inhuman fear seized him and cut off his breath. For a moment he stood rooted to the spot and then he began to run, to flee for his life towards the city. He stumbled and fell, got up and went on running, without noticing that he had already passed the first tram stop. He did not stop until he was in the suburban streets, among the first rows of houses and the occasional cheap café or tavern. He stood and glanced rapidly around him, as if to make sure that he was not being followed. All of a sudden he realized the insanity and senselessness of his flight, and once more he felt a tremor of fear, but a different fear this time, not of anyone outside him, but of himself — at the mercy of every passing wind to buffet him as it would, without his being able to offer the least resistance. He felt a dull pain in his head, which was as heavy as a lump of lead. He picked up a handful of snow and pressed it to his forehead. "Ah, I'm mad, mad!" he groaned, walking on, but calmly now, like someone out for an evening stroll. He went mechanically into a small restaurant, had something to eat, and then walked to the nearest tram stop and rode home.

34

THE next morning — it was a Saturday — he carried
out his wife's commands like a sleep-walker, without
a word and without looking at her, in a stupor so extreme
that no spark of light could penetrate it. When Thea left
he got undressed again and lay down for some reason in
her bed, which still preserved the warmth of her body. He
fell asleep and did not wake up until three o'clock in the
afternoon, his body tingling numbly with the exhaustion
of a sick, excessive sleep, and his feet feeling as if they were
made of cotton wool. After washing and dressing, he was
overcome with the boredom of enforced inactivity. He had
nothing to do and nowhere to go, like a traveller obliged to
wait for hours for a train in some remote village, to which
he was completely indifferent. The sharpness of the pain
which had flared up suddenly and devastatingly from time
to time during the past two days had somewhat dulled,
to be replaced by total indifference to and disinterest in
everything. Lotte was no longer among the living — this
was quite clear to him now. And this certainty had settled
into his soul like a heavy lump of rock, pressing him to
the ground. He sensed that something very important was
about to be decided, without knowing what it was about or
what the nature of the decision would be. At the same time
he was haunted by a feeling of guilt which did not leave
him for a moment, and he hoped unconsciously that this
guilt would be expiated by the decision about to take place.

For a while he paced about the room in increasing
impatience, and in the end he went out to the street.
Twilight was approaching. There was no trace of yesterday's snow. The pavement was wet; there was a penetrating cold in the air, and the wind ploughed through the
street, rattling ill-fitting window-panes and making the
shop signs dance. With sheaves of slanting rain lashing

intermittently at his face, Gurdweill hurried down the streets, taking no notice of his surroundings. When he crossed the canal, he cast a quick glance at the black, wrinkled water and immediately looked away again, deliberately averting his eyes as if there were something extremely disagreeable about the sight. He even unconsciously quickened his step until he had put the water behind him. His shoulders stooping, his mind a blank, he strode through the labyrinth of the Innere Stadt. Suddenly he found himself in Herrengasse, and he felt a shudder run down his spine. Without turning his head to look at the café, he crossed the road, passed the Burgtheater and the Parliament, and turned into Lerchenfelder Strasse. The city was already steeped in the black of night, broken by the light of the streetlamps. Gurdweill reached Myrtengasse, and turned into it. It was a short, lifeless street, which seemed to have been lifted up and transferred here bodily from some provincial town. In front of number 15, Lotte's house, he stopped. For a moment he seemed undecided, then he crossed to the other side of the street and fixed his eyes on the second-floor windows. Two of them were lit, the windows of the salon, according to his calculations. For a long time he stood there looking up at the two windows. Once or twice he felt an urge to go up. Lotte must be lying there on the sofa, wrapped in her blue silk kimono with the flowers on it, reading a book. Perhaps even that book by Arthur Merling, no, Lerchner (that damned name, he could never get it right!), which had been lying there a few days before. Perhaps it was even a good book in spite of everything! They would serve tea and little cakes, and a delicate steam would rise from the tea, and the air would be full of the fragrant breezes of a distant, early spring, shot through with yearning for something marvellous and undefined, for something which did not exist, and for Lotte, too, who was close enough to touch, and for him, himself, too . . . And as for her telling him that last time to go away . . . why should that stop him . . . he wasn't going to be insulted by something like that! Then she was upset — and it was all his fault! But now, now he was coming to put things right! Now it was already plain as day to him

460

that it was her and only her he had always loved! And she would surely not bear him a grudge because of it! Up to now he had not known his own mind, he had been blind ... As long as she didn't lie there like that staring at the ceiling ... From now on they would always be together and nothing would ever separate them again ...

These thoughts flickered through his mind, mixed up together and, as it were, simultaneously. And suddenly a girl turned into Myrtengasse who resembled Lotte in both her figure and her gait, or so, at least, it seemed to Gurdweill, whose heart stopped at the sight. And strange to say, at that moment he felt a sudden terror, in case the girl really was Lotte ... When she came closer, he recoiled instinctively, and with such force that she turned to look at him. Then he saw that she was definitely not Lotte, and he began walking back to Lerchenfelder Strasse, in disappointment and despair. It was now raining steadily, a light, dreary rain. Suddenly Gurdweill was seized by a feeling of desperate urgency; he wanted to get home as quickly as possible, as if he were afraid of missing something. He hurried to the nearest tram stop and waited impatiently for the tram to come. Throughout the journey he racked his brain in vain to remember something which he had meant to buy when he left the house. In the end he gave up in despair.

In his room he lit the lamp and began by force of habit to tend the fire in the stove. It was about seven o'clock. The rain drummed on the window-pane like a swarm of flies. Apart from a small slice of bread there was nothing in the house to satisfy the hunger which suddenly attacked Gurdweill. He went into the kitchen and put the kettle on, and a few minutes later he was sitting in front of the open stove, dipping the bread in a cup of black coffee and chewing it without tasting anything. When he was finished, he added coals to the fire, shut the stove door, and went over to the window. The rain, perceptible now only in the jumping of the puddles in the street, increased his feeling of utter bereavement. Turning away, he glanced casually into the mirror above the washstand. He saw the upper half of the room shrouded in shadows

461

due to the shade of the oil-lamp, and his own face, sharp, hollow and unshaven, which looked to him like the face of a stranger, and which he found so disagreeable that he had to avert his eyes. He lay down on the couch, and waited tensely for something which he was unconsciously anticipating. At the same time he felt a distinct aversion to being with Thea. He could not bear to be in the same room with her now. Something inside him had revolted against her since Lotte's death, something had exploded, even if it did not show on the surface and he was barely aware of it himself. Incapable of reflection in his present stupor, he did not think of her at all, but whenever her image crossed his mind an elemental, animal fury flared up in him, burning his breath and making his heart beat erratically. His whole being rose up in rebellion against her. And although he did not pass judgement on her in lucid, rational terms, he knew with an intuitive certainty which needed no proof that she was to blame for all his misfortunes, she was to blame for the death of the baby, she was to blame for Lotte's death and for everything else. And suddenly Gurdweill felt in his bones that something was going to happen between them in the immediate future; there was no force in the world capable of stopping what was about to happen — and he waited. Without knowing what he was waiting for, he waited.

Worn out and exhausted by all that had happened to him in the past few days, he could not move a muscle, but neither could he bear to go on lying there. He jumped up from the couch and began walking around the room. Suddenly he felt stifled, and opened the window wide, letting a current of cold, wet air burst into the room. Leaning out, he saw that the rain had stopped, a fact which for some reason afforded him a slight relief. Listening attentively to the night he heard, as through a seashell, the distant city roar, which was rather subdued at this hour of night, and then he closed the window again. He sat down at the table and took a clean sheet of paper and pen and ink out of the drawer. Isolated phrases began to run through his mind — but the next moment he realized the madness of what he was doing and leapt up from his chair, terrified to the foundations of his being. Feverishly he began to put on his coat.

At that moment he heard the passage door opening and recognized Thea's voice saying: "Just a minute, I'll put on the light and show you the way!" And she immediately opened the door of the room. "Oh, you're at home! I've brought a visitor."

Gurdweill for some reason began taking off his coat again, as his wife ushered Franzl Heidelberger into the room. The latter immediately produced two bottles wrapped in thin, cream coloured paper from his pockets, placed them noisily on the table, and said to Gurdweill, who was standing in the middle of the room, unable to believe his eyes:

"Well, Herr Doktor, I'm delighted to visit you in your palatial residence!"

And he added immediately, as if he felt the need to apologize:

"The Frau Baroness met me in the street and invited me, and I took advantage, so to say, of the opportunity."

And he twirled his moustache with a meaningful smile.

"Why are you standing there like a dummy?" scolded Thea, taking off her outer garments. "Hang up Herr Heidelberger's coat! And the stove — is it lit? Go and get the glasses! And make coffee!"

The guest, who was apparently already a little drunk, dropped on to the chair next to the table and grinned in agreement:

"The Frau Baroness is right. We want to wet our whistles a bit. We've brought some good stuff with us, hee, hee!"

Mechanically Gurdweill took the tumblers from under the washstand and set them on the table. He was sorry that he had not gone out earlier. Now he had missed his chance.

The guest remarked:

"We haven't seen you for ages, Herr Doktor. You've forgotten your friends, eh? And Gustl asks about you night and day!"

"I'm busy," muttered Gurdweill unwillingly.

"But still! I always say: a friend is a friend! No excuses!"

463

Thea placed the parcel she had brought with her on the table and opened it, revealing a tin of sprats, pickled cucumbers, sausage and rolls.

"Bring the corkscrew!" she commanded her husband.

"No need!" Heidelberger intervened. "I've got a pen-knife with a corkscrew attached!"

And he began uncorking the bottles: a bottle of "Three Star" brandy, and one of old white Bordeaux wine, with a dusty label upon which the year 1905 appeared. He pointed this out to Gurdweill triumphantly:

"You see, twenty years old! It must be excellent!"

Thea poured brandy into the glasses, one for her husband too.

"Drink, idiot!" she scolded him, when he tried to excuse himself on the pretext of feeling unwell.

After taking an obligatory sip, which tasted like a bitter medicine, he put his glass down again. He did this standing up, as if he had not a moment to waste. Thea and Heidelberger emptied the brandy in their half-full glasses in one gulp.

"Not bad!" said Thea, swallowing a piece of sausage.

And to her husband:

"Where's the coffee? Go and make it at once! And make it good and strong!"

Gurdweill obeyed. A few minutes later he came back from the kitchen with the coffee pot and put it on the table. Then he tried to withdraw to the couch, but his wife would not have it.

"Sit here with us! And drink!" She jerked her chin in the direction of his glass.

"I'll drink l-later," stammered Gurdweill.

"You mustn't shame us, Herr Gurdweill! What a pity Gustl isn't here. If she only knew, she would come running on all fours, and then we'd have a foursome! She's a great admirer of the Herr Doktor's, hee hee!"

"And Lotte?" In the middle of making herself a sandwich, Thea suddenly turned to her husband. "Tired of it all, was she? An unhappy love affair, perhaps?"

Gurdweill's blood rushed to his head. In a quiet but firm voice he said:

"Leave Lotte alone. I don't want you to talk about her!"

"And why not, my precious? If she was such a fool! She got what she deserved, the silly fool! Why are you staring at me with those calf's eyes, as if you wanted to swallow me alive? You can join her if you like! The world will get along very well without the pair of you! And if it will make her happy, just imagine how happy it will make me!"

"You haven't ... you'd better ..." began Gurdweill in a trembling voice and left his sentence unfinished.

"What? What? Speak plainly and stop bleating like a calf! To life, Herr Heidelberger! To the healthy and the brave!"

Gurdweill bowed his head in silence.

"Help yourself, Herr Heidelberger!" Thea pushed the rolls and sausage in his direction.

The guest was not unwilling. He took another hefty gulp of brandy, and topped it off with the proffered delicacies.

"The Herr Doktor seems a little glum. It isn't worth it! I always say: You want to mope — count me out! A man is not a beast! So there you are!"

And after a short pause:

"Here, have a drink and you'll feel better!" He slapped Gurdweill on the shoulder. "Take the Frau Baroness, for example! She could teach a few men a thing or two! And she's only a woman!"

Then he poured out the wine. Gurdweill tasted it, too, in order not to provoke his wife. He wished he was somewhere far away — anywhere but here, with these two half-drunk people conspiring together against him. It was almost midnight. Thea's and Heidelberger's faces were flushed. Their skin was like a thin film artificially plastered on to their faces, and from time to time they rubbed it with their hands, as if to stick it down and stop it from splitting off. Gurdweill had moved away and gone to sit on the couch, while the two of them went on drinking, eating, chattering and laughing light-headedly. The room was opaque with clouds of smoke. Thea remarked that it was stuffy, but refused to let her husband open the window. She stood up and took off her blouse, remaining in her

465

petticoat with her arms and shoulders exposed.

"You're actually quite good-looking, Herr Heidelberger, ha, ha!" she cried and jumped on to his lap, where she began twirling his luxuriant moustache.

Gurdweill felt as if he had received a heavy blow on his back. Something black began spinning giddily in front of him. For a moment he hoped that his eyes had misled him. But no! She was really sitting on his lap — Thea, his wife, on this Heidelberger's lap! He leapt noisily to his feet. "What's the matter, Rudolfus?"

"I-I think . . . the heat . . . shouldn't we open the window . . ."

"No! There's no need!"

"It's late . . ."

"What of it? There's plenty of time! Go and pour us some wine, and hurry up about it!"

"Why? You've had enough already . . ."

"Pour it, I said, idiot!"

He took the bottle and poured.

"More! Fill them up! To the brim! That's it! Now bring them here! To your health, sweetheart!" she turned to Heidelberger laughing wildly.

Gurdweill went up to the window and stared out at the deserted street frozen in silence, at the dark windows of the hotel opposite, but he could not keep his back to the room. He turned around again and saw that his wife's naked arm was already coiled round Heidelberger's neck, and that the latter's face was twisted in a drunken grin. He wanted to scream, to scream soundlessly, to do something to separate them — but his limbs, as in a dream, refused to obey him. He stood and watched, spellbound. He could not take his eyes off them. And in the midst of the agony he felt at the sight, like a pip buried in a fruit, was a grain of perverse pleasure. He saw Thea planting her lips on Heidelberger's mouth in a long kiss. Then she slipped off his lap. Gurdweill went over to the washstand, wet his handkerchief in the water jug, and passed it over his brow and the rest of his face.

Heidelberger rose heavily to his feet.

"It must be late. I'd better be going."

466

"Why? Stay here with us. You can go to bed at once if you're tired."

"But there's no room for me here! And the Herr Doktor . . ."

"The Herr Doktor will sleep on the couch, as usual."

And in a tone of command:

"Herr Doktor, make the bed for Herr Heidelberger! Hurry up!"

And Gurdweill obeyed. He took his bedclothes and threw them in a heap on to the couch, and made his wife's bed while she washed her face, as she always did before going to sleep.

The guest asked Gurdweill where the lavatory was.

"Go and show him where it is!" said Thea, who had apparently overcome the effects of the alcohol. "Go on, take the lamp — no, wait! Matches will do!"

Gurdweill led him down the passage and waited for him. For a moment he had the crazy idea of locking him in from outside, so that he would have to stay there all night . . . Unconsciously he slipped his hand into his trouser pocket and fingered a hard object, which he did not at first recognize. It was a long object. Not his pipe, nor a pencil: its thickness and shape meant it could be neither of those — and it was important to know exactly what it was. Suddenly he remembered that it was the folding penknife with the rough, brown, horn handle, which he had purchased a number of weeks before — and his fingers tightened around it convulsively. A connection between this knife and something unclear flashed through his mind, but a kind of screen immediately descended, leaving him with a feeling of regret for something important which he had been on the point of discovering when it slipped away. When they returned to the room Thea had already finished washing, and she was pacing about the room in her green petticoat, a cigarette between her lips.

"You can put your clothes here, on the chair," she said to Heidelberger.

The latter undressed slowly and got into bed, a crooked, drunken smile fixed on his puffy face.

467

Gurdweill sat on the couch.

"Aren't you going to bed?" inquired his wife. But she received no reply. He sat without moving, the pile of bedclothes on his left, at the head of the couch, his eyes staring blankly in front of him, seeing and not seeing. One thought darkened his mind: "Something's going to happen in a minute, something's going to happen in a minute . . ." Empty bottles, glasses, the coffee pot, the leftover food lay scattered over the table; the empty tin of sprats was at the edge nearest Gurdweill, demanding his attention as if it were a symbol of something or other. The air was saturated with cigarette smoke and the sour smell of alcohol in the process of being digested. "Perhaps he's already asleep, and then . . ." He wanted him to be asleep, and then again he wanted him not to be asleep, so that what had to happen would happen in full. Unconsciously he anticipated Thea's actions and movements and, as it were, guided them. Without looking at her as she stood opposite him, on the other side of the table, he saw her taking off her petticoat and hanging it over the back of the chair. Then she took off her bodice, cupped her breasts in her hands, glanced at the bed, and let them go again, smiling a twisted, vicious smile. He saw all this from a distance, as if it were taking place in the house across the street; he saw clearly enough and at the same time as through the definite barrier of two windows and the width of the street in between, which prevented him from making the least move to stop her. Thea stood there for a moment completely naked. She drained the dregs of the wine in one of the glasses. Then she took a last puff of the fag end of her cigarette, which she took from the table, and crushed it out in the ashtray — all of which she did naked. Her movements seemed to conform to some regular routine. Now she took her nightgown, which she had previously placed in readiness on the side of the bed, an orange nightgown still folded from the laundry, and slipped it over her head. She cast a sidelong glance at Gurdweill, smiling the satanic smile which might in itself have driven a man to murder, took a step towards the table, bent down and blew out the lamp. The flame flared

468

up, agitating the air in the room, and died. In an instant they were blind. A shudder ran through the man on the couch, but he went on sitting as if turned to stone. The silence increased seventy-fold. In it the light tread of bare feet could be heard, like the scampering of a mouse, and a faint, abortive creak from the bed, more like the abstract idea of a sound than the sound itself. There was a soft rustle, a turning over in the bed — imperceptible tremors which Gurdweill nevertheless picked up quite distinctly, and after that once more a moment, the merest fraction of a moment, of silence, broken into, as into an empty frame, by the distant whistle of a train. Gurdweill sat like a man imprisoned in an iron mould made to measure for his body. His heart beat in every part of him, his arms, his legs, his skull, and seemed about to break free and detach itself from the still body at any moment, to roll like dull thunder through the darkness of the night until it disappeared forever. And now his ear caught a smothered sound from the bed. Something strange, full of mystery, oppressive and terrifying as death, burst into the room, and gave rise to a movement which lasted an eternity, which would never stop. The body of the man sitting on the couch was suddenly drained of the marrow of its life by a vast, invisible hand. His body instantly grew very light, as if it were made of air, expanding and overflowing its boundaries and merging with the air of the rest of the world. His heart stopped. He lost his balance and fell over backwards on the couch.

He did not know how long he lay there. Perhaps a moment, and perhaps an entire day — in any case, when he woke and recovered his senses, the first thing he noticed was that it was night, black and silent. Afterwards, when his hearing became sharper, he heard a faint, barely perceptible breath coming from the direction of the bed. "Yes," he said to himself in order to confirm the fact that he was awake, "it's night now and Thea is sleeping." He lay on his back, where he had fallen, with his legs dangling to the floor. They felt curiously heavy, and he could hardly move them. He overcame his exhaustion and sat up. As soon as he sat up, the thing which had happened a few

469

moments before lashed at him in all its terror. And to prove to himself that he was not dreaming, he rose wearily to his feet, walked to the bed and bent over it. After peering through the darkness for a moment he made out Thea's head quite clearly, on the side of the bed nearest the window, and next to it another head, its moustached face turned up to the ceiling — Franzl Heidelberger's face. There was no room for doubt: it was all true! Gurdweill turned away in horror, took his hat and coat automatically from the stand by the door, and ran from the room.

35

HE opened the door and he went outside and began walking rapidly along the cold, empty streets without knowing what he was doing. Only one thought pulsed incessantly in his mind: "She did that to me!" driving him on and on. A clock struck three — "It's already three o'clock and she did that to me!" The sewage carts parked on the corner of Heinestrasse and Taborstrasse gave off a suffocating stench, but Gurdweill walked past them without even sensing it. He was to be seen in Taborstrasse, in Obere Augartenstrasse, running, waving his hands, perhaps even talking aloud — and in the end he found himself in front of number 18 Rembrandtstrasse, where Ulrich lived. His feet stopped in front of the house of their own accord, as if seeking a refuge here for their owner. Gurdweill stood and looked at the house, which seemed to him familiar, and it was only after some time that he realized that he was standing in front of his friend's apartment. He began walking to and fro in front of the door, as if waiting for someone. His footsteps rang rhythmically in the empty street, giving birth to a hollow echo. Nightmarish thoughts pounced on him like wild beasts, thoughts capable of driving a man out of his mind. Everything he had kept buried inside him since meeting this woman, everything he had always known in the depths of his heart and not allowed to cross the threshold of his consciousness — now burst into it like a torrential flood sweeping through the shattered wall of a dam. Everything, everything was true! Everything he had always known by signs which did not lie, the hints of his friends, the gossip of strangers — it was all true! And the things he had only guessed — they were true too! From now on there was no hope of denying a single detail. To and fro Gurdweill

471

paced in front of number 18 Rembrandtstrasse and talked to himself, almost aloud . . . With anyone! Without any discrimination! From the first day she met them! Before his eyes there appeared a legion of men, some of whom he had glimpsed talking to her or walking with her and others whom he had never seen at all — all of them huge as giants, all of them smiling at him scornfully, pointing at him. And the baby — now it was as plain as day — was not his, but her boss Dr. Ostwald's. Martin was not his son! And she was to blame for his death — she and she alone! She had not treated him as a proper mother would! But for her — the baby would still be alive today! And she had killed Lotte too! She and she alone! Everything dear to him in the world she had killed! Gurdweill once more drank to the dregs the bestial, gratuitous, humiliating cruelty of their life together. She alone had undermined his soul, ruined his life, turned him into a broken reed! And why? Why had she needed to do it? When he had loved her so much! And after all that she was lying there now with a strange man — in his room.

And as if he had only now realized the horror of it, he was suddenly seized by an endless despair, together with a strange fear, and he began to run straight down the street, too terrified to look behind him. He ran across the Augarten Bridge, and turned right at the Police Station, where he suddenly had the insane idea of going in and asking for protection and help. But he immediately abandoned this idea. "Not the police!" he said aloud and continued running. At the entrance to a little side street he saw light in the distance, above a hotel door, and it occurred to him that he might be able to find a refuge there. He went up and rang the bell loudly.

After a while a sleepy servant showed him to a small room on the second floor. There was an iron stove standing in the corner, but the fire was not lit. Gurdweill sat down on the bed and stayed there for a long time without moving. It may have been about five o'clock when he suddenly stood up, as if he had come to a serious decision, pushed the blue and white striped quilt up to the head of the bed, and carefully inspected the sheet. It seemed clean enough, but by the time he had finished his inspection Gurdweill had forgotten what he wanted, and he sat down again. There was a muffled creak from the next-door room, which immediately subsided, but Gurdweill shuddered at the sound and looked wildly round the room, without, however, discovering anything suspicious. He stood up again, went up to the wardrobe and opened it. The wardrobe was empty. It exuded a dull, stale smell of cheap perfume — the smell typical of loose women. For a moment he regretted coming here, but the next minute the feeling was gone. He picked up a yellowing piece of old newspaper, which was lying on the wardrobe floor, shut the door, and began to read it. When he saw that it was two months old, he crumpled it up and threw it into a corner. All of a sudden the memory of the night's events hit him like a slap in the face, and he began rushing around the room like a caged animal. The room suddenly seemed to have had all the air drained out of it, there was nothing to breathe, and Gurdweill opened the window wide. Shafts of cold whipped his cheeks. He felt a sudden urge to run home and do something. It was impossible to leave things the way they were! What on earth was he doing here? He did not know exactly what he had to do, but a vague feeling told him that he should be there now, where matters could be mended, something could be changed. He banged the window shut and started to leave the room. But when he passed the bed he was overcome by a great weakness, a sudden paralysis seemed to have attacked his limbs, and he was obliged to sit down. He was incapable of moving a muscle. He sat with his head on his chest, withdrawn into himself, like a lifeless dummy. Something buzzed incessantly in his head, seething and bubbling like boiling water. He distinctly heard a voice behind him saying maliciously: "The Herr Doktor will sleep on the couch, as usual!" . . . and he felt mortally insulted, furious, and in actual physical pain. He needed to turn his head and deny something, to protest, to shout at the top of his voice, to hit out in all directions — but his body was made of lead. Iron whips could not have made him move a muscle. But the voice said again, this time to his face: "He's not a man at

473

all . . ! Could anyone really call that little creature a man? He's nothing but an idiot! Look at him sitting there! I can do what I like to him and he won't open his mouth! What a joke!" Gurdweill suffered inexpressible torture, but he did not have the strength to move. He knew the voice well. A voice which required no words to insult him to the depths of his being — he knew it well. But where and when had he heard it? If only he knew! And then another voice spoke, and this time he knew for certain that it was Lotte's. He even saw her standing in the corner, between the wardrobe and the washstand, wearing a blue, silk, flowered kimono, and she said: "What? You won't do a thing to him! Nothing, you hear? From now on he belongs to me and me alone — and you have no part in him!" . . . This was very strange . . . So, there was still a way out — all was not yet lost! Ah, Lotte, Lotte! If not to her, whom could he turn to now? But Thea — suddenly he knew it was Thea, even though he could not see her — responded by bursting into loud laughter, which cut into his flesh like a blunt saw. "Yours, is he? Yours? Don't make me laugh! Who married him, you or me? And who gave him a baby? And who made a man of him? Answer that if you can! Ask Herr Heidelberger — he knows everything!" Gurdweill shuddered at the name. He was afraid that she would tell Lotte something else, something he would rather she did not know. But he could do nothing to stop her. And Thea went on screaming: "You think you can just walk in and take over, do you? You'd like that, wouldn't you? But I'm still alive! And I tell you again, and Herr Heidelberger is my witness, that I'll do as I wish with him! No one can prevent me, least of all you!" Lotte took a step forward, and pleaded in a voice choked with tears, to which Gurdweill could hardly bear to listen: "Please, don't, be so cruel. Haven't you got a woman's heart? I beg you, let him go . . . What do you need him for? Take Herr Heidelberger instead — it makes no difference to you, after all — and let him go. Look, I'm begging you on my knees" — and Lotte actually dropped to her knees — "let him go! Don't be so hard hearted!" "Never! I'll never let you have him! And I'll take Heidelberger too!

474

I'll take whomever I like — and you'll have nothing! And now enough! Why are you still alive? There's nothing for you here . . ! Why don't you go away and die? The world will get on perfectly well without you, won't it, Herr Heidelberger? Prepare yourself, we're going to put an end to it right now!" Gurdweill saw something flashing towards the kneeling Lotte, and suddenly he knew that it was a knife and that Thea was going to kill her. He made a tremendous effort and hit out with all his strength in the direction where Thea should have been standing. His hand hit the corner of the bed, and Lotte disappeared.

There was silence all around. Gurdweill sprang to his feet. His knuckles, which had hit the wooden frame of the bed, hurt. The scene was still vividly before him; he imagined that he could still hear the voices. His body was bathed in a cold sweat and his heart beat fit to burst. He was certain that he had not been dreaming, that he had seen the whole scene with his eyes open, and he was afraid to sit down again. He was now standing near the bed, next to the place where previously he had been sitting, but facing the window, afraid to turn his head to the door in case he saw something unimaginably horrifying there. For some time he stood without moving. In the end he recovered and inched slowly round the bottom of the bed, which stuck out into the middle of the little room, and sat down on the other side, facing the window. "No!" — he said to himself — "This time I'll be on my guard! I won't let any harm come to Lotte!" Suddenly he took fright at the sound of his own voice and fell silent. He stared straight ahead of him at the window, set into the wall like a black square with its cheap greenish curtains drawn to the sides. That green colour clashes with the red wallpaper — the trivial idea came into his head — he really couldn't stand that shade of green . . . And he lay down absent-mindedly on top of the quilt, fully dressed and without taking off his shoes.

When he woke up, a milky day was shining through the window. The electric light was still on, too, getting in the way of the daylight. At the beginning he did not know where he was, and he looked around for a moment

475

in bewilderment. All of a sudden he remembered, and started up from the bed. The fearful night was over, and he ran to switch off the light, as if by so doing he could obliterate something from his memory. But nothing was obliterated. Everything was quite clear, and seemed even more real by the light of day. His body felt sore and exhausted, but he took no notice. Suddenly he was in a great hurry, he had not a moment to lose. He took out his watch, which said three o'clock, put it mechanically to his ear and realized that it had stopped. Then he went up to the window and looked outside, at the little street with the two grocery stores, one next to the other, which were both shut. Gurdweill was unable to decide what the time was. He picked up his hat, which had fallen to the floor while he slept, and as he passed the mirror over the basin next to the door he saw a strange, shrivelled, unshaven face, with two feverish eyes in it. This face meant nothing to him, he was completely indifferent to it, and he walked out of the room.

Downstairs, in the office, the round clock on the wall said half past two. This clock must have stopped too, concluded Gurdweill, it was inconceivable that it could be so late! Suddenly he realized that the valet was staring at him, and he was overcome with confusion, as guilty as if he were hiding some crime.

"What . . . what's the time?"

"It's half past two."

"Half past two in the afternoon?"

"Yes, of course," the valet smiled in polite amusement.

"But the shops . . . the grocery stores opposite, I mean, are still closed . . ."

"Today is Sunday. Yesterday was Saturday, which means that today it's Sunday. And in the city of Vienna the shops are closed on Sundays. We're Social-Democrats here."

"Ah, of course! You're quite right, sir! In that case, it's all clear!"

And as if to correct some unfavourable impression, he took ten groschen out of his pocket and offered it to the valet. To the latter's astonishment, he even shook hands with him, and then hurried out of the hotel.

476

It was not very cold. From time to time the sun even peeped out of the clouds, like an unexpected stranger. The Sunday streets were dull and quiet. Gurdweill walked quickly, he had no time to waste. The previous night hovered distinctly in front of him, barring his path, this night and many other nights and days before it, and he hugged the walls and pushed his way through. In front of the church on Serviten Platz it occurred to him that he should eat something, even though he was not in the least hungry. He stood still and inspected his surroundings, looking for somewhere to eat. With exaggerated care he subjected building after building to his scrutiny, as if everything now depended on this alone. His old, deeply rooted fear of ostentatious places prevented him from going into the large restaurant diagonally opposite him. In the end he discovered a simple working men's café and went inside. There was nothing left to eat. Lunch was over, he was told, but if he cared to wait a while, they could make him an omelet or something of the kind.

"No, no!" protested Gurdweill. He wasn't in the least bit hungry and there was no need to go to any trouble on his account. He left the little restaurant and went into a café nearby.

Afterwards he directed his steps to Porzellangasse, and got on to a tram. Although he did not know where to go, he was driven to flee the city, which had grown alien and hostile. It seemed to him that people were looking at him in a special way, as if there was something strange about him. The tram was going to the suburb of Nussdorf. Gurdweill sat with a solemn expression on his face, as if some important business awaited him at the end of the journey. When he reached the last stop, it was evening. The air was cooler here, with a cold wind blowing from the Danube nearby. As soon as he alighted from the tram he was struck by the full force of his calamity, as if it had been waiting here at the terminus to greet him. A black shadow flashed before his eyes, and he almost fainted. He was standing next to a streetlamp which had already been lit, and he leant against the post for support. He wiped away the cold sweat which had

477

broken out on his brow with his handkerchief, and then passed it over his eyes which suddenly seemed to have lost their sight, and his dark, unshaven cheeks. Gradually his momentary faintness evaporated, and the strength returned to his body, as if powers which had been scattered through the air were one by one resuming their rightful places. He even sensed a new determination awakening in him and rising from his depths, a resolution of crucial importance whose precise nature escaped him for the moment, but which he could feel stirring inside him like a palpable thing. His right hand, which was still holding the handkerchief, clenched convulsively into a fist, with such force that the fingernails dug into the pad of flesh below his thumb. He put his handkerchief back in his pocket, glanced absent-mindedly at the full moon hanging tenuously in the dark-blue heavens as if about to fall to the ground at any moment, and set off with a resolute tread. Unknowingly he took the road leading away from the city towards the village of Klosterneuburg, a gravel road running along the Danube and the railway line on one side, and the foot of Leopoldsberg on the other. He walked rapidly. He passed and left behind him low, isolated houses nestling against the mountainside; little taverns full of uproar in the summer, which were now sunk in slumber and dimly lit. Afterwards the houses stopped completely and Gurdweill was alone. Only the moon accompanied him tirelessly, vanishing momentarily behind the mountain and reappearing again like a faithful dog. Sometimes a speeding car came from before or behind him, roaring and hooting and blinding him with a glare like Bengal lights, pushing him to the side of the road and racing on, leaving a stench of petrol and a dwindling din behind it. From time to time a train passed on the tracks next to the road, going to the city or in the opposite direction, to the many little villages dotted over the countryside. For a moment a chain of squares of light would flash by in the darkness, with an occasional human head and shoulders silhouetted against an orange background. Gurdweill went on walking rapidly, impervious to his surroundings.

478

After walking for about two and a half hours, the first houses of Klosterneuburg came into view. Gurdweill reached the big square in front of the railway station and came to a halt. For a moment he imagined that he was still in Vienna, but he immediately had second thoughts. The square and all the buildings around it were completely unfamiliar. He could not remember ever having seen them in any of the quarters of Vienna. How could he find out where he was? He stood there for a moment at a loss, and then he noticed the railway station and directed his steps towards it.

There were only a few people in the smallish hall, some of them standing in a short line in front of the ticket office and others wandering about or sitting and waiting. A train must be about to depart, Gurdweill concluded mechanically. He scanned the hall and discovered a railway clerk in the corner. He approached him hesitantly.

"When . . . when does the last train leave?"

"For where?"

"For . . . er . . . for . . ." stammered Gurdweill.

The clerk looked at him suspiciously.

"Where do you want to go?"

"Me? Home . . . that is, to Vienna, of course. I live in Vienna and so obviously that's where I have to go . . ."

"Your last train leaves at twenty-three hours fifty-eight minutes," said the clerk laconically.

Gurdweill could not bring himself to inquire any further, and walked away. At least he knew now that he was not in Vienna. And then he had a wonderful idea: he went up to the ticket office and bought a ticket for Vienna. Then he went outside and read in the light of the lamp: Klosterneuburg — Vienna. Franz-Josefs-Bahnhof. Aha! — concluded Gurdweill triumphantly — so he was in Klosterneuburg! He was suddenly overcome by exhaustion, and dropped on to the steps of the station building. For a while he sat there without moving, his head in his hands and his elbows on his knees. Fragments of thoughts flitted through his mind. He had to go to Vienna — that was where he lived. Now he was in Klosterneuburg, where he did not live, where it was out of the question that he lived . . . Lotte was not with him now . . . what a pity! If she were here, they could have continued their journey in a little while, once they had already come so far . . . He already had his ticket, too . . . If only his head hadn't started hurting so badly . . . It always had to interfere and spoil everything . . . Yes, and he would have to see Thea before he left . . . And for this he would have to wait until after midnight . . . she was never at home before midnight . . . And Heidelberger, he would have to see him too . . . He would definitely be with her, they were always together — he had seen them with his own eyes . . . This last thought made him start up like a spring, and he began running across the square, waving his hands threateningly at some invisible person. When he reached the other side he found himself standing right in front of the brightly-lit entrance to one of the cafés surrounding the square. All of a sudden he felt sure that he had lost something while he was running, without knowing exactly what the lost object was. And he retraced his steps, scanning the ground with his eyes. In the middle of the square he stood still and began turning out his pockets one after the other. His search produced crushed and crumpled bits of paper, old tram tickets, cigarette stubs, small change, his wallet, the big penknife, his cracked, sooty pipe, a box of matches, and so on. He examined each object intently before putting it back. He even put the old tram tickets back in his pocket. In the end he took the train ticket which he had just purchased out of his coat pocket, and instantly realized that it was this very ticket for which he had been searching, and which he had been afraid that he had lost. Somewhat calmed by this discovery, he put the ticket away for safekeeping in his wallet, as if he really had lost it and found it again. The train left at twenty-three hours fifty-eight, in other words, at nearly midnight, and it was now — he glanced at the station clock — nine o'clock, which meant that he had three hours to wait! Gurdweill was overwhelmed by despair at the idea of not being able to return to Vienna sooner (he had forgotten that the clerk had distinctly said the "last train") — because it was suddenly quite clear to

480

him that he was in a great hurry, that he did not have a moment to lose. He had to be in Vienna at once, at this very minute! If anyone had asked him the reason for his haste, it is doubtful if he would have known what to reply, but his impatience nevertheless increased until it felt like an actual physical pain. And as if to reach Vienna more quickly by these means, he began to run towards the station entrance. But before he reached it he appeared to change his mind, and retraced his steps to the café. It so happened that the building which housed the café on its lower floor stood apart from its neighbours, with a rather steep street on either side, and an alley joining them at the back. And Gurdweill, without having the faintest idea of what he was doing, began rushing round and round the building, like some kind of moving fence. After he had completed his tenth or twentieth round, the village policeman, who unknown to Gurdweill had been following his movements from a distance, approached and stationed himself in front of the café. When Gurdweill came round the corner again he stopped him. Gurdweill gave him a dazed look and tried to hurry past him.

"Stop! What do you think you're doing?"

A note of suppressed anger quivered in the inexperienced young policeman's voice, as if Gurdweill were his sworn enemy, or as if the latter's unusual behaviour was an affront to his personal honour as the local representative of public law and order.

Gurdweill explained: "What do you mean ... I — I'm going for a walk ... In any case I'm taking the train to Vienna today ... I have a ticket for Klosterneuburg — Vienna ..."

This reply served only to increase the anger of the policeman, who thought he was being made fun of. He called sternly:

"That's all very well! Have you got papers?"

No, he had no papers with him. Fortunately for him, however, he found a letter with his name and address on the envelope in one of his pockets, and showed it to the policeman. The latter took it and turned it this way and that, looking alternately at the envelope and at Gurdweill, as if to ascertain whether the name and address were really those of the small, unshaven man before him. After a short pause for reflection, he returned the letter to Gurdweill.

"Good! And now be off! And don't walk round the building again!"

"Why shouldn't I?" Now it was Gurdweill's turn to lose his temper. "Haven't I got the right to walk where I please? I think I know my rights!"

"I'm warning you, don't be impertinent! Or else I'll have to ask you to come with me to the station!"

Gurdweill decided to obey, since he did not want to risk missing the train. In the distance he saw the hands of the station clock pointing to ten o'clock, and unconsciously avoiding the café he had been encircling before, he turned into the one next to it. The entire incident with the policeman was instantly wiped from his mind, and once again he felt profound regret at not being in Vienna at this moment. For while he was here, something dreadful was without a doubt taking place there, and afterwards it would be too late to do anything about it . . . When he had finished drinking his coffee, he supported his head on his hands and the next minute he was half asleep. A very long train, endlessly long, was flying past him at a tremendous speed, and he had to jump on to it — which in itself did not seem difficult. But on the steps of every carriage which passed him stood a policeman cracking a long whip and preventing him from getting on. First it was the policeman who had accosted him outside the café, and then it was Heidelberger. On the platforms of all the countless coaches of the train stood the same policeman, in other words, Heidelberger, with a long whip. All the passengers — their heads were sticking out of the windows — laughed at his plight. In the end he managed to jump on to one of the last carriages. He was overjoyed. Now he would be able to rush to the aid of Lotte (for Lotte was in great trouble!). But suddenly he saw that the carriage into which he had jumped was standing still. And the reason for this lack of motion was immediately clear to him: he had forgotten to buy a ticket, and as long as he had no ticket the carriage would refuse to budge. On the other hand, he could not get off to buy a ticket, first of all because he was in the middle of the journey, several miles from the station, and secondly because he was sure that the minute he got off the carriage would begin to move and leave him behind. It also transpired that the inside of the carriage was not in the least like a normal railway carriage, but resembled an empty room, with no furniture in it but for one broken chair standing on its head with its three legs up in the air. He was not particularly surprised by this, however. The crux of the matter was, how to get the carriage to move. The conductor came in, and Gurdweill began searching hopelessly through his pockets. Suddenly he found an old tram ticket, which although it did not resemble the usual elongated tickets — it was large, green and square, more like a large envelope in shape — was nevertheless a tram ticket, of that he was quite sure. Hoping that it would help, he offered it to the conductor. But at the sight of the ticket the latter broke into terrible laughter, coming out of his mouth in one burst after the other, each of which hit Gurdweill like a hard object. He knew that if he did not hide, this laughter was perfectly capable of killing him. Every burst hit him like an iron bar, and he began scurrying about the empty room like a mouse, keeping to the walls and corners, while the conductor pursued him and hit him with his laughter. There was nowhere to hide. The room had no windows or doors — it was sealed on all sides. With the last of his strength he beat against the wall, trying desperately to make a breach in it.

"What can I do for you, sir?" inquired the waiter, who thought that Gurdweill's banging on the table was intended for him.

Gurdweill looked at him with a dull, demented stare and said nothing. The waiter stationed himself next to the table and waited. Gurdweill's eyes strayed here and there, he saw people sitting at the marble-topped counters, and drop by drop reality filtered through to him. In a faint, strained voice, he blurted out:

"Can you — perhaps you can tell me, what time it is exactly?"

483

At the waiter's reply, that it was now five minutes to eleven, he started up, hastily settled his bill, and left the café.

The fresh air sent a chill running through him, but he did not feel it. The square was bare and deserted. High above, the moon still hung like a seal on the night. Gurdweill turned into a long street leading from the square and walked along it slowly, until a fit of restlessness overcame him again, like the sudden onset of a feverish disease, and he ran back to the station. He passed through the hall and went out on to the platform, where he paced back and forth for what seemed like a very long time. But the hands of the station clock stayed stubbornly where they were. Time stood still. The silvery tracks ran gleaming into the depths of the night. The high signal lamp turned red. There was a long, low ring — a message from the station down the line. Then came a whistle from a freight train, which loomed hugely out of the darkness and passed without stopping, puffing strenuously and making a deafening noise. Long barrel-cars slid past, cages with cattle standing in them, roofless cars piled with stones or stacked with planks, and closed cars with huge numbers, or occasionally words chalked on their sides. The noise receded into the distance. The rails went on humming quietly for a while, and far away something throbbed in the night, with a tender, touching sound.

In the end the long-awaited train emerged from the darkness and received Gurdweill together with a few other passengers. The compartments were packed with people, for the most part dozing, going back to town after a day in the country, and Gurdweill stood in the corridor, leaning against the wall and looking outside without seeing anything. He felt nothing but one blind, consuming urge — to get home as quickly as possible. For some reason he did not take a tram from the Franz-Josefs-Bahnhof, but ran home by foot, and the closer he came to his neighbourhood the faster he ran. It took him three-quarters of an hour to reach Kleine Stadtgutgasse. Bathed in sweat he stopped and stood looking up at the windows of his room, which were in darkness. There was no way of telling if she was

484

already sleeping, or if she had not yet come home. He rang the bell, groped his way up the stairs in the dark, carefully opened the passage door, and entered on tiptoe. In the passage he stood still and held his breath, listening. All was silence. Then he crept up to the door of his room, opened it, and stepped soundlessly inside. Thea grunted unintelligibly in her sleep. He waited motionless by the door until she was quiet again. There was not a sound to be heard, apart from his own heart beats and Thea's very faint breathing, which seemed to be coming from somewhere below him, as if it were rising out of the floor. After a few moments he dared to take a step towards the couch, and sat down. The moon spread a broad, slanting band of radiance across the bed and over the opposite wall. Gurdweill listened, straining every nerve, and keeping his eyes fixed on the bed, as if to make sure that nothing happened on it without his knowledge. And for a long time nothing, indeed, did happen. Only the ray of moonlight moved from the foot of the bed to the middle, almost touching the sleeping Thea's breasts. And suddenly someone in a white shirt raised himself on Thea's right side and sat up in bed. Gurdweill heard not the faintest sound, but he saw everything so vividly that there was no room for the shadow of a doubt. "So he's here again tonight! He was here yesterday and he's here again today!" He waited with bated breath, and Heidelberger waited too. The latter sat woodenly, looking straight in front of him, his head sunk slightly on his chest and the bristles of his heavy moustache covering his lips, as when Gurdweill had first seen him in the tavern in front of his tankard of beer. In the end he turned his head slowly towards Gurdweill and gave him a long stare. He seemed to be smiling beneath his moustache. After looking at him for a few moments, he lay down again. Gurdweill went on waiting for a little while longer, but no one stirred. Then he rose silently to his feet and approached the bed, but from the other side, the side where Thea was lying sprawled on her back, the open penknife glinting in his hand. There was a brief groan, a shudder in the bed. A distant clock struck two.

485

At eight o'clock in the morning Gurdweill appeared in Ulrich's room and woke him up. On his thin, unshaven face was a strange, frozen smile. He sank on to the edge of the bed and sat there for a while as if turned to stone, while his friend looked at him uncomprehendingly. In the end he said softly, as if talking to himself:

"Thea died last night."

About the Author

David Vogel was born in Russian Poland in 1891. Living in Vienna when World War I began, he was imprisoned by the Austrians as a Russian enemy alien. In the twenties, he began to publish the Hebrew poetry for which he is now admired in Israel and to write his only novel, *Married Life*. The book was published in 1929 after Vogel's arrival in Palestine. A year later he returned to Europe, settling in Paris, where after the outbreak of World War II he was imprisoned by the French as an Austrian enemy alien. Several years later he was arrested by the Nazi occupiers as a Jew, and died in Auschwitz in 1944.

Temple Israel

Minneapolis, Minnesota

IN MEMORY OF

LOUIS LAZAAR

BY

MRS. S. A. PINK